WHEN SHE WAS BAD...

Also by Louise Bagshawe

Career Girls
The Movie
Tall Poppies
Venus Envy
A Kept Woman

WHEN SHE WAS BAD...

Louise Bagshawe

First published in Great Britain in 2001 by
Orion
An imprint of Orion Books Ltd
Orion House, 5 Upper St Martin's Lane, London WC2H 9EA

A CIP catalogue record for this book
is available from the British Library

ISBN: 0–75282–150–4 (cased)

ISBN: 0–75282–152–0 (trade paperback)

Typeset by Deltatype Ltd, Birkenhead, Merseyside

Printed in Great Britain by
Antony Rowe Ltd, Chippenham, Wiltshire

I would like to dedicate this book to my Granny
and my Great Aunt Polly Youldon

My first thanks must go to my editor Rosie de Courcy for her outstanding work, as always, on this book. Her touch is light but assured. I need also to thank my excellent raft of agents: Michael Sissons is captain of my team, and indeed a very benevolent dictator, as whatever he decides for me is invariably right. I need to thank my American agent Peter Matson, my film agents Brian Siberell at CAA and Tim Corrie at PFD, James Gill at PFD for his soothing touch and general ability to sort anything out, and my fabulous manager Alan Greenspan (not *that* Alan Greenspan but only fractionally less influential). I must also thank my translation agents ILA.

My family and friends were very supportive, mostly in the form of making me get off the internet and stop procrastinating: my darling husband Anthony, my parents Nick and Daphne Bagshawe, my brother James, sister Tilly, Teen Cib (sic) Alice, and Jacob Rees-Mogg, John and Gina Florescu, Dawn Harris, and Fred Metcalf.

It's a good job I'm not giving an Oscar speech or they'd have started the music by now.

At Orion, my wonderful publishers, I must thank first the inspired art director Claire Heggarty, who came up with the title; Susan Lamb for her great covers and advice; and Kirsty Fowkes whom I am looking forward to working with, and who really helped out with the search for a decent title (never my strongest suit!).

Chapter 1

'Lita!'

Lita Morales stopped scrubbing off her parents' scratched Formica counter-top and turned around to see her mother smiling and proudly waving an envelope.

'Happy birthday, sweetheart.' Mama kissed her on the cheek, tugging on her gloves against the Bronx November cold. Outside their tiny apartment, the street lamps of Wheeler Avenue were silhouetted against the pale gold, icy dawn sky. It was half-past six and Mama had to head out to take the subway to Manhattan soon. 'Your father and me got you a gift.'

Lita smiled and took the card in the crisp paper envelope. It had a picture of a hedgehog holding some balloons; a kid's card, really. Mama had probably gotten it cheap, because one corner was frayed, and in the Morales household, they watched every cent. Inside the card was seventeen dollars, one for every year of her life, her traditional birthday present. It looked like a lot of money to Lita.

'Thanks, Mom.' She hugged her.

'I got to go. Try to get back early, OK?'

'OK,' Lita agreed.

Mama left quickly and, of course, Pappy had already gone. He might be back to snatch a little sleep some time this afternoon. Lita couldn't resent that nobody was here for her birthday. Her parents had to work, and Chico, snoring in his room, didn't count. She carefully put her seventeen-dollar fortune away in the old sock under her bed, reserving two dollars for emergencies today.

Now it was time to clear away the breakfast dishes. Lita worked quickly, not wanting to be late for school. The city, in the dawn, out past her kitchen window, depressed her. There was some new graffiti from one of the gangs on the Chinese laundry across the street. She hoped it wasn't Chico's gang. For once.

Lita loved her brother, but he really annoyed her. He had a serious aversion to using his brain.

She was going to be eighteen next year. She really had to start thinking hard about a job, about some way out of here. Otherwise she'd be stuck in a dead-end job like her mother, or else start hanging out on the corner like Chico, causing nothing but trouble, wasting time.

That wasn't the life that Lita wanted.

To wind up like Mama and Pappy, dark-skinned and dark-eyed, looking ten years older than the thirty-seven they actually were. Mama's fine bones held up well, but her face was sallow from lack of sleep. Mama had a stoop from being bent over her sewing machine all hours at the garment sweatshop in Alphabet City, a place that paid her slave wages and no benefits, that ruined her health and her eyesight, so now her lovely dark eyes were hidden behind Coke-bottle glasses. And Pappy drove that cab up and down the city, day and night, working double shift, his skin paper-thin from smoking and stress.

In a way, it was no wonder that Chico didn't want to work. Pappy yelled at him. If they were ever going to get accepted in this country, he said, to be more than 'wetbacks', to get respect and not insults, they needed more men like Pappy, more guys prepared to do an honest day's work. Chico said that was for chumps. His entire generation was opting out of it. Besides, wasn't there supposed to be an honest day's pay in there somewhere? Which *they* obviously weren't making, crammed into a three-room apartment in the worst part of town.

Pappy's answer was to strike Chico. So far her brother had not responded, just balled up his fists, glowered and strode off. But it was coming. Lita knew it.

She stayed in school, which Chico had not done, promising his father that he'd work construction. Pappy hadn't taken much persuading. Book-learning didn't seem to benefit the family much; you couldn't say the same for that good, off-the-books construction money. That was manly work. Besides, it wasn't good for Chico to be idle. So Pappy said it was OK if Chico didn't finish high school. Pappy hadn't, and he'd done OK, hadn't he? A roof over their heads, the same place for four years, rent always on time, and even a little stashed away for emergencies. Maybe his son could do better. That was what every father hoped for.

Carlos Sr didn't think much about Lita. She was blossoming, but her mother dressed her nice, in long, shapeless skirts and blouses, so that the boys didn't try and get too fresh with her. Since Lita had turned down her Mama's proposal of a job at the sweatshop so angrily, he had backed off suggesting she follow in her brother's footsteps. If Lita wanted a high-school graduation, maybe that was OK, too. It was true she was another mouth to feed, one that made no contribution to the house, but he worked her hard enough that it seemed fair. Their cramped apartment was spotless; the windows gleamed, even though the neighbourhood was filthy. Lita had to do her chores before she got to start her homework.

For her classmates, homework was a drag. For Lita, it was a reward. She didn't get to sit down at the tiny desk in her minute bedroom until the apartment sparkled like an ad for kitchen cleaner. The Bronx might be dirty and covered in graffiti, but the Morales' apartment was clean enough for Betty Crocker to cook in.

Pappy liked it that way, so there was nothing more said about Lita going to the sweatshop.

Besides, as she grew, he started to hope there was something more for her. Maybe, with that fancy high-school diploma, she could learn to type, get a job as a secretary. They had women in the front office at the cab company, making coffee and filing. That was a good life for a girl. Soft clerical work that didn't ruin their hands. Plus, not even Carlos Morales could ignore the way his daughter was developing.

At thirteen, she'd been the prettiest girl in school. At fifteen, she'd been the prettiest girl in Soundview. And at seventeen, she might just be the prettiest girl in the entire Bronx.

The long skirts and shapeless blouses were just no match for Mother Nature, who was shaping Lita up in a most unmotherly way. Her breasts had budded early, grown and just kept on growing, until she could fill out a tight sweater like Lana Turner, not that Mama would ever give her a tight sweater. Hand-me-down brassieres from her cousins didn't fit Lita any more. She had to go to Marshall's and pick up special ones, with Mama wincing as she doled the money out carefully from her pocketbook. Lita possessed only three bras at seventeen, functional, sturdy contraptions that held her softness tight against her chest, without a whisper of lace or a suggestion of silk. But they could not stop her feeling sexy.

Lita felt the eyes of the boys on her whenever she walked down the street. They lingered on her breasts when she was coming, and on her butt when she was going. The exercise revolution would not start for another ten years, but Lita was trim, naturally firm, and her glorious butt, jutting out from her tiny, handspan waist, was high and tight, and it rolled just a little when she walked with that natural, disturbing sway to her hips.

Lita didn't want to encounter her father's belt. She didn't bait him the way Chico did. She submitted to the ankle-length skirts and wrist-hugging blouses, but it was no good – she made whatever she wore look sexy. The narrow, straight skirts just emphasized all that shape – her tiny waist, her firm, flaring ass, and the breasts the sturdy cotton bras fought to confine. And she didn't bother with drugs or booze, not because she was a good girl but because she was arrogant.

Lita wasn't going to wind up like her brother Chico. She wasn't going to wind up like Elena Ayala down the street, nineteen and already the mother of twin screaming brats.

Lita Morales was going to get out. And this year was the year she was going to do it.

'Oh, baby, where you goin', lookin' like that? You sure are wearin' those jeans, girl. Sure are.'

Lita walked on, her face impassive, her banged-up satchel slung over one shoulder. She got just as many compliments in her skirts as in her Levi's, and just as much trouble, too. Boys on the street corners yelling and whistling as she walked by. The one good thing about winter was that she got to wear her large, cheap blue coat, the one Mama had handed down to her. It covered up all that shape, as Rico Gonzalez called it, and it enabled her to walk the eight blocks to her building without too much trouble. The white boys were the worst, man. Yelling out that she was a hot tamale, mamacita, and all that jive. Lita despised them. They lumped all Hispanics into one basket, the Cubans, the Mexicans, the Puerto Ricans – everybody except the Domies, whom they thought of as black. Stupid bastards. If you weren't lily-white, to most of those boys you weren't anything. They thought of all Spanish girls as hot like pepper, heavy-lidded, exotic-looking toys for them to fuck and forget. There was no considering how they'd feel if it was their sisters being leered at. What, did they really think those catcalls would make her stop and speak to them? Lita turned down twenty dates a week.

She had a kind of boyfriend anyway, Hector Fernandez. Hector was ambitious, which was one reason she liked him. He was respectful, most of the time, though he pretended to ignore her when he was hanging out with his boys. Hector's father owned two rental apartments, and his family had a little money. Hector himself got to drive his older brother's 'Cuda, a flash convertible. Lita loved to get driven around in it when she had time before she had to get home, even if Hector liked to try and slide his hand up her knee. And Hector was a jock, which kept the worst of the school catcalls away. She was looking forward to seeing what he'd gotten her for her birthday. She'd had to get back home today, but Hector was going to see her tomorrow, nice and early. They were meeting up before school.

He'd been in class today, and leaned over and told her he had to meet her then.

'It's really important, baby.'

Lita smiled back at him, her dark eyes flashing over his. 'You got something for me?'

Hector had grinned, that same sly, easy grin he flashed at the cheerleaders when he thought Lita wasn't looking.

'Yeah, I sure do. Drop by tomorrow and pick it up.'

'I will,' she promised, then spun in her seat to face the blackboard before Mrs Meyer turned around and bawled them out.

Lita marched onto the corner of Wheeler and Seward. There was a bodega on the corner, and she ducked inside.

'Lita.' Mr Perez, the owner, was a friend of her mother's, sometimes even giving them a little credit. 'How you doing today, *querida?*'

'Pretty good.' She flashed him one of those million-buck smiles that had gotten pretty disturbing of late. Jose Perez had played with Lita when she was a little girl. He hastily turned away as she selected some eggs and bread and riffled through his magazine rack.

'Here, you want this?'

He offered her a dog-eared copy of *Vogue*. 'Somebody spilled coffee on it. I didn't see, or I'd have made them pay. I can't sell it.'

She picked up the treasured object gingerly by the corner. 'For real? You don't want it?'

'You take it, you take it,' he said, hurriedly giving her change for her purchases and shooing her away. Carlos Morales would kill him for what he was thinking. 'See you again.'

Lita stuffed the magazine into her satchel and ran down the block to her building. Her key twisted in the lock and she bounded up four sets of stairs as though they didn't exist. A quick look around told her her mother wasn't back yet. Chico would be down on some corner with his boys, looking to scam a dollar, if he wasn't at the site, and Pappy wouldn't be back until it was time to eat. Chico's dishes from breakfast were stacked high in the sink, because she'd left before he was done. Lita felt a pang. She wanted to get out and read her magazine, but she had never skipped out on her duties and today would not be a first. Quickly she ran the water, squeezed a tiny bit of liquid onto a rag and cleaned up the sink. When the dishes were dried and put away she swept the floor, washed down the table and made her parents' bed. Chico's room was clean, mostly because he was never there, and her own tiny space was immaculate.

She might want to skimp, but she never did. Roaches didn't take the day off. Theirs was the only place she knew that had no infestation – the bugs didn't come because Lita left them nothing to eat. She was mad that Mama had left dirty dishes out for four hours, but she knew her parents would blame her. Lita had gone to school early today to take an extra class. Drama. Her father would say she should have waited here instead to wash up.

Whatever. The apartment was clean, and now she was free. Lita went into her room, peeled off her clothes and grabbed the beach towel they used in the bathroom because Mama had found it on sale five years ago. It was great to have the place to herself, to be able to take a shower without Chico or Pappy banging on the bathroom door. They had no money for luxuries like shower gel, but that was OK. She soaped herself up, revelling in the hot water, scrubbing the dust of the Bronx from her skin. Cheap shampoo and conditioner lathered up her glossy hair, and Lita dried off quickly, hanging up her school clothes and picking a dress. Her mother was nowhere to be seen, so she chose the red one she kept in the back of her closet, the one she never wore in front of her. It came to just below the knee and had a V-neck, dropping to show just a hint of her cleavage. It was thin and badly cut, but it clung to her curves like a second skin and the fluted hem whipped around her thin legs. Lita picked her black cropped jacket to wear over the top.

She didn't dare put on make-up; the thick blue eyeliner and fake lashes that her girlfriends liked to wear were totally forbidden in her mother's house. But she blasted her hair with Mama's dryer until it swung choppy and sexy around her face, grabbed her stacked sandals that she'd got from the bargain basement at J.C. Penny and raced downstairs with her purse and her magazine. *Vogue*. She loved it. Sometimes she got to read a copy her friends might have bought to share, but money was tight everywhere. Lita's dollars she saved and hid in a sock under her chest of drawers. Every cent she had went there. She didn't trust the bank. Sometimes she did the homework of one of the richer chicks, or wrote a study paper for a senior, and cleared a couple of dollars. If it was an all-night deal for a test the next day, Lita charged a flat ten bucks. They complained, but they paid up. They had no option – it was better than flunking.

Today there was over six hundred dollars in that sock, not counting the ten dollars she'd slipped into her purse. Someday she would need that cash. Lita hoped it would be someday soon.

Lita raced down Westchester Avenue to the subway station. She bought two tokens and jumped on to the six train. It was filthy, covered in obscene graffiti and anti-war signs. She didn't like to think of the war. All those young boys dying. Thank God her mama had bribed the doctors to write Chico up as mentally unfit. They had been going to get a used car with that money, but it was better to have her brother alive, royal pain in the butt that he was. She was passionately against the war.

'Don't you think these men should fight for their country?' Mr Richards, her political science teacher, asked his angry class. 'What do you say, Lita Morales?'

Lita knew he'd turned to her because she was the quiet one, the only student in his class that had a shot at honour roll.

'Sure, they should fight for their country. But this ain't their country.' She waited till the cheers had died down, then added, 'And this war is illegal.'

'I suppose you support the Commies, too,' Mr Richards sneered.

'No, sir, I support the Constitution of the United States. And under the Constitution, the President has no power to declare war. There is only one body that can do that, and that is the US Congress. Congress never declared war on Vietnam.'

There were low whistles around the room. Lita knew that being smart didn't always mean you were popular, but she didn't care. She faced her teacher down.

'Well . . . technically this isn't a *war*,' Mr Richards replied.

'Tell that to all the boys who are dying. Tell that to the men coming back with their brains fried,' she said.

The class cheered, and nobody louder than the boys, finally showing some enthusiasm in Social Studies. They reached their majority pretty soon, and nobody wanted to join up. Some of them were heading for Canada. Others tried to get discharges and still others joined the National Guard. Those were the real smart ones, she thought. But some of her classmates wouldn't be coming home.

'America has never lost a war. It's young people with your attitude who are going to make this the first,' Mr Richards said. He had a ring of red blood around his shirt collar, like the blood vessels were going to pop.

'No, sir. It's old . . .' she nearly said 'jerks', but stopped herself just in time . . . 'men like President Nixon who are going to make this a first. He's going to lose a war that Congress never authorized. And now he wants to blame kids for it.'

Mr Richards stared at her with fury, but he had no reply. The class had moved on and Lita got an 'F' for that week's study paper, a paper which was well reasoned and lucid. She had only grinned. Mr Richards wasn't going to beat her generation like that.

The train rattled out of the station, getting her away from Soundview, away from the Bronx. She was going to Grand Central, to head out to the Village. She'd find a coffee shop and sit in the sun, on the sidewalk, and read her magazine, and dream of all the clothes she'd buy when she was a rich lady.

Which Lita Morales was determined to be.

Chapter 2

The Village was a trip. She thought it was her favourite part of Manhattan, not that she got out here too often. There was too much studying and cleaning to do. Lita had her heart set on a scholarship, maybe to NYU, maybe to Columbia. Anything that would qualify her for more than the dead-end jobs Pappy had marked out for her, or the married-before-she-was-old-enough-to-drink route that so many of her girlfriends had taken. But if it was a weekend, a Sunday, after Mass, she liked to get on the six and get into the city. Manhattan had such a vibe to it. Sure, it was dangerous after dark, and there were needles in the parks from the hippies, and graffiti over the buildings, but still . . . the concrete and glass canyons stretched up, almost for ever, and they affected Lita like a hit from the drugs everybody but her seemed to be taking.

Adrenaline crackled across her skin when she came here. She wanted an apartment on Park Avenue, on one of those buildings with silk awnings and a doorman in livery. She wanted to be like those rich young wives she saw walking out of Saks, with flunkies carrying their purchases on garment hangers and in stiff cardboard boxes. Lita could almost see inside those boxes. Delicate satin and lace lingerie wrapped in folds of gold-embossed tissue paper, tied with tiny ribbons perhaps, or a funky Fiorucci mini-dress, a swirling print with a flared hem, something Mick Jagger's girlfriend Bianca might wear with a fabulous pair of oversized white sunglasses and a large velvet hat. Lita loved fashion. Just because she didn't get to wear much of it didn't mean she didn't want it.

And the Village *was* fashion. It was as in as flared jeans and beaded shell tops. The flower children and the black power students moved side by side through the leafy streets with their low-slung brownstones that looked as though they'd come from another age. Hip, new cafés were full of guys with long hair and guitars, pumping the latest hits from England – 'Abbey Road' was her favourite record right now – and serving fancy coffee at a quarter a cup. Ridiculously expensive, but worth it to sit on the sidewalk on a sunny day like this and watch the world go by. Lita was an expert in making her coffees last an hour, maybe more. Nobody ever told her to hurry up either. She was gorgeous. A beautiful girl could do whatever she liked.

She turned onto Christopher Street and headed into Incense, the best joint on the street. Pushing her way in through the curtain of gaudily coloured glass beads that jangled and flashed, Lita strutted up to the counter and ordered a black coffee with cinnamon sprinkles.

'Ten cents,' the boy behind the counter said, spooning a liberal amount of sprinkles on to the frothy drink.

Lita blinked. 'But it's a quarter.'

The guy smiled at her, flipping his long curl, back over his brown corduroy collar. 'Honey, for you it's a dime.'

'Thank you,' Lita murmured, rewarding him with a rare smile. It lit up her face like a flash of light on the water, and the kid mentally dumped both his blonde girlfriends and proposed to her all within the space of two seconds. But she was gone, dropping the coin on the counter and heading outside to the street, and all he could do was watch the sway of that amazing round booty as she sauntered out of the door.

'Your mouth is open,' said the guy who had been sitting at the bar, sipping a whisky sour even though it was only five o'clock. He wore the kind of real expensive suit that meant you didn't make smart-ass comments about the hour when he asked for booze, not if you lived on tips.

The barkeeper sighed. 'Can you blame me? Did you check out that ass, man? That is one hot chick. I dig that, I tell you.'

'Yeah, she had nice skin.'

'Nice skin! Forget the skin, did you see the set she's dragging around? And those eyes. Damn.'

The man glanced at him in an assessing way he found kind of off putting.

'This should take care of the check,' he said, pulling out a crocodile wallet and laying a twenty on the counter. 'Keep the change, OK?'

'Are you sure? I mean, thanks,' he said, instantly regretting the question and pocketing it before the man could change his mind. That was the better part of a week's rent. And with that huge gold Rolex, he looked like he could afford it. The guy got up and followed the hot chick into the sunlight in a rattle of beads, blinking as he emerged from the dark, smoke-filled café.

The barkeeper shook his head. Eye-candy and bread. Pity neither one of them had stayed. He liked money and he liked hotties. Oh, well, he was twenty bucks to the good. He started to hum a Stones number.

He had no idea he'd witnessed a moment that would change two lives.

Lita sat in a patch of bright summer-evening sunlight and stretched out her calves. The delicious scent of cinnamon wafted up to her from the table and she breathed it in, enjoying every second as she flipped through the magazine. There was Jane Asher, snapped in an awesome orange minidress with thigh-high leather boots, and there was Twiggy, exotic and limber in a long knitted skirt and a little pussy-bow blouse against the London cold. Swinging London was so hot. She wondered if she would ever go there. Maybe someday, when she had some money. Paris, too. Paris was more violent, though; it was still recovering from those student riots last summer. Lita preferred how the English girls dressed, with that thick, chalky white eyeshadow and extra-dark mascara. Dusty Springfield was rumoured to wear seven coats. She flipped the pages, drinking up the skirts and leather-bead waistcoats and almost-sheer white blouses with the broderie anglaise at the collar. All the models were lily-white, skinny like Twiggy with no butt and no boobs. Row after row of California girls with long blonde hair and light tans. Lita felt a little insecure and tugged her coat around her to hide her breasts. She knew she could only drool over these dresses. Even if she travelled to some alternate universe where she could actually afford them, she wouldn't be able to fit into them.

It was easy to drop weight on drugs. Lita was sure half these chicks never ate real food. They inhaled their sustenance through tiny silver spoons, like the whacked-out dealers that hung round Soundview. Anyway, she tried to reassure herself, she wasn't fat. She had curves. It wasn't her fault that women's bodies were out of style now. She was still a woman. She could diet herself to death, but she'd never have the ass of a ten-year-old boy. Lita smiled ruefully. She'd need to have one of those plastic surgeons chop it right off for that to happen.

'Excuse me, miss?'

Lita glanced up. A man of about thirty-three was standing over her. He wore a fancy suit and a gold watch. She stiffened. This was her time out, and it was precious. Why did men think they had the God-given right to hit on any female that happened to be sitting on her own?

'Peace and love.' Yeah, that was cool, that was all right . . . and that was a good line for getting girls to drop their panties, Lita thought cynically. Just like it had happened to Elena, and nine months later she had two babies that you couldn't take back to the store for a refund.

'I'm kind of busy,' she said waspishly, 'mister.'

'You look like you're sitting reading a magazine,' he said mildly.

'Exactly. Like I said, I'm busy.'

He grinned, liking her fire. Man, she had some looks on her. Bill was gay, so he had an objective opinion, and this girl was hot. In the daylight you could see it all the clearer. Straight guys would sit up and pant whenever that body walked by, but he was more concerned with her face. Her skin was just fantastic. *Café au lait*, with long, glossy hair, pouting lips and angles on her cheekbones that meant she would keep her beauty well into middle age. Her heavy-lidded, chocolate eyes reminded him of . . . who was it, he could almost see it . . . Oh, sure – Sophia Loren. That was exactly who she looked like. A teenage Sophia Loren, with slightly darker skin and a Bronx accent. A real tough-girl. Of course, she'd be too short for catwalk work, and that was a bummer, but he just could not pass up the face. It was different, and at Models Six, different was what they were looking for, at least theoretically. It was true that every girl seemed to be a skinny blonde beatnik from Frisco, but he just had a feeling about this one.

'I won't take up too much of your time, miss. I'm not here to hit on you. I don't swing that way, OK?'

He fished out a card from an inner pocket and handed it over. 'This is for real. My name's Bill Fisher, and I work for a model agency.' Seeing the look on her face, he added quickly, 'A legit model agency. None of that nudie stuff. Some of the girls take their moms along to shoots.'

She didn't say anything, so he bent forward and gestured at her dog-eared copy of *Vogue*. 'Page sixty-seven – that's Tabitha, she's one of ours. And on the next page, we rep Samantha, she's the redhead on the left.'

'So? What do you want with me?'

Lita told herself to be cool, but her heart was hammering at a million beats per second.

'I'd like to take some shots first. Test shots.'

'Tests for what?' Lita demanded.

He looked at her like she was crazy. 'To be a model, of course.'

Lita told herself she shouldn't go. She had taken her break, and now it was time to get home to her books. Mama would want help with dinner. And what if they stacked the dinner plates in the sink again and left them? The apartment would get roaches. Roaches the size of mice . . .

It was no use, though. She was acting like she didn't care, but this might be the most exciting thing that had ever happened to her. Things like this just didn't happen. Of course, there was no way she'd make a model. Hadn't she just finished *Vogue*? Almost every girl in there was a white-bread, skinny blonde, not to mention tall and willowy. The kind of chick with money, with no roaches in her kitchen. But this gay dude, and from the way he was checking out the boys in tight pants on

Christopher Street, he actually *was* gay, this dude thought she had a good face. Good enough that somebody might pay her to take pictures of it.

Lita imagined Melissa Menes, the snotty girl at school whose father owned a run-down apartment building, hearing that she'd had a test to be a model. Melissa got her hair dyed platinum blonde in Manhattan every six weeks and had spare money for clothes. She never failed to sneer at Lita. Lita burned, remembering when Melissa scored tickets to see the Beatles and brought them to school, waving them around so the other girls could ooh and aah and crowd around her just to touch them. Lita hadn't bothered, even though she loved George Harrison with a passion.

'Not interested? Maybe you got your own seats,' Melissa had said, then added, with that light little laugh Lita hated so much, 'but . . . no, I guess not, huh, Rosalita?'

Melissa always liked to draw out her full name, like she was making a mockery of it. She thought she was Lita's natural superior. But smoking made her skin thin and her constant tanning in the salons had made it a bit weathered. Besides, there was a lot of acne under that expensive foundation she liked to wear.

Lita told herself to make sure to get the guy's card when they were all done here. If she didn't bring back actual proof, nobody would believe her. And she wanted to show off. She wanted Hector to be proud of her.

'OK, baby. Turn a little to the left. Smile. Nice. Now look at me as though I'm your worst enemy.'

Lita was too polite to do that. She gave the cameraman a slight frown.

She hasn't got it, he thought, mentally shaking his head, and she's too short. And what do we do with all that T and A?

He paused. There was still half a roll of film left. He couldn't really use it for much else, didn't like to get his rolls mixed up. Let the kid dream for a few more seconds, anyway. He hated it when the handlers cut a session short. The unpromising prospect inevitably started to cry and plead and strike stupid, embarrassing poses. Like this Spanish chick. She was as stiff as a board.

'OK, thanks, Mizz Morales. We're going to cut loose now. Don't bother posing, just look at the camera and move naturally.'

'But . . .'

'Don't think. Just move, baby, enjoy it, OK?'

Suppressing a sigh, he moved back behind the lens of the Hasselblad and moved to press his button and get rid of the rest of the film.

Lita started to move.

With a rising sense of excitement, he snapped his pictures, the Models Six back room exploding in a sea of light. Hell, she was hot. Really hot. Now she wasn't being directed, she moved like a star. She almost writhed. Sexuality oozed out of every inch of her golden skin and he didn't think she even knew it. She was tossing that glossy dark hair, twisting at the waist, eyeing the lens like it was a lover, challenging it, daring it, defying it, those dark eyes flashing, those haughty cheekbones tilted up at him. His mouth had gone dry. He was getting a twitch in his pants. Oh, man, please; boners in the office were a definite no-no. Of course, photographers got to bang girls all the time, that was a perk of being in the model business. But not at a first session, and certainly not at Models Six. You got blacklisted for that kind of stuff. He bit down on his inner cheek to distract himself.

'Thanks.' He stood up hastily, and gestured to the door. 'If you go back out there, Bill will take your details.'

'OK,' she said flatly.

The hot babe had gone. She was beautiful still, but she had gone back to that quiet, studious teenager that she'd been before. He started to tell her that the session had been great, but it was too late. She'd already walked out.

Outside the studio, Bill took down Lita's phone number.

'It takes a while for the shots to get developed. I'll pass them on to Mr Jack Hammond, he's the boss around here. If we're interested, somebody will give you a call, so there's no need to call us back.'

'Don't call us.' Lita shrugged. 'No sweat, mister, I get it. Can I have a copy of your card with the appointment on it?'

'What for?'

'I want to tell my friends,' she said shamelessly.

Bill chuckled. He liked her. Maybe the pictures would come out good. One in every fifty times, that actually happened.

'Sure, miss. Here you go. And here's thirty bucks for cab fare.'

'Thanks,' Lita said, pocketing the fortune without blinking. She never turned down free money. Manners only went so far. She rode the elevator out of the impressive marble building with its smoked-glass walls and caught a subway on the next block.

She wasn't going to waste money on a cab. Lita didn't believe in wasting money. She could do better things with that thirty dollars than pour it down the drain.

It was seven-thirty when she finally got home. Mama was in a bad mood.

'I left your plate, but it already got cold. You'll have to wash up after yourself, too.'

'Don't I always, Mama? How was work?'

She blew the air out of her mouth. 'Work's work. You know how it is. Your father already left for the night shift.'

'I'm sorry,' Lita said, feeling guilty.

'Just don't be late again. Chico's always late, but Pappy relies on seeing you.' Her face brightened. 'Chico gave me some money today. He did good overtime on the site.'

'That's great,' Lita said, wondering whom her brother had jacked up to get an extra twenty bucks for the house. Maybe she was being too cynical. Maybe he had actually done some work. Anyway, money was money. 'I'm going to be hearing from the colleges soon, Mama.'

'College. That's good, honey. But you know it'll be hard to pay for,' her mother said. She meant it would be hard for Lita to pay for. There had never been any suggestion that her parents could possibly afford it.

'But they offer scholarships.'

'Those things don't pay rent, Lita.'

'I can take a job.'

'You? You don't work,' Mama scoffed. She loved her daughter, but sometimes the sight of her, her hands still delicate, the nails not chipped and torn, unroughened by honest labour, maddened her. Mrs Morales did not count book-studying as real work.

'I'm pretty good at typing already. There are people who need that.'

'If you're at college all day you can't be no secretary,' Mrs Morales snapped, then instantly regretted it. It was Lita's birthday today, after all.

Lita sighed. They had this fight almost every time Mama came home. She helped herself to chicken and rice and grabbed a fork. She would eat it cold so she could kiss her Mama and get away into her tiny room quicker.

'But I could type stuff up at night. Reports and stuff. They farm out that work.'

The phone rang and her mother jumped on it, holding up one hand. '*Hola. Si.* Who is this? What do you want with her?'

Lita jumped up, her heart pounding. Her mother glanced at her.

'Yes, OK. Yes, I guess you can talk with her.' She held out the receiver gingerly. '*Querida*, it's some gentleman from the city. For you.'

'Oooh, Hector, *ayy babee*,' Melissa moaned, sitting astride him, grinding away rhythmically. Her parents were out for another hour and she had the place all to herself. It was the second time this week that Hector Fernandez had come over to 'study', and Melissa was triumphant.

Hector had that cool-ass car, and it had been driving her nuts to watch him squiring Rosalita around in it. Missy couldn't stand that arrogant bitch, anyway. She wasn't even popular, despite her glossy hair and her figure, because she was, like, a superbrain swot. Plus, what was she putting on airs for when everyone knew her dad drove a car and her mom worked in a sweatshop? Plus, she wore second-hand shit they bought at the Salvation Army, ridiculous baggy clothes. She had no pride in her appearance, but Missy thought Rosalita considered herself all superior. Didn't her brother Chico run with the gangs on the corner like the rest of the boys in the neighbourhood?

Melissa squeezed her slightly heavy thighs on Hector and bounced up and down so he could get a better view of her tits, blonde hair flying. Mmm, that bitch didn't know what she was missing. Did she want to die a virgin? Whatever. It was her problem that she couldn't keep a man.

Hector grunted, looking away, an expression of fierce concentration on his face as he thrust into her.

Melissa smiled, reaching her long, polished fingernails behind her to tickle Hector's balls lightly, the way she knew men liked. Rosa Morales was the one girl in school that had never seemed impressed with Melissa, never paid court to her expensive blonde hair and her nice make-up and her money. Once Melissa had announced that she'd just *die* if she wasn't married by twenty-five, and Rosalita had laughed and said she'd just die if she wasn't in a good job by twenty-five. Like she was Golda Meir or something. Like she was too good for Melissa.

'Hey, that's good,' Hector gasped, 'just like that—'

He stared up at Melissa's jiggling tits with those dark, perked nipples, and felt the wave of lust and pressure start to build up. Melissa Men[illegible]s was not his ideal, but what the fuck, Hector was eighteen and it didn't take much. The thought of what Lita might be hiding under those shapeless duds her Mom made her wear had kept him going for months, but he'd been starting to feel ripped off. Man, she *never* put out. And Melissa had made it clear she was good to go. Mind you, his friend Jack Metcalf said he'd banged Melissa, too, but any port in a storm . . . and she *did* have real big titties . . .

Hector grunted, gripped Melissa round the waist and exploded inside her. *Yeaaahhh* . . .

Now he had to break up with Lita, but so what? Lita wasn't gonna give him anything. Melissa had been nagging him to do it for weeks, and now she was gonna get her wish. He didn't need no uptight broads. Melissa said Lita had all the makings of a bra-burner, and Hector thought she was right.

'Let's cuddle,' Melissa suggested.

Hector grimaced. Hell, no. 'You should shower, sugar. Your folks will be back soon. Anyway, you want me to meet Lita, huh?'

'Yeah.' Melissa's red-lined lips curled up into a victorious smile. 'It's about that time.'

Lita walked to their spot on Castle Avenue – there was a little island on the service road leading down to the Cross-Bronx which had a statue on it. Kids liked to meet there; you could tell, because the base of the plinth was littered with cans, cigarettes and marijuana butts. Hector always met her here and this morning he was waiting for her, too. She squinted to see if he was holding a parcel or a bunch of flowers, but she couldn't make anything out. Never mind, maybe it was small, like a gold pin or something.

She was almost skipping. Wow, wait till she told Hector they actually wanted her to be a model, wait till he heard the kind of money they were talking about, enough to let her drop out of school, enough so that she could put college off for a few years, maybe even get a house—

Wait. There was someone else with her Hector. A *girl*. Oh, man—

'Hector?' Lita ran across the little road and looked uncomprehendingly at Melissa Menes, wearing even more foundation than usual and a pair of little gold studs in her ears. 'What is this? Did you bring my birthday gift?'

Melissa burst out giggling. 'It's your birthday?'

'It was yesterday.' Lita stared at her. 'What are you doing here, Melissa?'

'I came to wait with my boyfriend.'

Lita's eyes rounded. Hector was staring at his shoes.

'Your boyfriend?'

'That's right. Hector don't want to see you no more.' Melissa shoved an elbow in Hector's ribs. 'Ain't that right, baby?'

'You didn't give me nuttin',' Hector grumbled.

Lita shook her head. 'I thought we had something, man.'

'Well, you didn't.' Melissa's eyes flashed triumphantly under her mop of blonde hair.

'You blew it, Hector.' Lita blinked back the tears that threatened to spring to her eyes. 'I told you we could get out of here together.'

'That was always bullshit, Lita.' Hector looked at her sullenly. 'This is good enough for me.'

'And me,' Melissa piped up.

Lita shrugged. 'But not me. See you two around.'

She turned on her heel and walked off.

Chapter 3

'A thousand,' the young woman said.

Richard Jenner, the President of Women's Magazines, stared helplessly at the model. He looked at Bill Fisher for help, but the booker just shrugged his shoulders powerlessly. Models weren't supposed to negotiate their own rates. Please. They were there to show up, shut up and smile. But everybody knew about Rosalita Morales. She was a fly in the ointment. She had never had a cover, never graced the front of *Cosmo* or *Glamour,* but she had attitude like she was Ali McGraw. Somehow she'd gotten hold of the rate sheet for regular jobs like this one, and she charged a full fifteen per cent more than the going rate. His deputies had warned him that she was non-negotiable, but he'd thought he could charm her.

He'd thought wrong.

'That's a little high, isn't it, Rosalita?'

Lita narrowed those lovely dark eyes. 'Your circulation is a half-million copies per issue. You can afford it.'

He would have bristled with rage if another woman had spoken to him this way. But what could he do? She was standing there in that sprayed-on silver miniskirt riding high and tight on those golden thighs, with a vest made of mesh links pulled across those glorious breasts, held together by nothing more than a piece of tape. It was hard to be mad with her. Jenner was concentrating on not losing his professional cool. She was also wearing outrageously stacked cream thigh-high boots, which brought that arrogant, slanted face right up to his. A dusting of sheer pink over her eyebrows, white eyeliner to brighten her pupils, and a slick of gloss on her lips, and she was ready to shoot. He couldn't recall when he'd had another model do an editorial for *City Woman* wearing so little make-up.

What was the scoop on this one? Discreet sources at Models Six had assured him she didn't put out. Models that hadn't made it all the way were usually so pliable. He could drop Si Newhouse's name, mention Condé Nast, assure her of a push for that coveted *Vogue* cover. If that didn't work, usually a piece of jewellery was enough to see the little lace panties sliding down. It was a fabulous perk of being in the fashion business. Jenner allowed the corner of his eyes to take in the sides of those tantalisingly concealed breasts, quivering as her chest rose and fell with her anger. It was a mistake. He started to get hard.

She'd never make it in modelling, he thought. Not even if she put out. She was a man's woman. All those curves. Short and luscious. But middle America didn't aspire to the skinny-minnie look as much as the city chicks. He thought contemptuously of his own readership. He sold to milk-fed farmers' daughters in Des Moines.

'And it's Miss Morales, Mr Jenner.'

Arrogant little wetback, he thought, his groin tightening. He'd have to call in one of the blonde interns he had come up to his suite on the twelfth floor and get some head. It wouldn't be the same as having this Chiquita do it, but he needed something.

'There are lots of other models.'

'And there are lots of other magazines. I think Bill told your people the price. If it's too much, we'll wish you good day and be on our way.'

The almond-shaped eyes were staring him down so coldly he felt his erection subside.

'Pay her,' he said furiously to his assistant. He stormed off the set.

He vowed he'd never use the bitch again. But he knew that wasn't true. The last two times they'd featured her – in sprayed-on Levi's and a backless evening gown – sales had improved by ten per cent. Using her *café-au-lait* skin and large-breasted, firm-assed shape next to all the heroin'd-out stick insects gave his magazine a certain erotic daring, and his readers something to identify with.

When he used Rosalita, sales went up. And his bosses were happy.

For Jenner, too, it was all about money.

'You gotta be careful,' Bill Fisher said, as they emerged from the *City Woman* building. Lita wore a pair of tight black pants with a gold belt, kitten heels and an off-the-shoulder black silk jersey. The silver outfit was neatly packed into the black leather holdall she brought along with every job. In addition to her extra money, Lita insisted that each shoot let her keep the clothes. That was unheard of, but if they wanted Lita, they had to agree. Even if they shot her in Chanel.

'If you cop that much' tude, baby, they might stop using you.'

'They won't. Sales are up.' Lita looked at her booker with all the confidence he didn't feel. 'Besides, they always give me grief over there, and still come back for more.'

Bill didn't argue. Besides, he was getting better commissions for Lita than any of his other mid-level girls, and she was doing all the negotiating. After two weeks he'd learned to stop giving advice and start taking it. The most Models Six could do was to keep her up to date on circulation and rates. He had never known a chick to take an interest in that kind of thing. What most of them wanted to know was which photographers were straight, so they could try and get into their pants and maybe get a better shoot, nicer lighting or an in at a big magazine. Morales lived in her own little world. She even checked out the advertisers. She knew, being Hispanic, that the big campaigns were probably beyond her, but she didn't seem to care. She took every job that paid her price, and made sure that it kept going up. She took receipts for everything. He had an idea that she even kept a log of her subway tokens. Come tax time, she was going to screw the government out of every last dime.

Bill found her intensity a little scary.

But it was exhilarating, too. He'd 'discovered' Morales, but that was the extent of it, he thought with a rare burst of honesty. Lita was a freight train, and he'd just jumped on board.

'Costa Rica Coffee,' she said.

'What about them?'

'They've just fired Carmen Liena,' she said flatly. 'I heard it from Marcel LeBroux at the *Seventeen* shoot last week. I want that campaign. It has TV spots coming up, the whole deal.'

'That's a serious deal, Lita . . .'

'They're considering Rachel Diego, Consuela Benes and Tina Mendes,' Lita said, ignoring him. 'All those girls are in their late twenties. My family's from Puerto Rico, so I have the looks, plus I'm eighteen years old. They'll want somebody fresh.'

'You don't have experience in TV.'

'Just set it up, Bill, OK? This is my stop.'

He looked up. They were at Penn Station. 'At least take a cab.'

'Call me when you have the audition, honey,' she said, kissing him on the cheek.

Was she really eighteen? he wondered, watching her go, that sexy little sway in her walk. She acted like she could be thirty-eight.

He adored her. She almost made him wish he were straight. Maybe not, though; the guy that wound up with her was going to have a spitfire on his hands.

Lita took the train out to Jamaica, Queens. The first thing she had done with her money was to get out of Soundview. She'd done it quietly, using a real-estate agent to get around the red-lining. If you wanted to move somewhere tony, you needed to be white. That was the first thing she learned. Black people, even black people with money, weren't acceptable in certain places. The real-estate agents suddenly had nothing to show. The prices went up fifty per cent, and previously 'unforeseen difficulties' came up in the surveys. For Hispanics, it wasn't much better. She'd burned when she'd found this out.

'That's just the way it is, honey,' one buyer's agent said to her, right before she fired him.

But Lita had come to accept certain things. Her parents were not cut from the same cloth she was, she knew that. If she was confronted with prejudice, she fought it. Mama and Pappy would not. Stick them in a racist, white-bread, country-club community in a good part of Brooklyn and the hostility would make them miserable. It might almost be better to be back in the shoe-box in Soundview.

There were better destinations. She chose a nice two-family in Queens, in a Hispanic section, one with low taxes and a big yard in the back. Mama could do gardening there – something she'd always wanted. There were four bedrooms, which meant Chico could get some space. She took the lower, two-bedroom apartment and had steel bars run over the windows. Once it was secure, she would live in it, and when she'd made some more money, she could rent it out. Some veteran with a war pension could take it. Then she would move to the city. Manhattan was the place to be, and Lita was moving there as soon as she could afford it.

She had the lawn mowed, cheap, attractive flowers planted and a bottle of Sangria chilled in the brand-new fridge. Then she brought her parents to see it.

'It's amazing, Lita. Is this your boss's house?' Pappy asked her doubtfully.

Her parents no longer complained about her 'dirty' photos. For her father, any photo in clothes other than the long shapeless skirts was indecent. At first he and his wife had been so ashamed that they threatened to kick Lita out of the house. But it only took one week for Lita to come back and count five one hundred dollar bills into his hand.

Carlos had never even seen a one hundred dollar bill. He held it up to the light, then looked at his wife. They never complained about Lita's career again.

'No.' She passed him a set of keys. 'It's your house.'

Lita let herself in. She switched on the lights and carefully unpacked the bag of clothes, smoothing down the leather and holding up the mesh vest so that it sparkled. Mr Wong owned the dry cleaner's two blocks away; she'd take them to him in the morning. Right now her place was little more than a storage rack for clothes. Mobile garment racks were in every room, neatly stacked against the wall. Because of her insistence that she keep all the pieces she modelled, Lita was one of the best-dressed women she knew and it all cost her nothing.

She fixed herself a light salad with a glass of white wine. Gradually the chilled alcohol seeped its way into her bloodstream, relaxing her. Lita turned to the *Village Voice* and the local *PennySaver.* Demand for apartments in this area was increasing. Tomorrow she would speak to a rental agent. This place could fetch a decent rent, and it would defray the costs of her move across the bridge. If she wanted to get the Costa Rica campaign, she needed to be where the action was.

And that wasn't Queens.

She marched into Bill's office the next day.

'Costa Rica,' she said brightly.

His face fell. 'Honey, I asked the agency, they said the girl has to be at least five ten, and they said they don't have a screen test of you.'

'So let them take a screen test,' Lita said impatiently.

Bill blenched. He had no desire to tell her the truth. 'They just decided to go in another direction. We'll get the next one.'

'Bill, if you want to remain my agent, I suggest you tell me exactly what they said,' Lita replied coldly.

He did want to remain her agent. 'Don't take it personally. The guy said that he didn't want a minor model, that he wanted somebody well known, he had a big brand to sell, and Models Six should know better than to waste his time.'

What the guy had actually said was that he didn't want some two-bit fat chick from the inner pages, but Bill wasn't brave enough to relay that message to his client.

'What's the name of the account executive?'

'Rupert Lancaster. A limey.' Bill realized too late what that look on her face meant. 'But you can't go over there, Lita. He works for Benson Bailey and we do a lot of work with them. Renee has a shot at an Estée Lauder ad with them . . .'

'I have to,' Lita said.

Bill folded his arms and studied his feet. 'Lita, I hate to break it to you. But we have bigger clients than you, cover girls, that do a lot of work with Benson Bailey and you're going to jeopardize our relationship with them if you start causing a scene. We'll just have to work twice as hard to get you another TV campaign.'

He looked up. She was already gone.

Lita had chosen her outfit carefully this morning. She threw together pieces from her last ten or so shoots. Nothing stereotypically South

American – that wasn't the impression she was aiming for. Teetering shoes by Gucci in pale pink leather with rhinestone straps, a one-shoulder halter-necked top by Fendi in clinging white jersey, to bring out her golden skin, and a swirling, bias-cut printed skirt by Mary Quant in eggshell blue and ivory. Her hair had been blown out by Roberto at Elizabeth Arden and blew glossy and perfect in a loose mane around her shoulders. She topped it all off with a pair of huge white Chanel sunglasses set with crystal and bright glittery silver eyeshadow. Even her underwear was Dior – a tiny wisp of coffee-coloured lace, a thong, with a matching underwired bra. Over the top she threw a belted cotton Burberry raincoat.

As she reached the lobby of Benson Bailey, Lita examined herself in the mirror. Perfect. She looked like a dusky flower child, like a groupie with a million bucks. She could have stepped off the back of a Rolling Stones tourbus with no problem. It was so, so, so . . . sixty-nine. With money.

The receptionist fairly quailed when Lita strutted up to her desk.

'What floor is Rupert Lancaster again? I work with Bill Fisher over at Models Six. I have some details I need to discuss with him on an account.'

'Eighth floor, ma'am,' the girl said hastily.

'That's right. Floor eight,' Lita agreed, and stepped over to the elevators. A suited man dived to press the button to hold it open for her. Lita minutely inclined her head. Long ago she had learned not to thank men for things. You always had to act like it was your right. Otherwise men assumed it wasn't, and they wanted you to pay for it.

Her adrenaline started to race as the floors ticked off. This was taking a risk. Even though she had ignored Bill, what he said was true. If she pissed off this Rupert dude enough to cost Renee that campaign, a million-dollar job that would net hundreds of thousands in commission for Models Six, they might drop her. And even though she'd get new representation, the jobs would lessen, would drop in price. Nobody wanted to work with 'difficult' girls. As much as she refused to budge on the money and the clothes, Lita was not known as difficult. She showed up on time, she was polite to the photographers, she stole nobody's boyfriends, she didn't shoot up, she didn't come to work with bags under her eyes and she didn't try and get out early. She did what she was told. If Lita Morales was your model, you could expect to pay, but you could also expect no disruption.

She was about to be *very* disruptive.

She took a deep breath and walked out of the elevator.

Benson Bailey was one of the biggest advertising firms in New York, and it showed.

The eighth floor was as impressive as the lobby had been. Photos were mounted on the walls – she thought they were original David Baileys. There was also a Hockney and a massive Jackson Pollock. Futuristic silver-leather furniture that looked like the miniskirt she'd worn yesterday was everywhere. Discreet stills from their more famous TV campaigns were mounted on every office door right over the name-plate.

Lita marched up to the polished girl with the pearls sitting at the kidney-shaped reception table.

'I'm here to see Mr Lancaster,' she said smoothly. 'I have an appointment.'

The girl looked up sharply.

'*Mr* Lancaster? I don't see anything in *Lord* Lancaster's book.' Her eyes darted towards a corner office. 'I'll have to check with his assistant, miss.'

Damn. *Lord* Lancaster. She should have checked; Bill said he was a limey. Rookie mistake, Lita thought, angry with herself. She followed the suspicious girl's line of sight.

'I can't help it that you don't know how to keep appointments written down,' she snapped, and marched across to the corner office. She heard the girl getting up from her desk and padding across the thick white carpet after her, but she didn't look back. Lita was used to running the streets of Soundview and this Upper East Sider was no match for her. Her hand closed on the office's brass door and she pushed it open.

A tall, thin, dark-haired, utterly gorgeous man in a pinstriped suit, his curly hair coming over his collar, was standing there with his assistant, a plump woman of forty. He stopped speaking, and his eyes flickered over Lita, taking in every inch of her, finally resting on her breasts.

'I'm sorry. I couldn't stop her. *My lord*,' the girl said, flirting with him heavily even though she was out of breath. 'I don't know how she got past the lobby . . .'

'Entirely my fault,' the young man said smoothly, in an aristocratic English accent that turned Lita's bones to water. 'I forgot to notify Mrs Smith about this appointment. So nice to see you, Miss . . .'

'Morales,' Lita said.

'That's it. Miss Morales. Won't you come in?'

Chapter 4

He closed the door behind her.

'Have a seat.'

Rupert Lancaster gestured to her to sit down. His brows were slightly raised, and he was smiling slightly. Lita was used to beatnik art directors and account executives in flares and orange-and-purple print shirts. This classic look, the English tailoring and the sober tie, almost made her nervous. He looked damn good in it. He also looked serious.

He was the first man she'd felt attracted to since Hector, and suddenly the last small pangs she'd felt for Hector disappeared. She knew they would never be back either. Rupert Lancaster was in a difference class.

Lita sat down. 'You're Lord Rupert Lancaster?'

'I'm Rupert, or Lord Lancaster. In your case, Rupert. I make it a point of not being stuffy with brave young women.'

Lita blushed richly. She had been expecting him to say 'beautiful young women'. The compliment was so much better this way. She *had* been brave. 'Well, thank you anyway.'

He settled back in his chair and looked her right in the eyes. Normally their gaze went straight to her breasts and hovered there throughout a meeting. Lita found she was breathing a little heavier. Man, she loved that accent. She loved those dark eyes, the aquiline nose and the dark hair just creeping over his collar.

'Now. I assume you have something you want to say?'

'Yes. You manage the Costa Rica account. You're looking for a new girl for the TV campaign.'

'And you want to be considered.'

'No. I don't want to be considered. I want the job,' Lita said boldly.

He chuckled.

'My clients are a big brand. They think it's better to be associated with a well-known model.'

Lita brushed the objection aside. 'Rachel, Consuela and Tina are the girls on your list?'

He nodded. 'You have good information. How did you find that out?'

'It's not important,' Lita assured him. 'But Rachel has never even had a *Vogue* cover, and the other two girls only picked up their covers after they got their first TV slots. It's TV that makes a girl well known. If you use me, I will be well known the first time you show the commercial.'

'Hmm. I'm not sure they'd go for it, Miss Morales.'

'Lita, please. May I take my coat off?'

As she stood, he came around the desk and peeled it from her shoulders. She heard his faint intake of breath as his head came close to her one bared, bronze shoulder under the clinging white knit, as he took in the glorious curve of her back and her high, tight butt. She smiled softly. She was going to get him.

Rupert hung her coat up on a mahogany rack in the corner of his office. Lita turned to face him, so her silk skirt could flare up a little and show off her calves and the rhinestone pink Gucci straps could flash. She was the height of fashion and they both knew it. Delicately she folded herself back into her chair. Her top clung to her curves and her hair was trailing over her one bare shoulder.

'Maybe you could also tell them that all three girls they are thinking of are in their late twenties. I'm almost ten years younger than some of them. If Costa goes with me, they'll get young and fresh. And it's all about that today.'

'I know. You might have a point there, Lita.'

She loved hearing her name pronounced with that aristocratic accent. She leaned forward to close the deal.

'Look – Rupert – I'll make a deal with you. You don't have to give me the campaign right away.'

'Very good of you,' he said dryly.

'But give me a screen test. Thirty seconds. You take that to your clients, and you'll have discovered a fresh face. Plus, I'll work cheaper than Rachel or Consuela.'

'You certainly will, if you want the job.' He grinned. 'Well, you sold me on the test. However, please understand I'm not promising you anything. Your enthusiasm and . . . presence may not translate to the screen. I think they will still prefer Consuela. But I am prepared to offer you a test for the part.'

'Great. Where do we go?'

'You go home.'

He walked over to the coat-stand, took her Burberry off it and shook it out for her. Lita reluctantly put it on.

'I'm a busy man, surprising though that may seem to you. Right now I'm ten minutes late for my next appointment. Leave your details with Mrs Smith, and when I'm ready to set it up, I'll call you.'

'But wouldn't it be better to do it—?'

'No, it wouldn't.' Rupert opened his door. 'Mrs Smith, would you see Miss Morales out?'

Lita caught a cab for once. She needed the privacy to collect herself. She felt elated, but a little humiliated. And strange. What was it about him that made her feel like this? Her heart was thudding. He had been so rude, almost dismissive, when he turfed her out of his office. But it made her all the more attracted to him. Why?

It dawned on her slowly. He had refused to take her shit.

They were going to do the screen test, but they were going do it on his terms and his schedule. She felt a squirmy sensation in her chest. Then there was his eyes . . . those dark eyes with the black lashes, and the black hair that was almost as glossy as her own. You could stick him in a pair of flares and he could be Mick Jagger. But the dark, insistently businesslike suit just made him ten times as attractive to her.

She felt like she was floating all the way back to Models Six.

When she got there, Bill wasted no time bursting her bubble.

'How could you do that to me? You can be such a bitch, Lita, you know?'

'I did what had to be done, Bill.'

'You did what could have cost Renee her Estée Lauder shot. I do have other girls, you know, toots. I could just walk away.'

'I won't do it again.'

'Damn straight you won't. What happens to me if I have to go to my boss and say I just lost them a campaign worth a hundred Gs, not to mention all the future business Benson Bailey wouldn't do with us, all because I can't control one of my clients?'

He didn't say 'one of my smaller clients', but it hung in the air between them.

'And,' Bill continued, not drawing a breath, 'what do you think happens to agents that lose accounts? They get the can, and it's not like other agencies are banging down their doors to get them to sign up. You have no idea how fickle this business is, Lita. Right now you're hot. But when you're cold nobody wants to know your name. All those great friends you thought you had really don't give a shit about you. So I don't need you going around screwing things up on some crazy mission!'

Lita swallowed. She felt bad. Bill was her friend, and she had put his career in jeopardy. She said in a small voice, 'It didn't go so bad. He told his people that I had an appointment, and we talked, and—'

'Was that before or after he asked you to give him a blow job?' Bill passed a hand over his hair. 'I'm sorry, baby. You didn't deserve that. I know you're not that way.' He grinned. 'If you were, we'd have at least had the cover of *Elle* by now.'

'He offered me a screen test,' Lita said proudly.

Bill rolled his eyes. 'Of course he did. To get you out of his office without causing a scene.'

Lita felt her face crumple. 'You think so? You think he lied to me?'

'Why not? You lied to them, didn't you?' Bill shrugged. 'I guess he might arrange a test for you, but it won't do you any good. He'll pick Rachel or Consuela, that's the word around town. He most likely warned you that they were still the favourites.'

Her heart dropped to her boots. 'He did.'

'See, he gave you what you wanted so there wouldn't be a scene, but put his firm in no danger of getting pressganged by us. He's a limey, very polite and proper. Hates scenes. You know that's how Rupert Lancaster is.'

Suddenly, despite her aching disappointment, Lita was very interested. 'I don't know anything about him. Why would I?'

Bill remembered who he was talking to. Lita was the only one of his girls that didn't pack her little vial of coke with the tiny silver spoon attached and hit the Manhattan clubs as soon as she exited the bars. She packed up her things and rode the subway out to Queens. Crazy, but he had stopped trying to figure her out long ago.

'He's, like, a big figure on the club scene here. Goes to gigs, hangs out backstage, always in the VIP bars at the best places. He knows the Wall Street crowd and the hipsters. Film premières, that kind of thing. I saw him at the party for *The French Connection* last week. He's super-polite to everybody. The middle-aged mamas adore him, of course, because he's got that fancy title, and it's kind of hip to hang out with a lord, too. That's why the rockers love him, because they're really snobs like everyone else at heart. It wouldn't surprise me that he acted like that to you. He's one of those chivalrous types. On the surface. A real smooth ladies' man. I see him with a different chick every other week.'

'He has a girlfriend, then?'

Lita knew it was ridiculous that her heart was thudding with adrenaline as she waited to hear the answer to this. She was eighteen. Too old to have crushes, right?

'Girlfriends. Nobody special.' Bill shot her a sly look. 'Ah, princess, don't even think about it. For your own good. He's strictly a four-F guy.'

'Four F?'

'"Find 'em, feel 'em, fuck 'em, forget 'em",' Bill told her. 'You don't have the right stuff to wind up an English lady, sugar. So just skip this one, huh? You could have anybody you wanted.'

Yeah, Lita thought, but I want Rupert Lancaster.

She knew exactly what Bill meant. She was Hispanic. It wasn't so much that she didn't have the right look to be an English lady. They both knew that if Lita put her mind to it she could find some stiff tweed skirts and pussy-necked white blouses and dress exactly like Princess Margaret. It was more that she didn't have the right *skin* to be an English lady.

Lita stole a glance at herself in the large mirrored door to Bill's office. She looked hip and gorgeous, but she also looked exotic. She loved her own looks, she had never lied to herself about that. But for the first time in her life, she examined her exquisite *café-au-lait* complexion and wished it were just a little lighter. But, hey, maybe Fisher had it all wrong. He was gay. He'd underestimate just how far a man would go for a woman he loved and lusted after. Mick Jagger had married Bianca, hadn't he? And Lennon was all loved-up with Yoko. It was true that the upper-class Brits didn't seem to cross boundaries that much, but there was a first time for everything. Some of their old kings had married Spanish and Portuguese queens. So why not a lord? They were marrying commoners all the time. If she went to England, she'd just be seen as an American model; nobody would know she was from the Bronx . . .

'Lita. Quit it. I know what you're doing. Don't.' Bill stood. 'If he calls, you can go to the screen test, but don't become another notch on the bedpost. You'll thank me for it one day.'

'Sure, Bill. Whatever you say.'

'I fixed up some appointments for you to go see apartments,' he added, trying to distract her.

'Apartments?'

'You said you wanted to move into the city.' Bill tossed her a *Village Voice* with various addresses ringed in pen. 'Forget the Costa Rica campaign and the limey. This is gonna take you all day. And one more piece of advice? Wear flats.'

He was right about the shoes, Lita reflected. She'd ignored his advice the way she usually did, but after the Gucci straps had rubbed off a layer of skin she'd given in and taken a cab to Macy's. Now she was in blessedly comfortable, hideously un-hip white sneakers. The sun had sunk over the towering glass-and-concrete forest of the city. She had seen eight places, and she had five more to go before she called it quits.

They were dumps. Pretty much all of them. One was about as large as her room back in Soundview; another had a concrete ceiling so low that anyone over five-eight would have to stoop; then there was the walk-up that involved seven flights of stairs, the basement apartment with the leaky pipes running across the ceiling, and the former hostel that she ran right out of because she could actually see the bugs scuttling across the floor.

But she was hooked. With each shitty apartment, Lita got a little more excited. No way was she going to live in one of these dumps, but they were all *here*. In Manhattan. Where men like Rupert Lancaster did the club scene. Where girls schmoozed with the power players and got the big jobs and the big cheques. The fact that landlords thought they could get away with asking outrageous rents for these places excited her; they were on the market only because people were desperate to live here, to be part of the cool set. If you could make it here, you could make it anywhere, went the song, but what it didn't say was that unless you made it here you went nowhere.

Manhattan was the brass ring. If it weren't, Bill wouldn't have sent her to these dives with a straight face.

Lita made up her mind. She wasn't going home without a signed lease. She was moving to Manhattan, and she was moving there today.

The next place she looked at was another dump. The one after that was only a dump-ette. Lita pinned the owner down and signed with him.

'I can only give you six months,' he said, reluctant to take the lease out of his pocket. She had jumped on it so quickly it probably meant he could have asked for an extra two hundred a month. 'And there's no rent control on this place.'

'That's fine. Sign the lease, please,' Lita said.

'Maybe I need to look it over first,' he said, eyes narrowing.

'And maybe I need to call the Housing Department. This place doesn't even have a full kitchen, which means you're trying to rent an illegal apartment. My brother works for them over in the Bronx. I could ask him to investigate this for me.'

The man paled behind his moustache. 'Sure, kid, whatever. Sign here.'

Lita took his leaky ballpoint and signed with a flourish. What did she need a kitchen for? She was going to be eating out every night. She folded the lease neatly into her purse and held out her hand for the keys.

'Wetback bitch,' her landlord muttered just loud enough for her to hear as he stormed out of the apartment.

Lita grinned. Music to her ears. She wouldn't have any trouble from him. If he'd had any balls, he'd have said it to her face.

The phone was wired in. She wiped down the receiver and called her mother. Let Pappy be in charge of renting the place downstairs. Mama agreed placidly. They had been expecting Lita to move out for some time now. Their roles had been totally reversed – her parents were in awe of her, and did whatever she suggested.

Lita was going to sleep here tonight. She thought about her clothes. Chico could bring them in the truck tomorrow. Within one week, she'd be totally settled in.

She locked up and headed for Filene's Basement.

'Veree nice.'

Chico lit a cigarette and stood in her living room, taking it all in. His sister – his stuck-up, arrogant sister – was living like a millionaire. He ignored the small size of her place, and the fact that most of her furnishings and drapes came from thrift stores in the East Village. He only took in the style. Lita had gone for an Indian effect, very Ravi Shankar, with Paisley drapes and purple and gold cushions on her bare couch. There was a hardwood floor, already meticulously clean, covered with a threadbare, cool-looking oriental rug, and mismatched pieces thrown together. She had a lot of closets and they were all full of her clothes. There was a scent of sandalwood and spices.

'Makin' a lot of *dinero*, Lita.'

It was a statement, rather than a question.

'I do OK. I send half to Pappy.'

'Sure you do.' Chico burned with resentment. Miss Goody Two-Shoes, now she was acting like a tramp, getting her picture took and living like a movie star. To get money, he had to work on a building site or jack up some chump. Why her? There were prettier chicks than her. 'You got too much cash. You should give me some. At least get me a job. I can manage you.'

'I got an agent.'

'Who can look out for your needs better than family?'

'I can't do that.' Lita burned with embarrassment. She felt so removed from her brother it wasn't true. He had taken from their parents, bummed through his life, and now he wanted a free ride off her. 'But Chico, I got an idea.'

'I'm waiting,' he said, annoying her even more.

'My place downstairs. I was going to rent it out, but who knows what damage a tenant would do. Tell you what. You can have it. Live there yourself or rent it out to somebody responsible. You could keep the rent.'

He shrugged. 'Yeah. You need me to do you a favour.'

A favour! She had only put it that way so he could save face. 'If you don't want it . . .'

'I want it. I'll tell Pappy. I got to go, Lita. See you some time,' Chico said.

He walked out, not bothering to shut her door.

Lita flopped on a cushion and tried to calm herself. Forget her brother. He was a good-for-nothing and he'd always be that way. She knew she had to move on. Her family was in her past now. She loved them, but she was heading for a new life.

She wished Rupert Lancaster would call.

Chapter 5

'Come in,' the young man said. He had lanky blond hair coming over his collar, and he wore a pair of tight jeans and a flower-print shirt with wide lapels. Just another hippie, Lita thought dismissively. She shrugged off her Dior swing coat and glanced around the room.

'Where's Rupert?'

'Who? I'm Freddie Wilson. The director.'

Lita shook his hand, a little impatiently. 'Rupert. Lord Lancaster. From Benson and Bailey.'

She hadn't heard from him all week. In fact, she hadn't heard from him at all. Yesterday, at seven, just when Bill was going to head out for the night, he'd gotten a call from some woman at Zane Productions, the hot commercials house, for Lita to come in for a test this morning. She had hardly been able to sleep, thinking he would finally be here.

'Oh, the client? They never send people to the shoots. Just watch the results, I guess.' He gestured to a chair in the corner. 'Sally will see to your make-up, OK?'

Lita slipped into the chair, annoyed. Great. What a frigging snub. He wasn't even here, and she'd wasted at least four hours of sleep on nothing. She had hollows under her eyes and she was extremely tired.

With an effort, she focused on Sally.

'How are you doing.' Lita gave her a grin. Make-up people could be a girl's worst enemy; the snotty models that treated them as though they didn't exist always seemed to look just that bit worse than the others. 'I hope you got some strong concealer in that bag.'

There was no point getting annoyed. Right now she had a job to do.

Bill had obviously been right about Lancaster just going through the motions with this test. It was her job to shake him out of his complacency.

'What's your name, sugar?' the director asked when they'd finished. He had a thin sheen of sweat on his brow. The way that model had swung her hips, smoothed the fabric over her tits, flashed those dark eyes . . . she was an out-and-out diva. She was a carnival in Rio all on her own.

He wanted her so bad it hurt. Screw Bill Fisher and his warnings to stay away.

'Rosalita Morales,' she said.

'You got something. You really got something.'

'Oh, I know,' she said.

Then, before he could offer her a spliff, she grabbed her coat and sauntered out.

Bitch, Freddie Wilson thought. She could at least show him some gratitude for this amazing test he'd just shot of her. Who did she think she was, some kind of movie star or something? He wished he could just junk the test, but Benson and Bailey wanted results. And, besides, he had a nasty feeling that she was going to make it. If so, he didn't want to be on her bad side. He shot a look at Sally. She was ten pounds too heavy and no model, but she was pliant. She'd have to do. He needed *something.*

•

'But she's *perfect,*' Rochman said. 'You're a genius, Lord Rupert.'

Rupert smiled lightly and didn't bother to correct him. 'She is rather good for the brand. I can negotiate an excellent rate for you, too.'

'Hmm,' Rochman said, not taking his eyes off the screen. Lita was smiling invitingly, dancing against a white backdrop. In the actual commercial there would be rows of coffee plants, she would be wearing a garish, fake Costa Rican costume and she'd be shaking a fistful of coffee beans. But he totally got the girl. She had liquid eyes and a slanting, arrogant face. Pure sensuality. Housewives would run to get his jars of weak instant coffee; they'd see it as exotic and daring. Maybe he could even start selling to teenagers and those drugged-out college kids. She was young, fresh and still somehow knowing. He wanted her himself.

'Cast her. Maybe I'd better attend the shoot if she's so inexperienced.'

'She seems to be doing OK there,' Rupert pointed out. His aristocratic face was impassive. 'I normally supervise the commercial shoots. But if you have a personal reason to be there . . .'

'No. Nothing personal,' Bob Rochman said hastily. He couldn't afford any rumours; his best friend had just got taken for almost fifty per cent in their nasty divorce settlement. 'You'd better go. Set it up soonest. I want to get this baby on the air.'

'Certainly, Mr Rochman,' Rupert said, and stood up, smiling.

He was looking forward to this.

Lita tried to stop her heart thudding and act casual. This was such a big deal – her first TV campaign, with Bill and the agency suddenly falling over themselves to lick her boots, and real money for the first time, and having an assistant drive out to the Passport Office to provide her with an emergency travel document – but all she could think about was the limey account executive.

She had never been on a plane before. A limo arrived to take her to the airport, and she rode out to JFK in air-conditioned silence, trying to calm herself. She'd dressed like Audrey Hepburn – little cut-off white pants, a silk shirt, huge wraparound sunglasses, a string of fake pearls. Her luggage was Louis Vuitton. She had bought it with her signing bonus, without even looking at the bill. Sure, an insane indulgence, but Lita wanted Rupert to be impressed. It mattered more to her even than saving money.

She checked her small suitcase in and was instantly greeted by an airport rep.

'Miss Morales? Baron Lancaster asked me to take you right to him.' He put her on a little cart and drove her right through the throngs of people, down a semi-empty corridor, and stopped right before a little door. 'Have a great flight,' he said, hovering for a second before disappearing. Too late, she realized he'd been waiting for a tip. She still wasn't used to that. Giving money away was a foreign concept to her.

Lita pushed the door open. It was a small, luxurious haven, with chairs and couches upholstered in velvet, a bar with coffee, tea, alcoholic drinks, fruit and snacks. Women lounged around in Chanel and Fendi. Papers and magazines were suspended from mahogany racks, and a butler moved around, offering refreshment to the bored, monied crowd.

She loved it.

Lita breathed in, deeply. This was it. She had arrived.

'Lita.' She spun around to see Rupert Lancaster standing there. He towered over her. He wore another well-cut dark suit and carried a neat briefcase in maroon leather. She noticed a discreet coronet with his initials under it embossed on the front. 'I take it is Lita, not Rosalita?'

'Yes,' she muttered. Suddenly she didn't want to look him in the face. He was so achingly gorgeous. What was it Bill had said? Strictly a four-F guy? She remembered her brother Chico, that pig, literally scoring notches into his bedpost. Rupert Lancaster was too European to do that, but the concept remained the same. This man was all clubs and gigs, and everybody knew how the groupies gave it up. Lita had watched the TV news shots of Woodstock totally mystified. Drugs, mud, naked girls letting themselves be groped and ogled, all in the name of love.

But she knew her brother and his friends too well for that. It sure was free. For men. And who was to say Rupert wasn't just the same thing, except in a suit?

She didn't want to look at him. She was almost afraid to.

But there was no getting around it. Reluctantly Lita raised her eyes to his.

'Maybe I'm getting ahead of myself. Would you still prefer Miss Morales?'

'No, that's OK. Uh, my lord.'

He grinned. 'Rupert and Lita, then. Never say that again. Only servants say the "my lord" stuff. And I hope that we're going to have an excellent working relationship.'

'Absolutely,' Lita said, feeling a fresh stab of disappointment. Working relationship. Of course. She had caramel skin, and she was a girl from the Bronx. What else could he possibly want with her?

'And after that, a friendship. If I'm not being too presumptuous.'

Lita felt his smile break over her like the sun blazing through the clouds. A wash of warmth rushed right across her skin.

'I'd like that,' she said.

They took three days and two nights to shoot the commercial. Lita turned in a relentlessly professional performance, not even wincing at the cheesy costumes. The light was blackish, gathering storm clouds sweeping over the green mountains, so that they had to take an extra day. Lita loved it. She got to stay in the hotel with Rupert. She wished they could be marooned for ever.

Benson Bailey had booked them in at the optimistically named Hotel Superior. The crew and the director bitched about the lack of air-conditioning, the wooden walls, the local food, but Lita ignored all that. From her window, there was a glorious view sweeping down to the valley; the mountains, deeply, wetly green, thrusting up to the clouds, and the sun brilliant in the sky the colour of a robin's egg. She loved goat, and chicken, the local cheeses and the unnamed, heady red wine. And best of all, Rupert's room was right next door.

On the second night, he invited her to eat with him.

'I didn't see you in the cantina last night,' Lita ventured, when she got into his room.

'Rice and beans?' Rupert lifted a brow. 'I'm not a rice and beans kind of chap.'

She wanted to ask if he'd ever actually tried rice and beans, but she didn't dare.

'Please, sit down.' He indicated a small table in the middle of the room. It had been set with a white linen cloth, silver cutlery and crystal wineglasses. Lita's eyes rounded.

'Where did you get this? I didn't think this was that kind of place.'

Rupert pulled out her chair, and Lita nervously sat down, trying to remember from the TV shows she'd seen what rich people did at dinner. Self-consciously she shook out the thick napkin and gingerly smoothed it across her lap. She tried to relax and 'be herself'. Except that suddenly she wasn't sure if herself was really good enough.

'It's not.' He gave her a sly wink. 'I make it a rule never to touch the local cuisine. I had this shipped from London.'

He indicated a small trunk in the corner of his room. It had linens and silverware in the lid, and a wicker hamper of food from somewhere called Fortnum & Mason underneath.

'Only trouble is it's all cold, but one must make do.' He brought over delicate dry crackers and pâté in a silver dish. 'Fois gras. Ever tried it?'

Lita spread it obediently on her cracker. It was smooth, very good. 'No.'

'It's made from a goose liver. They force-feed the bird until its liver explodes.' Blithely he lashed it on his cracker and bit in. Lita felt nauseated, but managed to swallow the rest of it. She didn't want him to get put off.

'Have some more.'

'No. No, thanks, I . . . have to watch my figure.'

'I suppose that's wise, for a model. Have a glass of champagne, though. They call it the jockey's drink. No calories.'

Lita allowed him to pour the Veuve Cliquot into her crystal flute. It was room temperature, but still absolutely delicious. She gulped at it. Rupert's dark eyes twinkled. He poured her another.

'Excellent. I do like a woman with a zest for life,' he said softly.

The alcohol went to her head. Lita's tension seeped out of her. She relaxed in her chair and smiled at Rupert. Man, he was handsome.

'What's the next course?'

He grinned. 'Smoked salmon, brown bread and a squeeze of lemon juice. Have you ever tried that?'

'No.' Emboldened now, she looked right back at him. 'We don't get much fois gras and smoked salmon in the Bronx.'

'That's where you're from?'

'It sure is,' Lita said, defiantly. 'My father drives a cab and my mama works in a garment shop. Worked. I send her money now, so she doesn't have to.'

There wasn't a flicker on Rupert's face. 'And was that what you were going to do before you realized how beautiful you were?'

It took a second for the compliment to register. Then Lita felt a slow flush creep all along her cheeks.

'No. I was going to go to college,' she said. 'And have a career.'

He chuckled. 'No chance of that, my dear. Some lucky chap would have snapped you up for a wedding miles before you got to be a typist in some little office.'

Lita didn't quite see how having a career had to equal being a typist, but she kept her mouth shut.

'I don't think I'm the type to sit at home with babies,' she ventured.

'That's only because you're so young. I hope you haven't been reading that Germaine Greer crap. The female eunuch, and all that. Let me tell you something, Lita. Women are all the same. They're made for love. Just love.'

She smiled at him uncertainly.

'Some women have to work, you know.'

'I know. And I think it's a tragedy that men aren't taking up their responsibilities. Of course, an unmarried woman must take care to secure her financial future, if she can.' He sounded doubtful about that. 'But when a young woman marries, her husband ought to take up the slack. Children, and making a happy home. Those are significant, you know. Don't you think so?'

'Of course.' She felt a bit confused. 'The most important thing.'

Rupert beamed. 'Absolutely. The most important thing. Love doesn't get its full due in our modern world. We can send cosmonauts into space, but we can't explore our own hearts.'

Lita gazed into his dark eyes.

'Oh, yes,' she said.

After dinner he walked her to her room and kissed her hand gently. Lita drifted into her bedroom, drunk with more than wine. She felt that squirming sensation in her belly, and she was moist between her legs. She had been half hoping that he would push her into her room, thrust her down on the bed and rip her virginity from her. It couldn't hurt as much as the girls said it did. But, no, he was too much of a gentleman.

She got it together just enough to drink two bottles of the French mineral water he had brought with him. That sobered her up, and she peeled off her clothes and fell into bed, pulling the mosquito net shut tight around her.

Just before she fell asleep, Lita remembered why Rupert had confused her. She wanted marriage, and someday kids. But why couldn't she work, too? Why was it one or the other?

It didn't matter. The image of his gorgeous, thick-lashed eyes staring into hers lingered in her brain.

He said he was all about love. Maybe Bill had it wrong. Maybe he wasn't such a wolf after all.

They wrapped up the shoot the next day. Rupert had to take an earlier flight home, because he had a meeting.

'It's a lawyer thing. A frightful bore,' he told her, shrugging.

'I hope nothing bad,' she said.

He grinned. 'Quite the reverse, actually. But I have to take care of it.'

She missed him badly when the car came to drive him away. It was ridiculous. But she still managed to concentrate on the shoot. After all, Rupert would see it, and there was no way she was going to disappoint him. They wrapped up just as the sun began to sink, rosy light spilling all over the mountains. It was spectacular, but all Lita wanted to do was get home. New York city was where Rupert was.

They landed at JFK at half past one in the morning. Lita dragged herself off the plane, stacked her luggage on the little cart and wheeled it out to where her driver was waiting. She had half expected to see Rupert there but, of course, that was just foolishness.

I mustn't lose my head, she told herself. I'm Rosalita Morales. He likes me, but I'm not a smoked salmon kind of chick. I can't jeopardize everything over some crush like a screaming girl at a Beatles gig.

When she got home, there was a card in her mailbox. Lita ripped it open, a surge of excitement blasting through her exhaustion.

It was a Valentine's Day card, stiff, heavy, gold-embossed edges. Inside there was a barely legible scrawl in blue fountain pen.

'The calendar says September, but it feels like February to me. R.'

She hugged it to her chest and didn't fall asleep until the sun crept up over grimy lower Manhattan.

Chapter 6

The campaign was a huge success.

The sight of Lita sashaying across the screen, her dark eyes flashing defiantly, her firm butt encased in a gaudy swath of bright green, fruit wound into her hair like a Victorian stripper, moved jars of instant coffee off the shelves all across America. Costa Rica followed it with another Lita campaign, this time featuring her in a suede dress with tassels, sitting in an opulent hotel lobby, sipping the nasty brew out of a bone china cup. 'Authentic Costa – Authentic Class,' screamed the slogan, and their market share went up four per cent.

Lita had money. She bought her parents a house of their own and gave them the two-family as an income property. They retired without further fuss. As far as Pappy was concerned, only a fool worked unless he had to. Chico sidled up to her for money, too. Lita offered to take him to Barney's, to get him some suits, get him a position of some kind at Benson Bailey. But he refused.

'Jus' give me the money, sis. I got me some *investments*,' Chico insisted.

'What kind?' she said suspiciously.

His face darkened. 'I don't want to say. I could blow it. You know how it is.'

Not really, she thought.

'Are you going to give me the money or not? I'll pay you back. It's a good opportunity for you. Of course, you don' *have* to. I'm only your brother,' Chico said with heavy sarcasm.

Lita gave him the money. Four thousand in cash. She wouldn't dream of handing Chico a cheque. What did he know from banking? It wasn't their way. She still had the money she'd saved up in that sock. She didn't ask for a receipt, because she knew she'd never see a dime of it ever again.

But it was worth it to pacify Chico. He wasn't exactly thrilled about her success. Whatever she could do to ease his simmering anger, she wanted to do. Lita racked her brains for something Chico could do to get him off the track of becoming her 'manager'. She thought about buying houses with two or three apartments . . . 'three families', the real estate people called them. Then Chico could be a handyman, run them for her. If only she could be sure he wouldn't shake down her tenants for money . . .

But it was hard to think too much about her brother. Lita was being swept along in a cloud of money, fame and aching hipness. Not to mention love.

Rupert had asked her out the day after she got home. Lita had sat there, staring at the phone, willing it to ring. When it had, she jumped on it before it could even complete its first trill. It was him, and a shudder of pleasure rippled through her to hear his voice.

'I suppose you must have thought that card was incredibly corny.'

'No, no, it was just perfect,' Lita sighed, thinking he was, too.

'I'd have sent flowers, but you wouldn't have been there to receive them.'

'That's OK,' Lita murmured.

'I take it that it wouldn't be too presumptuous to hope you'd go out with me?' Rupert said.

'Oh, no.'

'No, you wouldn't? Well, I can't blame you. I wouldn't either.'

'Of course I would. I meant . . .' Lita flushed.

'I know what you meant, sweetheart. I'm just teasing you. Tell you what. You get yourself ready, and I'll pick you up around ten.'

'Isn't that a bit late?' Lita said, then winced. She could have kicked herself. The first date was not the time to start criticizing. What did she know? He was the sophisticated one.

Rupert laughed. She loved the crisp, limey accent that he had. Like a prince or something. He was a nobleman, of course. It was a whole different world, and Lita suddenly longed to be part of it.

'Maybe for a bourgeois dinner for two. But we're going to a late supper, and then we're hitting the clubs. I want to show you off. Wear something dramatic, darling, won't you?'

I sure will, Lita thought after she hung up, utterly excited. She raced to her shower. Hair first . . . you couldn't look great unless your hair was glossy and gleaming. She soaped every inch of her body, rubbing Chanel No. 5 body lotion into her smooth-shaven legs. Frantically she began to go through her extensive wardrobe in her mind. It felt about as important a decision as choosing a wedding dress. Lita slipped into a luxurious white towelling robe from Saks – one she'd had delivered in that glorious thick cardboard box lined with crisp tissue paper – and padded over to her closets. Sexy, but not too sexy. Even though he'd said dramatic, Lita was going to be careful. She knew she could pour herself into thigh-high white boots, a leather miniskirt that looked like a belt with pretensions and a halter-necked mesh vest with two discreet copper-wrought flowers to cover her nipples, and she'd have Rupert, and every other man she'd meet tonight, drooling at her feet. But after he'd drooled, and gotten her into bed – maybe with presents of diamond rings, the way some of the magazine guys had tried to bribe her – he'd fuck her a few times, then dump her. And Lita wanted to be more than that.

She wanted to be Rupert's wife.

Maybe it was crazy to think like that, and on the first date, too, but Lita didn't care. She believed in Destiny, and Rupert Lancaster had Destiny written all over him. From that first encounter in his office, with her heart in her mouth, to him making he wait so long she thought he'd forgotten about her, to that romantic evening in Costa Rica . . . Oh, man, what would Mama say . . . her little Chiquita an English Lady, a Baroness . . .

Lita went through her wardrobe like a general planning a strategic attack. Something sexy, but not tarty. Hmm . . . She tried a minidress in silver leather, a backless ruby gown in crushed velvet and a clinging pantsuit in lemon silk, but nothing was quite right. She settled on a fitted silk top in a soft pink, set with tiny silver beads, and a white swing skirt that came to just above the knee but which lifted and moved around her legs when she walked. She spritzed herself with more Chanel, tugged on a pair of teetering high pumps and she was ready to go. Carefully, Lita tugged her robe back on so she wouldn't stain her outfit, then went to her kitchen and fixed herself an omelette. She had a feeling Rupert would be impressed if she didn't eat too much. Lita saw the models around her getting skinnier every day. The restaurant he'd take her to might be a steakhouse, who knew? But she'd do better if she just ordered a grilled chicken salad. The thought of rabbit food made her starving. She threw peppers and fried-up steak strips and a little cheese in her omelette and devoured it. A glass of Cabernet Sauvignon, and she was more relaxed.

I'm ready for this, Lita told herself.

Rupert arrived with the largest bunch of red roses she'd ever seen.

'Five dozen,' he said, when he saw her trying to count them. Mmm, she was a looker. Check out those tits in that tight pink top. He glanced and checked out the slight puckered shape of the nipple against the silky material. Her little white skirt showed off the curve of her calves; he imagined the firm, satiny thighs. Would her pussy be trimmed, or shaved right off? She was so young. Completely fuckable. He couldn't wait, really.

Oh, well. Softly softly. She was almost ready to drop into his hands like a ripe plum. She'd be begging for it like every other piece of ass in New York soon enough.

Lita was overwhelmed. 'Let me just put them in some water.'

He chuckled. 'I doubt you have that many vases. Here, let me.' He took the heavy blossoms from her, ran a sink half-full of cold water and dropped them in there. 'After work tomorrow, maybe we'll go to Bloomingdale's and get you something to put them in. But don't stare at them all night. We've got places to go.'

He tugged her after him out on to the street. He slipped her into a cab – for some reason she'd expected him to come in a limo, but this was refreshing. Maybe he was just trying to show her he was a regular guy. In the car, Rupert turned to her admiringly.

'You've got real style, Lita,' he said.

'Style is my business,' she said, basking in the compliment.

He took her to Tavern on the Green and ordered caviar and blinis, which she loved, and a chilled bottle of champagne.

'You shouldn't spend so much money on me,' Lita protested.

Rupert took her hand, turned it over in his, and kissed the back of her palm, slowly and deliberately. She felt herself instantly slick up between the legs and pressed them together.

Not on the first date. Not if you're playing for keeps, said the little voice in her head. Her mother's voice.

'You're worth every cent, and more. Besides . . .' he gave her a wink '. . . it's all on expenses. The ad is testing wonderfully. You're going to be a huge star.'

'So what are you doing in America, Rupert?' Lita asked.

He smiled.

'Would you believe that I'm marking time?'

She blinked. 'You're a major executive at Benson Bailey.'

'That's true,' he said smoothly. 'But I have interests in England.'

'With that title, you must be rich,' Lita said, then regretted it. She didn't want him to think she was a gold-digger. Silently she thanked God that the Costa Rica campaign was paying her two hundred thousand, all in. She had money of her own. Not in his league, of course, but enough to differentiate her from all the other hippy chicks and fortune-hunters that Bill said liked to hang on his every word.

'There's more to it than money. I have a place, a family house. It's belonged to the Barons Lancaster ever since King James I gave us the title.'

His face darkened.

'So . . . that's good, isn't it?'

'It would be, if the house were in my hands. There's a small legal problem. But I'm having it resolved.'

'That's why you flew back to New York?'

'Exactly.' He ran his manicured thumb lightly over the palm of her hand. Lita's nipples tightened instantly. She shifted forward, hoping he hadn't seen it, but Rupert's dark gaze was fixed on her chest.

'It's cold in here, huh,' she said.

'No,' Rupert said, grinning. 'Not particularly.'

Quickly she took a gulp of her wine, covering herself.

'But let's not talk about me. I'd much rather discuss you and your brilliant prospects,' he said.

'But I *want* to talk about you, Rupert,' Lita said earnestly.

Hell, she's young, he thought. She made him want to lick his lips. What a glorious body she had. And almost certainly untouched. She was for too uptight to ever have gotten properly laid.

Rupert was bored of the skinny-minnie coke junkies he took home from all the nightclubs. No tits, no ass, and nothing to say. This one was reasonably intelligent and, more importantly, was eminently pliable. Just eighteen. She carried herself well, too. He thought with a wardrobe from Chanel, some proper clothes from Dior, a string of pearls or two, nobody would really notice her background. She looked exotic, and wasn't that all the rage in London at the moment? Of course, he'd have to get her voice coaching. But that would be easy to arrange. She had money, and the house – once he got it back – would need fixing up. He could parlay his grace and favour Benson and Bailey job into four or five campaigns for Lita, get her into the multimillions, and then marry her. She'd get a title and he'd get money, not to mention the finest ass he'd seen in five years.

It would be a lot easier because she worshipped him. Something she made no effort to hide.

But then again they all worshipped him.

He checked out the taut nipples under the silk beaded top. Gorgeous. He wondered if they were cherry pink or dusky rose. Mentally he flicked a tongue over them.

'I want to talk about your love life,' Lita persisted.

Rupert shrugged. 'What love life, darling? Apart from meeting you, my life has been a desert. A boring desert of work.'

'My agent told me—'

'Bill?' Rupert waved his fish-knife at her dismissively. 'Bill's a sweetheart. But he's gay. He really doesn't understand that straight men can have female friends without sleeping with them.'

'He said you were really popular in the clubs.'

'It's the title. I know it's childish, but some girls seem so fascinated by it. And it was only something I was born with, not something I've earned.'

Lita sighed. He was so perfect.

'I think that you should only be rated for who you are, not how you were born. That's one of the things that attracted me to you. Your drive. You burst into my office and wouldn't take no for an answer. I admire that in a woman. We need more girls like you around.'

'Thank you,' Lita said. She almost glowed.

'Eventually you'll get married and give the modelling up, I know. But until then, you're going to be a big star.'

'You think I have what it takes?' Lita asked.

Rupert gave her a slow wink.

'Baby, I think you have everything it takes.'

After dinner, he drove her out to the Lions' Den. It was the hot new place in the East Village, packed full of minor rock stars and film executives, with girls in thigh-high minis three deep on the sidewalk, begging to get in. They exited the cab, and Rupert walked up to the gorilla of a doorman. Lita walked behind him, her heart thudding. This kind of place was something she had never tried before. Sally, another girl at the agency, had gotten turned away from this place just last week. She would never allow herself to be humiliated like that.

'Come in, your lordship,' the gorilla grunted, and removed the red velvet rope. The crowd outside howled, but Rupert, ignoring them, whisked Lita inside and up a flight of steps.

'You forgot to pay.' Lita gestured at the booth.

'Don't be silly, darling. I never pay. Ah, Alessandra, *cara*, good to see you.' Rupert kissed the air at the side of a woman's cheeks. She wore a sheer white dress in chiffon, dotted with flowers. She was nude under the dress. Lita bit on her cheeks to suppress a gasp.

'Rupert, dah-ling. I have the lounge all ready for you. And your woman. Who is it this time?'

Rupert's smile didn't fade. 'This is Rosalita Morales, a big star at Models Six.'

'Wonderful. I was a model, too.' Alessandra didn't even glance at Lita. She was heavily made up, and her boobs were sagging. Lita guessed the woman wasn't far shy of fifty. A shiver of fear ran through her. Was this what awaited the ex-model? Refusing to realize you were over the hill? Displaying a beauty that wasn't there any more?

That's not going to happen to me, she vowed silently. She'd have to find something else to do. She was quitting on her twenty-fifth birthday.

'You were *the* model, sweetheart. And now you own this fabulous place.'

'*Si*. Come, dah-ling. Your table is waiting, like always.' She turned on one of her teetering stilettos and led them up a flight of metal stairs. There was a velvet-covered door at the top, with another gorilla outside it. Alessandra swept through the crowd as the heavy pushed the door open.

Lita breathed in sharply. Two rock stars she recognized, with teenage blondes draped over them, were doing lines of cocaine openly off a glass-topped table. There was a daytime soap star on a plush maroon bench, feeling up the tits of a gameshow 'assistant' Lita had seen once or twice. Pappy was a fan. She lifted her eyes from the girl's exposed nipples, trying to hide her shock. She didn't want to come off as some little naïve kid.

'Here, my angel.' Their hostess gestured to a corner table, mercifully dark, with a bottle of champagne already chilling on it. She sat down and realized that one wall of the VIP room was a pane of tinted glass. They could see the crowd dancing and sweating below, but none of them could see in. It was weird. Lita slid into the booth.

'Thank you,' she muttered.

Alessandra ignored her and kissed Rupert on the cheeks. 'I see you later, baby, OK?'

'Rupert.' A young girl bounced up to their table, wearing a white crocheted minidress and no knickers, from what Lita could see of her bony ass. 'Baby, baby, it's been too long. At least a—'

'Poppy, hi.' Rupert cut her off, shaking her hand. The girl looked disconcerted. 'Have you met Lita Morales? She's with Models Six.'

'I'm with Ford,' Poppy said, looking at Lita coldly. 'Are you a friend of Rupert's?'

Lita felt a sudden wave of jealousy crash right through her. She hated this skinny white girl with the platinum dye job, dressed like a total slut. The old hag was bad enough, but this bitch had to be even younger than she was. Jailbait with a crush on Rupert. In Soundview, the girls didn't sit around and let other women make an open play for their men.

'No, I'm not his friend, I'm his girlfriend,' she snapped. 'Nice to meet you, OK, Poppy, but could we get a little privacy? We're trying to have a romantic evening here.'

She ignored the soap star manoeuvring the dolly bird front and centre on his lap. Poppy looked at Rupert, enraged, but all he did, Lita was glad to see, was shrug.

'Run along, Poppy. I'll see you soon.'

Tears formed in the corner of her eyes. 'You fucking bastard, Rupert,' she wailed.

'We don't want any scenes,' he said coolly, but he glanced over at the security guard. Both girls saw it, and Poppy straightened up.

'I'm going,' she said. She looked at Lita. 'You poor bitch.' Then she flounced off, the crochet rising dangerously high on her bare ass.

'Who was that?' Lita demanded.

Rupert shook his head, gently. 'I'm sorry you had to see that, darling. She's a girl from another agency who's been after me for quite some time. I let her down as gently as I could, but whenever she sees me around she propositions me.'

'Oh,' Lita said, feeling foolish.

Rupert reached up and gently traced a fingertip on her cheek. 'I loved how you handled that, though. Especially the part about you being my girlfriend. I was thinking I'd have to talk you into that.'

Lita smiled.

'We're going to be so good together,' he said. 'You'll see.'

Chapter 7

Lita didn't even remember losing her virginity. Not much of it, anyway. Her life with Rupert was a whirl of activity, ad glamour and pure, glorious romance. The Costa campaign bowed to heady sales, and Lita was in demand. Rupert seemed to be on hand with every job she booked – Tasty Tuna, the Mama Assunta Spaghetti Sauce and Nestlé coconut milk. Bill glowered, but he had to suffer his presence. Benson Bailey was still a big client and, besides, he couldn't afford to upset Lita. The dollars were flowing into her account like a waterfall crashing into a pool. Bill noticed that his client no longer saved every dime or even demanded an accounting of her rates. She was too busy for that.

Lita Morales was head over heels in love.

Rupert took her everywhere. He introduced her as his girlfriend, his love, his soul-mate. They went to Upper East Side dinner parties, and nobody condescended to her even once. In fact, all the bankers' wives and doctors' fiancées wanted to be her best friend. They took her shopping, they took her out for manicures. They fawned on her, and Lita loved it.

It was heady, because she knew what they were thinking. They were utterly transparent. They wanted to be buddies with a future English peeress. Goddamn snobs. She hated that, and she loved Rupert for admiring her for herself, not who she'd been born. Lita thought it was ironic that Rupert was so much less snobby than the people who hung around him.

But she let herself be fawned on. Why not?

Lita didn't want to admit it, but she was mostly doing it for her lover. His effortless polish and sophistication were qualities she sometimes felt she could never match. Rupert hated any kind of a 'scene', and Lita wasn't about to make one because some of his friends were stuck up.

The weather turned cold. For Thanksgiving, Lita invited Rupert home. To her surprise, he accepted.

Rupert was welcomed into the house in Queens by a glowing Maria, a glowering Chico and a glum Carlos. Maria had refused to allow him to drink before the meal in case he embarrassed her in front of the lord, as she continued to refer to Rupert despite Lita's silent pleas with her eyes to stop. Chico had been forced into an ill-fitting suit and stared at Rupert, saying nothing.

'Are we gonna watch the game?' Carlos demanded, as Rupert was manfully chewing his second helping of overcooked turkey.

'Of course not.' His wife looked shocked. 'The lord don' watch no football.'

Carlos went a shade of puce, but said nothing, glancing at his daughter. These days he was almost scared of her, the way she ran the family's lives at eighteen, but Thanksgiving was Thanksgiving. Even though his wife made every other mother in the neighbourhood miserable by telling them her daughter was about to become a *Marquesa*, and he liked to see her bursting with pride, Carlos wasn't about to let some limey ruin his Thanksgiving.

Lita took the hint and stood up, thanking God for her escape.

'Mama, actually, Rupert and I have to be getting back to the city.'

'Yes. I'm taking Rosalita out for dinner. We're going to see a play. And if I stay here, Mrs Morales, I'm afraid I'm going to eat all your delicious turkey, and you'll have none left to make soup.'

Maria giggled and smiled. Wait till she told Gloria down the block that the English lord loved her cooking. 'I wish you could stay.'

'Oh, so do I.' Rupert managed to look heartbroken. 'But unfortunately the curtain up won't wait for us. So goodbye, Chico—'

'Later, man,' Chico muttered.

'Goodbye Mrs Morales, and thank you for the wonderful dinner. It was sublime. And goodbye, sir,' forcefully shaking hands with Carlos, who managed a smile. The English lord called him Carlos Morales, sir. Very respectful. That was good. And he was leaving, so Carlos got to watch the game. That was even better.

'Goodbye. I show you out,' Carlos said, with a rare burst of manners.

He watched his daughter grab her coat at lightning speed and leap for the door. His wife hurried to get up and shake hands as Rupert left, all smiles, closing the door behind him.

Maria jumped up and down with pure joy.

'He loved us, *querido*. He'll be back for more of my cooking. Maybe we'll invite some people over.'

'We'll never see that man again,' Carlos replied flatly. He could read Rupert better than his wife. 'We're not his kind of people.'

'Our Lita is, though,' Maria said stubbornly. 'We'll see him because of her.'

'Maybe.'

Carlos doubted it somehow. Maybe his girl could pull it off. She had surprised him with this modelling, with all the money. But there was something in the Englishman's eyes he didn't like. Ah, well – he had his own house, with his own garden, and his son had a job. So let Lita waste her time with this man. As far as her father was concerned, she could do anything she wanted to.

His girl was tough as rawhide. She wasn't going to get hurt.

'Thanks for that,' Lita said, as they climbed into the cab Rupert had paid triple time to wait for them.

He kissed her on the cheek, gently. 'What are you talking about? Your family are delightful.'

Lita felt a burst of pure love explode inside her. Oh, he was so wonderful.

'Let's skip the theatre,' Rupert said, as though he actually did have theatre tickets, 'and just have a romantic dinner at my place. I want to give thanks to *you* for coming into my life.'

'That would be lovely,' Lita said.

Rupert's apartment was a fabulous Upper East Side penthouse, with a glass wall that looked towards the park. Everything seemed serene, like you were floating above the bustle and grime of the city. He had a small marble table set for two, rather like their first dinner in New York. There was a silver ice bucket on a stand, filled with half-melted ice, with a magnum of Krug champagne nestled inside it.

'That's a lot of wine,' Lita said lamely, because her heart was going so fast she had no idea what to say.

'That's just the first bottle. Plenty more where that came from,' Rupert told her.

He served her caviar, salmon mousse, a whole hen lobster and smoked oysters, with a chocolate soufflé for pudding. Lita barely tasted any of it. She got drunk on Rupert's compliments and champagne that he never allowed to hit the bottom of her glass. Her head swam, and she told him she loved him and that she would always love him.

When Rupert took her into the bedroom and peeled off her dress, Lita stumbled back on to the bed, and had nothing but a vague, warm memory of his lips on her throat, her collarbone, and her breasts, working their way downwards.

She woke up the next morning with such a violent hangover that she hardly even noticed the soreness between her legs. She was desperately thirsty and staggered to the fridge, where she drank an entire bottle of Evian before promptly throwing it up again.

Rupert emerged an hour later as Lita sat nursing coffee. Usually she would have asked for his permission to make it, but today she felt too ill.

'I see you took a shower already.'

Lita was wearing one of his white towelling robes, which completely smothered her. She nodded; there had been a reddish stain on her inner thigh. She blushed.

'Did we . . .?'

'Yes, we did. Don't tell me you don't remember it.'

Lita shook her head.

'Oh, poor baby. You have a hangover. I didn't realise you were even tipsy, or I'd have waited. But I assure you, it was glorious.'

He smiled at her, and suddenly Lita felt a little less sick.

'I know it was,' she lied.

Excellent, Rupert thought. She really is very pliable. And the sooner I get her out of America and away from that god-awful family the better.

Rupert asked Lita to move in with him. She accepted joyfully. He bought her an entirely new wardrobe and made her donate all her fashionable clothes to charity. He went through her jobs, making 'suggestions' – no more thigh-high minis, swimsuit shoots or deep cleavage. Benson Bailey used her for several more TV campaigns. The money flowed in, and he found her an accountant to handle it.

She bought houses, and gave her parents and Chico a life estate. Now she would never have to worry about them again.

Rupert became more romantic as the days passed. He stopped taking Lita to nightclubs, and contented himself with dinner parties, the Met and the ballet. Lita appeared at theatre premières in ankle-length silk dresses with long white gloves. Sometimes she even wore her glossy hair high in a tight bun, a style Rupert approved of but Lita hated. Still, she put up with it. She was smart enough to read the signs.

Lord Lancaster was taking this relationship seriously. He was moving her out of 'girlfriend' territory.

When he proposed on Valentine's Day, with a beautiful single-carat princess-cut solitaire from Tiffany's, and one hundred red roses scattered around the apartment, Lita was thrilled, but not all that surprised.

She had read the signs. It felt like it was meant to be. Nothing but good things could happen to her. It was destiny.

Lita put Rupert's preoccupation in March down to stress. Benson Bailey lost a couple of accounts and, ridiculously, it seemed they blamed Rupert for it. He didn't discuss his work with her, but Lita heard it from the girls in Bill's office. Rupert became withdrawn, and was often closeted with his lawyers for long hours in the afternoons, not coming home until eight or later.

She pressed him for a wedding date, but Rupert put her off. 'Plenty of time for that, darling,' he said vaguely. 'I can't concentrate on the wedding the way I'd like to just yet. Couple of things I have to take care of.'

Seemingly, he also could not make time for the engagement party her mother was so desperate to throw. Lita couldn't persuade him to drive over the bridge to see her family, but she tried to understand. If his work was suffering, it was hard to be social.

But she couldn't rob Mama of the joy of seeing her in her triumph. Lita went home for a weekend and showed the ring to her parents.

'It's so beautiful,' Maria cooed. 'The lord has such good taste.'

'You must call him Rupert, Mama. He'll be like a son to you once we're married. What are you going to call me, the lady?'

Maria glowed. 'Say your married name again, *chica*.'

'Lady Lancaster,' Lita said for the umpteenth time.

The doorbell buzzed and Maria ran to let in five middle-aged ladies, her new friends. Lita good-naturedly flashed the ring, and talked about how badly Rupert had wanted to come. She lied and said he was on a business trip. It seemed easier than telling the truth.

Chico muttered that it was great, but he had a night shift at the site to go to. 'Maybe you give me some money for a wedding gift, for investments.'

'Sure,' Lita said, softly. He was meant to give *her* the gift, but she knew there would be no point saying that.

After dinner, Lita cleared the table and washed everything up, like before. It was less than a year ago that she had done this, but it seemed like another life on another planet. She vowed quietly not to let herself get too distant from her family. They were more important to her than Rupert's smart friends, and she was a little ashamed that she was starting to feel embarrassed by them.

When Pappy examined the ring, after dinner, she could see he wanted to say something.

'It's OK. You can tell me, whatever it is,' Lita reassured him.

'The ring, it's very pretty. But it's a little small, no?'

'It's a one-carat diamond.'

'I know. For our friends, that's a nice ring. But this man is supposed to be rich. When he come to our place for Thanksgiving he didn't have his own car.'

Lita paused. 'Pappy, he has a big apartment and real nice suits, and he eats caviar . . .'

'That's nice. But does he pay for them?'
'Does it matter?'
'You have a lot of money, Lita,' Carlos said slowly.
'But he started going out with me before I had anything.'
'OK.' Her father kissed her on the cheek. 'As long as you're happy, baby. You're a good girl.'
Lita nodded and looked away. She was thoughtful on the ride home.

A week later Rupert was back to his old self. He resigned from Benson Bailey.
'They don't appreciate what I do for them, so why bother?' he said, rubbing the back of Lita's neck. 'I don't need to waste my time like that. I think I'll start my own business.'
'That's a great idea.' Lita was instantly interested. 'What are you thinking of?'
'I'm going to found my own advertising agency.'
'Lancaster Advertising?' Lita smiled.
Rupert looked shocked. 'Good lord, no. I'd never use the family name like that. What if something went wrong? I was thinking more of "Modern Commercials".'
Lita thought the name was hardly inspired, but what did she know? Rupert was the commercials whiz.
'I have a lot of clients that want to jump ship,' he told her over dinner. Rupert's apartment boasted an actual working fireplace and as December started he had taken to having glorious, crackling pine-log fires each night. Tonight he was stretched out on the Persian carpet in front of the grate, with Lita snuggling up against him, luxuriating in the warmth and the flickering play of light. Maybe they would make love later. Rupert was an exacting, careful lover, but she thought she enjoyed the sense of closeness with him a lot more than the actual sex. This was a naughty little secret Lita knew to keep to herself. Was she maybe not normal? Rupert would probably say she was repressed. Her Catholic upbringing, perhaps. Lita told herself it was OK; they were getting married, and after the ceremony she would relax and enjoy it more. Maybe sex wasn't really all that important, anyway.
'They're going to come to Modern and bring their accounts with them. We'll make a fortune.' He kissed the tip of her nose at her look of surprise. 'You're included, of course. You don't think I'd keep it all for myself! You're going to have a stake in the company from day one.'
'But you don't need me for a stake, do you?'
Rupert chuckled. 'Of course I don't need you, darling, but I don't want you to lose out on this. Weren't you always talking about how

you wanted to be in business before we got married? Well, the wedding's a year away, probably, so this is your chance.'

A whole year? Lita thought with a sharp stab of disappointment, but at least it would give her a chance to make sure Rupert came out to Queens for that engagement party. She didn't say anything. She didn't want to spoil his mood, now that he was back to his charming, outgoing self.

'You'll be modelling, so you'll be a silent partner, but you can see how the business works. Maybe help me with a few campaigns. Would you like that?'

Lita kissed his chin. 'It sounds like a lot of fun, darling.'

'I'll bring you all the documents to sign tomorrow,' he promised.

Lita got in from a Chanel shoot to find four slim pieces of paper stacked on the walnut desk in their bedroom. She read them carefully and was immensely relieved. They offered her forty per cent ownership of the company, with very fair provisions for any flotation on Wall Street. They also offered her access to a company bank account as one of the officers and approval on major campaigns.

She signed, cross with herself for the shadows of doubt about Rupert that had started to creep in.

'That's terrific, darling,' he said when she presented him with the papers. 'I've set up some accounts that channel money from our personal accounts into the company account.'

'How much are we putting in there?'

'It's not a set figure. Rather than stake too much cash, I thought it would be sensible if we had a drip-feed system, and take out only what's needed. If that's acceptable to you, of course.'

'Absolutely.' Lita signed the banking forms he handed to her, feeling warm and reassured. It was good that Rupert was so conservative. It probably went with his background. She wouldn't have liked to blow a lot of money on a start-up, even with all his new clients.

Rupert swung her into his arms and twirled her around. 'Come on, let's go to Tiffany's and do some early Christmas shopping.'

They had a blissful afternoon. Lita was wrapped up against the biting New York cold in her new Balenciaga mink coat; it was soft and comforting, like Rupert's presence. He bought her pearls from Cartier's, big drop earrings, and *sachertorte* with hot chocolate, and took her to 21 for dinner.

Lita was too sleepy to make love that night. She fell asleep, in Rupert's arms, by the warmth of their dying fire.

It was the last good day they ever had.

Over the next weeks, Rupert withdrew into his shell. Lita put it down to the pressure of work. He took several late-night calls at his desk that involved a lot of shouting. When she asked about the business, he told her, curtly, that it was just teething problems. When Lita asked what kind, Rupert told her to just be supportive.

She ignored his attitude. Starting your own business was hard, there was no denying that. She organized their Christmas, spending a few pleasurable hours at Barney's shopping for just the right stocking fillers for Rupert, and a few more at Zabar's with her mom, getting the perfect ingredients for Christmas lunch.

A week before the holidays, Lita walked into Rupert's apartment to find him on his way out the door with a suitcase in his hand.

She blinked. 'What's all this? You're not running out on me, are you?'

'Don't be foolish,' Rupert said coldly. 'I've been summoned to England on urgent business. I'll be back on Monday.'

'If it's urgent, let me come with you.'

He kissed her gently on the cheek.

'Darling, it's a legal bore I have to sort out. Nothing to trouble you with. Back Monday.'

She didn't have to wait until Monday. Rupert sent her a telegram on Saturday. It was faster than a letter and less personal than a phone call. Lita read it, read it again, then folded it neatly and put it in her purse.

It was the only thing she took from his apartment. She left the fur and the pearls on his bed, which she made carefully. Then she took a cab to a hotel.

The telegram read: 'Dear Lita. Stop. Things not working out between us. Stop. Best to call off engagement. Stop. You may keep the ring. Stop. Apartment is owned by Benson Bailey you must be out by the twentieth. Stop.'

Stop. Stop. Stop. Just like her life had.

Chapter 8

Becky looked down at London and sighed.

From thirty-five thousand feet and the first-class cabin of Pan Am Flight 24, it didn't look all that impressive. She was tired, and the grey fog that hung over the grimy city seemed to sap her energy even more. The Thames didn't sparkle, and it wasn't nearly as wide as the Hudson River. Becky tried to tell herself that she would be glad just to get on the ground. After an hour's delay on the runway at JFK, condemning her to cheesy chat-up lines from the businessmen seated next to her, and the bumpy, uncomfortable flight, she felt in need of a long shower and a bubble bath. The news back home had showed Great Britain in the grip of union strikes that were causing electricity blackouts. Becky was booked into the Ritz. She vowed grimly that she would have those uniformed flunkies fanning a fire with bellows if necessary. There was going to be hot water for her in this miserable, cold city, or else there'd be hell to pay.

'Champagne, ma'am?'

The air hostess with too much blue eyeshadow and a face that had seen too much sun leaned dutifully over her with the bottle of Moët. She hadn't seen to Becky's needs much during the flight, but Becky was used to that, too. Hostility from other women was as normal to her as the tired old chat-up lines from men old enough to be her father. It didn't make any difference that these women didn't know anything about her. The key factor wasn't personality. It was her long, tanned limbs, golden and firm from swimming in the ocean and tennis in the Hamptons; the fountain of blonde hair, naturally pale, but streaked discreetly with platinum at Elizabeth Arden's Red Door salon on Fifth Avenue twice a month; the nails, deliciously natural with a delicate French manicure; the high cheekbones, the slim model's body with its lean lines and little bud breasts; the full lips and striking green eyes – in short, just about everything. On a flight like this the hostesses would normally be the centre of attention. Since when did any woman other than a society matron fly first class? But ever since Becky had walked through the airplane door and turned to the left, eighteen years old and achingly beautiful, with her kitten Chanel heels and her silk Pucci wrap-around dress, no man had had eyes for anyone else.

'Sure, why not?' Becky said, lifting her glass. The golden wine fizzed into it, and she sipped, letting the icy bubbles play on her tongue. Strictly speaking, she wasn't supposed to drink till she was twenty-one. But the lack of questions came with the price of the ticket. Didn't the Brits have the legal age as eighteen? About the only good thing you could say for this place, she thought morosely.

'So where are you staying when you get to London?'

The old guy on her left leaned into her. His skin smelled unpleasantly of the eight Scotches he'd downed since take-off. The weak sunlight glittered on his wedding ring.

'With my boyfriend,' she snapped. 'Maybe you're staying with friends of your wife?'

He turned away, muttering something under his breath that sounded like 'bitch'. Yeah, right. A bitch. Wasn't that defined in Webster's as 'woman who shoots down a jerk'? She heard that a lot, too. It might be an exaggeration to say men were all the same, but a lot of them were very similar. The girls at Mount Holyoke were probably on a protest march right now. A feminist thrill ran through her. I'll miss them, Becky thought, even Claire Hoyden, the ugly Boston Brahmin chick that had publicly burnt her bra in the courtyard and set alight a hundred-year-old chestnut tree while she was doing it. With Claire's boobs, a generous C cup and already starting to sag, Becky thought that had been a bit unwise. But her sorority was caught up in the sexless glamour of Germaine Greer, Susan Sontag and women needing men like fish needed bicycles. Most of them had secret posters of hunky dudes up on their lockers, though. Bobby Fischer, the chess champion, was pretty popular. Becky had no posters. After Richard, she was sour on all men.

Becky tried not to dwell on Richard. The bitter disappointment was still lingering. She had wanted something special with him. After all, Richard was supposed to be The One. He had a skinny, intense, poetic look, floppy dark hair and a notable Connecticut family. They had dated steady for almost a full year before he'd talked her into 'doing it'. It was supposed to be incredibly romantic, a symbol of their eternal love for each other. Richard had prepared her a picnic lunch – with wine – and brought along a leather-bound volume of love sonnets by John Donne to get her in the mood. But the late summer weather had blown up with a fall chill, the mayo might have been a touch off, and Richard, when he peeled off his shirt, was a nine-stone weakling. Becky had suddenly felt revolted, but the half-bottle of Pouilly Fuisse had had its effect. Richard pushed her back into the grass, which was kind of itchy, and not satiny like it looked, and spread her thighs, thrusting into her.

Becky had gasped in pain, which Richard had muttered something sympathetic about, but he kept thrusting. The only good thing was that it was over in two minutes . . . he had taken longer to find exactly where to put it in, shoving himself against her like a drunk trying to jam his key into the lock. Richard moaned loudly and collapsed on her, and so they'd lain there together, with Becky half-heartedly stroking his head and wishing he'd get off her so she could wash herself in the stream nearby, get dressed and never see him again.

'Wow, that was great.' Richard kissed clumsily at her. 'Let's do that again.'

Becky lay underneath him, her wonderful long, slender legs, her apple-breasts and tiny, delicate pink bud-nipples trapped beneath his pale, gangly limbs.

'I don't think so.' She moved her hips firmly, pushing out, away from him. Her gorgeous platinum blonde hair caught the pale sunlight, and she wanted to cover herself with it, like Lady Godiva. 'I'm kinda sore. We'd better get back.'

'OK. But we have to do this again, soon.' Richard stood up, his stick-thin arms at his sides, ogling her firm ass that pointed north, the result of summer tennis matches. He reached out a hand and ran it through the silky blonde hair, not noticing her flinch.

Becky shuddered again at the memory. Ugh. She'd known she was coming to England when the news of the court case reached Aunt Mindy, but that had certainly made leaving the States a little bit easier. No tears at the airport.

'Please fasten your seat belts for our final descent into London. The ground temperature outside is sixty degrees and it's a cloudy day . . .'

No kidding. Becky shivered and made to draw the fabric strap tight around her tiny waist.

The chauffeur was waiting for her as she came out of customs; they had taken one look at her passport and waved her through.

'Let me get your bags, miss.' He had an accent Becky recognized from the movies as being Cockney. 'The car's this way, if you'll just follow me.'

'Of course.' She hoped it wasn't too far into the city. She felt amazingly tired, and the travelling wasn't done yet. In the car park, the driver pulled up in a gleaming Rolls Royce and lifted her heavy Louis Vuitton cases into the trunk without blinking an eye. He held open the door, and Becky slid into the back seat with an elegance born from months of deportment training at Mrs Porter's on the Upper East Side. The driver noted her slim calves with appreciation, but Becky was too exhausted to notice. They pulled into traffic and hit the motorway, the car gliding over the road as smoothly as a gondola in Venice.

The chauffeur touched his cap in the mirror.

'Well, Miss Lancaster,' he said cheerfully. 'Welcome 'ome.'

'When exactly is she going to get here?'

The Honourable Mrs Henry Whitlock tapped impatiently on the mahogany dining-room table in front of her and fixed her husband with a look. It was very important to know exactly when her niece was arriving. There would be nothing lacking in Fairfield, she thought bitterly. She and Henry had cleared out of the rooms she'd occupied for the last seventeen years to that new and ordinary house in Gloucester; an attractive enough townhouse with a garden full of roses, but not Fairfield, *her* Fairfield. She still couldn't think of the place as belonging to her niece. But it did, that was the law, and she wasn't going to allow Christy's daughter to have any complaints; her brother's orphan heir, maybe, but marrying that dreadful American woman had been Robert's mistake.

As far as Victoria Whitlock was concerned, his daughter Rebecca was just an extension of that mistake. Who knew, with Christy's dismal record of jazz parties and martini lunches, if Rebecca was even her brother's child? Victoria thought furiously. The snapshots she had seen showed a young woman with every indication of taking after her mother. Indecently long blonde hair and swirling print dresses – what was there of Robert in that, except maybe her almost masculine height? Rebecca was five eight and still wore heels. Obviously she liked to attract attention to herself. And that was most certainly *not* the Lancaster way.

When Lord and Lady Lancaster, Rebecca's parents, had taken that motoring trip around the Riviera and been killed by a drunk driver it had been a black day for Victoria. Of course she mourned her brother, and even Christy hadn't deserved to die. Divorce had been more along the lines of Victoria's daydreams. And little Charles, just six months, strapped into the back seat of Robert's Aston Martin and killed instantly. Leaving the direct line with no male heir. Victoria tried hard to suppress the occasional thoughts of what-if that drifted through her mind unbidden. What if the nanny bringing Rebecca out to the airport to join her parents, one year old and the apple of Robert's eye, had not hit that traffic jam? What if she hadn't decided to take the next flight? Of course Victoria hadn't wished her niece dead, but there was no denying that if Rebecca had been in that car, she, Robert's only sibling, would have inherited Fairfield.

If wishing the girl had been in that car was beyond the pale, resenting her for coming home was not. Rebecca had been the owner of Fairfield, unknown to herself, as soon as her poor father's car had smashed into that lorry. But her mother's wretched relatives had swooped down and carted her off to New York right after the funeral. Victoria had not put up much of a fight. She blamed Christy and her fast ways for Robert's death. The baby would only remind her of her hated sister-in-law, with those large green eyes and that mop of blonde, un-Lancaster-like hair. Victoria was good with dogs and horses, but not with babies. Certainly not one that didn't even belong to her. So for Jack and Mindy Rogers to take their sister's baby seemed a natural choice. If Rebecca inherited Christy's aggressive American ways, Victoria reflected, America was the best place for her.

But now she was eighteen, and the trust had matured. Victoria and her cousin William, the head of Lancaster Holdings PLC, were no longer the executors. Fairfield Court, the family company, and everything that went with it had passed into the teenage hands of the Hon. Rebecca Lancaster. Everything except the title. That was Rupert's, and Victoria shuddered anew and decided not to think about that particular problem just yet.

'She should be up around six. Barkin was to pick her up at the Ritz by two, so not later than that, I'd say.'

Henry Whitlock regarded his wife nervously. Her steel-grey hair and thick tweed skirt were especially crisp and unforgiving today. A bad sign. When Victoria dressed like this, you didn't want to be in her way. Whitlock just liked his port, his *Times* crossword and being left alone. Of course it was too bad to be turfed out of Fairfield, but it wasn't as if they hadn't known it was coming.

'Did you tell the maid to make up the master bedroom?'

He nodded.

'And did you have her put roses in the vase?'

'She picked some red ones from the garden, from the large bush as one goes into the kitchen garden.'

Victoria's skin prickled as she remembered what those roses were called. 'American Beauty'. An omen. As though Christy's brat were already laughing at her.

'Everything's ready, then,' she said.

Barkin glanced behind him at Miss Becky. She'd asked him to call her Becky, but he thought, for the sake of his job, it would be safer to stick with 'Madam', at least when Mrs Whitlock was in earshot. She was staring out of the window at the Cotswold countryside and didn't seem to notice him discreetly checking her out. She was too young, too rich and too posh for him, and if his Maisie could see him now she'd be furious. But Maisie wasn't around, was she? He was free to check out those amazing, coltish legs that poured out of a tiny white miniskirt into itsy-bitsy, strappy white leather heels, pale against her golden brown skin, and the rigid, tight white military-style jacket on top, buttoned up against the chilly English summer evening, with gold buttons and that all over it. Barkin wasn't big on fashion but he knew when a girl looked amazing. Hair the colour of melted butter spilled all over the soft leather of the passenger seat. He couldn't see her eyes, they were hidden behind oversized Jackie O. sunglasses. And it was a pity she was wearing that rose-scented perfume . . . he wanted to smell her natural skin. She was so clean and fresh, her plucked, styled eyebrows complementing her delicate hands. And no tights on those endless legs. She looked like Twiggy, but prettier. He wondered what kind of underwear a girl like that had on. If she'd shift in her seat maybe he could see it. That skirt was so damn short, but somehow she always managed to keep her legs together or at some infuriating angle so he couldn't see. Soft lace, he was sure, a little wisp of something pink or peach . . .

Barkin felt himself getting hard. He swallowed and focused on the road ahead. The last thing this lass needed was another car crash.

Besides, she was a nice chick. Asked him to put the radio on so she could listen to the Bee Gees. She wasn't going to like it up at Fairfield. That much he was sure of.

It wasn't his habit to feel sorry for millionaires, but when he considered what Becky Lancaster was letting herself in for, he almost had a twang of pity.

'Owen, how far away are we?'

He wished he could break her of that habit. If Mrs Whitlock heard her, he was for the high jump.

'Only another fifteen minutes, Miss Becky. And if you don't mind, I prefer Barkin.'

'Oh. Sure. Thanks.'

Becky sank back into her seat. Tears prickled into her eyes behind her Fendi sunglasses, but she blinked them back. Damn the goddamn English. She was tired still, and nervous, and he couldn't even let her use his first name? The Ritz had been soothing – a luxurious bath, a soft white towelling robe, perfumed soaps and decent food – but she hadn't slept at all. Her body clock was totally off-base. There had been thunderstorms all night, too; lightning and rain driving against her windows. It had been relief, when dawn had finally come as she lay awake tossing and turning, to see that the sun was out.

Her aunt had sent her a telegram. 'Dear Rebecca, welcome to your home. Barkin will arrive to collect you at two. Please do not be late. We look forward to seeing you shortly.' She had read it five times straight, and still didn't know what to make of it. Was this what people talked like over here? Her aunt sent Christmas and birthday cards each year, all simply signed 'Love Aunt Victoria', And now they were finally going to meet.

She dressed carefully, a white leather mini-suit by Fiorucci and shoes to match, did her make-up very lightly and repacked. God forbid she should be even a little bit late. She missed her friends back home. They'd have made this fun, an adventure. Instead, it was starting to feel like being packed off to boarding school for the first time. The front desk checked her out with impersonal efficiency, and then there was Barkin, the family chauffeur, grabbing her bags and steering her towards a Jaguar for the long drive north. Becky tried sleeping, but it just didn't work, and conversation was heavy going. Now even the driver wouldn't let her use his first name.

Her mom's relatives had always cooed over Fairfield Court, what an incredible place it was, how lucky she was to own it and live there some day. Becky hoped so. She ached for the hot weather in New York – why had she ever complained about the summer heat? Watermelon by the pool, boy-spotting on the golden beaches, her friends taking long drives down the coast, raising hell. Fairfield Court was what she got instead, for the rest of her life. And right now she was wondering if it was worth it.

Her father's relatives had approached her about a year ago. When she hit eighteen, she would become the sole executor of her own trust. The house would be hers, the companies would be hers. But there was no need to uproot herself, her uncle's lawyers had argued. The Lancaster family would make Rebecca a handsome cash offer. Fairfield would go to Mrs Whitlock, the business to her cousin William, and Rebecca could stay in the United States with more money than she would ever need.

They had been surprised when she turned them down. In fact, she had almost surprised herself. But Rebecca couldn't forget, not quite, that she was actually English. She had never known her father, only seen pictures of him – a young, straight-backed man with dark hair and laughing eyes, his arms linked through her mother's, a face she saw more clearly in her own mirror each day. Her father had left her the house should her brother die. He had wanted his children to have it. He had wanted her to have it. And she felt that coming here was fulfilling his wishes.

She had booked the ticket for her eighteenth birthday. No matter if England was damp, and cold, plagued by industrial unrest; a country which was actually contemplating asking the IMF for a loan. Her father's family company operated from here. And now it was *her* company.

'Here we are, Miss Becky,' the driver said. He made a left, turning through two half-rusted gates next to large stone pillars, from which twin lions reared up; she recognized them from her coat of arms. The car trundled noisily on to a long gravel drive. Becky leaned forward, craning her head, and took her first look at her home.

Chapter 9

Becky gasped.

It was incredible. Like something from the movies. A huge manor house built from warm grey stone rose out of the gravel drive. It had bay windows, latticed with lead, a lavender path leading up to the front door and a great spray of blood-red ivy climbing up one wall. To her right and left lawns stretched away, terraced in one place, punctuated with steps that looked slippery with moss and lichen. There was a tall, ancient wall to the right of the house, covered in glorious wisteria dripping with lilac flowers. The house towered over the wall. It had gables and spikes. Behind it she could see a gnarled orchard of some kind.

'Welcome to Fairfield, miss,' Barkin said, with a small note of pride.

Becky couldn't think of anything to say.

'What's behind that wall?' she managed.

'That's the kitchen garden, miss. It's very nice. All sorts of herbs and flowers and that.'

A kitchen garden. A walled garden. Becky felt her mood transformed, as though somebody had waved a magic wand over her head. It was the most romantic thing she'd ever seen. She half expected Prince Charming to come riding around from the back with his armour properly shiny, mounted on a white stallion. And looking nothing like Richard.

'Do you like it?'

'It's beautiful,' Becky said. 'Just beautiful.'

'Mr and Mrs Whitlock are waiting inside for you, miss. I'll bring your cases up to your room.'

He climbed out and opened her door. Becky suddenly longed for a full-length mirror. She wanted to check herself before she met Aunt Victoria. Was her lipstick on straight? Had her mascara blotted? She felt butterflies start to writhe in her stomach. This was Daddy's sister. The first member of her father's family she'd ever met. Nervously, she walked up to the door and rang the bell, trying not to scuff her white leather shoes.

There was a pause that seemed like an age to Becky. She heard the bell sounding inside the house. She shifted a little from foot to foot. Finally, there were footsteps clip-clipping down the stairs and over stone, it sounded like. Becky swallowed slightly. The heavy door swung open slowly.

'You must be Rebecca,' Victoria Whitlock said.

She was a middle-aged woman in an unflattering, neat, purple suit with a cream blouse. The shapeless skirt cut off at mid-calf. Her hair was coiled into a bun and looked as though it had half a can of hairspray holding it in place. Her lips were coated with a very precise slash of red lipstick, which looked out of place on her pale face. There was a large string of soft pearls at her neck, and she smelled of violets.

Becky smiled warmly. 'And you're Aunt Vicky.'

'Victoria, please. Yes, I'm your Aunt Victoria. Do come in and see your house,' Victoria said.

Becky followed her aunt in. She didn't much look like Daddy, from the photographs. She was certainly a lady. She seemed a little cold, but that was probably just cultural, Becky told herself. She glanced around the entrance hall. Yes, there were flagstones on the floor, and dark, rich wood panelling, and a marble bust on a plinth . . . oh, how lovely it was. She wanted to hug herself. Becky found she was wearing a ridiculous grin.

'This is the library,' Aunt Victoria said. 'And this is your Uncle Henry. Do come and say hello to Rebecca, Henry.'

Becky took it in – the huge bay windows looking over a long lawn leading down to a lake, the tall walls lined with leather-bound books with gold letters on the spine. Most of them probably hadn't been opened in a hundred years. She loved it. There was a short, plump man standing by a card-table covered in dark green baize; his *Daily Telegraph* was lying on a weathered burgundy leather armchair.

'Uncle Henry!' she said gaily. Would it be out of order to hug him?

Henry Whitlock stared at her. His niece was the most stunning woman he had ever laid eyes on. She was a gift-wrapped parcel of long blonde hair, golden skin, clear eyes and coltish legs that went on for ever. She wasn't his *blood* relative, of course. Thank heaven, because he found her attractive. So damn attractive . . . and so wrong, all wrong for the family, for his wife, for Fairfield Court. Was this the new mistress of the house, then? Wearing that outrageous white leather skirt? She looked like one of those rock chicks. That skirt was so high round her narrow hips it looked like a belt . . . and then the military jacket, tight round her waist and slashed low around that golden neck of hers. And the teetering heels, pale against her tan, that threw her slim body forward, giving her the faintest suggestion of curves and elongating those already endless legs . . .

'Henry,' Victoria said sharply.

'Ah, yes.' He cleared his throat and approached the amazing creature, leaning forward to kiss her cautiously on the cheek. She smelled of baby powder. Henry flushed; his world was not used to being disturbed by desire, not at this stage in his life. He had a dreadful feeling that Rebecca meant trouble for him, and lots of it. 'Welcome to Fairfield. I hope your journey wasn't too bad?'

'Oh, no, it was fine,' Becky said.

There was a pause.

'Lovely weather for it,' Victoria said blandly. 'Are you hungry, Rebecca?'

'No, not really. Thank you.'

'Well, it will be supper in half an hour. Barkin has already taken your things up to your bedroom. What I suggest is a bath, and then I will collect you for supper, and we can go over the details of the house to settle you in. I'm sure you'll find everything is in order.'

'Oh, sure – I wasn't worried about that, I—'

'Excellent.' Victoria cut her off. 'Follow me, please.'

Her bedroom was on the second floor.

'I'll leave you to it,' Victoria said. 'Just follow the stairs all the way down to the ground when you're finished. The dining room is immediately to your left.'

'Thanks,' Becky said.

'And, Rebecca – you may want to change for supper. What you're wearing . . .' She took a long, disapproving look at Rebecca that made her want to tug her tiny miniskirt down her thighs. 'It isn't really suitable. But I'm sure you'll learn.' Victoria flashed her niece a quick, pained smile, and left, closing the door behind her . . .

The bedroom was high-ceilinged, with beams running through the plaster and a huge carved wardrobe of dark wood that looked hundreds of years old. The vast bed was brass and neatly made up, with feather pillows and a vase of fresh roses by her bed. A door opened into a bathroom that overlooked an apple tree covered in moss and lichen. Becky's cases were at the foot of the bed. She looked out over the large lead-paned bedroom windows at her estate.

The manicured lawns were dotted with small, winding gravel paths that were bordered with flowers of every description; statues here and there, ancient and weather-worn; an orchard, and the other side of that the kitchen garden. Half the garden stretched down to the lake, with terraced steps leading from a sundial. Becky flopped down on the bed. It was like living in museum, except it wasn't one. She could touch everything, run everywhere, pick the flowers, swim in the lake . . . It had been Daddy's, and now it was hers.

Becky forgot Brad, and Richard, and all the teenage boys who had broken her heart back home. She fell instantly and completely in love.

Becky pushed her aunt's behaviour to the back of her mind and ducked into the bathroom. There were dry towels and some tiny bottles of scented bath oil from Floris. No bubbles, but when she poured them into the hot water the entire room was filled with the scent of gardenias and jasmine. She knotted her long blonde hair up on the crown of her head, lowered herself into the water and started to think. Now she was here there were things to do. Papers to sign, all that stuff. She owned a company Uncle Henry and some cousins were running, and that was what would pay the heating bills at Fairfield, so she guessed she'd better check that out. Plus, even though Aunt Mindy promised she'd be over at the end of next month, she had to realize she had no friends here. If she was going to live in England she had to make some. Despite the hot water, Becky shivered as she thought about the driver, and the air hostesses, and her aunt. All so cold. Aunt Mindy had told her about Mom's legendary parties here. She could do the same thing. She soaped her long legs and started planning – Christmas parties in the Hall, with a blazing fire and crackling pine logs, and a dinner next month with all Daddy's relatives, maybe a marquee in the garden with champagne and—

'Rebecca.' There was a sharp rap on the door. 'Are you in there?'

'Yes. Sorry, Aunt Victoria,' Becky called. She'd lost track of time. She scrambled to get out and swathed herself in a vast white towel. 'I'll be right down.'

The dining room was long, impressive and formal. Her aunt and uncle had positioned themselves at the head of the table, flanking Becky's seat. She hurried in, dressed in a long, clinging blue silk number by Balenciaga, the most conservative thing in her cases.

'I'm sorry to keep you waiting.'

'It's quite all right,' Victoria said, making a face to show that it wasn't. 'You'll learn that we do things rather differently here from the way you're used to.'

'Sure.' Becky felt her nerves creeping back. 'Why I am at the head of the table? You should be sitting here, shouldn't you, Uncle Henry?'

'No, indeed,' Henry Whitlock said heartily, but his smile didn't reach his eyes. 'I'm not the head of the house any more. You are the owner of Fairfield, Rebecca. You are the hostess.'

A Mrs Morecambe, a wizened old cook, served them supper – a rather delicious roast chicken, with golden brown skin and roast potatoes. There was a side-dish of crisp green beans.

'These are wonderful,' Becky said, desperate to make conversation.

'They're from the kitchen garden. I planted them in the spring,' Aunt Victoria said tightly.

Becky saw her opportunity. 'Of course, of course. You've been living at Fairfield all this while.'

'I was born here, and I grew up here. And, yes, I have been living here while you've been in America with Christina's relatives.'

'I know that,' Becky said, giving her a warm smile. 'And I really don't see why you should move out. There's plenty of room here. I'm only one person . . .'

Victoria held up a hand. 'Thank you, Rebecca. Very kind,' she said shortly, 'but Uncle Henry and I have our own house. Tempting though it is to be offered guest rooms at Fairfield, I think we'll stay there.'

'Sure. Whatever you want. You're always welcome, though.'

'Very good of you,' Uncle Henry said thinly.

Becky was silent. There was no avoiding it. They hated her. Everything she did pissed them off.

Well, she told herself, at least I tried. I can't do any more than that.

She forked the chicken into her mouth quietly. Forget making conversation. Why should she bother?

Aunt Victoria led her back into the library after dinner. She had laid out a large stack of papers on a walnut desk.

'You must be tired, but if you could, please review and sign these when you get a chance. They are trust papers from the trustees. Now it has matured, you must sign off in order to claim your beneficiary status. I have included some maps of the house, names of the staff and other things of that sort to help you to settle in. Your uncle's phone number is listed there – you may call us if you have questions, or need help. The result of the legal battle with Lord Lancaster, your second cousin, is listed in there, too.'

Ah, yes. Lord Lancaster, her second cousin Rupert. He had tried, and failed, to get Fairfield. Thank God.

'Thank you. I'll look at them.'

'The address to which to post them is listed on your contact sheet. If you want anything, ring the bell for Mrs Morecambe. Her bedroom is just below yours on the first floor. You'll need to tell her if you're expecting breakfast, that sort of thing.'

'I will. Thank you.' Becky remembered what they had said. 'Very – very kind.'

'And now,' Aunt Victoria said briskly, taking her husband's hand as though to tug him out like a dog on a leash, 'Uncle Henry and I are going to our home. I hope you had a pleasant evening and you like Fairfield.'

'Yes, thanks. And I love it. I love Fairfield.'

'Well, of course you do,' Aunt Victoria said, as though she were some kind of simpleton. 'Rebecca. Everybody loves Fairfield. Goodnight.'

'Night, Aunt Victoria, Uncle Henry,' said Becky. She made no move to hug them. She was quite sure it wouldn't be welcome.

She followed them out to the Hall, shook hands, and watched them climb into a stately Rolls-Royce and drive away. Her aunt did not turn around and wave goodbye.

'Will you be wanting anything else, Miss Becky?'

Becky turned to see Mrs Morecambe hovering by her elbow.

'No, thank you.' It felt awkward having a servant. Aunt Mindy had a maid come once a week, and that was about all. But that was this woman's job. What was she going to do, fire her? 'Let me help you clear up.'

'Oh, no, miss.' The older woman looked shocked. 'I already did all that. Let me get you a hot chocolate at least. You've had a busy day.'

Suddenly Becky found she wanted to cry. It was the first kind thing anybody had said to her since she landed. She swallowed.

'Thanks, that'd be nice,' she said.

She closed the door behind her and glanced around. Now she was practically alone in this vast, old place, she expected it to be a little spooky. But it wasn't. The portraits of her ancestors seemed warm and friendly. The grandfather clock was beautiful. She loved books, and the house was overflowing with them. Even the flagstone floors of the entryway seemed warm and comforting.

Maybe it was the ghost of her father. This was the home he had wanted her to have. The place she was born to. Aunt Victoria had been born to it, too, but it wasn't hers. Becky understood how she must hate that. But if Victoria refused to share, she thought with an arrogant little toss of her teenage head, she, Becky, wasn't going to eat her heart out over it. And she wasn't going to sell it to her either.

Fairfield's mine, Becky told herself. And it's going to stay that way.

Mrs Morecambe, smiling, brought her a large mug of warm, soothing hot chocolate.

'Mr Morecambe takes care of the grounds, miss. He can lay a fire in here if you want.'

'That's OK, really. I'm not going to stay up long. And thanks so much for this,' Becky said, smiling at her. 'I don't need anything else tonight.'

'Goodnight, then, miss,' Mrs Morecambe said, nodding and backing out.

She was amazed. The young lady had manners, very nice manners. Mrs Morecambe liked to see it. She was well disposed to like her anyway for upsetting that old witch Mrs Whitlock, who never thanked you properly for anything and was always ringing the bloody bell late at night. Imagine, a Lancaster offering to help clear the table! It was a wonder, that was what it was. Mrs Morecambe felt a pang of pity as she laboriously made her way up the stairs. Mrs Whitlock was already drowning the young lady in papers. No doubt she'd soon give up and move out. Nobody resisted Mrs Whitlock for long.

Becky curled back into the burgundy leather armchair, luxuriating in its softness. She picked up the piles of papers and began to sift through them, one at a time. Trusts . . . maturation . . . Fairfield . . . And then the business, Lancaster Holdings . . . The small print all started to blur. She would finish it another time. More important were the maps of the house. She saw there was a conservatory, a drawing room, a reading room, many bathrooms . . . She would have a party, and use all those dusty bedrooms and bathrooms. What was the point of having space you didn't use?

There was a billiards room. Billiards . . . that was a fancy word for pool. She was good at eight-bail, played it in bars for two-dollar bets sometimes. She saw markings for two fountains, a pantry, servants' quarters, a wine cellar and a second library on the first floor. It really was heaven, Becky told herself. Now she just had to find somebody to share it with.

Chapter 10

'What do you think?' Becky asked.

She turned to Sharon Jenkins, smoothing the dress down around her waist. Sharon was twenty, and Becky, lonely and homesick during her first month in England, had happened to meet her in the village pub one night. Sharon had been a lifesaver for her. She was attending Oxford University, one of the women's colleges, Somerville, reading English. She wore hip-hugging, bell-bottomed jeans with funky little bead fringes, and tight T-shirts made for nine-year-old girls. None of Becky's American friends had English relatives or acquaintances outside London, and she hadn't come to Fairfield to drive all the way down south whenever she needed some company. When she found Sharon, Sharon was blind drunk and needed scooping up and pouring into a cab. Becky struggled to lift her into the car because Sharon had a healthy, strapping, Nordic-milkmaid kind of body. The important thing, though, was that she got Sharon's phone number. She'd called the next day, in the afternoon, to give the hangover a chance to wear off, and they went out for dinner. Finally, Becky had a friend.

'What the hell . . .? You *own* this?' Sharon asked, amazed, when Becky finally had the guts to invite her up to Fairfield.

'I do. I know it's kind of far out,' Becky said, blushing.

'Fuck that. Let's hang out here all the time. It beats the hell out of our shitty little council flat,' Sharon said robustly.

Becky had had great pleasure in introducing Sharon to her aunt when Victoria made one of her rare forays to Fairfield for dinner, with Henry trotting obediently behind her. Becky gave up trying to win her aunt's affection after the first week – Victoria wasn't interested in anything more than propriety. She saw her niece twice a month, no more and no less. There were no telephone calls; business was conducted through the lawyers. Becky figured she just didn't want people to be able to say she'd abandoned her.

And then, of course, there was Fairfield. Victoria wanted her to be lonely and unhappy. That way she might give up, sell out and go back to America. They had made it very clear that that was 'for the best'.

That it was best for them went without saying. Becky knew she'd get just the minimum of human contact from her father's sister. It had been that way throughout her childhood. Her only error had been in expecting that to change now.

'Aunt Victoria, this is Sharon, a friend of mine. Sharon, this is Mrs Whitlock.'

'How do you do.' Victoria peered down her nose at Sharon, as though amazed that Becky should have a guest in the house. It *was* amazing. Where had she picked up this . . . young woman? 'Your name is Sharon, is it? What do your people do?'

'My dad has a butcher's shop in Hawsham,' Sharon said, smiling.

Victoria paled, and Becky hid a small grin in her soup spoon.

Sharon wasn't fazed by Victoria. She was smart and cultured, but she also drank and smoked and loved to dance in the seedy third-rate nightclubs in the local town. Plus, she had friends. Lots of them. Guys and girls. Some of them were dweeby, some were jocks, some wanted to be politicians. Becky didn't have that much in common with most of them, but at least she now had company. Sometimes all you wanted was a pint of cider and a plate of bangers in the pub with your 'mates', as Sharon called them. It made her day-to-day work in the castle bearable.

And it *was* work. Becky seemed to have the phone glued to her ear constantly. Untangling her rights and, more importantly, her money seemed to take for ever. She was still living on the allowance she'd been paid at her aunt's house in the States, because nobody could wok out just how much she was due. Becky found it totally frustrating. She owned Fairfield, and the raft of UK companies that was Lancaster Holdings. But they all had trustees, and debts, and shares outstanding and she wasn't all that sure of anything.

The lawyers told her to stop worrying her pretty little head about things.

'Mr Henry Whitlock and Mr William Lancaster are doing a splendid job of running your interests. Simmons & Simmons are arranging for more dividend cheques to be placed in your personal account, Miss Lancaster. Why trouble yourself further?'

Mr Alexander Simmons, grey-haired and wearing a neat, worsted suit, steepled his fingers and looked at his young client expectantly.

It was unusual to have such a peach sitting in his office. He admired the tight-fitting dress with the swirly print; it was silk, and it showed off those endless legs and the outline of a small bra. He imagined it as lacy and snapping off easily under his hand. Pale pink or strawberry red on top of those firm little breasts? And was that blonde natural? He'd *love* to find out.

Becky felt a sudden surge of annoyance.

'I'm troubling myself because I want to take control of my own companies,' she said flatly.

'But that's ridiculous.'

Becky blinked. 'Excuse me?'

Mr Simmons snapped back to earth, recognizing his mistake. 'I didn't mean ridiculous, Miss Lancaster. A natural desire, of course.' His face showed that he thought it was anything but. 'But . . . forgive me . . . unless you know a lot about shipping and exports, I fail to see why you would want to run Lancaster Holdings. It is a pretty complex business.'

Becky paused.

'You're right, of course,' she said. 'I'll research it, and get back to you.'

'You do that,' he said blandly.

Meanwhile, she had another aim in mind. Nobody wanted to acknowledge her, or take her seriously. But Becky could change their minds about that. She was here, and she was eighteen years old. Even though she was not yet twenty-one, she had come into her trust. She had to show the Lancasters . . . Victoria, William, the lawyers, the corporate executives . . . that she was in control. Even though they all just wanted her to go away, it wasn't going to happen.

Fighting words. But she had no idea how to do it.

Sharon had come to the rescue yet again.

'Throw a ball,' she said one day when they were sitting in the drawing room, watching the BBC announce the latest round of power outages.

'Throw what?'

'A ball. A dance. You got the dance floor, you got a perfect place to set up a marquee . . . all the toffs do it. Sixteen, eighteen, twenty-one, hunt balls, any excuse really.' Sharon scrutinized her friend, imagining the cool East Coast babe in a posh ballgown. 'You'd be a big hit. And you'd be the hostess. They'd all have to come. After that, they'd all have to write you thank-you letters. My sister in Colchester's a caterer. It'd be a great party, and afterwards, you could hang out with some of your own kind of people.'

'You're my kind of people.'

'In one way,' Sharon said, without malice, 'not in another.'

Becky was quiet, because she knew it was true.

'Could you help me with that?'

'Absolutely. And,' said Sharon, who always refused to accept a penny from Becky, 'you can get me a dress.'

'You're going to wear a ballgown?'

'Maybe,' Sharon admitted.

Becky looked sceptically at Sharon's orange and blue eyeshadow. 'I'll believe that when I see it.'

But she was excited. A ball. How very *limey* that was. And Sharon was one hundred per cent right – all her stiff-necked relatives would have to attend. They'd see she was here to stay. And if Becky was honest, a tiny little voice in the back of her mind said that Sharon was right about something else, too. She *did* want to mix with her own people. Maybe that made her a snob. Maybe she was as bad as Aunt Victoria. But she couldn't help it. Part of her wanted to see the world her father had been born into, to force those people to notice her. Accept her.

'Let's do it,' she said.

It took two months to organize. Becky travelled down to London on a rickety BR train and took a cab to Smythson's, in Bond Street, to get just the right heavy, creamy paper for her invitations. She went to Dabett's for the party decorations, and personally selected each paper lantern, floating candle and sparkling web of fairy lights. Zeile's handled the flowers, Sharon's sister had charge of the food, and that just left the dress. Becky had gone everywhere from Chanel to Harrods before finding a perfect creation in a vintage-costume shop off the King's Road.

Becky pirouetted for her friend.

'Man.' Sharon sighed. 'You just look . . . awesome.'

Sharon was wearing a pretty dress she'd picked up at Peter Jones, a dark blue silk ballgown with little puffed sleeves and gold embroidery at the bodice, which emphasized her large breasts and did a creditable job of covering her butt. She had felt gorgeous when she put it on, certain that Jack, her boyfriend from college, would come over all light-headed when he saw her in it. But the problem with being friends with Becky was that you had to deal with how *she* looked. Most of the time, Sharon could handle it. But she was only human. Did Becky really have to look quite this . . . edible?

'You like it, huh?' Becky asked, examining herself.

Wow, Sharon thought. She really has no idea how good she looks.

In that gown, Becky was a goddess. It swept down from her tiny breasts in a whisper of palest pink chiffon, ruched and gathered over a tight whalebone corset to push her cleavage together, so her breasts resembled tiny, tight little plums, pushed up for inspection, a suggestion of curves on her slender body. The Victorian corset cinched in her already minuscule waist; now a man could circle it with his hands. Maybe a hand and a half. Over creamy layers of silk and four stiff petticoats, her skirt ballooned out around her, the pink chiffon delicately layered with pale golden satin. Tiny roses of red lace were scattered across her gown, like poppies in a cornfield. Her platinum hair, usually draped freely around her face, was piled on top of her head. She looked stately, like a Victorian duchess, and yet so young, so sexy . . . the delicate dress matched only by the fresh bloom of her complexion and the sparkle of her eyes.

She might be a Yank, Sharon thought enviously, but tonight she was the perfect English rose. She could have walked straight out of Sharon's set texts. She was the kind of girl that made you want to start reading a lot of John Donne sonnets.

No detail had been overlooked. Becky's shoes were satin, dyed palest pink, like a blushing white rose. She was tall enough that she only had to wear flats. Tiny flaxen tendrils framed her aristocratic face, and she had just the smallest touch of make-up on – sheer foundation, a whisper of blusher and white liner under her eyes to make them sparkle. Becky looked as though she had stepped right out of a Gainsborough portrait. She had no evening bag – her room was right upstairs, and anything else would have been overkill – draped over the elegant wrist. But . . . and only a real blue-blood would have done this, Sharon thought; her mate *was* a blue-blood, even though she sounded like Jacqueline Smith . . . Becky had a fan dangling from her left hand. A real fan, an antique thing made of feathers, with a white ivory handle patterned as intricately as lace. Becky had already fanned herself twice, and she flicked the handle sharply, without seeming to try, so that it spread out like a white peacock's tail . . .

Sharon swallowed hard. She liked Becky, she reminded herself. There was no point in acting bitchy just because she was so gorgeous.

'What time do you think the first people will arrive?'

'Well, invitations said seven, so I'd better be down there five of.'

'No one's gonna get here till half past at the earliest.'

'But if somebody does . . . I can't keep my guests waiting,' Becky said firmly.

Sharon flopped onto a seventeenth-century embroidered chair. 'The hostess with the mostest. I should have known this would happen. You can be ruthless, you know.'

Becky laughed. 'Me? I'm not ruthless.'

Sharon looked at her levelly. 'You are, hon. You might not realize it yet, but you are.'

'What makes you say that? I'm a pushover.'

'Really? Rupert's coming, isn't he?'

That was true, and Becky felt the butterflies take flight, seething around in her taut little stomach.

It had been her greatest triumph since coming to England. No, she corrected herself, her *only* triumph. As soon as Sharon had mentioned the possibility of bringing the family together . . . with herself as mistress of Fairfield . . . Becky had thought about Rupert. Her cousin. Or, to be really accurate about it, her second cousin, once removed. Which wasn't that close. But Rupert had one thing to recommend him that she didn't – he was a man.

The family had a title. Rupert had it and she didn't. He was Lord Lancaster. Her great-grandfather, Gerard, the fourteenth baron, had had a younger brother. Much younger, some twenty years perhaps. The Hon. Herbert Lancaster had had issue, four sons, the eldest of which, John, was technically her grandfather's first cousin. But with the age difference, he had grown up with Becky's dad. And his son, Rupert, who was just two years older than her, was Dad's second cousin, and her third cousin once removed.

But Becky, with no sisters or brothers, had never got to know the only relative she had of her own generation. And it was all because of sex.

She was the wrong one.

Dad had only had a sister, and his father had two sisters. So her brother had been the last hope for Gerard Lancaster's line. Three only sons, the last one dying with his father, a toddler who couldn't even pronounce his own name.

Herbert Lancaster had no such problems. He had four boys, and William, the youngest, was currently managing Lancaster Holdings, along with Uncle Henry. Becky didn't know any of those brothers. She'd meet them tonight. But the one that had concerned her, growing up, was John.

Mr John Lancaster had noticed the lack of Y-chromosomes in the senior branch of the Lancasters. He had no expectations that his cousin Robert was going to die, or that his son would. But once he had teased him about making provision. What would happen to Rebecca if disaster struck?

Becky had only seen her father's face in photographs, but she liked to imagine the scene. Her dad, looking coldly at his cousin. Saying, 'Then Becky would inherit Fairfield.'

'Oh, no,' John said, 'Robert. Fairfield is entailed. Then it would come to me. The house must go with the title. Of course you see that.'

But Daddy hadn't seen that. Not at all. And he'd told his cousin so, and the argument got more and more heated, until John stormed out of the house and never spoke to her father again.

John had died after Robert did. Too much steak-and-kidney pudding, too many helpings of cheese and biscuits. Nothing as dramatic as a car crash – more your bog-standard heart attack. Becky felt sorry that they had never reconciled. It was poignant to die angry, unreconciled. Had John regretted it, as he clutched at his chest? she wondered. Had Dad?

Rupert Lancaster had not taken the opportunity for any reconciliation. His father had succeeded to the title, but not the house. Furious at his dead cousin because, after all, the infant daughter wasn't even in England, not even using Fairfield, John Lancaster filed suit. The house was entailed on the male line, with the title, and if the male line was dead in one branch, it was to go to the other. So what if the law was five centuries old? It was still the law.

Prove it, her father's executors had said. Prove it.

And John tried to. He died trying.

But Rupert, now Lord Lancaster, the shadowy figure she had vaguely heard of throughout her childhood, over there on the East Coast of the US, had not given up. He was still trying. For years, and with barely enough cash to pay the lawyers, Rupert had taken his case through the English courts, with no success.

And then there was last year.

Becky had been playing a round of tennis, her blonde hair streaming out like a banner as she ran around the court, enjoying the sunshine and the gentle thwack of the balls on the warm tarmac, when Aunt Mindy ran out looking worried, waving a telegram. The courts had received notice of new evidence in the Fairfield case. Rupert Lancaster, the young Baron, had unearthed a seventeenth-century document in his grandfather's papers.

It was a writ of entailment.

Issued and stamped by James I, the new Scottish King of England, at the request of the then Baron, it stated that the land, manor and estate of Fairfield were to be forever indivisible from the title. And that would mean one thing.

No women.

Rupert was quoted in issues of *The Times* that winged their way across the Atlantic to an anxious, teenage Becky. 'Ladies are looked after in my family,' he'd said. 'Excellent matches are made for them. They marry well. They receive dowries. But if you split the land from the title, you destroy hundreds of years of tradition. I'm fighting to preserve that. I'm sorry Miss Lancaster's representatives don't see it that way. After all, my cousin is really an American.'

Becky recalled that moment now with an icy splinter of anger deep in her heart. The reason she wasn't in England was that the family, the wonderful *family* Rupert prated on about, had abandoned her.

But the panic subsided six months later when a High Court judge, in session at the Old Bailey, threw out the case. The paper was determined to be 'unreliable evidence'. They hadn't gone so far as to say it was a forgery, Becky noted. That would accuse an English peer – young, dashing, seen at Annabel's and Tramp – of perjury, of perverting the course of justice, and that would never do. Besides, Becky knew from the English press that Rupert Lancaster was considered a hero – poor, gracious, noble and the underdog, fighting against her and her high-priced team of Yank lawyers. The Court wouldn't want to tarnish his reputation.

At least they had thrown out the case. Three months before her eighteenth birthday, when she would, finally, reach the maturity of her trust fund.

Becky had given 'no comment's to reporters until she was blue in the face. But she had been worried. Very worried. It was amazing, the amount of value she had attached to Fairfield before she had even laid eyes on it.

And now she knew why. The house was in her blood, baked into her genes. She made a note to send some flowers to the trust lawyers. They had done a good job for her. Rupert might have the title, but he couldn't take her house.

She was amazed he had accepted the invitation. But she was also glad. Rupert was her cousin, the only living family she had of her own generation, however distant. He bore her father's title, and it wasn't good that they should be enemies.

Well, he was coming tonight. Becky felt a distinct shiver of nerves at the thought.

She was finally going to meet him.

Chapter 11

Fairfield Court was ablaze.

Rebecca had had torches placed along the driveway, driven into the ground, sending sparks and smoke up into the early evening twilight. Across the front court, before the marquee, pillar candles had been placed in the close-cropped grass in clear glass bowls, lighting up the ground with a gentle, flickering glow, setting the shadows dancing across the mossy stone steps.

The marquee was a gorgeous fantasy, an Arabian Nights-style tent in soft cream silk, with the tables inside painted in gold, the chairs covered in pure linen and red satin cushions with gold embroidery heaped against the walls. There was a small dance floor and a space for the string quartet to set up, and later a DJ, with his booth hidden from the diners by an ornate wooden screen. Each person's table was set with sprays of roses and white baby's breath, beeswax candles scented with white musk, crystal and silverware.

Outside the tent, along the side of the house, she and Sharon had had the caterers range out tables, laden with hors d'oeuvres and large silver buckets crammed with ice to chill the Perrier-Jouet and Krug. There were tiny blinis heaped with glistening mounds of Beluga and Sevruga caviar, smoked salmon and cream cheese speckled with dill in rolls, tiny sandwiches of cucumber and cress with the bread thinned by a rolling-pin, minute slices of a fresh truffle omelette, oysters, both fresh and smoked, and shellfish kebabs of king prawn and hen lobster cooked with ginger. As she walked past, lifting the skirt of her ballgown so the chiffon didn't trail over the flagstones, Rebecca breathed in the delicious scent, but her nerves were so great she wasn't even tempted to pick.

The place looked sensational. She looked sensational. But she was still scared.

Sharon had gone home, despite her friend's pleas.

'I have to,' she said. 'Can't stay here. You have to do the receiving. You're the hostess. You don't want some of these people thinking I'm Rebecca Lancaster. Besides, I need a gin and tonic. Be back around eight.'

And she'd kissed her on the cheek and left, without even looking guilty about it.

Rebecca positioned herself at the top of the terrace. A row of candles lit a path directly to her. She adjusted the thin lace shawl around her bare shoulders, and waited. For a second, an icy panic took hold of her. It was already seven thirty-five by her gold Patek Philippe watch, and nobody was here. She had two fields below the garden marked off for parking, with attendants, and more torches for light.

What if nobody came? What if the English side of the family decided to punish her by making her look like a total fool, a teenage reject, an upstart Yank with no idea? Maybe all it would be would be Aunt Victoria and Uncle Henry, who would patronize her and make her feel even worse than she did right now. Rebecca felt slightly sick. She had spent over twenty thousand pounds on this party. She didn't even want to think what that was in dollars.

Suddenly there was a new sound in the twilight over the cellist tuning up. Rebecca lifted her head and saw two sets of headlights sweeping down her drive. A Rolls-Royce followed by a Jaguar. She took a deep sigh of relief and breathed out to steady herself.

Here we go, she thought.

'This is great.' Sharon grinned. 'Fucking 'ell. Look at this. It's like something out of *Pride and Prejudice*.'

'Hold on,' Rebecca hissed. 'Mr and Mrs Hope? How nice to see you. Yes, a lovely evening. Do have a glass of champagne . . . some caviar? And this is your son? Jocelyn, good to see you.'

Sharon hung back, watching Rebecca press the flesh. She was so self-possessed, it was hard to see her as only eighteen. Her hair swept up, diamonds at her earlobes glittering in the firelight, and a whisper of chiffon all around her, half her male guests could barely take their eyes off her. They might be stodgy old goats, like Mr Hope here, fifty if he was a day, in his black tie, with his pimply son with the pudding-bowl haircut, but he had a hard time taking his eyes off Rebecca's face. Mrs Hope, who had the reddish face of somebody who liked her port a little too much, and whose complexion matched her voluminous burgundy Laura Ashley ballgown with a huge bow on her bum, dug her elbows into her husband's side and dragged him off to the food tent.

Guests were milling around, arrayed in ball dresses and cocktail sheaths, the deepening night illuminated as much by their jewellery as by the candles. Everywhere Sharon looked the crowd glittered. There were hundreds of people here, with waiters circling endlessly, carrying magnums of champagne, and the low hum of conversation rose over the liquid sounds of the string quartet. Yet nobody, herself included, shone as brightly as Rebecca. Sharon found herself slightly taken aback by how at home her friend was here. Of course, this *was* Rebecca's place, and these people were her relatives and stuff . . . but maybe it was the American accent. Sharon had never really thought of Rebecca as one of *them*, despite what she'd said to her.

But Rebecca made the Queen look common, the way she stood there, waving and nodding and pressing her hand so lightly over everyone else's. Her gorgeous gown, her dangling diamonds, the fan, the aristocratic cheekbones . . .

You would never tell she was an American. No way, Sharon thought.

She reminded herself firmly that Jack said he liked bigger girls, and anyway, Jack would never be Becky's type. He was here somewhere, Becky had said. She thought she'd drift off and find him.

'See you later,' she hissed at her friend.

Rebecca didn't hear her. Her feet and legs felt sore from standing up, it was starting to get chilly and there seemed to be an endless line of people coming up to shake her hand. Lords, ladies and Hons galore, with lawyers, and bankers, and their wives; all apparently thrilled to be here. Shaking her hand and wishing her well. As she glanced around at the crowd, swilling her drink and scoffing her food, she felt strange. Her party was a complete success, and yet she knew nobody here. She resisted the temptation to glance at her watch as another set of third cousins trooped past her. Surely soon it would be time for dinner, then dancing. Oh, hell. She'd probably get stuck dancing with her Uncle Henry to lead things off. Apart from Sharon's boyfriend, and some guys in the village, he was the only man she knew here.

She waved the third cousins toward the champagne and tugged her thin lace shawl tighter around her waist. The stream of people thinned to a trickle and then to a halt. It was almost nine o'clock now. Perhaps she could go inside and sit down, rest her aching calves.

Not yet, apparently. There was a young man coming towards her, without any obvious wife or children. He was tall, dark-haired and dressed in an immaculately cut dinner jacket, with a crisp white shirt and neat bow-tie. Becky automatically straightened herself a little further. She felt a slight blush creep into her cheeks as he came closer.

Damn, he was handsome. Look at those eyes. Dark, and fringed with thick black lashes, almost Latin-looking. He was well muscled without being too much of a jock, and he bore himself well. She saw the eyes of her well-heeled guests sliding over to him, the conversations around him seeming to halt as he walked past.

She racked her brain. Had she invited any film stars or TV people?

Maybe he was some kind of English star she'd never heard of. Or an athlete or something.

The young man strode up the steps and gave her a minute bow. 'Rebecca Lancaster, I presume?'

He had a low, sexy voice. Rebecca felt her blush deepen. His cheekbones were high and arrogant, and he had a sensual, slightly cruel mouth. She tried to collect herself.

'Yes,' she said, smiling at him as formally as she knew how. 'Welcome to Fairfield.'

'Thank you,' he said dryly. 'I'm Rupert Lancaster. Your cousin.'

Becky reddened. She had no idea her meeting with him would feel this way. She hadn't recognized him at all. In two-dimensional inky newsprint, nothing of his magnetism had come across. Not these chocolate eyes, not the sheeny jet of his hair, and certainly not the arrogance of his bearing.

'L-Lord Lancaster?' she stammered.

He smiled briefly. 'I think it should be Rupert and Rebecca, unless you have a strong objection. We may be distant relatives, but we don't have to be that distant.'

'I agree.' She held out her hand. Instead of shaking it, though, he curved the fingertips and lifted it gently to his mouth, kissing the back.

'I'm sorry I'm late,' Rupert said. 'I ran out of petrol.'

'The car did, or you did?'

'The car. I never blame myself for anything, if I can avoid it.' He smiled wolfishly. 'So kind of you to invite me, by the way. I always felt badly that we weren't reconciled.'

'The court case . . .' Rebecca said awkwardly.

'Yes. Hard to come together when you're in dispute over legal matters. But, as much as I may not like it, that's been resolved.'

'Absolutely,' Rebecca said. She suddenly felt embarrassed. It had been really good of Rupert to show up at her party as she played chatelaine in the house that he thought he was entitled to, that he had spent his entire life fighting for. She moved hastily off the top step so as not to seem quite so queen-like. 'I'm very glad to see you. I – I hope we can have dinner together.'

'I'm not invited to dinner? I thought it rather went with the ball.'

She blushed again. 'Absolutely. You are, yes. But I've seated you with some distant cousins.'

'Even more distant than us?'

'Even more distant than us. I didn't know if you'd want to sit with me.'

'You silly girl, I came all the way from London just to see you,'

Rupert said softly, and Becky felt her insides turning into melted butter. He looked at her intently for a second, his dark eyes roving over her gown. It felt as though he were ripping it off her skin.

'What a ravishing dress,' he said, putting a faint but discernible emphasis on ravish.

Oh, I wish you would, Becky thought suddenly. I sure wish you would.

'Thanks. Shall we go into dinner? I – I need to switch around some place cards.'

'Absolutely,' Rupert said. He offered his arm, and it looked like the most natural, chivalrous thing in the world. 'I wish I had my friends from London here. I always like to be seen escorting the prettiest girl in the place.'

Even in the darkness of the night, Becky felt a wave of pure sunshine wash over her. Oh, man, was he gorgeous. And definitely distant enough for romance. If he was interested, that was. He was the perfect English gentleman . . . courteous, confident, well built . . . and his eyes, his eyes were just hypnotic . . .

She smiled back up at him, and threaded her slender arm through his. Everybody stared as they walked into the marquee together.

I suppose I could hack it, Rupert thought dispassionately. Of course, the accent will have to go, but that could be worked on. A few years here, and she'd probably lose it altogether. The tan was attractive certainly, but also a little vulgar. Then again, what could you expect, with that upbringing? She probably chewed gum, too, and swore. American women were very pushy. He knew that from first-hand experience.

He regarded her out of the corner of his eye as he shook hands with various nonentities milling around the marquee, which was over-decorated and sumptuous. She was quietly switching the place cards with the minimum of fuss and the maximum of grace. A wash of resentment flooded across his soul. Look at her, so beautiful . . . he could not deny she was beautiful . . . so regal, and welcoming all these people into *his* house. And spending all his money, when he had to have frank conversations with his bank manager at Coutts just to get him to honour his cheques.

Rebecca's father had been a wastrel without any regard for the family. Marrying that tramp, threatening to divide the house from the title, and then speeding on the open road, killing himself and his heir, so that today it had come to this. For the first time in ten generations. What a bloody joke. And now his daughter looked as though she was going the same way. What was the point of all this ostentation? Rupert thought enviously as he looked around. American show boating.

Well, he'd soon get that out of her.

She was highly fuckable. That dress couldn't hide the slimness of her figure – never mind the full skirts, he could tell from her slender wrists and delicate collarbone. Her hair was thick and glossy. It couldn't be natural, but it looked good. Real good. Rupert imagined those long, coltish legs wrapped around his waist. Was she a virgin? He'd love to break her in. Each thrust would feel like a victory.

When Rebecca was his wife, safely pupped up with a boy, preferably two, everything would be all right again. He would be master of Fairfield. His son would be master of Fairfield. He would set up a proper 1970s entailment that no strident Yankee female and her barrage of lawyers could break.

And he would have nobody to thank but himself.

'I got it,' Rebecca said, coming back to him, holding up the small, thick triangle of card. She smiled, a wide, healthy smile full of white teeth against golden skin. Rupert saw the flush of her cheeks, the glitter in her eyes. It was a look he'd seen on countless young girls, from sixth-formers at St Mary's, Ascot, to that hot tamale of a model, Lita Morales. Rupert grinned. He had her already. All he had to do was reel her in.

He felt lucky. He had no doubt he could get Rebecca Lancaster. As soon as the invitation arrived in the post, it had been a done deal. She obviously wanted to 'make friends'. Yeah, right . . . like he would ever be friends with the woman who had stolen his inheritance. But she was American. She'd be touchy-feely, and on top of her desire to reconcile with him he had a title. All women liked that, especially Americans. And with an American, you had the accent. As successful as he'd been with babes in the London clubs and at country balls, Rupert had never known anything like the ease of getting Yank chicks. In New York they just couldn't wait to drop their little panties. Only Lita had made him wait, and probably only as a ploy to get him to marry her.

And it had nearly worked. Rupert shook his head; he had actually told himself he could have smoothed over Lita's rough edges. Foolish, for ultimately she was . . . Hispanic. Working class. Unsuitable to be Lady Lancaster, and the mother of a Baron.

Besides, he'd lost the case, and then it had all become moot.

The pool of eligible wives had shrunk to one. Just one. It was his good fortune that he'd actually enjoy banging her. Maybe he could work out some arrangement with Lita, too, when he was in New York. But maybe not. It wouldn't do to have got that far and then to risk everything.

He'd have to cut Lita off completely.
'Let's sit down,' he said. 'I really want to get to know you.'

Chapter 12

Lita checked into the Pierre. It was sinfully luxurious, but she needed it. She needed comfort, and reassurance. The gilt lobby of the hotel, with its massive Christmas tree, soothed her slightly.

She took a bubble bath and swathed herself in the warm, white, voluminous towelling robe. Then she sat by her window overlooking the cold, grey, leafless stretch of Central Park and reread the telegram.

There had to be some mistake. Rupert couldn't mean it. If he did, wouldn't he have said something? At least called?

He had been so warm when he'd left. Was it the stress of the new business?

Oh, hell. The business. Lita snuggled deeper into her robe, trying to overcome the sudden surging feeling of panic. What had he said about her money . . . that he would set up a drip-feed and only take what was needed? The business was brand-new, though. It couldn't have needed that much. Besides, Rupert was rich.

Wasn't he?

Lita pressed her manicured nails to her forehead and tried to think. She didn't want to consider this, but she had to. It was the same feeling she'd had the first time Pappy took her up to the observation deck of the Empire State Building. She was afraid of heights, but somehow she couldn't resist walking to the rail and looking over the edge, watching the sickening drop and feeling as though she were falling, even though her feet were planted on the concrete, even though she was perfectly safe.

She always looked out over ledges. And she had to think about this.

Her father's words rang in her ear as she examined her engagement ring. It flashed prettily. How much would a one-carat solitaire go for these days? A thousand dollars, maybe? Two, if it was a nice stone? Two thousand. It wasn't that much of a stretch. Lita had assumed that Rupert had picked the ring for its classic elegance, rather than its size. But what if he couldn't have afforded anything more?

The apartment. Unless this telegram was a horrible practical joke, it wasn't even his. Benson and Bailey had leased it for him, with the lease running out at the end of the year. And now he'd been fired, they'd have to take it back. But his gifts to her. The pearls, the fur . . . the hampers from Fortnum's. No doubt luxurious. But, said the nagging doubt in her head, wouldn't it be easy to afford status symbols if you didn't have to pay rent?

Rupert had never paid when they went out. Maybe a dinner here and there. But that was always charged to 'expenses', because she was working for the agency. Clubs let him in free, and they dined at friends' a good deal. Of course, he dressed immaculately. But he had no car. No car of any kind. They took cabs everywhere.

So assuming he paid for the things people noticed . . . suits, shoes, cufflinks, flowers, the occasional gift . . . what were his other expenses?

No rent. No car. No entertaining. Without that, a fancy suit became affordable, even on mediocre money.

Lita thought harder. OK, let's work this out, she told herself, trying to stay calm. Rupert's job, before he was fired, would have given him a good salary, because firms didn't give employees sensational corporate apartments if they weren't getting paid at top level. So where had Rupert's money gone? He had next to no expenses.

Lawyers, said the little voice in her head relentlessly.

That was why Rupert had gone to England. He had that thing he called a 'little legal problem'. Something about a house. And maybe the case had not gone as well as he had hoped – lasted longer, and taken more money. Otherwise why would he have come to her for cash for the new business? Which, she remembered, she had been pretty unimpressed by. But Rupert had reassured her, because he'd managed to poach all those clients from Benson Bailey.

Well, he *said* he had.

Lita shivered in her warm robe. She shook her head to clear all the bad thoughts. Yes, this was a mess, but she'd go back to her parents' tomorrow, call her bank and figure it out.

She ordered room service. Roast duck, new potatoes, string beans and half a bottle of red wine. What she really needed to do was to talk to Rupert and sort out the whole mess. The wine relaxed her, and Lita climbed into her soft, warm bed and drifted off to sleep.

But her last thought was that she had no way to track Rupert down.

Lita woke early, checked out and took a cab out to Queens. Her father was home; he told her Mama was out shopping for dinner.

'He left you, baby?'

Lita nodded. 'I think it's some kind of mistake, Pappy.'

'It ain't. He wasn't our kind of people, Lita. I knew he was a bum when I first saw him.'

Lita smiled. 'Whatever else he was, he wasn't a bum.'

'He sure was,' her father said stoutly. 'The kind of guy that skips out on the fare. Seen his kind a thousand times.'

The smile vanished. 'Pappy, I need to use the phone.'

'Use it all you want. You paid for it,' her father said.

Lita put her cases in the hall and dialled her bank manager.

'How nice to hear from you again, Miss Morales,' Paul Wilson said. He had acquired a great respect for his young client's financial acumen over the past eighteen months. And who wouldn't enjoy having a foxy young model as a client? All his colleagues were totally jealous of him.

'Good morning, Mr Wilson. I have a question about my balances.'

'Yes. We had noticed the unusual activity on the account. We're hoping to get a lot of your business back shortly.'

Lita felt the perspiration dew across her brow.

'Exactly how much do I have left in the accounts with you?'

'Let me see now.' She heard him rustling through some papers. 'I make it seven thousand.'

'Seven thousand dollars?' Lita repeated blankly.

He heard the dismay in her voice. 'There's nothing irregular, is there? We have been transferring the money to the company account as per your written instructions.'

'No, that's quite correct.' Lita's pride came rushing back to save her. She was half in shock. 'However, I do want to cancel that order now. I think we've transferred enough across.'

'I'd say so. Almost three hundred thousand dollars.'

'Right,' Lita said faintly.

She steadied herself against the wall.

'Is there anything else we can help you with today? That standing order is cancelled.'

'No, thank you. Have a good day.'

Lita hung up. She wanted to rush to the bathroom and throw up. Her father came and stood in front of her.

'Is something wrong, *querida*?'

'Nothing, Pappy. I'm getting the flu maybe.' It was a lie and she knew he wasn't buying it. 'Everything's gonna be fine.'

'If you say so, Lita.'

Lita hugged her mother when she came back and fended off her excited questions about Rupert. She washed and chopped vegetables for the salad and helped Mama fix chicken cutlets for dinner. Chico wasn't around, a small blessing.

'How long are you staying for, honey?'

'Just a few days. I have to take a business trip to England. I wanted to leave my stuff here if that's OK.'

'Why don't you leave it with the lord?'

Lita sighed, looking at her mother's bright, expectant face. Getting out of the garment store had peeled back some of the years that no money and no hope had added to her skin. She hated the thought of disappointing this woman.

'Mama, me and Rupert are having some troubles right now. I can't leave my things with him.'

Her mother looked horrified. 'Lita, honey. You aren't leaving him, are you? That wouldn't be right.'

'No, I'm not leaving him,' Lita said, grateful to be telling the truth for once. 'I'll let you know what happens, OK?'

'OK,' Maria said suspiciously, glancing at Lita's left hand to check that her engagement ring was still glittering there.

Lita ate her mother's tough chicken with every appearance of enjoyment, but she was restless. She slept fitfully in the guest bedroom and didn't bother to unpack. She could take her clothes with her to England.

Rupert had better have a good explanation for this.

Lita's father insisted on driving her to the airport.

'Of course you're not gonna call a cab. What am I? I didn't forget how to drive in one year.'

'I know you didn't, Pappy.'

'So, what time's your flight?'

'Twelve o'clock,' Lita lied. She didn't have the money to blow on a first-class seat. She was gonna need to wait at the standby desk for as long as it took.

He dropped her off at the kerb with a dark look. 'Lita, don't believe anything that boy tells you till you seen the proof. Promise?'

'I promise.'

'Sometimes parents aren't as dumb as they look to teenagers,' Pappy said sternly, then drove off.

Lita thought about that as she walked up to the standby desks to see what her chances were. A teenager. She was one; she had almost forgotten it, with the pressure of her career, and the relationship, and moving out. But she was a teenager, and she had fallen for a pretty face just like any young girl with a crush on a rock star.

She refused to let herself believe it could be that simple. How could Rupert have spent her three hundred thousand? He had invested it in the business, and she owned part of that business. So if the worst came to the worst, she could get it back. Just like she could get him back. He said it wasn't working out between them, but what did that mean, really? She could make it work. She knew she could.

The Pan Am ticket seller smiled politely at her and told her he had one seat available. It was in the centre of a row, and it was for the red-eye overnight. She would be cramped and blocked in and exhausted.

Lita took it. She had no choice.

When she landed in London, there was a small booth with a list of hotels. She booked one of the cheapest ones she could find. It took two and a half hours to get through the morning traffic into town. It was Lita's first time in Europe, but she was so shattered she didn't even look around her. The hotel was in Lancaster Gate, and it was depressing – cramped little rooms with ugly patterned wallpaper and a shared bathroom at the end of the hall. She didn't even bother taking a shower, just tugged the thin curtains closed, crawled into bed and fell into a sluggish twilight sleep. The tooting horns and rush of cars outside might have kept her awake, but Lita was from the Bronx. She was used to it.

She woke up at three p.m., and the sun was already setting outside. It was chilly even inside her room. Lita took the small, scratchy towel the hotel provided, padded down the hall and took a long bath, washing her hair and body, making herself clean. She had no idea where to start looking for Rupert, but if she found him, she wanted to look good. She got changed into her black leather pants and cashmere poloneck, blasted her hair dry, made herself up lightly and went downstairs.

The clerk at reception blinked. This chick was nothing like the girl who had checked in. Without the dirty hair and the bags under her eyes, she was a stunner.

'Yes, miss?' he said hopefully.

Lita gave him one of her most melting smiles. 'I need some help, but I'm not sure exactly what to ask for.'

Good. Maybe she would stay at his desk a little longer. Look at that rack, he thought. Was she a hooker? Naw, couldn't be . . . too rich-looking. And not hopeless enough, although there was a slight desperation about her.

Pity. He might have stumped up the fee for a piece of that.

'Why don't you tell me and I'll see if I can 'elp.'

'I need to track somebody down, but I don't know where they live.'

'Phone directory,' he said brightly. Yanks – didn't know they're born, did they?

She shook her head. Her shiny hair bounced around like in a shampoo commercial.

'He's got quite a common name. Lancaster. But he's a lord. A baron, I guess. Lord Lancaster. And I don't know that he'd have a number listed anyway.'

'You could try the House of Lords. But I don't fink they let people in. No . . . wait. There's a book that lists all the dukes and that. Lords, too.'

'What's it called?'

'I can't remember. But you should go to the local library,' he said with a rare burst of inspiration. 'They'll be able to help you. I'll write down the address for you.'

'Hey, thanks.' Her American accent was like melted butter. He basked in the warmth of it. Maybe she'd like to stop looking for that lord and go out with a regular bloke. Maybe he should ask her.

But she was already out the door.

'Oh, yes, madam.' The librarian was a small woman with mousy hair and a neat navy skirt. 'That's *Debrett's.* And you may also find him listed in *Who's Who.* Let me show you. Will you be wanting to borrow the books?'

Lita shook her head. 'I'll just be taking notes.'

She was set up at a small reading desk with an overhead lamp. The silence was so thick it was oppressive; the flipping of the wafer-thin pages seemed very loud in there. It made Lita nervous.

She looked Rupert up. And there he was, with a huge coat of arms topped by a coronet and supported by two bears with chains around their necks. Rupert, an only child, Baron Lancaster. Educated at Eton, blah, blah, blah . . . no university, she noticed . . . Family seat . . . That was it, right, the house? Fairfield Court, Shropshire. Where was that? She could look it up. Lita wrote it down. London clubs . . . the Shooter's . . . that was worth trying, too. And a flat in Eaton Square.

Lita copied it all down carefully and got out of the gloomy building as fast as she could manage. On the street outside, it had started to snow. She ducked into the nearest restaurant and ordered a steak. She had to fight the impulse to rush right over to his club in a cab and demand to see him. That wasn't the way to go.

She ate the red meat when it came and felt the energy rush back into her. OK. Take a train to Fairfield Court? But what if he was in London? She could hardly go to his townhouse and wait for him to show up. It was too cold to do that.

She looked at her own reflection in the mirror. Yeah, she looked good, but she also looked hip. This was not the way to storm the citadel.

She knew Rupert's friends . . . stiff-assed jerks, all of them. And this was his world.

Back at the hotel, Lita examined her case carefully. She had packed everything between sheets of tissue paper so that it didn't crease, and that effort paid off for her now. She had a beautiful, below-the-knee pink tweed Chanel suit, the string of pearls he'd picked up for her at Cartier and her fur. She paired them with low heels from Dior in pink leather with little gold buckles, and swept up her hair into a severe bun.

Perfect.

Lita waited until the clock hit eight, then took a cab down to the West End. The club was exactly what she had expected – discreet, with a small brass plaque outside and a door with ornate cast-iron bars carved into lions' heads. Lita waited for the liveried doorman to open the door to admit her, politely touching his cap. She swept in without even looking at him.

'Yes, madam?' asked the man at reception.

There was no challenge in his tone. Lita congratulated herself; she looked like she belonged.

'My name is . . .' Quick, think of something rich and anglo. 'Elizabeth—' well, it was good enough for the Queen, wasn't it? '—Astor. I'm meeting Lord Lancaster for dinner.'

'Certainly, Miss Astor.' He riffled through his little book. 'Ah – I don't see your name . . .'

Lita sighed. 'Good Lord. Rupert's so forgetful. He *is* here at least, isn't he?'

He consulted another book. 'I'm awfully sorry, madam, but I don't think so.'

Lita pouted.

He was only human. 'You could probably find him at Miss Lancaster's residence in the country if you called, madam. Fairfield Court. I believe he mentioned last week that he was going up there for a birthday ball.'

Lita snapped her fingers. 'Silly boy. And not even a phone call. Well, thank you, you've been most kind.'

'My pleasure, madam,' the man said, signalling to the doorman to show her out.

That Rupert Lancaster is one lucky bastard, he thought enviously.

Lita waited while the doorman flagged her down a taxi, then tipped him. She waited until the door had closed behind her before letting herself start to grin.

Tomorrow she would go back to the library, find this Fairfield Court and get the train there. And then she'd speak to Rupert, and it would all be sorted out.

She had to believe that.

Chapter 13

Becky woke early and smiled.

Despite the warmth of the goose-down comforter on her bed and the cold of her room, she jumped out of the sheets. Her cousins had given her a cashmere robe to take to England, and she wrapped herself in it and walked to her bay window. The lead-panelled glass looked out over the terraced lawn going down to the large lily pond. It was just as though there had been no party. The marquee had been cleared away, the candles and torches were gone from the terrace. In strike-ridden Britain, she'd got exceptional service by simply paying the workers more money.

Dawn was breaking, and her window faced east. The sun was red, but getting brighter. There was a gorgeous, luminous quality of winter light in the pale sky; it would be clear and cold today. Becky thought idly about getting her Christmas tree in and throwing another party. A smaller one this time. Last night had been an exceptional success. Whether they had come out of kindness or pure rubber-necking curiosity, her entire guest list had showed up and hadn't left until the small hours. Exhausted, she had sneaked off to bed at four a.m. She didn't know why she wasn't exhausted right now. What had she had, maybe three hours' sleep?

But deep down, she knew why she woke up so early.

Rupert. It was excitement about Rupert.

Becky had been so nervous about meeting him – the possible scene, the hostility. Last night she had felt, finally, with Fairfield full of guests, not so ridiculously empty, that she truly belonged here. She was a hostess, and she was letting people into *her* home. Which Rupert had thought was his home.

But he had behaved so well.

Becky hugged herself and looked out over her beautiful grounds. Was that the right way to put it . . . that he had behaved well? You couldn't sum up his gorgeous, slim, dark-eyed looks with that, nor his charm, nor the way he'd watched her and made her stomach flip. You couldn't ignore the way he'd danced with her, so graceful, so commanding, as though he had done nothing but waltz from the day he'd come out of the womb. How about the way he'd defended her in conversation, when Aunt Victoria came up and made a snide remark about the cost of the party? He was . . . so English. The consummate gentleman. And that accent . . . boy . . . cut-glass. Becky remembered some of the people fawning on him over the title, and how Rupert put them at ease. She thought she'd fitted into his arms like she'd been made for them.

It was good to have her hand kissed. To be made to feel so welcome and so liked. It was as though he hadn't spent all that money fighting the court case, as though the court case had nothing to do with her whatsoever.

Rupert had looked deep into her eyes when he discussed it with her, so she could feel his sincerity.

'I can't lie to you, Becky. I did feel that I had a right to Fairfield, and it was my father's wish that I should fight for the house. So I did. I hope you can respect that. But as it's over, I don't hold a grudge, and I hope you won't.'

'Not at all.'

'If I had won, you'd always have been welcome here. You're family. Even if you are *very* distant,' he added, glancing at her breasts.

Becky felt her nipples tighten.

'And you're always welcome here. Any time. I have eight spare bedrooms.'

'Actually, you have ten,' he said lightly. 'Don't forget the extra two over the servants' quarters.'

Then he grinned, and his whole face lit up.

My God, Becky thought, he's so handsome. And she thanked heaven that the tent was only bathed in a gentle glow so that he couldn't see her blushing.

'I hope your dance card isn't filled already, or else I shall have to rip it up and get you a new one.'

She smiled. 'It's not.'

'Good,' Rupert said confidently, 'because now I've seen how beautiful you are I shall be monopolizing you all night. I've always been selfish.'

He leant over and refilled her champagne flute.

'Why don't you tell me about your childhood?'

Becky shook her head. 'It was very boring.'

Rupert took one sinewy hand and pressed it on top of her soft one. 'Nothing about you could ever be boring,' he replied.

Becky sighed with pure happiness. She didn't even feel tired. She'd gone from being a lonely cuckoo in the nest to being accepted overnight. And now Rupert.

Maybe she was mad to think he was interested in her, though. These English gentlemen were all notoriously charming. Maybe it was just good manners on his part. Of course, she was beautiful, she knew that. But men decided what was beautiful. Maybe she wasn't his type of beautiful. Her boobs were tiny. It went with being tall and slim. Becky opened the cashmere robe and examined them critically. They were small and exquisite, with tiny bud nipples, but certainly not curvy. Maybe she should get a push-up bra. But, then, wouldn't he be disappointed when she took it off?

Easy, girl. Not even one date, and she was already planning to jump into bed with him. And he hadn't even called yet.

Becky shook her head and padded into her bathroom to take a shower. She wanted to blow-dry her hair with a round brush in a flip, and pick out her best cosmetics to lose the bags under her eyes. Because if he called, she wanted to be ready for him.

The train up to Hawsham took two and a half hours. Lita paid through the nose for a seat in first class – she thought she could have taken a shuttle to Mexico cheaper – but it gave her a relatively clean seat, an empty carriage and a place to think.

The pain of Rupert's telegram had softened with distance. Nobody forced him to propose, right? She looked at the ring on her left hand and comforted herself with it. Obviously the business had put him under extreme stress. And why assume that her money was gone? If it was in a business account, she could get it back. Or even leave it there, and invest in Rupert. After all, Benson Bailey had invested in him pretty heavily, with the comp apartment, the expense account and everything. He must have been good at his job. Why not think he'd make a go of Modern Commercials?

He'd been so great with her parents. Very polite. Even trying to make small talk with Chico. Which was hard.

A man in a neat uniform pushed a trolley of very nasty-looking sandwiches past her and asked her if she wanted anything.

'No, thanks.' He was staring, so that was a good sign. Lita wanted to look her best. She'd tried on four outfits before settling on this one – her black Fendi pants in leather, with the off-the-shoulder sweater in white merino on top; it was warm and stylish and it showed off a sexy, but still decent amount of *café-au-lait* skin. Her hair was loose around her shoulders, curly and gleaming, and her lips were painted fire-engine red, matching her nails.

She didn't look as though she was afraid of anything. 'But you could tell me how long it's going to be till we reach Hawsham?'

'About another twenty minutes, now, miss.'

'And will it be easy to get a cab there?'

'You're an American,' he said, in the voice of one making a discovery.

'That's right.'

'Well, Hawsham isn't a big town, miss, but ask the stationmaster and he'll give you a number for a local taxi company, all right?'

'Yes, thank you,' she said, turning away and looking out of the window.

The guard thought that there would probably be little cards stuck up in the phone booth, but he wanted to do the stationmaster a favour. Check her out. Maybe she was a movie star or something. Gorgeous. Reluctantly he pushed the trolley away.

Lita glanced again at her book. *The Pocket Guide to Manor Houses of England and Wales* Fairfield Court had a two-page spread. It was beautiful, certainly, if you liked that sort of thing. Lita didn't. She was all about soaring modern architecture. She thought the canyons of Manhattan were the greatest sight in the world. But she could see why other people would gape in awe at something like Fairfield. It reeked of history, and to Lita, it reeked of hundreds of years of privilege. The owner was listed as a Miss Rebecca Lancaster, who had inherited it from her father. Not Rupert, then. Some relative, probably a maiden aunt or something. Lita wasn't bothered if Rupert paid family visits around Christmas. It was just that running back to his homeland was no way to confront teething problems in the business . . .

She thought she had figured out why Rupert sent her that telegram, too. Most likely something had gone badly wrong, or was going wrong, with his new company. And he had lost some money, and he didn't want to put her through it. He probably thought that asking her to marry a failure wasn't right. But Lita wasn't bothered. Even if Rupert had lost his money, she would still love him. He needed to see that she was there for him. And her money . . . well . . .

Lita watched the soft green English countryside roll past her window and wondered about that. Rupert was probably working on salvaging her money right now. That's why he had said he had to rush over for a legal matter. He wouldn't want to show his face to her again until he'd got it back.

Love was all about trust, and she trusted him. She just needed to show Rupert that he could trust her, too.

She got out at Hawsham, which was a tiny little station, a bit like something in Westchester. The station was small and cosy, red brick with a little table on which were mounted dog-eared leaflets for local tourist attractions. One of them, she saw, was Fairfield Court, which was open to the public in the summer. Lita picked it up. It had a little map on the back. She pocketed it, and asked the stationmaster for the number of a cab company.

'I'll call one for you, miss,' he said, wishing he could drive her himself. 'Where are you off to, then?'

'Fairfield Court. It's in—'

'Oh, I know where it is. Everyone does. You up for the party, then? I thought that was last night.'

'It was.' The guy at the club had said something about a party. 'I just have business with Lord Lancaster.'

'Oh, that Rupert Lancaster. Always in the papers, he is. Said nice things about Miss Becky that's taken over the house. Between you and me, I think he might be looking for a wife.'

'Oh, yeah?'

'You know. Someone suitable, someone like him. That lot stick to their kind, don't they?'

She muttered something noncommittal and went outside to wait for the car. What did that guy know about sticking to his own kind? Rupert told her it wasn't where she came from, but where she was going that mattered to him.

The call came at eleven, and Becky was ready for it.

'Thank you, Mrs Morecambe.' She took the receiver from the old woman and tried not to sound too eager. 'This is Becky.'

'Becky, it's Rupert. I hope I didn't wake you?'

'Not at all.' She couldn't help herself. 'It's nice to hear your voice.'

'It's much nicer to hear yours. Look, I'm staying at the Rose and Crown in town. I don't have any meetings back in London until tomorrow. I wonder . . . if you're not too tired . . . would you like to have tea?'

'Sure. That would be great. But, look, why don't you come here?' She wanted to have him all to herself. 'Mrs Morecambe can make tea. Can't you Mrs Morecambe?'

Her housekeeper nodded and smiled encouragingly.

'It'd be so much nicer. I can get some cakes at the village shop.'

'Wonderful. Three suit you?'

'Perfect,' said Becky, because it was.

She hung up and looked pleadingly at Mrs Morecambe.

'You don't want to be bothering with nasty shop-bought cakes, miss. I can make a nice cake. Fruit or sponge?'

'Sponge, please,' Becky said. 'I don't want to put you out, but—'

'Nonsense, miss. It's my job. But don't you go making that much of a fuss of him. It's better that the young gentleman should make a fuss of *you.*'

'Absolutely,' Becky said, then ran upstairs to spritz herself with Chanel No. 19. She would set tea up in the drawing room which looked out towards the kitchen garden, and fill a vase with winter jasmine and Christmas roses. This was it, really; there were no soft lights, no music and no alcohol. If Rupert wanted to ask her out, he'd do it today. Becky didn't think asking her to tea counted, because he could just be being friendly.

She went into the library with a stack of papers on Lancaster Holdings. It was hours until teatime, and she needed something to distract her. Trying to unravel exactly what she owned and what it did would fit the bill nicely.

Lita looked at her watch. It was half past two, and the cabbie said it would take them another quarter-hour to drive out to Fairfield. It was a good time to turn up, after lunch, giving them enough time to recover from their hangovers. Lita wasn't too concerned. She looked as though she fitted in. They would tell her where she could find Rupert. Lita looked appreciatively at the English countryside, relaxing in her seat. It was pretty, with the villages and little thatched houses and farms dotted around. Hard to see it as the same country as London, yet it was only a couple of hours away. She still preferred Mexico, though. When she'd sorted out this mess with Rupert, maybe they could go travelling somewhere. Go to Rome, and see the Coliseum.

'Here we are, miss. Been here before?'

Lita glanced up. She was being driven through two enormous stone gates down a long, bumpy drive.

'This will be a first,' she said.

They took the corner, and Fairfield appeared, imposing and ancient.

'Nice,' Lita said. She thought she still preferred Fifth Avenue. The cab ground to a halt in the gravel in front of the door; she tipped the guy handsomely. Better to make sure he would come back if she called him. Then she walked up to the door, which was dark, aged oak, and rang the bell.

Becky heard the bell ring and jumped. She tried to calm herself. It was ridiculous to get butterflies in her stomach like this over a guy she hardly knew. He was ten minutes early, but Becky had been ready for him for ages. Her hair tumbled around her neck like a platinum waterfall; her nails were manicured and buffed with a clear French polish, and she'd put blue drops in her eyes to get the red out.

Mrs Morecambe moved towards the hall, but Becky brushed her away.

'I'll get it.'

She opened the door, smiling.

There was a young woman on her doorstep. Becky blinked, her mind racing over yesterday's guests. She was almost certain she didn't know this one. She was so young and so beautiful Becky would have remembered her. She was also too dark to have been on Becky's list of pasty white English relatives and friends of the family. No, she didn't think she knew her.

'Can I help you?' Becky asked neutrally, hoping she wasn't committing some horrible social gaffe.

'I hope so. My name is Rosalita Morales.' She was an American, and Becky recognized the light Bronx accent. What was a Puerto Rican girl from the Bronx doing here? She stuck out her hand, and Becky shook it, reluctantly. She had a nasty sense of foreboding. Had something happened to Aunt Mindy?

'I'm looking for Rupert Lancaster,' Lita said, when the blonde social X-ray didn't introduce herself. 'I heard he was here yesterday. I need to talk to him, and I was hoping you'd know where he might be.'

Becky stared at her.

'What do you want with Lord Lancaster?' she asked, rather coldly.

'I'm his fiancée,' she said.

Becky's eyes widened. His what? He hadn't mentioned anything about a fiancée. Her mind did a quick inventory of the woman. She was dressed too well to be selling something. But then why wouldn't she know Rupert was here? Why wouldn't he have brought her?

'Come in, please,' Becky said.

'Thank you.' Lita stepped into the hallway and folded her hands, looking at Becky expectantly.

'I'm Rebecca Lancaster,' Becky said, after an awkward pause. 'Please, come this way. I'm expecting Rupert for tea here shortly.'

The girl smiled, a flash of white, perfect teeth. Becky thought she was very beautiful, but a little too short, too curvy, too obvious. That white jersey draped all over those massive breasts. Becky thought about her own tiny boobs and pulled herself up straight to compensate.

She marched ahead and showed Lita into the library, complete with flowers and a silver tray laid out with tea, scones, jam and a fresh lemon sponge that Mrs Morecambe was extremely proud of.

'Please, have a seat. Would you like some tea? Or I can fetch you ice water, or coffee?'

'Actually, do you think I could just go and freshen up?'

'Certainly. There's a bathroom in the hall. First on the left,' Becky said. She felt a stab of disappointment right in her chest.

'Thanks,' the Rosalita girl said easily, walking out of the room with a sassy tilt to her hips.

Becky breathed out.

The doorbell rang again. She marched out to the hall and opened the door.

Rupert was standing there with a huge bunch of red roses.

'Becky. You look ravishing,' he said, grinning at her.

'And so do these.' She smiled back lightly. 'Did you bring them for your fiancée?'

'My fiancée?'

Rupert looked totally blank.

'Yes. Rosa Morales, or something.'

'She's here?' he said.

'So you do know her.' The rush of hope that had come at his blank stare disappeared again.

'Of course I know her. I worked with her.' Rupert drew close and murmured into her ear. 'She's an ex-girlfriend, a common little model – a mistake. Unfortunately for me, she can't seem to let go. She's a bit nuts.'

'But she's in my bathroom.'

Rupert pressed Becky's hand. 'Look, I have no idea how she tracked me down here. I'm awfully sorry about it. But why don't you run upstairs? I need to deal with this as kindly as I possibly can. I'll get rid of her and call you when the coast is clear, OK?'

'All right, Rupert,' Becky said uncertainly.

'Where's your phone? I'll call the cab right now. And don't worry. Everything will be fine. Trust me.'

Chapter 14

Lita heard the doorbell go and the murmur of conversation in the hallway, and her heart jumped. The little bathroom, papered with a William Morris pattern that looked old enough to be original, was equipped with a two-faucet sink and a mirror that was spotted with age in its gilt frame. Her pulse racing, Lita examined her face as she washed her hands. She took out her lipstick and touched her lips up. Yeah, that was better. She wanted everything to be perfect.

She took a deep breath, then walked out.

Rupert was standing in the library and the blonde Boston Brahmin chick was nowhere to be seen. Lita smiled and ran to him.

'Rupert! Darling, I'm so glad to see you. It's been real tough trying to track you down.'

Rupert shut the library door.

'Of course it has.' His voice was ice. 'I didn't leave you an address. I sent you a telegram.'

'I know, but you can't mean it. We're engaged – you can't just break it off out of the blue like that.'

'I can't?' He laughed lightly, cruelly. 'And I thought I had. Look, Lita, it was fun, but now it's over. Don't make a scene.'

Lita stepped back two paces from him. She had never seen this look in his eyes.

'A scene? You told me you loved me.'

'Men say lots of things in bed.' He shrugged. 'I'm sorry you had a wasted trip, but I never asked you to come.'

Lita suddenly shuddered. Fear ran up and down her spine, scuttling over her skin like a spider.

'Rupert, what about my money?'

His eyes narrowed. 'What money? What nonsense is this?'

'The money you asked to borrow for Modern Commercials. You'd said you'd take it only as needed. And when I checked with my bank, they said over three hundred thousand was gone. Almost everything.'

Rupert looked her right in the eyes and shrugged. 'Yes, unfortunate. Your money wasn't a loan, it was an investment in the firm. I lost an account, and the money went in overheads. We all hoped the business would succeed, but that's life in today's market. I'm sure you can make some more.'

Lita steadied herself on a burgundy leather chair.

'Your "firm", if that's what it was, was only open a month. How can you have spent that much?'

'Investments. Overheads. Operating costs. They mount up.' He smiled slightly, and she found she hated him. 'If you think you have a case to sue, go ahead. I put the company into liquidation. But I hear that lawyers' fees get pretty expensive.'

Lita nodded. 'I will sue you, here and in the States. I'll get back what you stole from me.'

There was a sound from outside, a car pulling up. Rupert strode to the library door and opened it, not even glancing at her.

'That's your taxi. I think you'll find you can't say I stole what you gave me signed permission to take.'

Lita gasped; her eyes filled with tears. She couldn't help herself.

'Come on, please,' Rupert said louder and more firmly.

She walked out into the hallway, half-blinded with tears, and brushed them away with the back of her hand.

'Lita, there's nothing going on between us and there never will be. You simply aren't my sort of girl. Becky is, and that's why I'm here. I feel sorry you had to hear it put so plainly, but it's for your own good. You need to go away. You're just . . . embarrassing yourself.'

'Very well,' Lita said, red-eyed and loathing him. 'I'm leaving.'

'Good,' Rupert said crisply.

He turned on his heel and walked back into the library.

Lita saw that the blonde girl was watching her with a sort of curious detachment from the top of the stairs, like a car passenger rubber-necking at the site of an accident.

She wrenched the door open and stormed out. She hated Rupert and she hated that icy bitch, too.

Lita had packed a pair of sunglasses in her bag. She slipped them on before she was even through the porch. No way she wanted to let Rupert gloat over her crying, or explain herself to the cabbie. She got in the car, careful not to slam the door. Screw them! The tears dried up almost instantly.

'Where we going, love?'

'The train station, please.' Thank God her voice wasn't wobbly. Grief and shock had vanished; there was nothing left but a pure, icy anger. She couldn't kid herself any more. Now all she wanted was to *get them.* Rupert and his bitch girlfriend. Lita started mulling it over as the car eased down towards the road, already making plans. She was eighteen going on fifty.

Make that nineteen going on fifty, Lita thought suddenly.

Today was her birthday.

When she got back to London she had a day to kill before her return flight. She packed away all her rich-girl, Euro-lady clothes, and tugged on a pair of jeans and her comfortable red mohair sweater. The clerk at the desk, not sure whether the polished lady was sexier than the fresh-faced girl in the ponytail and clinging sweater, suggested as many excursions as he could think of, in the hope that maybe she'd stand there a little longer, and shift from foot to foot, so he could watch those glorious tits jiggle. But Lita wasn't interested in the British Museum or the National Gallery or the Tower. She just flashed him a smile and walked out, heading for the library.

Rebecca Lancaster. Rupert's name was Lancaster. The stuck-up snob had received her like it was her home. Lita pulled out her guide book and *Debrett's* and *Who's Who* and looked up Rebecca Lancaster. She wasn't listed, but *Burke's Peerage* had her as a footnote; Rupert had succeeded Robert Lancaster, his second cousin, who had issue, 1. *d.* Rebecca Elizabeth, and 1. *s.* Charles Henry, who died in infancy. So that *d.* Rebecca succeeded to the seat, Fairfield Court, which was also claimed by Lord Lancaster, Rupert . . .

She lifted her head in the silence of the gloomy library and started to write on the cheap yellow pad she'd brought with her.

What had Rupert ever told her about the house? That it was his . . . Legal troubles . . .

He had said the house belonged to him. And that there was a court case to be resolved. Let's say they found in favour of Rebecca. What would happen then? Rupert would no longer be inheriting the house and whatever came with it, so he'd have to make his own money. And instead of trying to earn it from Benson Bailey or somebody else, he'd just decided to steal hers instead. Lita felt herself flush hot with rage despite the cool of the library. That was when he'd started acting strangely to her, presumably. Because now he didn't want to marry her . . . he wanted to rip her off. Lita thought, with a sudden burst of insight, that Modern Commercials had probably never existed in any real way. It had been a new 'firm' he'd set up so that she would sign that fucking paper, the drip-feed paper, and give him all her money.

And now she was right back where she'd started, give or take a few lousy thousand bucks.

Lita glanced down at the diamond glittering on her left hand. He'd said she could keep it. Yeah right – very good of you. She tugged it off and put it in her pocket. First thing to do was to sell it off. She had no intention of sending it back. She couldn't afford grand gestures any more.

She needed every cent for revenge.

The vision of Becky, standing up above her, watching her crying and stumbling out with that cold, priggish expression of surprise made Lita's manicured fist ball under the table. She hated her, with her huge old house and her titled father and the guy at the station sounding so happy that she was taking Lita's man. Not that he knew, but . . . 'their own kind of people'. Right. Rebecca had been good enough, noble enough, blonde enough for Rupert, and she hadn't been. He wasn't prepared to take a chance on them making it when Rebecca was there. And what had Lita become? Just another girl making a scene, like that chick in the club that Rupert had blown off. Lita's cheeks burnt. Rupert's voice, so firm, like he was being fair, while his eyes had stared at her with total disdain. 'You're just embarrassing yourself.'

Now Lita knew why that chick at the club had called her a poor bitch. She *had* embarrassed herself. She'd let Rupert make her cry and let Rebecca Lancaster watch, like she was a science project Rebecca was observing.

Lita thought about Rebecca until she was so restless she had to get up and leave. She banged the books shut so sharply a cross-looking librarian padded over to her.

'I hope there's no problem here?' she whispered sharply.

Lita looked right through her.

'There won't be,' she said.

On the flight home Lita thought about how she would play it. She bought a copy of British Vogue and flicked through it. The obvious answer was to model, do more campaigns and get more money. But somehow she recoiled from that. It seemed like moving backwards. Lita remembered what she'd said to Bill about the Costa Rica shoot . . . putting the other girls down because they were in their late twenties. She didn't want to be considered over the hill, washed up, before she'd hit thirty. Taking less money, doing worse and worse spots . . . winding up in the J.C. Penney catalogue, and with her agency not even taking her calls . . .

No way. The life was not for her. Lita remembered school, wanting to use her brain. Her beauty would pass. She shuddered at the thought of hitting thirty. Man, that was old. She wanted to have gotten somewhere before she was *that* old.

She was in her last year of being a teenager right now, and it was going to be her last year of modelling. Let Bill get her a couple more campaigns. Just to give herself enough money to get straight, get a new apartment. She'd buy a little piece of real estate in the city, and use the time to find out what was next for her life.

Rupert was right. She saw that. She couldn't afford a lawyer to go after him right now. But, as the proverb said, revenge was a dish best served cold.

Lita could wait. She wanted more than three hundred thousand dollars. She wanted his total destruction.

And Rebecca Lancaster's, too.

'Retiring?' Bill Fisher looked at Lita with dismay. 'Baby, you can't. You're one of our top earners. You've made so much money.'

If only he knew.

'I guess.' Lita tried to look nonchalant. 'But, Bill, I'd kind of like to do something else.'

'You don't know how to do anything else.'

'And if I quit five years from now, I'll be twenty-five with no experience of doing anything else. And what happens then? I get a grace and favour job here as your secretary?' Lita shook her head. 'I don't think so. I'm moving on.'

Bill made a face. 'I already booked you in for the Country Fresh campaign.'

She thought about it. 'Country Fresh, the pasta people, right?'

'Correct.'

'Who has that account?'

'The ad agency is Doheny.'

Lita smiled. Doheny, with its large offices on Madison Avenue, was one of the biggest commercials firms in New York. They handled Nescafé, the Republican Party at State level, the Dairy Farmers of America, and de Beers diamonds, among others.

'I wouldn't leave you in the lurch, Bill. Country Fresh can be our last campaign together.'

Bill sulked. 'You haven't worked here long enough for me to buy you a gold watch, you know.'

'We'll be working together in the future,' Lita said, in her maddeningly mysterious way. Bill always felt he was on a need-to-know basis with this chick. 'Just not like this.'

Lita tried to keep her financial situation to herself, but it was impossible. She chose to tell her parents what had happened on a Saturday night, so she didn't have to deal with Chico – he'd be out drinking and partying till dawn somewhere. Her mother's wail of dismay ripped into her heart, but Pappy was a rock.

'Hey now, *querida.*' He patted his wife's hand and grinned broadly. 'He was no good. She's lucky to be out of it.'

'Why would the lord do such a thing?' she sniffled.

Lita forced a smile of her own. 'Sometimes two people just drift apart.'

'So now what are you doing?'

'I'm getting a new place in the city.'

'You should stay with us. We'll get you a nice boy,' her mother promised.

'I don't think so, Mama. I'm gonna take a break from boys for a little bit.' Lita lifted her head and breathed in appreciatively. 'Something smells good. What are we eating? I'm starving.'

'Of course you are.' Her mother leaned over and pinched her upper arm, frowning. 'You don't eat right. You should come back here more often for some real food . . .'

Pappy winked at her. It was the only subject that could possibly have gotten her mother off Rupert.

Lita found an apartment that was a little better than her previous one. The mortgage was no problem – she put down three thousand and had payments of eight hundred a month. It was a walk-up on West Fourth, a quiet, tree-lined street in the Village, near her old coffee-shop. It was small, only two bedrooms, but the living room had bay windows with a cute mahogany bench that she fell in love with instantly. Plus, it was hers. Assuming she'd be able to make the payments.

Lita thought she had about four months to find another job. Her nest-egg would cover her for a while, plus the Country Fresh campaign would net her twenty grand for the print campaign. A lot of money. Enough to cover her back.

But life in the Big Apple was expensive, and she had to keep up a certain look. No way she wanted anybody to know how badly she'd been ripped off. She'd thought she was too smart for that, but when it came right down to it she'd been taken like a kid at his first game of three-card Monty. The money wouldn't last all that long. She had to get some more.

But she had a pretty good idea how to do it.

'So she wants to see me.'

Harry Weiss took off his black wire-framed Lennon specs and rubbed them, which was his habit whenever he was perplexed about something.

He was a tall, gangly man, thirty-five and lean, given to wearing black pants and polonecked sweaters. The swirling colours of hippie fashion left Harry cold. He had about twelve black outfits in his wardrobe, with the occasional splash of what he claimed was blue, but which everybody else said was such dark navy it might as well be more black. Harry didn't care. He was an account executive, which meant he met with clients and hired copywriters. He also supervised graphic designers. He needed to project an aura of hip-meets-hardass to seem businesslike but cool at the same time. Therefore he always wore black. It saved time and made him look deep.

Nobody argued the point. Why would they? Harry had revitalized the old blue-chip Doheny. He was constantly bringing in the hot new advertising executives, the talent that landed the big campaigns. He knew what buyers needed, and he gave it to them. That was what paid for his townhouse on West Sixty-Ninth.

Harry prided himself on being ready for anything, but this request surprised him.

'Yes. She said she wanted to discuss creative matters with you.'

'Man, she already has the gig.' Harry sighed. 'Remind me. What's her file?'

'Rosalita Morales, booker Bill Fisher at Models Six, too short for catwalk work, couple of big TV campaigns, no covers, demanding but never blows a shoot.' Susie, his assistant, rattled off the information from memory. Working for Harry, you had to be prepared.

'I remember. Sold a lot of coffee. Mid-list model.'

'She's shot one day's worth of print ads already and there's another session scheduled for tomorrow. The photographer thinks you should talk to her, keep her happy.'

Harry sighed. 'So now I have to listen to a lot of inane suggestions from a bimbo.'

'The pictures have come out real nice, Harry. He doesn't want her playing up for the second session. And besides,' she shrugged, 'she's waiting outside. I told her you were in a meeting, but she said she'd wait. She's been out there for over an hour.'

'Send her in, then. And come in and get me in fifteen minutes. Urgent phone call, whatever you have to make up. OK?'

'Got it.' Susie nodded and left his office. She walked back in a moment later with the model. Harry stood, smiling warmly. The girl wore heels and a neat camel-coloured fitted suit that emphasized spectacular curves. She wore full make-up – foundation, eye-shadow, thick mascara, liner and neatly pencilled fire-engine-red lips. She seemed very self-possessed.

'Thanks for seeing me, Mr Weiss. May I sit down?'

'By all means. Please.' He gestured to the Eames chair in front of him, and noticed she had a briefcase. She also had a sensational pair of legs, but Harry was immune to her beauty. This was work, and he never allowed himself to get distracted. The girl was a model. She was supposed to be beautiful.

Lita lifted the neat black case, stamped with her initials in gold, on to her lap. She saw right away that Weiss wasn't checking her out, so she assumed he was gay. Whatever. That was a good thing. It wouldn't get in the way of her future job. She clicked it open.

'These are some mock-ups of the layouts we're shooting right now for the Country Fresh campaign,' she said. 'I wondered if I could talk to you about them. I have a couple of ideas.'

Harry repressed another sigh.

'Please go ahead, Ms Morales.'

And Lita did.

Chapter 15

'Who was that girl?' Becky asked. Rupert was standing in the hallway, listening to the car pull away down the drive. He looked upset.

'An old girlfriend. I'm very sorry you had to see that, Becky. I think the poor girl must be pretty disturbed to track me here. I hope she can move on with her life now.'

Becky winced. 'That can't have been fun.'

'It wasn't. Fiancée! She's even worse than I thought. I had to be a little nasty to her to get the message across.' He shook his head sombrely. 'Cruel to be kind, I suppose, but it hurts me to have to do it.'

'Do you think you got the message through to her?'

'I think I did, yes. I'm pretty certain she won't be back. She's American after all. She's going home.'

Becky felt a small rush of relief. She smiled. 'Is it always so dramatic when you come to tea?'

Rupert chuckled. 'Not normally, no. I'm afraid I'm frightfully boring.'

I bet you're not, Becky thought, enjoying the sound of his laugh.

'Let's have some of that tea, then, before it gets stone cold.' He opened the door of the drawing room for her.

Over tea and the excellent sponge cake, Becky relaxed. Rupert asked all the right questions; he seemed fascinated by her childhood, her adolescence, everything except her love life.

'Don't tell me about any of them. I'll get so sick with jealousy I shan't be able to finish my cake.' Mrs Morecambe was hovering behind Becky and he winked at her. 'Which is quite outstanding.'

Becky beamed. 'And don't tell me about any of your girlfriends.'

'Oh, I have a reputation for being a rake, but it's not at all deserved. I'm a dreadful picker of women usually. Look at the latest disaster.'

'So what does that say about me?' Becky asked him.

'Only that there's a first time for everything, I suppose. Or that with my luck you'll refuse to see me ever again.'

'Not much chance of that,' Becky said, ignoring Mrs Morecambe's disapproving frown.

'Last night was the most tremendous bash. Did you plan it all by yourself? You're very clever.'

'My friend Sharon helped me.'

'Then we should all be thanking Sharon, too. Who is she?'

'She's, like, a local girl. Her father's a butcher.' Becky watched Rupert's face, but he didn't wince like Aunt Victoria. 'I've kind of found it hard to make friends, so she helped me with this party. I hang out a lot with her friends right now . . .'

She let the sentence hang in the air.

'Well, now.' Rupert gave her that slow, sexy smile of his. 'I expect Cousin Vicky calls them frightful oiks.'

Becky nodded.

'I don't think that way, but I do think it's important to mix with lots of people. Different types of people. I can introduce you around, if you'll let me. I'm selfishly motivated, you understand. I want the kudos for bringing the most beautiful woman in England to other people's parties.'

Becky blushed crimson. 'Stop flattering me.'

Rupert looked her right in the eye and said, 'It's hardly flattery if it's true.'

Tea dragged on so long that Becky asked him to supper, but Rupert shook his head regretfully. 'I've got to get back to London. Business, I'm afraid. But look, I'm going to a party at Alice Pomfrey's on Friday. Why don't you come down? Better still, let me come up and get you. We'll have a fun drive, and you can stay with me.'

'It's kind of early for that,' Becky said, wishing she could stop the blushing.

'I have a spare bedroom. You'll be perfectly safe. At least for a bit.'

She hesitated.

'I promise I shan't molest you. I've got no desire to scare you off.'

'Well, I would like to meet some new people.' She had a vision of her phone starting to ring, of tennis parties, people in the house, general fun, the kind she'd had back in the States.

'Of course you would. Bring a case, stay the night. Perhaps we'll see a matinée the next afternoon. Walk round London Zoo.'

'I'd love that.'

Rupert stood and kissed her hand. 'Then it's a date, gorgeous. I'll come around six on Thursday to pick you up.'

'Wonderful. Oh, no, it isn't.' Becky's face fell. 'I have to have dinner with Aunt Victoria and Uncle Henry that night. It's their night.'

'So just add me to the list.'

'They can be pretty scary,' Becky admitted, not wanting to put him off.

Rupert laughed. 'I can handle Vicky.'

'She likes to be called Victoria,' Becky said.

'I know.' He winked. 'That's why I call her Vicky.'

As soon as he was gone, Becky dived for the phone, squealing with excitement.

'You don't want to tip them off like that, miss!' said Mrs Morecambe sternly.

Becky hugged her. 'Oh, I know, Mrs Morecambe, dear Mrs Morecambe. But he's so perfect!'

'No man is perfect, miss,' Mrs Morecambe sniffed, but she couldn't look that upset. She smiled at Becky as she rang Sharon. The young lady might be regal, but she was still a kid really. That Rupert was handsome, though. But it didn't do to let 'em know you'd noticed it.

'So what's the post-mortem?' Sharon said on the phone. 'Is this Capulet and Montague?'

'Basically. But without any parents to get in the way. You won't believe who showed up, though.'

'Go on.'

'His mad ex-girlfriend who said they were getting married.'

'Bullshit!' Sharon said happily. 'What a fantastic story. I'm coming right over.'

'I've still got some tea left over.'

'Fuck tea,' said Sharon stoutly, 'I'll get the beers in.'

She was as good as her word. She turned up with a six-pack and some cigarettes, which Rebecca made her smoke outside.

'It's bloody freezing out here. You're a Puritan. Bloody Yanks, everybody smokes.'

'I don't want my house stinking.'

'Snob. You can't help it, poor sod, it's your genetics, I suppose. So, Rupert. Good-looking bit of totty.'

'I'm sorry?'

'No need to be,' said Sharon, smirking. 'We'll have you speaking English in no time. Totty. Trouser. Hunk. A rather thin hunk, but a pin-up if you like that sort of thing.'

'He's delicious. I love that accent.'

'God knows why. Chinless wonder, we call that. But if sounding like Prince Charles floats your boat . . . and he isn't going to be cracking any mirrors, I'll give you that.'

'We're not that closely related.'

'You will be if you get hitched, though. How convenient, you won't even have to change your name.' Sharon started to tease her. 'Except you'll have to put Lady in front of it. Ooh, milady.' She dropped a curtsy. Becky hit her.

'He's going to introduce me all round London.'

'Because we're not good enough for you?'

'Oh, stop.'

'I think it's a good idea. You need someone to stick up for you, with that old bag and her husband—'

'Sharon,' Becky reproved faintly.

'Well. She's your family, I suppose.' Her friend looked doubtful about that. 'But she hasn't helped you settle in. Maybe she thought if you got lonely enough you'd pack it in and go home. But your cousin Rupert, now. He's no shrinking violet, he'll sort you out.'

'How do you know about Rupert?'

'I read the *Daily Mail*, don't I? Nigel Dempster writes about him. Bit of a party animal, dates models.'

Becky felt a stab of jealousy. 'The girl that was here looked like a model.'

'And you don't?'

'Of course I don't.'

Sharon snorted. 'Anyway, he disappears to America for a couple of years, I don't know why. And you know he came back here when the judgment went in your favour. He appealed it from the States, and I guess they said they couldn't hear it over there, which was this month some time. So it's big of him to show up to the party.'

'He didn't make me feel awkward about it at all. He said it was something he had to do for his father.'

'Sounds to me like he took one look at you and decided it didn't matter any more.'

Becky hugged herself. 'I hope so. I don't want to get over-excited, or anything—'

'Bit late for that,' Sharon said perceptively. 'When are you going to see him next?'

'Thursday night. I'm staying over with him for a party on Friday in London.'

'Just don't sleep with him. If you want to marry that sort of guy, you don't give it up.'

Becky lifted a brow. 'As if I would.'

'You're not fooling anyone, babe.'

Thursday was bitterly cold, but Mr Higgins, the gardener, laid a huge fire in the Hall that crackled and spat and smelled wonderfully of pine cones, and gave off so much heat Becky was walking around in her T-shirt. Mrs Morecambe helped her hang her Christmas decorations, and she spent a happy morning threading little strips of gummy coloured paper into paper chains. They pinned mistletoe to the ceiling in every room, so that Rupert wouldn't be able to avoid kissing her, and Mrs Morecambe showed Becky how to mull wine. It was so much fun, Becky almost forgot that Vicky and Henry were coming too.

She had learned to dread the visits that were as regular as dentist's appointments. Her aunt always had some criticism, some nasty little dig, and Henry always avoided her questions about the firm. They sat in Fairfield so easily, and discussed the house between themselves so that she had to bite her tongue to stop apologizing for owning the house. Becky thought it would have been better to have no family at all than to have these two, but she couldn't stop herself; she wanted to please them, to make Daddy's sister love her.

Oh, well, it was the season to be jolly. Maybe they'd be full of the Christmas spirit.

But she was worried. Rupert was coming to this dinner, too. Becky could take the endless needling, but what about him? He was the son of the guy that had fought with Robert; he was the enemy that had been trying to take Fairfield for years. Becky winced at the thought of Vicky turning her fire on Rupert. She might even put him off. One really nasty remark, and who knew . . . he might storm out. Which would be just what Aunt Victoria would love, because it would leave Becky back at square one.

Becky took a long bath with masses of Floris Gardenia perfume to relax her. She washed and blow-dried her hair, and picked out a Christmassy-looking dress – something dramatic, but still warm. There was nothing worse than looking like Missy Worth had back home, always going to Thanksgiving dances in her itty-bitty silk dresses, but with a bright red nose and chattering teeth! She selected a crimson velvet dress, floor-length with a deep V at the breasts, and a beautiful pale grey cashmere cloak to throw over the top of it when she walked out to Rupert's car. Her suitcase was already packed with crisp tissue-paper sheets between her suit, her silk nightgown and negligee from Janet Reager, and her Moroccan slippers, as well as a dramatic little silver number that she'd wear tomorrow night. Frightened of Aunt Victoria making some barb about her setting her cap at Rupert, Becky only wore a smidgen of foundation and some lip salve, just to make them glow. Firelight was soft enough, anyway. She thought she'd get away with it.

The bell rang and she walked downstairs to greet her guests, forcing a smile.

But it wasn't them. It was Rupert.

'You're early,' Becky said, trying not to sound as delighted as she felt.

'I thought you might want reinforcements. Bit of back-up.' Rupert produced something small from behind his back, wrapped in plain round paper.

'What's this?'

'Flowers are so boring. I saw this in a little shop in Jermyn Street, and thought of you.'

Becky tore off the paper. It was a wooden musical box with painted flowers on the top and a small gold key. She wound it and it started to play '*Au Clair de la Lune.*'

'It's beautiful. I don't know what to say.'

He grinned. 'I think "Thank you" is traditional. But don't bother – that look on your face is all the thanks I want. What's that smell?'

'That's mulled wine, your lordship,' said Mrs Morecambe.

'It smells incredible. Do you think I could have a small glass?'

Mrs Morecambe bustled off and returned with two glasses. Becky took a sip. It was sweet and warming and full of cinnamon and cloves.

'Do you know, I think that's the best mulled wine I've ever had,' Rupert said warmly. 'You're a sensational cook, Mrs Morecambe.'

Becky was amused to note that now it was her housekeeper who was blushing. How lovely of him to make Mrs Morecambe feel good. Aunt Victoria and Uncle Henry did nothing but hand her their coats and ignore her.

Rupert sat in the Hall by the fire, sipping his mulled wine and paying Becky lots of extravagant compliments. She enjoyed being with him so much that when the doorbell rang again she jumped out of her skin.

He reached out and put a manicured hand on her upper arm. 'Relax. I can handle these two.'

'You don't know what they're like, Rupert.'

'They're not as bad as you think. They just need to be handled firmly,' he said, 'like dogs.'

Becky giggled.

Rupert jumped up and walked out to the hallway. Victoria was already brushing snow from her felt hat vigorously.

'Rebecca, you really must start to light the porch lamps outside. There's ice on the gravel,' she said without looking up. 'I could have slipped and broken my neck.'

'Oh, nonsense, there's plenty of light going outside from the hall windows,' said Rupert loudly. Victoria's head snapped up, like a fox hearing the hounds braying in the distance. He sauntered forward and embraced her, giving her a smacking kiss on the cheek and shaking Henry's limp hand warmly. 'How nice to see you again, Victoria, Henry. You're looking very well, Victoria. What a lovely suit.'

She was wearing a boxy suit in heart-attack purple, with dark stockings and rather clumpy brown shoes.

'Rupert.' Victoria acknowledged him coldly. 'What are you doing here?'

'Dinner, and some of Mrs Morecambe's excellent mulled wine. You should try some.'

'Yes, thanks,' Henry said quickly. His wife shot him a disapproving look.

'You don't normally like anything but sherry before dinner, Henry. And, Rupert, you were here just last week for the dance.'

'Indeed. Amazing that Becky agreed to have me back so soon. In fact, I'm stealing her tonight.'

'You're doing what?'

'I'm taking her down to London. Alice Pomfrey's having a party tomorrow night. Becky hasn't had much of an opportunity to make friends up here, so we're going to hit the circuit.'

'Alice Pomfrey's?' Victoria's face tightened. Becky watched with interest. 'I don't think she'd enjoy that, Rupert. Rebecca is used to America, you know.'

'But she's not in America now. If she's to settle at Fairfield, she needs to make a go of it here. Wouldn't you agree? I expect you've been introducing her around all your friends' children, Henry, haven't you?'

'Not really. Didn't think they were Rebecca's sort of people.'

'What, none of them?' Rupert's eyes widened slightly in mock surprise. 'But with your work, and Victoria's famous dinner parties, I'd have thought you knew hundreds of people. Gosh, while the court case was pending, I'm sure I saw in the *Tatler* that you had Fairfield filled with parties.'

'Really?' Becky blurted out. Her aunt had told her that it was always 'very quiet' in the country.

'Hardly *filled* with parties,' Victoria said fiercely, looking at Rupert like he was something nasty she'd found on the sole of her shoe.

I really, really, like this guy, Becky thought.

'Shall we go in to dinner?' Rupert said innocently.

It was the first enjoyable dinner with her aunt and uncle that Becky had ever had.

'So, how was America, Rupert?' Henry asked. 'Glad to be back home, aren't you?'

'Of course he is. What could he possibly like about America? The people are so brash and tasteless. You're English, really, Rebecca,' Victoria added without conviction.

'Yes, I am glad to be back. But only because I found Becky here. To think that I was over there when she came over here. America's a lot of fun, you know. You should try it, Victoria – it loosens people up.'

'I hardly need to be "loosened up",' Victoria said tightly. 'Please pass the potatoes, Rebecca.'

'How are things going at Lancaster, Uncle Henry? I'm having a hard time finding out the information I need from some of the company officers.'

'Now, Rebecca, that's hardly a fit subject for dinner.'

'Oh, I don't know,' Rupert said easily. 'Becky told me she wants to take an active interest in running Lancaster, and she hasn't been able to make head or tail of it.'

'I finally got a couple of prospectuses,' Becky said, feeling emboldened. 'But I need more.'

Victoria sighed. 'Look, Rebecca, these companies have been run very efficiently by the trustees for years. They *did* manage to survive before you arrived.'

'But the point is that now Becky is going to take over. I have a suggestion that might help,' Rupert offered innocently. 'I know a couple of lawyers, Becky. Experienced in company law. They can help sort through the paperwork and get you the figures that you need.'

Becky lifted her head. 'Well, that would be—'

'Unnecessary,' Henry said. Becky noted her uncle had gone a mottled shade of puce. 'We can supply you with whatever you need, Rebecca, I'll get on to it. All right?'

'Yes, thank you, Uncle Henry,' Becky said meekly.

It was the first time in her life she felt like she'd had the upper hand with her family. She stole a glance at Rupert, but he was pretending to be engrossed in his salmon mousse.

Oh, well. She'd have a chance to thank him later.

Chapter 16

'But I still don't see why I have to start this way.'

Lita stood in front of him, glowering, her arms crossed over her impressive breasts. She had her long glossy hair tied back in a neat ponytail and wore a suit – a fitted jacket over a white shirt and a long pleated skirt, together with Maryjanes. The thick mascara and bright red lips were gone, he noted, and instead her silk shirt had a small pussy bow at the neck – the most outlandish thing she was wearing.

'You have to start this way because everybody starts this way.'

Lita looked up at Harry. He towered over her the way he towered over everybody else, much like the way he metaphorically towered over Doheny. All the other secretaries, even the junior executives, were terrified of Harry Weiss and scuttled back to their desks whenever he appeared, trying to look busy.

Not Lita. When she had turned up for work yesterday in a thigh-high mini and sexy lime green shirt knotted under her bra, Sadie, the receptionist, had sent her home. Lita had demanded to see Harry.

'Are you crazy?' Sadie whispered. 'If he sees you like that he'll fire you.'

Lita blinked. 'But this is an ad agency. Copywriters dress how they want.'

'Sure, but you're not a copywriter. You're Mark Smith's assistant.'

'I'm what?' Lita shrieked. She glanced down the corridor. Harry's office was at the end. The door opened, and Harry emerged, talking business with a couple of suits.

'Get. Out.' Sadie shoved Lita towards the door. 'It's for your own good. And hurry back, because you're already late.'

Reluctantly, Lita went back to the Village and changed.

When she got back to Doheny, she marched straight into Harry's office. Susie looked up at her coldly. There were a hundred job applicants for every position at Doheny, and this Hispanic cupcake with the smouldering eyes and bee-stung lips had just waltzed into the ground floor. Yeah, it was a real mystery.

'I want to speak to Harry Weiss right away,' the prima donna said.

'Well, isn't that nice? You can't – he left for a meeting.'

'When will he be back?'

'*Mr* Weiss won't be back until tomorrow.'

'Then I need to see him, first thing.'

'You can make an appointment. He doesn't have any time until eleven a.m. I'll call you if he agrees to see you. Now . . .' Susie glanced pointedly at the clock on the wall. 'Have you reported in to Mr Smith yet?'

'Of course not. There's been some mistake. Harry – Mr Weiss – didn't hire me to be a secretary,' Lita insisted.

Susie was a secretary and didn't like the way Lita said it.

'He certainly did. He discussed it all with me. Of course, if you don't want the job, I'll be more than happy to tell him you resigned,' Susie said icily. 'Plenty of candidates would love a shot at working for Mr Smith.'

Lita wavered. Suddenly, she felt unsure of herself.

'No, I'm not resigning.'

'Then get over to your boss's office *now*. Unless you'd rather be fired,' Susie snapped.

Lita swallowed hard and did as she was told.

Mark Smith's office was two floors and half a building distant from Harry's. It hummed with activity. Copywriters lounged in their offices with the doors open, %shouting out campaign slogans and script ideas for commercials. Art directors were ripping up magazines, pinning photos to pinboards and, Lita noted, flirting heavily with the assistants. She made a quick inventory. There seemed to be about twelve offices on the floor, two of them occupied by women. Everybody else in a skirt was typing, or over in the kitchenette making coffee.

'Excuse me.' She turned to one of the typing girls who was dressed conservatively like herself. All the assistants were. She guessed that the freedom from shirts and ties was only handed out when you got an office. 'Where does Mark Smith work?'

The girl indicated the office with a jab of her thumb.

Lita walked up to it. It was as chaotic as the rest of the place. In the room were two men, one big and beefy, wearing a tweed flared suit and a large gold charm in his chest hair, and the other skinny, with sideburns.

'Yeah?' the big one said.

'Mark Smith?' Lita asked.

'Who's asking?'

She stuck out her hand. 'Rosalita Morales. I'm your new assistant.'

He looked at it with withering contempt, and didn't take it.

'Is this some feminist shit? I expect you to turn up before me, toots. I need my letters typed. I had to borrow Barry's girl this morning. I had to get my own coffee. Why the fuck did Maria have to get herself knocked up anyway? She was never late. And look what they give me, some popsy who can't even get here on time on her first morning.'

'I'm sorry, Mark. It won't happen again.'

They looked at each other. 'Ooh,' the skinny guy said, meanly. 'Listen to *her*.'

'Who the fuck told you to call me Mark? Did I tell you to call me Mark?'

'No.' Lita paled. She really didn't want to get fired, not before she'd had a chance to talk to Harry and get this whole mess sorted out. She noticed that some of the other offices behind her were starting to quieten down and listen to the bawling Smith. With a flush of embarrassed anger, Lita realized that they were enjoying it. 'No, you didn't – *sir.* I'm sorry, sir.'

She lowered her eyes deferentially. The thin man chuckled. Lita thought she hated him. Smith relaxed a little.

'That's more like it. Here one day and think you own the goddamn place. Go get me and Bud a coffee before we die of thirst.'

'That's Mr Roberts,' the thin man added.

'Yes, sir.' Lita turned to Roberts. 'How do you take your coffee, Mr Roberts?'

'Milk, two sugars.'

'Same for me,' Smith barked. 'And get it back here in under five minutes or you're out of the door, baby. Got it?'

'Yes, sir. I got it,' Lita said quietly.

She hoped there was no rat poison in the kitchenette. Because she might just be tempted to put some in the coffee.

That had been yesterday. Lita had ignored the sly grins of the other secretaries, typed letters barely adequately and kept her head down. She gathered that Mark Smith wrote the copy, and Bud Roberts was the art director, one of several Smith was assigned to. Both of them called her 'baby', 'doll' and 'toots', and Lita didn't dare to object. She had swallowed her pride and counted the minutes.

This morning she hadn't made the same mistake twice. A conservative, sexless suit, arriving at work on time and excusing herself for her meeting with Harry Weiss.

That bitch Susie had shown her in with a sly grin.

And then, after he'd listen to her outpourings for five minutes, Harry had cut her off and told her that, yes, she was going to start as a secretary.

'But, Harry—'

'Mr Weiss.'

'*Mr* Weiss. You offered me the job because I came into your office and pitched you my ideas for the Country Fresh campaign.'

'That's correct. "Fresh from the heart of Italia" was your slogan, wasn't it?'

Lita beamed. 'Yes.'

Harry leaned on his desk, his wedding ring catching the sunlight that slanted on to his mahogany desk. 'And did you see us using that slogan in the TV ads?'

Lita paused. 'I guess not.'

'We went with "Mamma Mia, that's good!". A slogan that Lionel Forth came up with, one of our senior copywriters. I hired you because you talked intelligently about advertising, you have experience of visuals and you sounded like you wanted to take this job seriously. Now I'm doubting my judgement.'

'How can you be? I haven't had a chance to do any work.'

'On the contrary, you've had plenty of chances to do some work – to find out your position, to turn up on time, to strike a good relationship up with your boss and to do his paperwork and learn from him how the job runs.'

'I bet he was never a secretary.'

'He started as a mail clerk, actually.'

Lita tried another tack. 'But not many women make it out of the secretarial pool, do they? There are only two on my floor.'

'Winners make money, Rosalita. Losers make excuses.' Harry sighed. 'Look, you were a model making some dough, having people jump when you snapped your fingers. You can't jump in at the top here because you have a pretty face. Maybe this was a big mistake for both of us.'

'It wasn't.' Lita was seized with a sudden desire not to leave here like this. Weiss was an arrogant, sexist, selfish son of a bitch, but she wanted to prove herself to him. 'I guess it was just culture shock, but I'm over that now.'

'Then get back to your office. And no more histrionics. I'm too busy for that shit.'

'Yes, Mr Weiss,' Lita said, standing up.

As she was walking out the door, he said, without looking up from his papers, 'Call me Harry.'

There were days when Lita thought she couldn't take the humiliation. Smith was a boor who liked to swat her on the ass and talk dirty in front of her, but Lita soon had him pegged – he was a junior copywriter who hadn't had a promotion in two years, and she thought Doheny might soon let him go. He was a typical bully. He took it out on the people underneath him, and he was so low on the totem pole that that basically meant Lita.

He made her pick up his dry-cleaning and send tulips to his wife and roses to his mistress. He criticized her long skirts and lack of make-up – Lita went down to the opticians and bought a pair of Coke-bottle glasses with clear lenses. That worked. He stayed away from her ass and treated her like the older secretaries in the office – as, basically, invisible.

As best she could, Lita learned the business. Doheny covered print, radio and TV ads, with different writers specializing in each field. They hired directors, graphic designers and account executives, as well as a whole department that decided where to place the ads. Depending on the product, the commercials could be homely, aimed at housewives, featuring the typical white-bread, blonde-haired family with a sprinkling of freckled kids, or hard-hitting political slogans. For drinks and cars it was all about models – women in bikinis draped over bumpers, women in tight T-shirts with 'Budweiser' emblazoned across them. Lita listened to assholes like Bud Roberts discussing the 'look' they wanted for one particular type of motorbike and thanked God she'd gotten out of the game when she had.

'Big tits,' Bud said loudly, not bothering to look at Lita or lower his voice. 'Blonde hair . . . I like that new "flip" style. Who's that chick? Farrah Fawcett? Like her, but bigger tits. Not fat, though.'

'Hey, dude, I dig those clam-digger pants,' Mark suggested.

'Yeah. Tight white leather, no panties, shows everything without getting the censors on your ass. Hey, toots,' Roberts barked at Lita. 'Call the agencies and tell them we want a blonde about five-eight through five-ten . . .'

'OK, Mr Roberts,' Lita muttered. 'With what colour eyes?'

'Who gives a shit about her eyes? Just make sure she's at least a D cup.'

Both men burst out laughing.

'And no more than one-thirty. We don't want no fat bitches. Got it?'

Lita bit down on her lip so hard she drew blood. She made the call, and then stayed late that night.

'What got into you, Lita? You're normally out the door at five.'

'I wanted to get a jump on my typing for tomorrow, sir,' Lita said meekly. 'No need to lock up. I'll do it.'

'Good. And make sure the place is tidy, willya?' He gestured expansively at the papers and empty coffee-cups strewn across his office, which resembled the Canyon of Heroes after the Mets World Series parade a few months ago. Lita thought it looked like a fire hazard. 'Those lazy cleaners never get it right.'

'Yes, sir.' Lita smiled warmly at him from under the camouflaged safety of her thick, ugly glasses. 'You have a good night, now.'

'Sure,' he said, walking out without shutting the door behind him.

Lita did, in fact, work on her letters for twenty minutes – just long enough to be sure that the chump wasn't coming back. Then she filed her work away, took off her glasses and slipped into Smith's office.

There was no way she was going to turn into a borderline pimp for these sleazebags. Lita saw how Ellen Kovacs and Lucy Weldon, the two women copywriters, had gotten promoted – five years slaving for the chauvinist pigs from hell, then finally permitted to submit some suggestions, and getting their own offices eighteen months after that. And now they were here, nobody took any notice of them.

There were exactly three women in senior positions in the whole of Doheny – one senior art director, one senior copywriter and one account director. Window-dressing for the company report.

Lita was going to be the fourth.

She wasn't interested in staying in this office, but neither was she interested in quitting. What had Harry Weiss said? 'Winners make money, losers make excuses.' So Doheny didn't promote women. It was 1970. New year, new decade, and women were taking the same old crap, despite all the bra-burning and student protests. In the real world, they made forty cents on the man's dollar. They got their butts patted, and they mostly got given letters to type.

Determinedly, Lita opened up Harry's filing cabinet. There were notes for each client meticulously organized in colour-coded folders. Lita knew exactly where everything was – she'd had to file it herself. She cleared a space on Harry's filthy desk.

First things first. She extracted the Skin-Soft line for Kitten Cosmetics. One of Mark's campaigns that hadn't done well.

'Defy your age with a Dab!' said the slogan. Lita examined the image – an anti-ageing cream in a gold-coloured pot. The product looked nice and rich, but she saw the problem instantly. Not only did the slogan suck, the model must have been all of twenty-one. Of course it wasn't going to sell to older women. They weren't stupid. Something Bud and Mark didn't realize.

OK, what was next? Another motorcycle ad. A girl in a cheesecloth shirt draping her large breasts over a biker. 'Freedom' was the slogan. That worked. Lita could see that. Unfortunately, most of Doheny's product campaigns weren't aimed at bearded, unwashed slobs. The clock ticked quietly through the night, and Lita got to work. She took notes on her little typist's pad, analysing everything from ad copy to the client liaison . . . who ordered what, Mark's directives from Randy Strauss, his account executive, who ventured into the lions' den as little as he could possibly manage. Lita noted that Randy wasn't happy with a lot of it. He was the one who had to take the creative work to the clients.

No wonder this asshole never got promoted, Lita thought.

She glanced up at the wall. It was already nine-thirty. She wanted to get home, take a bath, review her notes. But first there was the 'Lucy' campaign.

Lucy was Mark and Bud's big shot. It was a new fragrance, launched by Kitten, who hadn't liked the way Skin-Soft had sold, but Mark's success with the Hard Rider bike company had prompted them to offer Doheny a second – and final – chance. Kitten was a serious client, a medium-sized cosmetics firm that sold its products in the North-East alone. They didn't have the distribution to compete with Elizabeth Arden and the other big boys, but they had plenty of dollars to spend for local advertising. And if Doheny didn't get them results, they'd go elsewhere.

Lita had heard enough office gossip to know Harry Weiss's reputation. He *hated* to lose a client. It made Doheny look bad. As if maybe they weren't the hippest, hardest, most in-demand firm on Madison Avenue. That got the other firms scenting blood, calling up their clients, looking to poach.

She checked out Mark's proposed 'Lucy' ad.

It was of a young woman standing on a restaurant terrace, looking moonily out at the stars. A handsome young man had his arms around her. Mark's slogan read, 'Get Him Interested – with Lucy.'

Lita filed the mock-up away, a huge grin on her face.

I've got you now, she thought.

Chapter 17

Lita didn't make it home until almost midnight. It took her two hours to get Mark's filthy office into some semblance of order. As used as she was to tidying up after Chico and Papa, and keeping a small space spotless, Mark Smith was a real challenge. Almost two years of the high life hadn't made her forget how to clean; she wanted to make Mark's space gleam and shine as though he had just moved in. When the cleaners arrived at five a.m. tomorrow, she thought they might die of shock.

She worked tirelessly, and now, if Mark wanted to, he could eat the jelly dougnuts he liked to scoff down for breakfast off his office floor. That would please him, she knew. In Mark Smith's world, most women existed for cooking and cleaning, and Barbie-doll types for sex, too. He'd be so surprised that he'd give her a break for a few days.

She jumped out of her cab – it wasn't safe to walk in Manhattan at night, so she was forced into the expenditure – and let herself into the building. Lita half ran up the stairs. Her metabolism was charged with adrenaline, despite the late hour and her exhaustion. Her knees and back and arms ached from crouching, bending over and scrubbing. Her eyes were tired and bloodshot. But she had her notes.

Inside her apartment, Lita went straight to the kitchen to fix herself a pot of coffee. It was going to be a long night.

Kitten Cosmetics. She understood them, and not just because she had been a model. Part of the reason she'd wanted to go into advertising was the stuff she'd picked up at shoots. Every product had an image, a target, a way it wanted to be sold. If the image in the ad designers heads matched the target audience, the product sold – and if not, it didn't.

Mark Smith and Bud Roberts understood pigs like themselves. They'd had success, Lita thought contemptuously, with pig things. Like motorbikes and speedboats and pool tables. Everything else they'd tried had mediocre results at best. And the way the advertising industry worked almost guaranteed you that – any advertising was better than no advertising, and Doheny's excellent team of buyers placed the print ads in just the right magazines next to just the right articles. To really *fail* at this company you'd have to suck even worse than they did.

But the Skin-Soft campaign hadn't exactly been luminous. Kitten was looking for better, but they weren't going to get it from Lucy. Not the way these boys were selling it. Mark did sort of OK at food items, because even though he didn't understand housewives he did understand food. But what women wanted, he had no idea.

Asking him to sell a perfume was like asking Joe Namath to sell diapers. Not a good idea.

Lita poured herself a black coffee and shook cinnamon on it. Then she went to her desk, a cheap black table from a Tribeca flea market, and laid out her notes, and the last two months' issues of *Vogue* and *Elle*.

She pictured the Lucy mock-up in her mind. What were they trying to say with that image? A bog-standard cosmetics message . . . attract boys. It put the girl in the supplicant position. 'Get him interested – with Lucy.' Blerch, Lita thought. What did that copy say? That he wasn't interested in the first place, and that the girl's whole aim in life was to attract a mate, if she could. And their visuals were lame. How many women-on-restaurant-terrace ads had she seen? Hundreds. What did either the copy or the visual say about Lucy? Nothing. Why not, 'Get him interested with Chanel No. 5.'? Why should women buy this perfume instead of a different one? There was nothing special about it.

All in all, what the ad said to her was, 'Ordinary scent for the ordinary woman.'

And that sucked.

Lita turned to her magazines. She pored over every single ad, whether it was for eyes-shadow, powder or lingerie. She didn't read the articles, but she flipped through the headlines. She had a copy of last Sunday's *New York Times* lying on her couch, and she skimmed that, too.

It was a new decade. It was an exciting time for women. Girls at universities were burning their bras, reading Simone de Beauvoir, asking for more pay, better jobs. The League of Women Voters was energizing women at the ballot box. There were definitely some man-haters out there, and when she thought about Mark and Bud she didn't really blame them. But if most women weren't quite so strident, they were still pissed off. They were listening to Karen Carpenter and Janis. TV shows were starting to feature them as more than wives and moms. But too much advertising still showed the early-sixties girl, the homecoming queen smiling pleasantly behind her football-playing boyfriend, as though the summer of love had never happened, as though young women weren't marching on Washington to demand an end to Vietnam.

'Get him interested.' The way that women were feeling in 1970, it was more like, 'Get him out.'

Lita grinned. She had a vision of a girl in a black leather catsuit booting a hapless chump with sideburns and a chest medallion on to the pavement. 'Get him out. Lucy.' Maybe not, but . . .

The idea sparked something, and she started to scribble fresh notes to herself.

The perfume was named Lucy. And what was that? A girl's name. A short, low-brow girl's name. Not Alexandra or Hortense or Elizabeth, but Lucy. So in order to link the perfume to something that young girls wanted, you had to provide something that they wanted to *be*. Someone, in fact. A 'Lucy' to match the name of the perfume. Something sufficiently different from all the skinny, white, gorgeous babes romping through flower-laden meadows in white chiffon dresses that all the big houses used to advertise their perfumes.

Kitten only sold Lucy in the North-East. Their ad-spend was targeted entirely in those areas. Lita thought about getting a 'Lucy' girl. She didn't really want to go that way, because once you picked one model to represent your line, the chick had you over a barrel. Lita had used it to her own advantage often enough. Kitten were a small outfit – they couldn't afford to be held to ransom. No, what if the Lucy girl wasn't just one girl, but several? All appealing to different markets, but all with the same outlook in common . . . ambitious, fashionable, socially conscious, spirited, independent. Her Lucy would never have a man in the picture with her. She might even play sports.

Lita went back through the magazines with a pair of scissors. She cut out figures and backgrounds and played around with them. She used the office paper, and stuck them to it with flour and water made into a paste, because she had no glue. Her coffee grew cold; Lita didn't even notice it.

By the time she was done it was three a.m. Lita packed up her mocks into her briefcase, the one she hadn't brought back to Doheny since she was hired, in case Mark thought she was getting 'uppity' again. Then she took a fast shower and laid her clothes for tomorrow out at the foot of the bed. She poured herself into the sheets, and barely had enough energy to set her alarm before she fell asleep.

'This is great.' Mark flopped into his chair, and regarded his gleaming office. 'You should do it more often, Lita.'

'Yeah. I wish my wife kept our place like this,' Bud added, oblivious to the look of hatred Lita couldn't help shooting him. 'You look awful this morning, Lita.'

'Oh, dear.' Lita wanted to say, And you don't, you greasy-haired fuck? But she bit it back. 'I think it's because I'm a little tired.'

She had dark shadows under her eyes big enough to make her look like a giant panda. Two layers of concealer hadn't done anything for her today. 'It took me a bit longer than I thought to get the place tidy.'

'You did good, toots.'

'Sir . . .' Lita put on her most submissive voice, the little-girl act that Mark liked. 'Do you think I could take an extra hour at lunch today? I need to meet someone. Only if it's OK with you, of course.'

'If all your work's done. But don't make a habit of it.'

'I won't. Thank you, sir. Would you and Mr Roberts like some coffee?'

She called Harry Weiss's office as soon as she got back from the kitchen.

'I'd like to see him. It's rather important.'

Susan's voice on the phone sighed. 'He only has one free half-hour, and that's right—'

'Before lunch, I know.' Lita had asked around and memorized Harry's schedule. 'I happen to have some free time then. Mr Smith said it was OK.'

The other woman hesitated. 'Well, if Mr Smith gave you permission, I guess I can fit you in. But you can only have ten minutes.'

'I thought you said he had half an hour.'

'Not for secretaries' requests,' Susan said coldly. 'Do you want this time slot or not?'

'I want it.'

'Then be here at one.'

Lita turned up at Susan's desk at two minutes to one. Her suit was neat, and her face was free of make-up, even though she had removed the fake glasses. She wore clumpy, ugly brown shoes. She watched as Susan nodded with approval.

'Ten minutes, Rosalita.'

'You got it,' Lita said sweetly.

Why, Susan thought, as she opened the door to Harry's office and showed Lita in, do I have such a bad feeling about this?

Lita turned around and politely but firmly shut the door in Susan's face.

Harry glanced up from his desk.

'This is about Mark Smith, huh?'

'Kind of. Yes,' Lita admitted.

'I'm surprised it took you this long to come to me. His last two girls only lasted a week each. They wouldn't stay even when I offered them a raise.' Harry sighed. 'Mark swore to me he'd keep his hands off the girls. I'm sorry if he's back to his old ways again . . .'

Lita coughed. 'That's not it.'

'You want more than an apology, huh? What do you want, money? You're at the basic typist's rate. I think I can squeeze in some more dollars for you, but not much—'

Lita held up one hand.

'Harry – you did say I could call you that – I gotta interrupt you. I only have ten minutes, and I don't give a shit about Mark putting his hand on my ass.' She withdrew her Coke-bottle glasses from her top pocket and put them on. 'See? I had no trouble since I got these babies.'

Harry blinked, then burst out laughing. 'That's initiative.'

'You like initiative?'

'Of course.'

'Good.' Lita drew out her mock-ups. 'Then you'll like what I've done for the Lucy campaign. If you show the client the shitty mock-up they have now, they're going to dump Doheny. Mark Smith and Bud Roberts never did any good work for fashion or beauty because they don't understand girls . . . and in the modelling scene, I know what's hip . . .'

Harry took off his Lennon glasses and rubbed them, then held out his hand.

'OK,' he said flatly, 'show me what you got.'

Lita laid her bits of paper down carefully over his desk. They were rough and ready, but they caught the spirit she'd been aiming for. There was a black girl with an Afro standing in front of the Sears tower, a redhead in a miniskirt and fitted jacket striding through Manhattan and a blonde girl fishing on a New England lake, laughing. She had written the copy underneath in magic marker. 'Lucy – when you make your own rules.'

Weiss examined the collages expressionlessly.

'See,' Lita said anxiously, 'Kitten only advertises in the North-East. So this makes it feel personal to the girls. And anyone buying a small fragrance when she could buy one from the major houses instead has to be looking for something different—'

Weiss cut her off. 'Now it's my turn to interrupt.'

'But if you'd let me explain my thinking—'

He looked at her like she was stupid. 'I don't need you to explain your thinking. The work says everything I need to know.'

'But—'

'It's brilliant,' Harry Weiss said, not listening to her. 'I love it. You're speaking to the urban chicks with jobs and the suburban chicks who want to be hip. You're branding it as rebel chic. But the girls are still pretty. I think it works on a lot of levels.'

Lita felt her thumping heart gradually slow down.

'I'm going to make you a copywriter,' he said. 'These images aren't put together well enough for you to be an art director, but I'll assign an art director to work with you. You'll start with the Lucy account. Let's see how that does, then maybe I'll let you go and pitch for more business.' He pressed a button on his desk. 'Susan – I'm promoting Rosalita Morales to copywriter. Better see if you can find her a spare office somewhere.'

'Yes, Mr Weiss,' Susan said, annoyed.

'What should I tell Mark?'

'Tell him and Bud to come and see me.'

Lita thought about taking this opportunity to complain about all the ass-patting and 'toots' and foul language, but she thought better of it. One battle at a time. That was the way to win wars.

'Thank you for this opportunity, Harry,' she said, pushing back her chair.

'Opportunity, my ass,' Harry said. 'If you lose me the client you're fired. What I'm doing here is allowing you to make me some money. Got it? That's your job. To make me money.'

'Got it,' Lita said happily.

He looked fierce. She got out of the door before he could somehow find a way to fire her instead.

'This is a joke, right?' Mark Smith roared.

Lita continued to pack her personal stuff in her cardboard box. 'No, it's not. I discussed some of my ideas with Harry Weiss and he seemed to like them.'

'Your ideas. You're my fucking secretary,' Mark yelled.

Lita noted the other girls were all listening keenly, though they had their heads down and were pretending to type.

'Actually, I'm not your secretary. Fucking or otherwise,' Lita said sweetly.

'Get me Harry Weiss on the phone!'

'Get him yourself. I don't work for you, Mark.'

Smith couldn't believe the wetback chick was talking to him like this. He went purple between the ears and jumped on the phone. 'Yeah, hi, Susie. It's Mark Smith. Is Harry in? Oh, good.' He shot a triumphant look at Lita. 'Sure, I'll hold. Oh, hey, Harry, Mark Smith here . . . My secretary is talking a lot of smack down here, man. Rosalita, yes.'

There was a pause.

'You did what?' Mark shouted, then got a grip. 'The Lucy campaign? That's my campaign. Harry, my client . . . No, I didn't know she was a model, but so what? You're a piece of ass, what does that make you, Ogilvy and Mather? I know she's a woman . . . OK, OK.'

He calmed down. His eyes now bore into Lita's with murderous hatred.

'If you want to give it a shot. But don't blame me if the client fires us, OK? Bud and I got you good work here. Oh, you didn't.' He swallowed hard. 'Well, we can't win 'em all, I guess. You got it. OK, bye.'

Lita watched him as he slammed the phone back into its cradle, obviously aware that the whole floor had seen him get shot down. He looked as though he'd love to reach those big paws across her desk and wring her neck like a chicken.

'Harry Weiss said that he didn't like the work we'd done. Except that I hadn't shown it to anyone yet. You went through my stuff.'

'I had to tidy your office, remember? I noticed a few things,' Lita said lightly. 'I thought the product might benefit from going another way.'

'You spied on me.'

'I got myself promoted,' Lita said coldly. 'If you don't like it, I really don't care.'

Smith spluttered. 'Where the hell are your glasses?'

'I don't wear glasses. I put them on so that you'd get off me.'

'You think you're smart,' Smith hissed, leaning across so close to Lita she could smell the reek of his aftershave. 'But you just made yourself an enemy. You better watch out, missy. You're playing with the big boys now.'

'Big boys?' Lita said loudly. 'That's not what your last girlfriend told me.'

Then, to muffled sniggers from the other girls, she turned on her heel and walked away.

Chapter 18

Dawn broke, and Becky was awake to watch it.

She propped herself up on one elbow and gazed through the lead-panelled panes of her bedroom window at the streaks of gold and pale pink coming up over the lake. It felt strange to be back at Fairfield. A month in London with Rupert, strike-ridden, cold, grumbling London, and she had started to long for the countryside. It was March, and still chilly, but Becky thought she felt spring trembling in the air. Masses of daffodils were everywhere in the orchard, and the kitchen garden was starting to bud again, and there was a soft green mist of baby leaves over the woods. Becky enjoyed the parties, the dinners, the nightclubs – Annabel's, and Tramp – and taking in a ballet at Covent Garden . . . Society was fun. But she was ready for a break. She was ready to take on Lancaster now.

She glanced at Rupert's sleeping form, the sheets crumpled round him in the bed beside her. He had rescued her, that was a fact. And I'm grateful, Becky thought, of course I am. Rupert was so well known in London society. He had introduced her to all the best and most important people. At the Royal Ballet she had even got to meet the very beautiful and chic Lady Tooley, the Director-General's wife, and sit in the Royal Box. But Patsy Tooley, though very kind and polite to Becky, had been a bit cold toward Rupert. That seemed to happen a lot. Becky guessed that people were just jealous of him.

Rupert had taken the job of getting her some friends very seriously. She had two Smythson's address books now filled with bright young things. Becky had wondered about Rupert squiring her round town day and night . . . time that he probably needed for his business. He had a position at some public relations firm, where he was a senior vice president. But Rupert didn't seem to mind. He'd told Becky that he wanted to help her.

'Somebody needs to get that old bag off your back,' he said casually.

Becky giggled. 'Rupert, you can't talk about her like that.'

'I most certainly can. And her husband isn't much better. He pretends to be henpecked and ineffectual, but he knows enough about business, and he doesn't want to tell you anything.'

'He sent over all that information.'

'Not enough. Why don't you let me look over the companies with my lawyer? I can get to the bottom of Lancaster for you, get you what you need.'

'You'd do that for me?'

He caught up her hand and kissed it passionately. 'Silly goose. I'd do anything for you. Don't you know that by now?'

That had been back at the end of January. Rupert had told her all last month that Lancaster was a mess, and his lawyer was sorting it out with Henry. They were back up at Fairfield now, partly to enjoy the fresh air and partly so he could show her all the results. Becky pushed her hair back from her eyes, and the diamond band she never took off flashed in the morning sunlight. Channel-set diamonds glittering in gold from Asprey's – the most beautiful Valentine's Day gift she'd ever had. Rupert had also taken her out to supper at Wilton's, the fish restaurant in St James's, and to Becky's embarrassment, they had run into Aunt Victoria and Uncle Henry. She had exchanged pleasantries with them, kissing the air on the side of their cheeks, and watched her aunt's face tighten up. Rupert had made it perfectly obvious they were on a date. Becky felt a small, cruel sense of triumph, of revenge.

What would they do if Rupert proposed? Sharon was teasing her about it unmercifully, and for the first time in her life Beck had imagined herself married. Up at Fairfield, occasional trips to London, life in this wonderful, glittering whirl that Rupert had snatched her into, uniting the family . . . Romeo and Juliet with a happy ending. Running her own companies while Rupert became a big PR whiz. Raising clever children and sending them to Oxford or Cambridge, and maybe getting a dog or two . . .

Rupert shifted in the bed and the linen sheets fell back, exposing his slender torso. He had the kind of lean, hungry body that looked well in clothes but which, if she was honest, she didn't enjoy all that much naked. Shades of Richard, in fact. There was nothing *wrong*, as such, with sex with him, but Becky was starting to feel uncomfortable with it. Just slightly, of course. Maybe because she wanted Rupert to think of her as marriage material . . . the double standard, sure, but it was true, even if she hated the idea of it. And then there was the boniness of him. She'd like to feed him up, get him a couple of weights. Becky couldn't see Rupert doing anything physical and she didn't know how to suggest it. Maybe she could install a gym in one of the rooms in Fairfield, and then Rupert would just join her when she started working out.

She wasn't sure how expensive that would be. Rupert had arranged, in short order, for his lawyer to get her a decent allowance from the businesses, but Becky needed to know exactly what kind of money she had to play with.

It was bound to be a lot. Lancaster owned shipyards, tin mines in Cornwall, even a small hotel operation in the Scilly Isles. The reports and accounting made it hard for her to understand how much it was all worth, but Rupert had been on the case for her. He and his lawyer could explain it all to her in plain English. Today was the day. Becky was glad. Despite all her new friends, she had started to mope with nothing to do.

Rupert was fast asleep. Becky slipped out of bed and grabbed her satin nightgown, putting it on before he could wake up. She wondered idly if she'd ever feel comfortable parading around nude in front of him.

'You look very . . . businesslike, darling.'

Rupert walked through the door of the conservatory, where Mrs Morecambe was serving Becky breakfast – a boiled egg, English Breakfast ten, and some toast with Marmite, which, as far as Becky was concerned, was England's only triumph in the food arena. She was reading a copy of *The Times* over a small vase of late-blooming crocuses and wore a neat suit, pinstriped, figure-hugging, finishing neatly just on the knee, together with a white silk shirt. It was chilly outside, but not too bad; the winters here were a picnic compared to New York, anyway.

Rupert was wearing slacks and a matching shirt and jacket. His dark eyes glanced over her, head to toe

'Well, it is a business meeting, darling.'

He grinned. 'You Americans take everything so seriously.'

'It is serious. I'm going to start running the companies today. They've put me off all this time.'

'I know.' He turned to Mrs Morecambe. 'Bacon and eggs, please. Thanks. Look, Becky, all I'm saying is you don't need to impress these people. They work for you. They're coming here.'

'I thought we were going into town.'

'Why should you go anywhere? Lancaster belongs to you. I told Mr Trout to come here, with his team.'

Becky smiled at her boyfriend. He understood her so well. Rupert was helping her to retake control of things, and she adored him for it.

Quentin Trout, QC, and his team – Marcus Rigby, Keith Jennings and Tristam Masters – arrived at eleven, wearing suits and carrying thick boxes bound in dark green leather. They were all about fifty, lean and formidable. They shook hands with Rupert and then Becky.

'A beautiful house, Miss Lancaster,' Trout said. 'Do you have a room we could go to review this data?'

'The library is this way.' Becky showed them in. Rupert had hefted a walnut table in from a sitting room for all the documents, and had helped her set out all the extra chairs and pads of paper with fountain pens laid neatly alongside. He teased her about being 'efficient', but he helped her out. Henry had just told her not to bother her pretty little head about it. With Rupert helping me, there's nothing I can't do, Becky thought.

'I have prepared some statements for you, Miss Lancaster,' Trout said, when his party had declined an offer of tea, 'summarizing the position at Lancaster, with its diversified interests across several industries. As you know, many industrial sectors in the United Kingdom have been hard hit by the recent waves of workforce unrest—'

'Strikes, you mean.'

'Exactly, Miss Lancaster. Strikes.'

'Try and speak plain English, Mr Trout,' Rupert interrupted, winking at Becky. 'We're here to make head or tail of this mess for Miss Lancaster.'

'Certainly, Lord Lancaster,' Trout said, bowing slightly to him. 'Plain English.' He seemed to struggle with this instruction. 'Er – due to the, strikes, as you put it, and the electricity shortages, Lancaster Holdings has suffered some losses. Shipyards are losing orders to the Americans—'

'Let me see.'

Becky lifted her papers and flicked right to the profit-and-loss columns.

Her heart did a small, slow flip in her chest.

'There's a lot of red ink here,' she said.

'Yes. Operating profits are down dramatically, and the Labour Party's taxation rates have meant that Lancaster Shipping has got into slight . . . hot water, let me say.'

'I've taken the opportunity to read through everything, Becky,' Rupert said. 'If you want, I could summarize, and then maybe the lawyers could take you through it afterwards.'

Becky pushed back in her chair. Despite the chill morning, she had broken out in a light sweat under her suit. This scenario had not been part of her planned golden life.

'I wish you would.'

'I think the shipping operations should be disposed of, leaving you to concentrate on mining, and we should lose the hotel business too. Right now we need something to counter these heavy losses. The stock price has been slipping despite your father's executors periodically buying back the stock.'

Becky breathed in sharply. 'In the States we hear about British strikes all the time. The place is full of strikes.'

'Well, the unions want a three-day week.'

'And I want to leap tall buildings with a single bound, but it's not happening any time soon.'

Rupert shrugged. 'The board has had a policy of negotiations to try and avoid strikes, and that's meant our workers get paid well over the going rate.'

'Our workers?'

Rupert coughed. 'Your workers, I mean. I've been working on this so long I started to think of myself as being involved.'

'But of course you're involved. You're helping me.'

'I'd like to help you,' he said, looking at her softly.

'Miss Lancaster.' Jennings shuffled his papers. 'It seems to us that Lancaster, because of its union policy, has such high operating costs and low productivity that they haven't been able to turn a profit for about three years now.'

'Then we must change the union policy. Stop over-paying. How is productivity?'

'Low. Look, Becky, you don't really understand industrial relations in England.'

'I understand when I'm being held to ransom,' Becky said, annoyed.

'You'll go through all the figures, but it may be a little late. If you'd got here three years ago—'

'I hadn't got any rights three years ago.'

'Mr Trout,' Rupert said, 'why don't you and the team take Miss Lancaster through everything, and then she can ask you whatever questions she has?'

He stood up.

'Where are you going?' Becky asked.

'I don't want to stay. I think it's your company, and I think you've had enough interference. You need to go through all the figures yourself.'

He gave her another wink and walked out.

Wow, Becky thought. He really respects me. What a difference. She turned to the lawyers, who were all watching him leave.

'I think Lord Lancaster's right. Gentlemen, take me through it. Let's start at the shipyards,' Becky said.

They left Fairfield after three p.m. Becky went out to the kitchen to get a lunch tray and found Rupert sitting on a stool, sipping a hot chocolate.

'Come back in. I need you,' she said.

'Here.' He passed her a tray of thinly cut ham sandwiches. 'I've made myself as useful as I can.'

Rupert was also waiting for her when she finally ushered the suits out at ten. 'I sent. Mrs Morecambe to bed. I thought you might want to be alone.'

'Yeah.' She tried not to let her feelings show, but she had tears prickling in her eyes. 'How could it be such a fucking mess? How could they let my father's company get ruined like that? I'm going to sue them.'

'There's no point in that. They probably did their best. They tried to buy Lancaster off you, after all.'

'I guess.' Becky flopped on to a chair. 'Rupert, I'm going to have to sell part of the company. I don't have time to turn it around. I feel sick, I just feel sick.'

'Maybe I—' He stopped himself. 'No, no, forget it.'

'Maybe you what?'

'You wouldn't like it, and I don't blame you.'

'Tell me,' she begged. Rupert looked thoughtful, like he was mulling something over. He's so reticent, Becky thought, he doesn't want to interfere. He respects me that much.

'I think I could help. I'd have to quit my job, but I do have something of a name in Britain. I could come in and do some PR, raise financing, work with you to dispose of small parts of Lancaster, nothing major. I think I could save the company. But only if you'd let me, of course. It's your firm.'

'You think you could do that?'

'I think so. I could make a horse-race of it, at least. And with you taking over the daily operations, we'd make a great team.' Rupert sighed, rather theatrically. 'I just hate the idea of the family company being dismantled.'

'Oh, so do I. Rupert . . . you'd really give up your job for me?'

'Of course, if you wanted me to.' He held up his palms. 'Only if you'd like to give it a shot, though, Becky. If you'd rather just pack it up and sell off the company, I understand perfectly. I don't want to force you into anything.'

'No! I'd love it. I'd love you to help,' Becky said. 'I can't thank you enough. I don't know what to say.'

'Don't say anything.' He drew her to him with a smile. 'Just kiss me.'

Chapter 19

Becky gazed out of her window at the winding streets of Oxford and tried to work out why she wasn't blissfully happy. Spring had finally arrived; it was May, and there were flowers everywhere, and she was in love. She was also sitting here in the Oxford offices of Lancaster Holdings, with everybody in the building reporting to her. Rupert had turned the perception of the company around. He seemed to be in his element, wining and dining half the newspaper editors in England, taking business trips to Europe and getting the message out there that Lancaster was still a force to be reckoned with, as he put it.

Orders were up, too. Rupert had shown her the new sheets for work to be done at the Yorkshire shipyards. So all his hard work, and the nice little write-ups in the gossip columns of the *Financial Times* and the *Telegraph*, must be paying off.

Rupert told her that shipping was deadly dull and also well in hand. He had suggested Becky turn to the hotel part of the business.

'What about the tin mines, though?' she had ventured. She didn't want to challenge Rupert too much, because she could see he was working his ass off. She was so grateful to him for giving up his job to help her out. Aunt Victoria no longer bullied her, and Uncle Henry and the rest of his cronies had been forced to back off from Lancaster, with Becky's consolation gift of a hundred thousand a man. Henry had sniffed at it, but she noted that he hadn't sent the money back.

'You don't want to get too into that right now. I'm still working on the mines. The hotel business needs work.'

'But the hotel division is such a small part of the company.'

Rupert had put down his tea-cup and looked her straight in the eye. 'If you want to blow it off and sell it, darling, be my guest. The whole shebang is yours to do as you like with. But your grandfather bought that hotel.'

Becky had nodded.

'My thinking is that no part of Lancaster is too small to save. But you might feel that a hotel is beneath you, and I fully appreciate that.'

She laughed. 'Rupert, of course it isn't.'

'If you're sure. The hotel business runs out of Oxford.'

'Why not London?'

'Maybe because it's so small. You'd have to make a sacrifice to save it, in that you'd be distant from the rest of the company. But it's a short hop down to Paddington, and I can drive up and see you every night.'

And he'd been as good as his word. Rupert schlepped up to town to see her every single evening, and commuted back down to London in the morning. They spent the weekends at Fairfield. He complained he hardly knew the way to his own house any more.

'I could come down to London, you know.'

'No need, darling. Why should you get up hideously early? Let me handle it.'

He was so considerate, Becky thought. So attentive, and protective, and chivalrous. He seemed to hit exactly the right note with her every time. He mixed up nights at the opera and ballet with movies and even the occasional concert. Last week he'd somehow managed to get tickets for the *Airport* première. When she complained she missed America, he took her out to see *Kelly's Heroes* and then got her a burger and fries for dinner, complete with French's yellow mustard. She knew she was lucky, and she knew that saving the hotel operations was a worthwhile thing to do. She just felt a nagging sensation in the back of her mind that something was missing.

'Miss Lancaster.' Ellen, her secretary, buzzed her. 'There's a woman here to see you.'

Becky glanced at her day planner. 'I don't see anything here. Isn't the designer due at ten?'

'Yes, she is, but this lady says she's a friend of yours—'

'Let me in, Becky, you old fart!' yelled Sharon's voice on the intercom.

Becky grinned. 'Send her up, Ellen.'

'Yes, Miss Lancaster,' Ellen said reluctantly. Becky could almost see her lips pursing. Rupert had hired Ellen Witherspoon. He said she was the most competent secretary he could find. But Becky didn't like her. She was twice Becky's age, and her stiff body language and total refusal to joke made it clear she didn't like working for a woman, especially one not much older than the students with their flares and sideburns that zoomed past on bikes outside their small lobby.

Becky looked down into St Aldgate's and saw Sharon's banged-up Renault 5 parked in front of a meter. She was suddenly very, very glad she was here. Whenever Becky had suggested they go and see Sharon, Rupert had been too busy for some reason or other. She felt guilty.

Despite Rupert always saying how much he liked Sharon, he didn't hang out with her a lot.

'Well, look at her ladyship,' Sharon said, bursting unceremoniously into the room and giving her a bear-hug. 'All dolled up. You look like Mrs Thatcher.'

'Goddamn it, I do not! Just because some people have to wear suits.'

'Yeah, very professional. What are you doing tucked away down here, though?' Sharon glanced around Becky's office, looking remarkably unimpressed. 'I thought you wanted to start taking over. We aren't going to win the revolution like this.'

'I don't want a revolution.'

'That's because you've bought into the Tory male capitalist oppression, sister.'

'Don't start with that sister shit.'

'I thought better of you, I really did. You're a Yank. But I won't hold it against you. You'll convert to radical feminism one day.'

'I doubt it,' Becky said. 'I like equal rights, but I don't hate men.'

'That's only because you don't know any better. You'll learn.'

'I take it you broke up with Jack?'

'Actually Jack and me are blissful.' Sharon grinned smugly. 'We're getting married.' She held up her left finger, with a small, pretty ruby surrounded by diamonds glittering on it.

'Let me look. Ooh, man, that's gorgeous.' Becky twisted her fingers over. 'When did he ask you?'

'Last night. I came right over here. Since I'd probably die waiting for you to come and visit me.'

'I know, I'm sorry. We've been really busy,' Becky said guiltily.

'So I've been reading in the papers.'

'How did he propose? I'm so happy for you guys. We have to throw you an engagement party.'

'He was very traditional,' Sharon said. 'We went out for a walk over some fields, and he kneels down and takes out the ring. Unfortunately two seconds later he also slipped on a cowpat. It was pretty funny.'

Becky burst out laughing. She'd really missed Sharon. She shouldn't have let Rupert keep her away so long. 'Oh, man.'

'And no engagement party, thanks. We're not the ruffles and pearls types. I invited you to the cheese and beer bash back threw, but I never got a reply.'

Becky was horrified. 'I never got the invite. You know I'd never blank you.'

'Do I?' Sharon said calmly. 'I've rung Fairfield a few times and left messages and nobody's got back to me. Ordinarily I'd think you were blowing me off, but as it happens I have skin like rhino hide, so I thought I'd come down here and check you out. See for myself.'

'Sharon . . . I never got those calls, I promise you.' But you never made enough of an effort to go down there and see her, did you? said the little voice in her head. 'This is awful. I don't know why Mrs Morecambe wouldn't—'

'Don't blame her. I spoke to Rupert.'

'But Rupert would have told me . . .'

'Sure about that, are you?' Sharon crossed her legs. 'Look, Becky, I know you're really into the guy—'

'I am. He's perfect for me,' Becky said defensively.

'All right. And maybe I should just butt out. But I have to tell you what I'm thinking first, and then if you want to tell me to sod off,' she added cheerfully, 'I'll be fine with that and I won't bring it up again.'

'Maybe he forgot about your messages.'

'That's possible, yeah.'

'He's been busy.'

'He has, hasn't he? A busy little bee,' Sharon agreed. 'And busy doing what? Taking over your companies. What do I read in the papers? A lot of overseas trips, a lot of partying, lots of impressive-looking statements made by "Lord Lancaster of Lancaster Holdings". I never used to read the business sections, now I'm glued to 'em. And you know what it looks like to me?'

'I'm sure you're gonna tell me,' said Becky, a bit sullenly.

'It looks like he won his court case. Not lost it. He's always at Fairfield, he controls who you talk to, and he acts like he's President of the company.'

'Rupert helped me get the board off my back.'

'And installed himself there instead. Now, what are you doing? Judging by the press, what you're doing is being the good little girlfriend in the background. You don't interfere with his work, you aren't doing the hiring and firing. You aren't even in London. You have no idea what goes on in the Lancaster offices—'

'Wait just a second. These are the Lancaster offices.'

'Not the main ones.'

'Every part of the company is important.' Why doesn't it sound as true when I say it as when Rupert said it? Becky wondered.

'Oh, su-u-re.' Sharon didn't bother to hide her contempt. 'Some shitty little hotel off the coast of Cornwall.'

'It's not shitty.'

'Well, it's not the Ritz, is it? And it's one hotel.'

'I'm doing a lot with it. I'll show you.'

'I'm sure you are, and I bet you're doing well. Seriously. I know you'd make a success of whatever you turned your hand to. You have that killer instinct, under all the tennis-tournament princess stuff. But you're not getting to turn your instincts to your company. Rupert is handling it all.'

'I keep an eye on operations. Rupert has gotten orders up, you know.'

'No, I didn't. And that's good, I suppose,' Sharon admitted grudgingly, 'but that's not to say you wouldn't have done even better. With less flash. And flash takes cash.'

Becky nodded slowly. It was true. Why did she assume she couldn't do better, when she hadn't even tried?

'One last thing, then I swear I'll shut up.'

'I'll believe that when I see it,' Becky grunted.

'He likes to have Fairfield mentioned in the stories in the press. I know you're beautiful, for a skinny cow. But I just keep seeing pictures of him, and you're in the background or hardly mentioned. He gets the company *and* the house this way. What if he marries you, and gets you knocked up, and you have a boy? What happens then? The kid gets the title from his dad and the house and company from his mum and Bob's your uncle. Rupert Lancaster gets what he always said he wanted. The title and the house reunited.'

'You think he's just using me?'

'I think it's very possible. Not certain. Maybe I just don't like him because he didn't pass on my messages. I might be biased.'

'Rupert gave up his own senior PR job to work at Lancaster.'

Sharon's eyes narrowed.

'I bet you didn't even check up on that, did you? Probably wrote him a fat salary without checking what he was making before. Gave it up, did he? I bet he laughed all the way to the bank. And the mansion.'

Becky had gone a bit pale, and Sharon checked herself. 'Look, hon, I'm probably way off. I don't think you should do anything based on a theory. But you should tell him to pass on my messages. Then maybe I won't have to dream up these wild scenarios.'

She fished an album out of her bag, the Jackson Five's 'ABC'. 'Look what I picked up, brand new. I got digs just off the high street. Why don't you take an executive decision and come over and listen to it? I got a kettle and a toaster,' she added temptingly.

'Hell, why not?' Becky buzzed Ellen. 'Ellen, I'll be taking the rest of the day off. Tell Lord Lancaster he can meet me at the flat tonight.'

'Yes, Miss Lancaster,' Ellen snapped.

They went back to Becky's flat first so she could get changed. It was a small, beautiful apartment in a sixteenth-century house, with oak beams in the ceiling and a nice view of Queen's College. She peeled off her business suit and grabbed a pair of embroidered bell-bottoms, her favourites – they were made of black denim with flowers made of tiny mirrors sewn on them. Becky had picked them up in Kensington market, but Rupert hated them so she didn't often get to wear them. She paired them with a plain white shirt and black leather jacket.

'How does that look?'

'Great. Not so stuffy. You're only twenty-one.'

'I'm twenty-two.'

'Whatever. You should hang out with people your own age.'

'Would you shut up about Rupert, please?'

'OK, I'm sorry. "Love is blind all day, and cannot see," as Chaucer put it.'

Sharon took Becky to her own tiny college room and they drank tea and watched children's TV. Sharon said she was a Wombles addict. She gossiped about Jack and college life and then took Becky out for fish and chips at her favourite chip shop at the top of St Aldgate's. She was a member of the Oxford Union 'You like debates?' Becky asked. 'No, I like subsidized beer,' Sharon said solemnly – and took her in there for more tea and a lot of sitting round with students talking about nothing. It was a lot of fun.

'I envy you,' Becky said wistfully.

'No, you don't,' Sharon answered. 'You're too ambitious for college. You wanted to get out there and rule the world. Yesterday.'

'That's not fair.' Becky blushed, because she knew it was.

'I don't understand you. You're rich, you're pretty, you got a title—'

'It's not a real title.'

'The Honourable Rebecca.' Sharon stuck her nose in the air mercilessly, enjoying watching Becky wriggle. 'You've got money and you've got a mansion. Why the bloody hell do you want to bust your guts all day working in an office? If it were me, I'd stay at Fairfield and just hire servants to feed me grapes.'

'Well . . .' The question was so direct it threw Becky off. She paused, thinking about it. 'My father wouldn't have wanted me to.'

'You never met the guy. How can you know that?'

'I just feel it. My father worked to build up something to leave his children. He structured his will so that his executors couldn't sell Lancaster before I came of age. I know I was born lucky,' Becky admitted, 'but somewhere up the line one of my ancestors worked to get what we have. And I don't want to lose it because I was lazy. I want to build it up, make it more than just a small British company. Make an impact in business, maybe the world.'

'*Noblesse oblige*?'

Becky coloured. 'If you want to put it like that. I guess.'

'Oh, stop. You don't have to apologize to me. I want to see women in power, even if they were born to it. It's better than nothing. And I suppose it's better than sitting on your backside. Like most of the landed gentry.'

'You're such a Bolinger Bolshevik,' Becky accused her friend. 'Wait till you start making some money and paying seventy per cent tax. I bet you shut up about the blood of the workers then.'

'Quite possibly,' Sharon conceded. 'Want a pint?'

Sharon left to meet Jack at St Catherine's at six, and Becky walked slowly home. She watched the sun set over the ancient grey stones of Oxford crammed up against the red-brick houses and shops of the modern town and thought about what her friend had said. Was Rupert too controlling? She had thought just the opposite. But Sharon wasn't lying about those phone calls, why should she?

But she wasn't going to rush to judge Rupert based on one friend's opinion. It made sense but, equally, who wasn't to say it wasn't coincidence? He sounded very sincere when talking about the hotel, and she'd done good work with the place. Becky had ordered remodelling, advertising, upgrading of the rooms and gardens – all things she'd enjoyed and thought were a real challenge. He was probably expecting her to fix the hotel and then move into the London offices . . .

But she couldn't stop the nagging doubt. It was in her head now. She had to know if Rupert was really in love with her, and not trying to win his case through the back door. It *was* kind of neat . . . Lady Lancaster, and any son would reunite everything. Class was important to Rupert. He had no Sharons in his life. All his London friends were smart, well spoken, 'people like us'.

OK, it was most likely bullshit. But she had to test him. She had to find out for herself.

Becky stopped at an off-licence and picked up a bottle of red for dinner, a cheap Beaujoulais which had got a good write-up in the *Sunday Times*. She entered her building, climbed up the stairs and knocked on her door.

Rupert let her in. She'd known he would be there. He had already showered and changed; he smelled faintly of Floris aftershave, and he looked gorgeous. Becky almost didn't want to say anything, but she steeled herself. She didn't want any clouds over the way she felt about Rupert. He was her boyfriend, her rescuer, her whole life. She had to be able to trust him.

'How was your day, sweetheart?'

He kissed her and took her jacket.

'Pretty good.'

'I heard you were playing hookey. I don't blame you. Business can be deadly dull.'

'I was with Sharon for half the day.'

Rupert didn't flinch. 'That's terrific! How is she? I haven't seen her for ages.'

'She's great. We caught up.' Becky didn't feel right telling him about the engagement, at least not yet. 'And then, you know, darling, I went to see a lawyer.'

She watched Rupert carefully. For the first time, she thought she saw his face tighten.

'That sounds . . . interesting,' he said neutrally, but Becky thought she detected a slight catch to his voice. 'What would you be seeing a lawyer about?'

'Fairfield, actually. I'm thinking that it's a lot of house for two people. I thought we should consider donating it to the National Trust,' Becky said lightly.

The change in Rupert was instant. She watched the blood drain from his face, then surge back into it. He looked unsteady on his feet. Then he bounded across the room towards her and slapped her, hard, across the face.

Chapter 20

Lita looked across the table at the clients and shook her head.

'I really don't think you want to do that.'

Norman Doyle, her account manager, was shaking his head and narrowing his eyes in what he thought was a subtle signal, but which looked to Lita like a mad squint, as though he had something gritty in his eye. She ignored him, the way she usually did. Since she had gotten her latest promotion to Senior Creative Executive, a post created especially for Lita by Harry Weiss, Norman had been trying to rein her in a bit. She was well known to be the copywriter that insisted on coming up with visuals, the woman exec who wouldn't keep her head down, the barely-there-for-a-year staffer who thought nothing of barging into a meeting of the Board of Directors to press her point. Anybody else would have been fired months ago, but Lita kept confounding her enemies by coming up with campaigns that actually sold stuff.

The 'Lucy' campaign, her first, had resonated with urban girls in the North-East and launched the scent to national prominence. Kitten Cosmetics had sold their company out, taken the money and run, but not before their chairman had given a grateful speech to analysts, citing 'the sterling work done by the Doheny advertising agency'. Commissions had gone through the roof. Clients requested Lita by name. Mark Smith and others had predicted she'd be a one-hit wonder, the novelty token female on staff, but Lita had shoved her success right down their throats. Coats, jewellery lines, more scent, lipsticks – everything that came into her office, she managed to find something new and different to say about them. Her famous commercial for Blood Orange, the daring fall shade from Chanel, had featured a broken stick of lipstick smeared across pebbles from the beach, not a girl at all. Her slogan was 'Think Out of the Box.' Harry let her run with it, though he had reservations . . . whoever heard of a lipstick sold without a model? But it took off, and the industry sat up and took notice.

Lita had made enemies. Lots of them, not just Mark and Bud. Many of the assistants were jealous and bitched about her in the restrooms when they knew she was sitting in a stall and could hear every word. Her male colleagues resented her. Word spread that she had gotten her promotion by crawling under Harry's desk. One morning, Lita opened her office door to find a hair-dryer laid across her desk with a note taped to it. 'For your next blow job,' it read. Lita, her face burning, had been reading this little message when she heard the sniggering from the typing pool outside her door. She looked up sharply, but all the girls had their heads bowed, pecking away at their keyboards like so many chickens. She slammed her office door shut, then kicked herself for letting her emotions show.

It would be the last time she made that mistake.

Lita forced herself to disregard other people's opinions. Your work wasn't your family; if they didn't like her, who really cared? She stopped wearing the 'acceptable' boxy suits and started to come in in bell-bottoms, jeans, T-shirts, brightly coloured dresses. She decided not to bother to play her sexuality down any more. Let them think what they liked. She wasn't going to hide her body for a bunch of assholes.

Lita decided to let her bottom line do the talking. She pitched for and got an assignment to work on a masculine product. Hex was a line of automatic drills and tools for the home. Lita took Eli, her art director, out to the DIY stores and talked to some guys, then came up with a no-nonsense pitch that worked perfectly. 'Hex. When you don't have time for mistakes.'

That was when Harry promoted her.

Now Lita was a senior executive, and at Doheny that meant she dealt with clients direct. It was no longer her account manager who conveyed the brief to her. Clients discussed what they needed in face-to-face meetings.

Norman Doyle had been a senior account manager for five years. He was used to massaging fragile egos, running nice, clean numbers, presenting the sober and responsible face of Doheny to big companies that wanted returns for their marketing dollars. He had made four sets of creative executives lose their T-shirts and sandals for suits and ties, and roped them back from scaring the clients. His job was to make sure things ran smoothly – the wild creative side was only allowed out once the clients had left the building.

Lita didn't allow things to run smoothly.

'Excuse me?'

Lita shook her head. She was wearing large dangling earrings and they sparkled as her neck moved. 'Your idea isn't going to work.'

'But you've had so much success with off-beat commercials.' Michael Gibson, Product Manager for Flexiclean, was almost pouting. Lita saw this all the time. Clients hired an agency to run advertising for them, but they secretly thought they could all do it better. They would come to meetings with 'a great direction' for Doheny to go in, which was really a version of the campaign they wanted to see. It invariably sucked. This was no different.

Flexiclean was a bargain washing powder, cheaper by about a nickel than its closest competitor. It wasn't selling well. It had a dingy box and no clear market image. Gibson had specially asked that Lita should get this job, and he'd come to the meeting all jazzed up about his own idea.

Norman Doyle had blathered that it was 'incredibly interesting'. But it wasn't, and Lita had said so.

Gibson's mock-up was of a young, hot babe with a blonde 'flick' hairstyle and a pair of sprayed-on red pants, tossing a box of the powder in the air. He'd come up with a slogan, too. 'Flexiclean. For the woman who's different.'

'This isn't one of my commercials. This is what you think my commercials are like, Mr Gibson. I go off-beat when it sells the product. Young women aren't interested in washing powder. Their moms do their laundry, and they're gonna feel alienated by some sexy chick being called "different". What are they, chopped liver?'

Gibson looked crestfallen. Norman interrupted. 'Lita, I really think that Mr Gibson's idea deserves serious consideration.'

'No, it doesn't.'

'Lita—'

Lita turned directly to Gibson and the suits ranked alongside him. 'Mr Gibson. You want to make a big splash with Flexiclean, and so do I. But this isn't the way to do it. Hip is no good when your core buyers are middle-aged.'

'So what do we do, then? The same old commercial? A mom pulls out her laundry and smells it and goes "Aah"?'

Lita giggled, and suddenly Gibson cracked a smile. She was so gorgeous. What he wouldn't give for five minutes, he thought. Amazing tits, a handspan waist and the kind of ass he thought had gone out with the forties. It was a stripper's body, hidden under the proper clothes. Gibson fantasized about Lita in a strip club, tendrils of dark, curly hair tumbling around a bare shoulder, her breasts jutting out at him, nipples perked, maybe with a sleazy wash of glitter on them, and a scrap of black lace all that hid that silky little triangle between her legs from everybody's view . . .

Hmm. Oh, man . . . He felt his cock stirring, and crossed his legs, firmly. She was talking.

'No. We need something unique, something for Flexiclean. My

commercials aren't really about hip. They're about unique. And you have something unique.'

They leant forward in their seats. Norman Doyle assessed the situation and bit back the retort that was bursting to come out of him. She was infuriating, but she had them hooked. Shit, look at her. They were dying to know what she had for them.

'Flexiclean is cheap. Cheaper than the rest of the powders on the shelf. Now this has worked against you in the past, because you've been seen as the poor woman's powder. Mrs Jones is embarrassed for Mrs Roberts to see her with Flexiclean because she looks like she can't afford Tide.'

'So?'

'So we switch it. Instead of making the price something to be ashamed of, let's make it a selling point. Mrs Jones doesn't look poor any more, she looks savvy. This is what Eli Green and I came up with.'

Lita reached behind her and laid out huge sheets of paper covered with sketches on the table, their storyboard for a TV commercial. The Flexiclean commercial would be her first on TV. And TV was the big time. Magazine ads were great, but TV was where millions and millions of units sold. A few years dreaming up successful TV campaigns, and you could write your own ticket.

'Let's have a look,' Michael Gibson said.

At the foot of the table. Harry Weiss watched silently. He had wanted to see how the Morales girl would do. He wasn't about to interfere. He thought she had a nose for selling.

The storyboard showed a thirty-something woman picking up a box of Flexiclean. Another woman passed her and selected more expensive washing powder. The first woman grinned and said she liked saving money. The second woman admitted that the bills tended to mount up. The first woman winked and said, 'Not in my house.' Then she patted the box of Flexiclean.

Lita went through the storyline frame by frame. She didn't even manage to get to the end before Gibson started thumping the table.

'I love it. That's brilliant,' he said.

'What actress shall we use?' Ed Dresden, their Vice-President, asked eagerly.

Harry scratched a note to himself on his yellow legal pad. He needed to get to know Rosalita Morales a little better. That much was obvious.

'I thought we could check with Family Models. They provided an interesting lead for the last Nescafé commercial,' Harry said, and all heads turned to him. Lita sat back in her chair. Harry was in control now. Her part in the meeting was over.

Harry went down to see Lita at five. It was the first break in his schedule that day. Doheny was getting busier, and it was Harry's job to juggle the creatives. He reported directly to Robert Dawn, the Managing Director. And Robert didn't care about Harry's workload. He wanted to see profits go up. It was all about bonuses in this game. And stock prices. Lita Morales was good for both.

He heard the shouting when he was two corridors away – Norman Doyle's high, reedy voice and Lita's low, insistent, warm, accented tones snapping back at him. Harry smiled to himself. Norman was a little staid for Lita, perhaps. He strode into the office.

'Norman, hello.'

The senior account manager stopped in mid-yelp.

'Hi, there, Harry,' he said. Weiss noted his cheeks were a dull purple colour, a colour he often saw around the men that worked near Lita Morales.

'Norman, could you give me a few minutes here? I need to have a quick word with Lita.'

'Yes, Harry,' Norman said smugly, shooting a foul look at his copywriter. '*Certainly*. I think that would be a very good idea.'

Lita opened her mouth to protest, but said nothing. Norman swept out of the room triumphantly, and Harry closed the door.

'I can explain,' Lita said immediately. Weiss saw her body language – fists clenched at her sides, back stiff. She was spoiling for a fight.

'Oh, can you?'

'Yes. This is the way I conduct my business. I don't tell clients that dumb ideas are great. That wastes time, and I need to get a good idea out there before some other guy has the same idea and beats us to it. My job isn't to [illegible]'

'Shut up,' Harry said.

Lita blinked. 'Excuse me?'

'I said shut up. You're excusing yourself for something I approve of. I don't want to hear you go blathering on like a scratched record. Get it? Got it? Good.'

Lita started to reply, then bit her lip.

'Quitting while you're ahead is one of the first rules of business,' Weiss said dryly. 'Now, I think we have some things to discuss. Are you free tonight for a working dinner?'

Lita looked at him warily. The rumours about the two of them hadn't abated. She could see the typing pool watching them through the glass walls of her office right now. If Weiss tried something on, this could be the end of everything she'd sweated for over the last year.

'I guess,' she muttered.

'Good. Then that's settled. Meet me at six-thirty in the Oyster Bar.' Harry ignored her lack of enthusiasm and left. Lita was like a spoiled child, he thought. Spoiled, but brilliant. He was not going to be influenced by her whims.

Norman had been waiting at the end of the hall. He scampered back into their office, lips pursed.

'I hope you took what he told you on board, Lita. You must try to behave maturely. This isn't modelling now.'

'Oh, I did,' Lita said. She wasn't about to admit to dinner. Why give them any more ammunition?

She arrived at the Oyster Bar at six-thirty exactly. Harry had reserved a table, and Lita slipped in to join him, thankful for the bustle of the commuters thronging out of Grand Central behind her.

You couldn't get more public than this, and that was a good thing. Lita's skin felt dry and flaky, the way it always got when she was extremely stressed. Copious amounts of shea butter rubs from L'Occitane didn't seem to help. She was so paranoid about her colleagues that she half expected to see a bunch of giggling, bitchy women peer around a corner and hiss loudly about her and Harry. He was sitting in a corner by the rail, his head bowed, in his usual black, the frames of his Lennon glasses glinting. Lita felt resentment bubble up like acid in her stomach. She had fought tooth and nail just to get out of the typing pool; she had come up with strong campaigns, she'd sold products, she'd gotten this firm new clients. And now Harry Weiss was hitting on her and treating her like a piece of ass, making all the stupid rumours that said some hot tamale wetback could never have a brain in her head – would never have gotten any further than making coffee without giving sexual favours out like candy – look valid.

Lita wondered briefly if she had enough of a reputation yet to quit. She didn't think so. Her success at Doheny had been stellar, but not so stellar that it couldn't be taken away by the firm's spin-meisters. Hubert West had quit, and the Doheny corporate PR machine went into overdrive, calling his clients and muttering dark things about colleagues carrying him, about cocaine use, alcoholism, wild mood swings. Lita had overheard some of the conversations herself. Hubert had been one of their biggest senior art directors, with major campaigns to his credit and industry awards on his desk. But by the time the Doheny machine was through with him, he'd had to accept a job with a much smaller firm for, it was reputed, only two thirds of his previous salary. And little firms didn't get clients. They got only other little firms, firms who didn't have the money to pay for proper advertising and campaigns. Nobody wanted to be Hubert West, and he'd had a five-year track record. Lita hadn't even been in her senior position for two months yet.

Bristling, trying to shove down her annoyance so she could think clearly, Lita marched up to Harry's table. He glanced up and smiled warmly at her, which annoyed her even more.

'Lita. Good to see you. Have a seat. Do you like oysters?'

'Not particularly.' She didn't see why she should make his easy for him. 'I had a bad one once and I was ill for three days.'

'I understand. Don't worry, they do have other things on the menu.'

'I'm really not that hungry,' Lita said flatly, pulling out a chair and sitting opposite him.

'Then you can watch me eat. I'm starving, so I'm afraid you're going to be here for a while.'

Lita edged her chair back a few inches so there was no possibility her feet would touch Harry's under the table and waited. He ordered twelve oysters, some caviar and smoked salmon with half a bottle of Pouilly-Fuisee, and her mouth started to water. Never mind, she could grab a burger on the way home. She regarded Harry as the oysters arrived and he started to tip them into his mouth. He was wiry but distinguished. The glasses looked good on him, and the black picked out his eyes. He looked like a cross between a professor and a rock star. She knew half the secretaries had crushes on Weiss. That was unsurprising. He was one of the most powerful men at Doheny, certainly the most powerful guy anybody saw on a regular basis. He had celebrity within the industry and every executive in the company wanted to be in his good graces. She admitted to herself, grudgingly, that he was fairly good-looking. Nobody had ever seen his wife, and he didn't keep photos of her in his office. Maybe that was why the rumours about Harry and girls in the office were so frequent. Her story was only the latest that she'd heard. It was the current one, though, and that gave it power.

Weiss lifted his head and looked her directly in the eye.

'I've got a proposal for you. Something that will really advance you in this company, Lita. It's hard for women to make it in business. They mostly need a little help. I'm prepared to give it to you.'

Lita swallowed hard, but her fury just wouldn't die down. The words spilled out of her as if she had no control over them.

'Oh, yeah? Why don't you go fuck yourself, Harry? I fought my way past two sexist assholes to get here and I'm not going to get involved with you. I make money for your shitty company and—'

'Lita.' Weiss paused, then started to chuckle.

'It's not goddamn funny,' Lita spat.

'You think I'm hitting on you.'

'What else would you call it?'

'Offering to mentor you. I'm not interested in you, Lita. Personally, I mean. I love my wife. Why do you think I picked the Oyster Bar? It's close to the trains. I have to be home in two hours.'

'Oh,' Lita said, in a small voice. She blushed purple.

'Why on earth would you think such a thing?'

'People in the office,' Lita muttered. 'They say I had an affair with you.'

Harry took off his glasses and rubbed the lenses. 'What?'

He really had no idea, she realized. Harry was one of those men who could be very focused in one area and completely oblivious in all others. 'Who says that? I'll fire them.'

'Everybody.' Lita sighed. 'Nobody gives me credit for a brain.'

Harry chewed his smoked salmon thoughtfully. 'And do you care what they think?'

'Yes,' Lita admitted.

'Good. Neither do I,' he said firmly, as though she hadn't spoken. 'Your ideas are bringing in clients. I want to see more of them. I want you to go away, do some research and get back to my office. Check out our competitors' ads, come up with better ones. I want to use you to go poaching.'

'If I can get you new accounts, I want a raise,' Lita said boldly. 'And I don't want to work with Norman any more. And I want to pick my own assistant instead of taking whoever the pool assigns to me.'

'We'll see. Get me the accounts first, and then we'll talk.'

Chapter 21

Becky staggered back. Rupert's eyes were hard, glittering, murderously angry. She glanced at the phone – it was all the way over the other side of the room. The door was closer. Becky wrenched it open. She heard people moving about in the lower apartment. Thank God.

'Don't come any closer.'

'Becky . . .'

Rupert struggled and seemed to master himself. He was breathing hard. 'I'm sorry, I lost it.'

'You certainly did. It's over between us.'

He paled. 'Darling, please. I said I was sorry. Truly. At least let me explain.'

He looked genuinely contrite, and for a moment Becky wavered.

'Becky!'

There was a shout from the street. Becky looked down wildly and saw Sharon in the lobby, about to come upstairs. Rupert's sorrowful expression vanished. He walked past Becky and barked, 'I don't think you'd better come up, Sharon. We're having a private talk.'

Sharon looked at Becky, bewildered.

'I said *go away*,' Rupert snapped.

Becky said quietly, 'Rupert, that's enough. It's time for you to leave now.'

Rupert's eyes met hers and saw the hard knot of anger there. He breathed in sharply.

'Very well.' His voice was equally soft now. 'I'll call you later, and we'll get past this.'

Well, I certainly will, Becky thought. Shaken, she drew back to let him get by her. Rupert took his coat from the door and walked down the stairs to the street, passing Sharon without ever glancing at her.

Her friend bounded upstairs and pressed her hands to her mouth. Becky's fingers touched her cheek in disbelief. The white mark of his hand had already vanished and was glowing red.

'He hit you? Are you OK?'

'I'm fine.'

'That bastard,' Sharon growled. 'You should call the police.'

'For a slap round the face? Don't be silly.' Becky rubbed the mark, wishing it would go down, but she could already feel it swelling. 'He packs quite a punch, for a thin guy.'

'Why did he do it?'

'I told him I was giving Fairfield to the National Trust.'

Sharon's eyes widened, then she burst out laughing. 'You said what? Oh, man, I meant for you to confront him, but not like that. Not right now.'

'He said he was sorry. He asked me to hear his explanation.'

'There is no explanation. You're not going along with that. He—'

'Relax.' Becky spoke calmly, but she felt the tears start to prickle in her eyes. 'I never understood women that stayed with men who hit them. I'm not going back to him. But maybe I was too harsh. I know how important the house and the family is to him. Not that that excuses what he did.'

'You think he's just about preserving the family honour?' Sharon snorted. 'I've got a bridge in London I'd like to flog you. Going cheap.'

'He said he'd call me tonight.'

'Let me stay with you, then. I'll call Jack—'

'No need. I can handle Rupert,' Becky said, suddenly wishing mightily to be on her own. Sharon was a dear friend, but she couldn't help her get through this. She could tell Rupert to sod off, but she couldn't tell Becky where she was going to find another man who could mean anything to her the way he had.

Her heart already hurt worse than her face.

Sharon could take a hint. She hugged Becky gingerly. 'Just make sure you lock your door, OK?'

'I promise,' Becky said, but she wasn't worried. Rupert hated scenes. He wouldn't try to kick down the door of her flat. She kissed Sharon on the cheek, which she took as just another Yank habit, and showed her out, then came upstairs and took a packet of peas out of the freezer, pressing it on her cheek. It was still going to be a nice welt. She wondered what on earth she could say back in the office to explain this.

She ran herself a bath, because she suddenly felt dirty. Becky brushed back the tears that were trickling down her cheeks, but it was no good. Rupert had been so much fun, he'd made her laugh, he'd gotten Aunt Victoria off her back, and he'd found her more friends than she could handle. Becky was a realist. She knew most of those 'friends' would drop her like a hot potato now. But she had hated her early days in strike-ridden, cold, damp England, and Rupert had shown her everything Sharon couldn't.

Romeo and Juliet. What a joke.

Was it really that bad, though? The side of her that longed to forgive him would not shut up. What if he hit her because he was enraged that she was betraying the family? She had it in her power to destroy what had belonged to the Lancasters for countless generations. Family was important to her, too. Couldn't she understand how he felt?

But what about what Sharon said? muttered the cynic in her other ear. Look at how much he was in the papers. You weren't. All the PR was about him and 'his' Lancaster holdings. And is that small hotel really important? Or is it just a device for getting you out of the main Lancaster offices?

He was just using me, Becky thought, and she started to cry in earnest. She was too intelligent to pretend that wasn't the case. In her living room, the phone started to ring. She ignored it. She wasn't going to let him see how much he had mattered to her.

Rupert wasn't going to give up and Becky didn't really expect him to. The following morning, she took delivery of five separate bouquets, alternating red and white roses, two dozen each time. She called a taxi and had them delivered to the cardio ward at Nuffield Hospital. There they might cheer somebody up, instead of making her want to cry.

She called the office and told them not to expect her in for the rest of the week.

'Lord Lancaster has called looking for you, Miss Lancaster,' Ellen told her. 'He keeps calling. What am I supposed to tell him?'

'Tell him that I'll be back at work on Monday, please, Ellen,' Becky said firmly.

'But where will you be?' Ellen insisted.

'Out of the office,' Becky replied. Then she hung up. She packed a small suitcase, locked up and stepped out into the street. Buses ran directly to Victoria Coach Station and there was one leaving in ten minutes. She couldn't do anything about her heart. The only thing left to do was work.

Becky stepped out at the grimy kerb of the coach station, delicately picking up her shoes to avoid getting them filthy, and walked out on to the street to hail a cab. She had spent the journey thinking hard, and in the middle of feeling sick about Rupert she also felt a little embarrassed. She had been in England for nine months now, and she still hadn't been into the headquarters of her father's company.

She had allowed Victoria, Henry and Rupert to push her away. She had let lawyers advise her, she had asked for briefs, she had finally taken control of the smallest and most insignificant part of the firm. But she had done nothing to establish herself. Nothing but allow other people to put her off.

Her father hadn't allowed her to inherit, and fought with his cousin for so long, so that she could be the puppet of grey men in suits.

If she had been sitting on the sidelines, whose fault was that? Her own.

I wasn't ready. I didn't feel old enough, Becky admitted to herself as the gleaming black car pulled over in the London drizzle. Part of me is still the kid playing tennis and sailing. Twenty-one is when most kids go to college or drop out and get an apartment and a drug habit. I let them shame me into thinking that older heads should make all the decisions, but twenty-one was when Daddy said I should inherit, not thirty-one.

Well, that time was over now. Sharon was right. She had to stop making excuses.

Lancaster Holdings was a large, modern building located on a narrow, cobbled hill that sloped down to the Thames. It was bang in the middle of the City of London, close to Canon Street Station, and Becky wondered idly how much the company paid in rent. Overheads must be massive. Was it necessary? It looked good on the front cover of the annual report, but . . .

She wandered into the lobby. It was decorated in the most modern style, with a large Andy Warhol print, black leather couches and a glass coffee-table perched atop a furry white rug. It reminded her a bit of the lair of any Bond villain you cared to name; she half expected to see Sean Connery stroll out from behind the desk. But there was a pretty girl sitting there in a suit and pearls instead. She looked Becky up and down curiously. Becky guessed she didn't see many twenty-something girls in jeans in her office. She smiled.

'Hi.'

'Can I help you?'

'Yes. I'm Rebecca Lancaster.'

'And whom are you here to see, miss?' The receptionist looked dubious, but wasn't actually insulting, Becky noted approvingly.

'I don't have an actual appointment . . .'

'Everybody needs an appointment. I'm sorry.'

'I own the company,' Becky explained patiently.

'Ohh-kayy,' the girl said, looking around slightly for a security guard. Becky grinned.

'Look, Lancaster Holdings. Rebecca Lancaster. That's me.'

'I never saw you before, miss,' the girl said patiently, as if Becky were a bit thick.

'Just call up to any member of the board.'

Who had taken over from Henry Whitlock? Most of them were previous vice-presidents that had been promoted until Rupert could find her some 'better executives', as he had promised. She tried to dredge up some names from her memory of the company report, but none came to her, except that of the accountant who had presented the thick pages of figures towards the end; she remembered him because Rupert had cursed the guy out so thoroughly. Kenneth Stone. Becky flushed. She had been so wrapped up in racing to London and getting her hands on her own firm that she hadn't actually thought about what she would do once she got here.

But what the hell. She owned this place. It was only her good-girl side that felt she had to explain herself to a receptionist.

'Kenneth Stone. Call his office and tell him Rebecca Lancaster is here to see him.'

'Hold on a second, please.' The girl lifted her receiver and dialled, keeping one eye on Becky as though she might start stealing the pot-plants. She spoke to someone in a hiss, then hung up, looking surprised. 'He'll see you. Fifth floor, room 506.'

'Where are the elevators?'

'The *lifts* are that way,' the girl said sternly, as though she'd had enough of Rebecca's nonsense.

Becky walked over to them and punched the button. The elevator car was a fantasy of brass and velvet and it looked as though it belonged in the Pierre back home. Obviously no expense had been spared in this place. No expense that came out of her pockets.

As the elevator whisked her smoothly up the building, Becky thought briefly about the girl in the lobby. That was how the world saw her. As a bit ridiculous, a teenybopper heiress who had no business sticking her nose in business. She was technically a college drop-out. It was amazing to people that she would even consider turning up at her own offices. Her own assistant resented her and had no fears about letting her know it. If she were ever going to change perceptions, she had a lot of work to do. A lot. And letting Rupert 'rescue' her had been just another way of putting it off.

She stepped out on the fifth floor. A small plaque on the wall, in brass, read 'Accounting'. It was much sparser-looking than the lobby, with thinner carpeting, no plants and no art on the walls. They were painted a cheerful yellow, and that was the sum total of the decoration.

Becky walked down the corridor and introduced herself to the secretary who sat outside room 506.

'I'm Rebecca Lancaster.'

'Yes, Miss Lancaster. If you'd come this way,' the woman said briskly. She was older and looked efficient. Her desk was very neat. She showed Becky into her boss's office and quietly shut the door behind her.

Becky took the place in. It was functional, with a dark wood desk, a couch, a chair and some family photos on the wall next to professional diplomas. There was a short, middle-aged man with a neatly trimmed beard sitting behind the desk. He stood up and offered Becky a damp hand.

'Miss Lancaster, please, take a seat.'

'Thank you.'

'I confess I'm a little surprised to see you.'

'I decided to do this at the last minute,' Becky told him.

'Indeed.' He nodded. 'I thought Lord Lancaster would have wanted to do it himself, rather than sending you.'

Becky paused. 'I think we're at cross-purposes. I came here to discuss the company with some members of the board. I wanted to take a more active interest. No, scratch that. A full interest. Control, in fact.'

'Then, if I may ask, what are you doing in my office? I run the accountancy division on this floor. As Lord Lancaster has probably told you.'

Becky tried to think of a good reason, but her wits deserted her. 'Honestly? Yours was the only name I could think of. I kind of rushed this.'

'And why my name?' His questions were penetrating, and the way he looked at her with that beady stare made her nervous. She placed his accent as lower middle class, a successful professional, but nothing like Rupert. He obviously knew and accepted that she was who she was, but he seemed to be rather combative. Becky squirmed a little.

'Your name is on the company accounts in the report, which I read.'

'There are hundreds of names in the report.'

'Lord Lancaster mentioned you once or twice,' Becky admitted.

He gave her a thin smile. 'I'll bet he did. And he wanted you to come here?'

'He doesn't know I'm here. Lord Lancaster doesn't own this company, Mr Stone, I do.'

'I know that, madam. But you appointed your cousin, didn't you? Personally? I have to assume you approve of what he's been doing here?'

Becky felt a nasty twist of foreboding in her stomach. She dodged the question. 'May I ask what it was you thought Rupert was going to do himself?'

'Fire me, Miss Lancaster,' he replied calmly. 'I have been expecting it for some days now.'

'Why on earth would he want to fire you? Is there a problem with the bookkeeping?'

Another thin smile. 'Your family in general doesn't seem to like the way I keep the books.'

'And how is that?'

'Accurately,' Stone said. 'I have given the board repeated warnings, both the previous board and Lord Lancaster's regime. I have been told to change the "presentation" of accounts to fit the new company policy, and to reflect the new orders that he has brought in. I have, of course, refused to do that.'

'I promise you, Mr Stone, nobody is going to fire you for doing your job. I'm not an accountant, and I have been relying on lawyers to give me a breakdown of what has been happening with the company. Lord Lancaster's lawyers told me that it was in urgent need of changes, losing money . . . was that false?'

'That was perfectly correct.' The accountant hesitated. 'Can I speak frankly to you about this?'

'Sure.'

'Changes were needed, but not the kind of change Lord Lancaster has implemented. The crisis has worsened substantially.'

'But what about all the new orders?'

'They are brought in with deferred payments. We undercut the competition to get those orders, and we are operating with a razor-slim margin. The amount of money spent on "public relations" is ludicrous. Wages are high, strikes are frequent, productivity is down, and our overheads grow every day.'

'Your offices don't seem to be too extravagant.'

'This floor is under my control. If you go to any other, you will see the waste that is endemic in this company.' Stone sighed. 'Frankly, I have been planning to resign. Being an accountant in a company determined to spend itself into the ground is . . . embarrassing.'

I'm embarrassing this nerd now, Becky thought.

Well, nerd he may be, but he sure sounded right.

'This office building—'

'A stupid expense. Real estate in Yorkshire would run our costs down by two thirds. But three successive boards have turned down flat my proposal to move. They said we needed the prestige of a London office, even though our interests are in Cornwall and Yorkshire.'

'There's no prestige to going bust,' Becky said angrily.

'I couldn't agree with you more.'

'So what should I do? Give me your advice, Mr Stone,' Becky said. Somebody was watching out for her. If she had met one of Rupert's glorified vice-presidents, she might have wasted a month in flannel before she found this out.

'There's not all that much you can do. The situation is beyond repair now.'

'Nothing is beyond repair,' Becky said fiercely. 'We'll start today. How often do we renew our lease here?'

'Every six months. It's up in June.'

'That's less than a month. Get rid of the lease. Find me something cheap in London. Sell all the paintings. If we have expensive perks, eliminate them. Anybody who doesn't like it, you can fire.'

'It's not in my power to hire and fire, Miss—'

'It is now. What is your title, exactly?'

'Vice-President of Accounting.'

'Now it's Chief Finance Officer. Personnel will report to you. You will start taking a board member's salary right away. I hope I can convince you to stay.'

He nodded. 'I'll stay, Miss Lancaster, but I warn you, I think it may be too late for this company.'

'Please,' she said, 'call me Becky.'

Chapter 22

Success never came quite as soon as she thought it should.

Lita didn't need Harry Weiss to tell her twice. She had gotten rid of Norman Doyle, hired her own assistant and aggressively gone after accounts. And it was working, within the system. Her job was her life. She worked late at the office, sometimes falling asleep at her desk. Men asked her out, some of her colleagues at Doheny even, once they got used to the idea that she wasn't going to quit or be fired. But Lita never even considered them. She was so brutal in turning them down that the rumour ceased that she was sleeping with Harry and one started that she was gay. The bitchy comments from other women didn't stop, not least because Lita made no effort to get any of the rest of them promoted.

That's their problem, she thought. I had to make it on my own, why shouldn't they?

Over the last year she had made her own way, and she had also become hard and bitter. Lita didn't think about that. She softened only on holidays, when she went back to her parents'. The rest of the time she thought she was just too busy to have an emotional life. She had tried that once, and it hadn't worked.

Love was unreliable. Success wasn't.

The only problem was that success wasn't coming as soon as she had hoped. Despite a year's worth of new accounts, sparkling successes with only one or two dips, a fancy company car that she never used because the subway was quicker, and a better apartment a few blocks away from the old one, she felt like she wasn't making any progress. She had been to Harry's office six or seven times, asking for a promotion, a small cut of the profits. Lita wanted to be made a partner. That wasn't a lot to ask, with the revenue she was making.

'Your campaigns have brought us a couple of million in new business. That's great, but it's hardly the lion's share of what we do here.'

Lita said impatiently, 'But what about all the indirect revenues? I'm making this firm hot.'

Harry had stared her down. 'All by yourself, huh? Doheny did survive before you got there. What about George Waters, Pete Bessel, Hank Abrams and Matt Lauder?'

'They do good work.'

'Not just good. They are bringing in countless new customers. You aren't the only one that does good work here, Lita. And these guys all have seniority on you. Keep doing good work, and we'll talk about it later.'

Later. Later. Later. Lita had worked her ass off all through 1971 and into 1972. She had built her reputation and Doheny's reputation. And now she was getting sick of it.

She sat in her latest perk, a corner office on the upper floor, and stared morosely out of the window. It was June, and her latest campaign, rather surprisingly, had flopped. Lita was kicking herself. She had let herself get seduced by her own press, let herself believe she could sell anything. Brite-White toothpaste was the latest release from a large pharmaceutical company, and had higher levels of fluoride than other toothpastes. Lita had fought for the pitch and gotten it, against the wishes of Hank and Matt, who both wanted a shot. What she hadn't done was wait for the Beta testing. She had persuaded the client to rush out with the campaign, get out there first . . . Lita loved to be first. Madison Avenue was all about new, fresh, attention-grabbing. But in this case it had been a disaster. The toothpaste didn't taste too good. People liked her catchy jingle and her pearl-toothed models, but they hated the product. After an initial sales spike, the toothpaste gathered dust on shelves nationwide. But much, much worse for Lita was the fact that she had tagged the name of the company on to the end of the spot she was so proud of. 'From your friends at Robinson, the family company.' Now not only was the R&D money on Brite-White up in smoke, but the other Robinson products were suffering. And so was she.

Robinson fired Doheny and hired Smith & Watkins, their greatest rival. Lita had been totally humiliated, and the boys in the company were letting her know it. She hadn't fully understood the depth of the resentment until she saw how much they all enjoyed watching her fall. Assistants hummed the Brite-White jingle under their breaths as she passed them in the corridors. The other senior creative execs, all men, used it as an excuse to get assigned all the plum jobs for more than a month. Even after her formal period in the doghouse, Lita was still feeling the effects. Instead of automatically being the first choice of new business, she had to compete with her colleagues to get it. She was no longer the blue-eyed girl. It was more than a bit embarrassing.

Manhattan glittered below her window, the sunlight gleaming on the windows of the cars crawling through midtown. Lita sighed and turned back to her latest campaign, a perfume for a large French house trying to break into the American market. Her work was good, but not outstanding, and she thought it was because she was feeling exhausted. A gorgeous girl was standing in front of the Eiffel Tower on her mock-up, with the slogan, 'European Elegance. Wear L'Amour.' It was OK, but it hardly rocked her world. It would do fine, but it wouldn't break any sales records. Lita wondered if she needed a vacation, a holiday from all the aggravation. Like she'd ever find time. She hadn't been out of the country since that long-ago trip to England. The image of Rupert and Rebecca flashed through her mind, with the normal burst of private, white-hot hatred. Flustered, she pushed her hair out of her eyes and pressed her hands over them.

Her phone buzzed. It was Janice, her assistant. Lita had picked Janice herself from the pool and they got on fine. In fact, she sometimes felt like Janice was the closest thing she had to a friend.

'Lita, Harry Weiss has called a meeting. Can you make it?'

'For Harry, of course I can.' Staring out at Manhattan's needles of glass and stone jabbing into the sky wasn't going to get her anywhere. 'Tell him I'll be right down.'

'It's not in his office, it's in the conference room. All the senior people are gonna be there.'

'Of course they are.' Lita sighed. 'OK, I'll be there.'

She picked up a pen and a yellow pad and made her way to the elevators. Lita hated being called to meetings with everyone else. She didn't think she should have to pitch for work against the others. Basically because she knew she was better than they were.

The conference room was packed. Lita was one of the last to get there. The polished oak table was set with glasses of water and a plate of cookies which nobody was touching. She nodded curtly at the usual suspects. Harry had obviously gotten there earliest, he was seated at the head of the table. All the senior copywriters and art directors and a couple of account managers were in there. She was the only woman in the room.

'What's the buzz?' Lita asked Pete Bessel, the best art director Doheny had. He glanced appreciatively at her short dress, which Lita ignored. She was used to the boys gawking at her. Bessel had once put his hand on her ass, but that was OK. She'd been wearing stilettos at the time and had trodden down on his foot so firmly that she'd cracked a toe. Ever since then, Pete confined himself to leering.

'Big new account. Harris Pharmaceuticals invited us to pitch. They want to see ideas.'

'Shit, that's big.' Pete frowned at the bad language, but Lita didn't give a damn. Screw him. She felt a shiver of excitement. Harris were huge. They had all kinds of household and cosmetic products, everything from diapers to shower gel to a range of cheap lipsticks. They had been using a much bigger firm, Young & Rubicam, to handle their advertising up to now. They were well known for spending tens of millions on all types of advertising . . . print, TV commercials, radio, billboards, the works. If the firm could get even a small slice of their work, it meant huge year-end bonuses for somebody. If it's me, Lita thought, I could double my salary.

She was making great money, but life in the Big Apple was expensive. If she had more of a cushion, maybe she could get into the stock market. Lita needed some assets. Right now she relied on her job just to keep her head above water.

'That's interesting,' she said.

'Forget it,' Pete said nastily. 'They heard about what happened with Brite-White. Besides, everybody wants first shot at this thing.'

'Go fuck yourself, Pete,' Lita snapped.

'Oh. Real ladylike. I can't imagine why a doll like you isn't hitched yet,' Pete said with heavy sarcasm. 'Do the *paisans* like that kinda talk?'

'Number one, there's more to life than getting married. And number two, I'm not Italian, I'm Hispanic.'

'Whatever.' Pete shrugged, just to show her that it was all the same to him. Lita thought of something suitably vicious, but was interrupted by Harry Weiss entering the room.

'Settle down, boys,' Harry said, and the murmur of voices subsided. 'You've probably heard that Harris is looking for new representation. They're considering us, a couple of boutique shops and Smith & Watkins. Needless to say, Bob Dawn, our esteemed MD, is determined that we should get the account. Harris has a soap they want us to pitch for. It comes in new packaging, a kind of bottle that you squeeze, and it comes out of a little spout.' He tossed a small bottle of liquid soap on to the table. It was white plastic with red and blue flowers on it. 'This is it. We have one week to put mock-ups together. They are starting off with a print campaign. You'll all come up with something, submit it to Bob Dawn's office direct. He picks the best three, submits them to Harris. God help you if none of them are good enough for us to pick up the account.'

'And what's the prize?' Matt Lauder called out across the table. The other men chuckled. Lita bit her cheeks. She couldn't stand these guys and their hearty, boys-club bonhomie.

'Apart from keeping your job?' Weiss asked flatly. Lita grinned. Harry

Weiss was the only one of these jerks she had any time for. 'Bob is actually putting up something pretty big. A hundred grand for the guy that gets this account.'

The murmur redoubled.

Or the girl, Lita said to herself. Or the girl.

'That's it. Go to it. They sent over twenty bottles of the product. Your assistants can come and get them.'

There was a rush for the door. Everybody wanted to get started right away. On her way out, Lita swiped the sample that Harry had thrown on to the table. She had a feeling that once Janice got down there, there wouldn't be any bottles left.

'Lita.' Harry Weiss stuck out his arm and stopped her as she was leaving. 'Janice told my assistant you wanted some vacation time. Is everything OK?'

Lita tossed the soap bottle in her hand. Look at how concerned he was over the idea she'd take a vacation. She really was a workaholic. 'It's fine, Harry, and I don't want any time off. Everything's peachy.'

'Good to hear it. You can come to me if you need to talk. Not about the soap, though,' Weiss added hastily. 'That wouldn't be fair.'

'Thanks.' She was quite touched. 'I'll keep that in mind.'

'I know you can do us proud on this one, Lita,' Weiss said quietly. 'If you get this account, Bob would forget all about . . .' His voice trailed off.

Lita patted the soap bottle. 'I know,' she said. 'I know.'

'So what are you going to do?'

Janice knocked and simultaneously walked into Lita's office. She was carrying a cup of hot coffee with cinnamon sprinkled on top of it, and it smelt delicious. Lita smiled gratefully; she needed something this morning. 'Come up with something perfect,' Lita said. 'Any ideas?'

The other woman blinked. Janice Cohen was almost thirty, rather plain and highly efficient. Lita was sure she could have gone to any good college – NYU, Columbia – if her parents had had the money to send her there. Janice was poor, but she never discussed her finances with anybody. Lita could see the signs, though. She herself had come from that world. Some of Janice's jackets and skirts were neatly darned in places. Lita had seen the same marks before, on her mother's clothes. The seventies were the 'Me' generation, everybody was about hot and young, and at thirty maybe life had passed a woman like Janet by. Yet she took immense pride in her work. She didn't rush out the door on the dot of five, she wasn't sloppy and she didn't gossip about Lita or anyone else. Lita had had a short list when she got to choose her own assistant. Janice's had been the only name on it.

'You're asking me for ideas?'

'Why not? You've worked here for six years, right?'

'Eight, actually.'

Lita motioned for Janice to shut the door behind her and sit down. 'You must have picked up a lot about the advertising business by now.'

Janice nodded. 'I would say so. But assistants aren't usually asked to give their opinions.'

'Well, this isn't a usual office. You heard about Bob Dawn's contest?'

'All the secretaries did.'

Of course. The secretaries knew everything before any of the executives did. They were faster than AT&T.

'Do you have any ideas on this?' Lita tossed her the liquid soap bottle.

'Other than to check the Beta testing?'

Lita groaned. 'Not you, too.'

Janice smiled, which was unusual. 'Yes, I do. I think that everyone else is going to be so desperate to get this business that they are going to forget to focus on the client.'

Lita leaned forward slightly in her seat. 'How do you mean?'

'They are going to be looking for ways to be new and radical and funky, but Harris likes to sell to wives and mothers. They like straightforward advertising, nothing conceptual.'

'Correct,' Lita agreed.

'So, look at this bottle. It squeezes. What Harris will want to emphasize is that it isn't messy. Maybe it gets more soap out, so it's economical. You always lose so much soap off the end of a bar, which is wasteful and untidy,' Janice said, with extreme disapproval. Lita imagined Janice painstakingly scraping soap mess from her sink and tut-tutting over it. 'So I would sell it for what housewives want in a soap. Value, efficiency and no mess. I think if you can do that, you'll be on to a winner.'

Lita grinned. 'So do I, Janice. Thank you so much.'

'You're welcome. And about that perfume.' Janice pointed to the mock-up of the girl by the Eiffel Tower. 'If I may speak frankly, that's rather boring.'

'Yeah, it wasn't my best effort.'

'Instead of deferring to the French as being so much more "hip",' and Lita could hear the inverted commas she put around the word, 'why don't you suggest that the American girl is the stylish one? Put a model in the same shot, wearing jeans and holding a large Stars and Stripes.'

'That's brilliant.' Lita was shocked. 'That's perfect.'

'And for the slogan,' Janice said, gabbling slightly now as though she was afraid of being cut off, 'How about "Have style. Will travel."?'

'I love it.' Lita leaned right over desk and hugged Janice. 'I was stuck on that one. I'm going to recommend you for a promotion.'

Janice turned purple.

'Are you OK?' Lita asked anxiously.

'I'm fine. I think I need a glass of water.'

'Just one thing.'

'Anything,' Janice said, with unaccustomed passion.

'Please don't leave me before we've got this soap thing done.'

Lita had somebody else on her team now, and she enjoyed it. Janice talked to the other assistants and reported back to Lita that her hunch was correct – the men were outdoing each other with outrageous ideas. Lita had Janice find out the results of the Beta testing and sample product names the company was leaning towards. She reported, from one of her opposite numbers, an executive's assistant at Harris, that the big company was almost settled on 'SoftClean' as the brand name.

'That's wonderful. You're a genius,' Lita almost shouted, when Janice got back to her with this nugget.

'But you can't use that name. They could trace the information leak back to Maria.'

'I'm not going to. But the name tells us things that Harris wants to point out. Clean is a given, but soft . . . They want the buyers to think about luxury.'

'And maybe that the soap doesn't melt and cake on to the sink.'

'That, too. Look, this is what I've got so far.' She held it up for Janice to see. 'What do you think?'

Chapter 23

'Oh, my goodness.' Janice sat down heavily on Lita's chair. 'That's perfect.'

Lita had a large mock-up on cardboard, done in her normal mode of using a collage to get an approximation of what she wanted. Once she was certain of her image, an art director would take it and produce something more refined. But the collages worked pretty well. They got the point across. Clearly Janice had gotten it.

An attractive, middle-aged woman in a neat pair of black pants with a crisp white shirt was fixing the coat on her angelic-looking, soft-skinned daughter. The door was open with a school bus in the background. The mother looked stylish and pulled-together. There was a picture of the Soft-Soap bottle in the foreground. The copy read 'No time for mess. No time for stress. No time for less than the best.'

'You think that would sell it?' Lita asked, rather proudly.

'Absolutely. She's a fox, but she's still a mom. You really hit it.' Janice peered under the slogan to read the small print. Lita had only bothered with a couple of sentences: 'Economy meets style. When you don't have time or money to waste, and you won't take anything less than the softest skin, use WonderSoap. Your family deserves it.'

'That's perfect, too. You're winning this easily.' Janice looked as smug as a cat with a dead bird. 'I guess that means I get my promotion, huh?'

'Absolutely. Just as soon as this is in the bag.'

'Then why don't you let me buy you lunch?' Janice asked boldly. 'I know this place where they serve the best soup in midtown.'

'That sounds perfect. Come on, let's go.' Lita grabbed her purse and they made a run for the elevators.

When they got back, she worked on her perfume commercial for the rest of the day. There was a temptation to go back to the soap, but Lita had learned that she had to trust her instincts. If she worked against her first instincts, over-correcting, adding stuff that wasn't needed, a campaign only came out worse. If your gut told you the initial campaign was right, it was better to leave it at that.

Soft-Soap was perfect. She knew it.

Janice worked quietly outside her office, taking calls from her existing clients and typing up paperwork. She only stuck her head round the corner when it was six, time to go home.

'See you tomorrow, Lita.' She paused.

'What's up?'

'Probably nothing. But Kathy Donalds was crowing some. She said Pete Bessel had an incredible idea.'

Kathy was Pete's assistant. They had offices just down the hall.

'Relax.' Lita was supremely confident. 'It can't be as good as mine.'

She went home, ran a scented Floris bath and then made herself some chilli with a large glass of Cabernet Sauvingnon. Maybe after she won the bonus and got Janice her promotion she'd take a week off. Go somewhere really warm and exotic. She would deserve it.

Next morning Lita was in the office early, putting the finishing touches to the L'Amour campaign. She hefted up her work and rode downstairs to Harry's office.

'Is he free?'

Susan nodded and indicated that Lita should go right in. She couldn't stand the girl, but there was no point fighting a losing battle. Harry obviously thought the sun shone out of her firm little behind.

'What's this?'

'The L'Amour campaign.'

'Let's have a look.' Harry hefted it up and regarded it in the light. 'Well . . . this is wonderful stuff. The flag is inspired.'

'You need to thank Janice.'

'Janice who?'

'My secretary Janice. It was her idea. The copy, too.'

'Your *secretary*?'

'I started out as a secretary. You might want to consider unusual routes for your copywriters. I think she should get a promotion,' Lita said, sitting opposite Harry and crossing her long legs.

Weiss regarded the work without looking at Lita's legs. Sexually, he always made her feel invisible. She didn't know whether to be grateful or resentful.

'I'll think about it. One good idea does not a copywriter make.'

'You could always—'

'I said I'll think about it.'

'At the very least she has to get a bonus for this work,' Lita said.

'I agree. Why don't you give it to her? Since you're getting paid for this.'

'Goddamn it, Harry. You're impossible.' Lita glanced behind him; he had a large sheet of cardboard propped up against his wall. 'Whose work is that?'

'Pete Bessel's. It's his shot for the Harris soap campaign. He gave me a copy – the original is already in the Managing Director's office. He's pretty proud of it.'

'Can I see?' Lita leaned forward curiously.

'I don't know. He might not like you looking at his work.'

'It's already gone through to the MD.'

'That's true.' Harry looked at his protégée thoughtfully. 'You aren't going to like it. This is a really great idea.'

'Let me see.'

He picked it up and turned it over.

'Oh, my God,' Lita said.

'What's the matter?' Weiss was concerned. Lita had gone pale. 'It's not that brilliant.'

'I have to . . . Excuse me, Harry,' Lita mumbled. She jumped out of her chair and ran out of his office.

That girl is nuts, Harry thought fondly.

Lita barged past the staring Susan and took the elevator right up to the ninth floor. Robert Dawn, Doheny's Managing Director, kept the entire ninth floor to himself. His office was more like a suite, with a private kitchen and bathroom, an executive chef and a private dining room where he entertained the CEOs of Doheny's top clients. The entire thing was surrounded by an enormous wall of tinted glass that enabled Dawn to watch the whole of midtown Manhattan spread out below him.

Nobody came up here without an appointment. But she had to try.

The elevator doors showed her red-faced and sweating. Frantically Lita tried to smooth down her hair and press the back of her hand to her cheeks. She knew she needed to be together for this. If she had any shot of being believed.

The doors hissed open, and Lita's foot landed silently on the thick pile of silver-grey wool that deadened every footfall up here. Mrs Higgins, Dawn's junior assistant, was sitting in front of Felicity Nonna's office. Nonna was the senior assistant. Higgins glanced up at Lita, taking in the sprayed-on jeans with the sequinned pattern at the hip, the cotton shirt knotted over her belly button, revealing half an inch of golden midriff, the stacked mules and the loose, glossy hair that tumbled around her shoulders.

'Can I help you?'

'Yes. I'm Rosalita Morales. I'm one of the senior creative executives downstairs.'

'Yes?' The older woman sounded remarkably unimpressed.

'I need to speak to Mr Dawn right away.'

'Can I help you with something?'

'I'm afraid not. I need to discuss this in person with Mr Dawn,' Lita said coldly. She was in no mood for bullshit from subordinates. Mrs Higgins took in her attitude, and backed off.

'I'll just get Miss Nonna for you,' she murmured.

Lita stood there and seethed. It was so quiet up here, everything so proper and calm, she thought that the woman must be able to hear the thudding of her furious heart.

Mrs Higgins retreated into her boss's office and the senior assistant came out a moment later. Mrs Higgins then absented herself into the kitchen. She doesn't want to see a scene, Lita thought. The woman reminded her of Rupert. She frowned.

'Mr Dawn only sees people with appointments, Miss Morales. Is there some matter I can clear up for you?'

Lita regarded Miss Nonna, who was about thirty-five and far more attractive than Higgins. That was probably why Dawn kept her nearest to his office, she thought cynically. Nonna was staring at her with quiet hostility.

'I'd like to see Mr Dawn. Maybe you can ask him if he'll make an exception.'

'I can't do that.'

'Why not?'

'Because he's not here,' Nonna said triumphantly. 'And he won't be back for two more days. He's on a business trip in Canada.'

'*Damn* it!' Lita almost spat.

'Excuse me?'

She pulled herself together. 'I'm sorry. The matter is urgent. I need to inform Mr Dawn that he can't accept submission of one of the mock-ups from the Harris soap contestants. Do you know what I'm talking about?'

'Of course.' Nonna gestured back into her office. 'I have three already in. Waiting for him to see them.'

Lita's heart thudded. 'Is one of them from Mr Pete Bessel?'

'I believe it is.'

'Well, you can't submit that to him!' Lita half shouted.

Nonna didn't flinch. 'And why is that?'

'Because,' Lita said, failing to control her anger, 'it's mine!'

'I just don't see how it could have happened,' Janice said. She was twisting her hands nervously.

'I do. We didn't lock my door.'

'I'm terribly sorry about that, Miss Morales—'

'Janice.' Lita sighed, exasperated. 'I don't blame you and you don't have to start calling me Miss Morales. I'm not gonna fire you.'

'Oh,' Janice said. She had gone very ashen.

'If that scumbag comes sneaking in to my office . . . I can't believe he would do something like that.'

Janet was still wringing her hands. 'But it *is* my fault. I told his secretary that you had the best idea I'd ever seen. I was mad at her boasting about how Mr Bessel had the whole thing wrapped up. I told her there wasn't even going to be a contest.'

'Did you tell her that she should come in here and steal the idea?'

'Of course not.'

'Then it's not your fault.' Lita seethed. 'That bitch upstairs. She wouldn't do anything about it. She actually said it was the first one registered.'

'I don't suppose there's any chance he came up with the same idea independently?'

'No chance at all.' Lita was emphatic. 'Pete's good, I don't deny it. But he doesn't understand the housewife market. He's always using models in their twenties to sell stuff to busy moms.' She scrunched a piece of paper viciously in her hand and threw it at the wire trash basket. It missed. 'Fuck,' she said.

'You aren't going to let them get away with it?'

'Me? Hell, no.' Lita stood up and picked up her mock-up.

'Where are you going?' Janice asked, bewildered.

'Just hold the fort. I'll be right back,' Lita promised.

She was going to see Harry. He trusted her. He would fix this.

'Lita, that's plagiarism. I don't get it.'

Harry took off his Lennon glasses and buffed them carefully. He put them back on, but the mock-up was the same as when he'd taken them off. A dead ringer for Bessel's work.

'Damn straight. But *he* copied *me*. I came up with this two days ago.'

'And you showed it to him.'

'No—'

'Then you discussed it with him. Told him your themes.'

'No—'

'Come on, Lita.' Harry was looking at her sceptically, and it drove her nuts.

'Come on? Come on?' She was standing up now and shouting. Susan was staring at her from outside Harry's office, but Lita didn't care. 'Harry, my assistant told his assistant I had a great idea. And we went out to lunch and didn't lock the door.'

'Lita. You're not being rational. Why would a great talent like Pete Bessel sneak into your room and copy your work?'

'Either he did, or I did.' She gestured furiously at her collage.

'If you had the idea yesterday, why didn't you turn it in to me then? Why did you wait? If it was ready in your office, why didn't you take it up to Bob Dawn? It makes no sense.'

'Hell, I don't know. I was busy with L'Amour. I didn't think there was a rush.' Lita stared angrily down at Harry. 'Are you saying you don't believe me?'

'What I believe doesn't matter. You've got no evidence, Lita, none. On the contrary, if it comes down to it, Pete can prove that you saw his work and copied it. I showed it to you.'

'You think I could have put this together that fast?'

'You could.'

'I can't believe it.' Lita sat down heavily. 'You're not going to support me.'

Harry paused. 'No, I'm not. I don't play favourites.'

Lita felt a wave of nausea wash over her. It was so unfair. That money was her investment money, her get-out-of-the-rat-race money. It was her chance to make Bob Dawn notice her, put her on a level above the rest. Maybe for her to get a partnership. And now Harry, the one person she trusted, was betraying her.

'I see.' She picked up her mock up and left the room without bothering to close the door.

Pete Bessel worked on Lita's floor, a corridor's length away from her office. Lita strode blindly past Janice, working at her desk, and over to where Kathy Donalds, the bleached-blonde with the orange skin that came from too much fake tan and who worked for Pete, was sitting.

'Is he in?' she snapped.

'Yes. Let me see if he can see you right now, Miss Morales,' Kathy said sweetly.

'He can see me,' Lita said, and barged into Pete's office, ignoring her. He was on the phone, but he excused himself and hung up.

'Lita. What a nice surprise,' Pete said smugly. He reached behind her and shut his door so Kathy wouldn't hear them. 'What have you got there? Oh, it's a copy of my campaign. Hoping to get some inspiration?'

'Cut the crap, Pete. We both know what you did.'

'Yes. I won the competition. That money's really going to come in handy for me.'

'Pete. You broke into my office, saw my campaign and copied it.'

Bessel put his face closer to hers, his eyes narrowing. 'Let me give you a little piece of advice, *mamacita*. Don't go around spreading libellous stories that only make you look pathetic. Bob Dawn got my work in a day ago, and don't expect Harry Weiss to back you up. I gave him a copy in front of his secretary. She saw me do it. So your little boyfriend won't be able to cover you this time.' He watched her face, and sniggered. 'You already went there, didn't you? And he told you to take a hike. You know what? I take it back. Go ahead and spread any wild stories you like. Nobody will believe you. Maybe they'll finally fire your cute little ass. Then maybe I'll let you come back here and make my coffee. You'd have to wear a shorter skirt, though.'

'Go fuck yourself, Pete.'

'I'd much rather you did. You know, you're wasted as a commercial executive, Lita. You're such a hot piece of ass.'

She trembled with so much anger her whole body shook.

'I love it when you do that,' Pete said laconically. 'It makes your tits jiggle.'

'I'm gonna get you for this. You asshole.'

'Oh, sure. I'm *reeeel* scared.' He leaned over her and opened the door. 'Good to see you again,' he said in a falsely cheerful voice. 'Thanks for dropping by.'

Lita pulled herself together, stood up and left his office. A strange calm came over her. She walked back down to her office, past the anxious-looking Janice and closed her own door. Then she spent the rest of the morning tidying her office. She had mascots, a bag of make-up, a couple of files of work-in-progress that she tore up and threw away. She cleaned her office thoroughly, the way she had cleaned her boss's office over a year ago. It was left clean, neat, almost sparkling. Then she walked out.

'Janice, take the rest of the day off.'

'Why?'

'I won't be needing you today, OK,' Lita said. Ignoring her assistant's worried look, she took the elevator downstairs and walked right in to Harry's office.

Weiss glanced up and sighed heavily.

'Look, Lita, I've made my decision. I can't help you on this one. I won't tell Bob Dawn that the campaign was your idea.'

'You won't have to. I quit.'

Harry paused, as though he hadn't heard her right. 'What?'

'I hope you will give Janice that promotion, Harry. She deserves it, she's talented. At the very least she's the best assistant in this shitty company.'

'I thought you said you were quitting.'

'I did.' Lita stared at him with eyes that burned with the white fire of her anger. Harry letting her down was the worst thing that had happened to her in her career. Worse even than losing all her money to Rupert's scam. 'Goodbye.'

She turned on her heel and walked out. She wasn't even going to shake his hand.

Chapter 24

Lita walked out of the Doheny offices on to Madison. It was a beautiful day, but she hailed a cab. There was no way she wanted to bump into even one other person entering the building. She thought she hated all of them.

Feeling impotent was worse than the actual theft. In a way, it had been a bold move of Pete's. Daring to come into her office. He must have worked pretty fast to get that collage together, copying hers, probably all through lunch. Then making a copy for Harry. But Pete was a weasel, and weasels were smart. She wasn't as mad about that as she was about Harry. Or having to just stand there and take the abuse that Pete dished out.

She would get him.

The cab driver was muttering to himself and blasting on his horn. Lita didn't care. It suited her mood perfectly. She hated the city and everything about it. She hated Pete and the sniggering secretaries and Mark and every asshole she'd ever worked with. She didn't hate Harry Weiss, but she felt betrayed by him, which was worse. Lita remembered, suddenly, that years ago she had also promised to get her revenge on Rupert and that snotty English bitch. The first humiliation came back to her, as fresh as the day it had happened, when she'd stood begging and pleading in that draughty English hall. But she had advanced her career – though not fast enough – and there hadn't been any time for thinking about revenge.

That would change now.

Lita wasn't sure exactly what her strategy would be. She had no idea. But she believed that if you looked hard enough, you could find whatever you want. It wasn't a question of trusting in the universe, but of trusting herself.

The cabbie dropped her off, and Lita ran upstairs and let herself into her spotless apartment. It felt so weird to be there in the middle of the day. Her place was clean partly because she was a neat person, but mostly because she was never there. Lita looked around at her sparkling counter-tops, the piles of cushions, the Moroccan lamps in filigree iron, the draped silks she had hung from the walls to create the feeling of a palace in a typically compact West Village apartment. She had eaten take-out for the last four days. She got a large plastic trash bag and threw out everything in her fridge that was perishable. The bills had been paid a few days ago, so that was one less thing to worry about. Lita needed a break and she needed it now.

She glanced at one of her gorgeous Moroccan lamps. She had created an exotic atmosphere to fight her stress at work. As far as possible, when she came home, she liked to be stepping into a different world.

But why not do it for real?

Lita packed her Louis Vuitton trunk full of clothes for warm weather, locked up and took a cab straight to JFK. She had all day to wait for a standby. She was going to Marrakech. Where none of the New York Doheny jerks would ever find her.

Lita's taxi from the tiny airport of Marrakech struggled and bumped along the dusty road, with her thousand-dollar suitcase precariously strapped to the top with a piece of string. She tipped the guy five American dollars, and he opened up, smiling at her with a sun-lined face and cracked teeth.

'You like hotel? Nice hotel?'

Lita felt a little nervous, but that was the trouble with being spontaneous – you had no idea where you were going.

'Yes. Thank you,' she agreed. 'Nice hotel.'

'My brother work. Nice hotel. Help cook. Small, but nice.' He sighed. 'Much dollar.' He blew out air from his cheeks as though this were an unavoidable tragedy. Lita took the hint and gave him another two dollars. She was exhausted after the flight, and even an expensive hotel was a lot better than nothing. From there, she could change some money and find out where there was something more modestly priced. She planned to stay at least a week, maybe longer, and do nothing very particular. Sunbathe, buy some more lamps, get a tan and find a swimming pool. Recharge, and wash the sticky, angry, frustrated feelings off her skin. She leaned back against the hot, sticky leather of the seats and let her eyes close.

The taxi juddered to a halt twenty minutes later, and Lita stepped out.

'Where is this?'

The driver handed her her case. 'Avenue Yacoub el-Mansour.'

'It's amazing.'

Lita glanced around her. Low-slung buildings that looked as though they had been baked right out of the mud crowded on top of each other. Men in long white robes and women wearing black cotton jellabas covered in jewellery made of long, glittering strings of coins pushed last her. There were push-bikes and donkeys drawing carts over the cobbles. There was also the sound of birds and the scent of flowers thick on the air.

Her driver gestured to a nondescript-looking wall with a faded brass plaque that read 'Hotel Fatima' above a black-painted door. He pressed on a buzzer and then jumped back in the car, roaring off.

Lita waited. She was wearing tight blue jeans and a white T-shirt, and every man was staring at her. She was beginning to feel very uncomfortable when the door opened. An older man in bagged, faded burgundy pants and a loose silk shirt bowed slightly.

'I'd like a room,' Lita said.

'Certainly, *madame*.' Like the driver, his English was tinged with a French accent. 'Come this way.'

She stepped into the courtyard, and he closed the door firmly behind her.

It was like stepping into an oasis. Lita gasped. The crowded, cramped bustle of the street had disappeared entirely. Behind the unimpressive doors lay a courtyard laid out in a formal Islamic style. There were four small fountains laid around a rectangular central pool, the paths, walls and fountains decorated with some of the most intricate mosaics that Lita had ever seen. The check-in desk, if that was what it was, was a small mahogany table under a fluted archway, where another man in white had a small book open. The older man had disappeared with her case, and Lita walked up to the desk.

'*Madame* wishes a room?'

Lita nodded.

'For how long?'

'A week.' She wanted to ask the price, but the place was so quiet and civilized that it felt unseemly to bring up money.

'Two hundred dollars a week, American.'

That's it? Lita wondered. Oh, well, maybe the rooms would prove to be a real flea-pit. But beggars couldn't be choosers. She pulled out a couple of C-notes and laid them down on a desk. The receptionist solemnly produced two small silver keys.

'This is for your room. Twenty-four, on the second floor. You will see it at the top of the stairs. This other one is for the front door, at night. Welcome to the hotel, *madame*.'

'My case,' Lita asked.

He made a sweeping gesture. 'All is taken care of. Please, do not have the concerns.'

'OK,' Lita said uncertainly. She took the silver keys and stepped back across the lush courtyard, ducking under orange trees and small palms, and walked up some stairs carved out of white stone. The second-floor corridor was full of more of the endless mosaic arches . . . The repeating pattern somehow very soothing. Lita found her door, curved and carved of gnarled wood. She tried the key – it worked perfectly.

The room was incredible. It showed her just how far off she'd been in her guesstimation of what a real North African room would look like. She decided that her pad back home was actually the height of tack.

There was a bed with carved posts and cool-looking white sheets. It looked deliciously inviting. The walls were plain white and looked very old, rather like a monk's cell. There were low stools and a closet and a chest of drawers, all carved from the same dark wood, and tasselled cushions to sit on. She had a small balcony with a view over the courtyard, and a glimpse of something green and lush beyond the hotel's outer wall. A private bathroom with marble in the tub and by the ornate sink had two tiny lamps in filigree silver, complete with candles, and two arrows in brass on the wall, with 'Mecca' written under them. So that she would know which way to pray, Lita realized. Obviously the hotel catered to rich Moroccans as well as Western tourists. She felt elation mix with her exhaustion. Her clothes had been unpacked and were hung neatly in the closet; her cases were laid at the foot of the bed. She peeled herself out of her sticky travelling clothes and headed for the shower. She washed her hair and combed it through, then clambered under the cool sheets and fell into a blissful sleep.

When Lita woke, she felt disorientated. It took her a few seconds to figure out where she was. Groggily, she got out of bed and padded over to the window. It was already dark outside. The courtyard below was lit with candles in the Moroccan filigree lamps, sending glorious, ornate shadows flickering across the trees and the pool. She looked up at the desert sky. The stars glittered, fiercely bright without any neon lights to block them out. The sky was almost savage in its clarity. She opened her latch to let the night air in. It was wonderfully cool, but not too cold. The mists of sleep evaporated; she was suddenly energized. Marrakech felt magic to Lita, as though she could start completely afresh here.

She ran to her closet and selected her uncrushable white rayon dress. It had three light layers, swept to the ground and had long sleeves. Admittedly it had a V-shaped neckline, but it was one of the most modest items she had with her. Lita picked out an orange chiffon scarf with gold embroidery and looped it around her neck to cover her glorious breasts, but she drew the line at covering her hair. That wasn't her style. She chose a pair of dangling earrings, citrines set in silver, and a pair of stacked sandals, and she was ready to go. She locked up her room, walked downstairs and changed some money.

'If you wish, *madame*, the hotel can provide a guide.'

'I think I'll just walk,' Lita said.

The receptionist looked disapproving, but offered her a small map. 'This is the city. The hotel is here,' he jabbed his finger, 'and Place Djemaa el-Fna is here.'

'Then that's where I'll go,' Lita said. 'Thank you.'

She left before he could press the hired help upon her. Outside the hotel, it was bedlam, much as it had been before. She slung her purse across her chest. The city must be crawling with pickpockets. Lita walked fast. It was a New York survival reflex. If you strode purposefully enough, you looked like you knew where you were going and people didn't mess with you. She had a good sense of direction and, besides, everyone seemed to be heading towards the square. The narrow streets were packed. She passed a man selling tiny tortoises, and chameleons that sat chained to a stick, their round eyes staring out at her. Wretched hens, about to be eaten, bloody where they had torn out their own feathers in misery, were stacked six deep in tiny cages. Wagons driven by donkeys clattered past her once in a while. Lita shivered. Obviously animal rights had not hit North Africa yet.

She found Djemaa el-Fna in just a few minutes. It was hard to miss. The narrow street with its hanging carpets and lamp shops twisted sharply to the right, and Lita stopped dead.

It had terminated in a vast, open square, glittering with the combined light of thousands of oil lamps and raw light bulbs strung between hundreds of stalls, an exotic market square with more to sell than waxed apples and tired string beans. There was an actual snake charmer, and to the side a belly dancer covered from head to toe in a light, Islamic costume. The scent that hit her was incredible – perfumes mixed with the aroma of roasting meat and nuts and what seemed like thousands of spices. It made her mouth water. Lita realized, suddenly, that she was starving. The square was surrounded by restaurants, many with terraces. She walked to the left and selected one that had a sign in English under the Arabic. A woman veiled in black from head to toe silently handed her a menu. Lita pointed upstairs.

'*La haut?*' asked the woman.

Lita started to shake her head, then realized she was speaking French. Of course. It had been a French colony. Lita's French was lousy, but she knew a couple of words. '*Oui, merci,*' she said. The woman nodded, and led her up a narrow, steep, curving flight of stairs in red brick with mosaic inlay. The terrace overlooked the square, the sparkling, fragrant bustle of it. Lita couldn't stop smiling. She pointed to a small table for two that was right at the edge of the terrace and the woman left her there with the menu.

Lita glanced at the place. It was spartan, but even the most spartan place here was covered in ornate, beautiful Islamic art. Miniature orange trees in terracotta pots, ripe with fruit, were dotted around everywhere. The place was packed, mostly with Moroccans in rich-looking robes. That was a good sign, like with the hotel. Lita hadn't travelled much, but it stood to reason that the best places would be frequented by the locals.

She started to study the menu and blinked. *Bastilla* . . . Flaked pigeon pie with salt, almonds and cinnamon. *Briouat* . . . Meat and spices in a square pie. Hmm . . .

'*Excusez-moi, madame.*' The woman was there again, bowing, with a small silver tray. There was a little glass with frosted blue paint and some kind of fragrant hot drink on it. Lita searched, but her lessons had fled her.

'Uh . . . I didn't order this.'

The woman looked blank.

'It's OK. It's complimentary.'

Lita looked up. There was a man sitting alone at the next table, an American. He looked about thirty-eight, he had salt and pepper hair and thick, dark lashes around dark eyes. Under the light summer suit he was wearing, she thought she saw muscles.

'Oh. Er, *merci*,' she said. The woman left the glass on her wrought-iron table and glided away.

'It's mint tea. They don't drink alcohol here, so this is the beverage of choice. Very traditional.'

'Thank you,' Lita said.

'My pleasure.' He turned back to his menu.

Lita sipped the drink. It was steaming, and very sweet, and nothing like the herbal mint teas back home. It was delicious. Strange, but delicious. Surreptitiously, she glanced across at the older man. His hands had no rings on them. Quite apart from his looks, he hadn't pressed his advantage with a corny line, and he seemed to know a lot about the place. She cleared her throat.

'Excuse me.'

He looked up at her. He had chocolate brown eyes that seemed to look right through her.

'I wonder if you'd like to eat dinner with me,' Lita said. Then she blushed. Was that too forward?

He hesitated for a split second, then smiled lightly. 'Thank you. That would be lovely.' He pushed back his chair, and came over to her table. He was tall, she noticed. Probably six feet. When she stood up, he'd tower over her. He offered her a large hand; he had a strong grip.

'I'm Edward Kahn.'

'Lita Morales.'

'Are you here on business?'

'Business?' Lita's brows lifted. 'Why would anybody be in Marrakech on business?'

'I couldn't imagine why else a woman . . .' he seemed to be looking for words '. . . uh, like you, would be eating by herself.'

Lita shook her head. She suddenly wished she'd put on make-up. 'No, I'm here on vacation.'

By yourself? That's very independent.'

She smiled, and her golden skin lit up. Damn, he thought, what a beauty. He had to steady an impulse to lick his lips.

'So are you here on business?'

'Actually, yes. I make a trip twice a year for buying.'

'And what do you buy?' Lita asked. The robed waitress appeared and hovered by their table. Lita glanced down at her menu.

'Have you tried Moroccan food before?'

'This is my first night.'

'We'll try the *bastilla*, the *kefta* and the *touajen de poisson*,' he said, nodding at the menu. He looked over at her. 'You'll just have to trust me.'

'Some people would say that's very sexist,' Lita said.

His dark eyes stared back at her. 'Would they?'

For the first time in months, she felt a tightening between her legs. She shifted on her seat and tried to distract herself. Romance was just bad news. Wasn't it?

'I import carpets, among other things. I run a design firm in New York.'

He lived in New York, Lita thought elatedly. 'That's interesting. What firm are you with?'

'Olympia,' he said.

'I've heard of them. They're the hottest interior design firm in America. Didn't they just get the contract to redo Gracie Mansion?'

He nodded.

'And they supervised the last redecoration of the White House. Even Sister Parish is jealous of Olympia.'

'You're very knowledgeable.'

'I'm with an advertising firm. Correction. I was. We're supposed to keep current on trends in pretty much everything. Besides, I read *Vogue*. Olympia is featured in there all the time.'

He inclined his head slightly. 'What firm were you with?'

'Doheny.'

'They're a very good outfit.'

'They're less good now,' Lita stated flatly.

He grinned. He liked her spark. 'You got fired?'

'I walked out. It's a long and boring story.'

The waitress came back, bringing a plate of Moroccan salad – minted leaves, tomatoes, diced spiced potatoes – and two glasses of iced water.

'This is so good,' Lita said, amazed.

'I think Moroccan is some of the best food in the world. Once you get past eating pigeon. So what did you do for them?'

'I was a senior creative executive. I worked on campaigns for print and TV. Some radio work. What about you?'

'I own the company,' he said.

'Oh.' Lita blushed again. Thankfully there were only the flickering shadows from the filigree lamps to show her complexion.

'How long ago did you walk out?'

'Yesterday.' Lita forked some mint and potatoes into her mouth as their waitress set down small square pastries. 'I went home, went to my apartment, packed a case and drove to the airport. I got here on the red-eye.'

He chuckled. 'You're adventurous.'

'I was mad,' Lita said. 'And I have a Moroccan lamp in my apartment.'

'Makes perfect sense.' He looked her over assessingly. Lita had a sense that her white dress was being peeled from her skin. She tugged her scarf lower. Her nipples were tightening, and it wasn't cool enough out here to blame it on something other than him. Of course he was too old, too established for her. 'And what did your boyfriend say about this unilateral trip?'

'I don't have a boyfriend,' Lita said, a little defensively, 'I was too busy.'

'Good,' he said, straight out.

Lita's blush deepened. 'Are you asking me out?'

'We are out,' he said. 'Try some of the bastilla. It's delicious.'

She obeyed him. It was.

'I'm here for three more days. Maybe we could explore the souks together. Then you can tell me the long and boring story.'

Lita hesitated. 'I don't know . . . I have a lot of plans.'

'No, you don't,' he said easily.

'OK.' She smiled, she couldn't help it. He wouldn't let her pretend to be coy.

He picked her up at the Fatima the next morning and nodded approvingly. 'You have great taste in hotels.'

'Thank you.' She bit her lip to stop herself from confessing she'd had nothing to do with it. She really wanted to impress this guy.

'I'm at the Palmeraie Golf Palace, just outside town. It's huge and modern. This is much nicer.' His eye swept her room.

'Getting ideas?'

He didn't smile. 'Of course. I'm always working.'

'I thought your company was huge,' Lita ventured.

'It is.'

'So don't you have vice-presidents to do this sort of thing?'

'The really important trips I don't delegate. This trip will lay up a stock of carpets for a year. For the small clients, the bread-and-butter clients, rich Wall Street wives and publishing moguls, we will be working the Near East look this year. And even an English country feel benefits from a Moroccan or a Persian carpet thrown in somewhere.' He looked around slightly impatiently. 'Are you ready?'

'Ready.'

'Let me see.' He stepped back and analysed her. Lita had chosen her most seductive dress, a silk wraparound number in pale blue that stopped above the knee and hugged her breasts. 'You can't wear that.'

'Excuse me?' she said combatively.

'I said you can't wear that. Let me see.' Ignoring her look of outrage, he went straight to her closet and riffled through her stuff. 'Try . . . this and this.' He handed her two hangers, one with her double-layered dark blue chiffon pants, the other with a loose, long-sleeved shirt in gold silk. 'A pity it's not high-necked, but you can wear the scarf over your hair and neck like this.' He took a white lace scarf of hers and looped it over her hair and neckline.

'I don't want to wear that,' Lita said mulishly.

'Display that much flesh, and the men here will think you're a hooker,' he said flatly, pointing to her dress. 'Save that for dinner. And if you don't mind, don't talk too much during this little trip. They will understand you are Western, but if you don't keep quiet, I will look like a man who cannot control his female.'

'And what if I do mind?'

He smiled. 'Then I will leave you to your own devices today. Business is business. I'm sure you understand that.'

'I guess so,' Lita said.

'Don't worry.' Edward looked totally confident. 'You'll love it.'

And she did. He led her though the winding, crowded, twisted streets of the city, packed into tiny districts each crammed with shops selling different goods: the leather-workers' souk, the jewellery souk, the fragrant spices souk where she stopped to buy a pound of pure saffron; the copper souk and the pottery souks, with bowls and dishes all covered with the intricate patterns of Islam, and the scents of nutmeg and juniper and cinnamon everywhere in the air; and finally to the carpet souk, where rugs and carpets, intricately worked, exquisitely beautiful, the blue of the Ait Ouaouzguite, the tribe that wove them, the reds of the Berber, the multicoloured Rabat and hundreds of other types, hung everywhere. Lita followed behind Edward, was offered countless thimbleful glasses of mint tea, shown carpets by women and generally ignored while he negotiated with the carpet-sellers in fast, guttural French. At each place they signed export papers. Edward bought hundreds of carpets, jabbing his large fingers, deciding lightning-fast from the vast selections in each establishment. By the time they broke for lunch, heading back through the chameleon-sellers to Djemaa el-Fna, she was exhausted.

'Follow me.'

'I'm always following you. Why can't I pick a restaurant?' Lita said.

Edward grinned. 'If you know a good one, be my guest.'

Lita shrugged. She wanted to stamp her foot, but he was right. How did she know she wasn't going to get food poisoning? Did he have to be so goddamn . . . dominant, though?

Edward led her to a nondescript wall in the corner of the square and rapped on a tiny door. This was a pattern in Marrakech – a door opening from some dusty street or square into a quiet oasis. This one led into a courtyard with tables placed under the shade of various fruit trees. Lita noted tangerine and pomegranate.

'This place is my usual restaurant in town.' A waiter materialized, and Edward ordered in French for them. Lita had to trust him – she had no idea what was in anything, and yesterday's dinner had been delicious. Another boy came over and bowed, bringing Edward several papers.

'That's the *Wall Street Journal*,' Lita said, astonished.

'Yes. I get them delivered here. A day late, but it'll have to do. I like to check on the news and stocks. Keep current. A glass of chilled lemonade here seems a good way to do it.'

'Why not read them at your hotel?'

'I keep my evenings free from work. They are devoted entirely to pleasure.'

Lita shivered at the way he said 'pleasure'. He was looking at her again as though he wanted to strip the chiffon from her skin.

'I also have *The Times* from London and the *New York Times.*' He passed them casually over.

A robed woman brought them still, iced lemonades, and Lita idly looked at the English paper. There was nothing in it to interest her . . . more news of electricity blackouts and industrial stoppages. Some kind of IMF loan was being talked about. Amazing how the papers could report so calmly while the country was falling apart at the financial seams. She turned to the business section. It would be interesting to look at some European print ads and compare them. Lita flicked through it idly, then, suddenly, stopped dead.

'Lancaster Scrapes Back Into the Black,' read the headline. And underneath it, there was a picture of Becky.

Chapter 25

She regarded herself critically in the mirror.

Becky needed to make a good impression yet, whatever she did, she couldn't avoid looking like a young woman. Despite the stress of the last two years, she was still in her mid-twenties, and it showed. She wore her long, golden hair up in an elegant French chignon, she kept her make-up light and professional and she wore flats so she wouldn't be too intimidating to the bankers, but that was OK – she was so slim that not even flats could make her legs look dumpy. Her suit was solid navy with a cream shirt; her briefcase and shoes matched it. She had chosen matt Wolford hose, which were comfortable and wouldn't draw too much attention to her. But, despite the crushing worry she had battled as hard as she could every working day for the past twenty-four months, and some of the weekends, too, her skin was still unlined, her eyes were still bright and she was still just a pretty young girl.

And that was a problem.

No matter what she did with Lancaster, no matter how deep or how drastic the cuts she had made, no matter what concessions she had been able to pull from the unions, in endless, mind-numbing negotiations, men still resented women in the workplace. Especially rich, attractive, young ones.

Becky had fought it. With Ken Stone as her hardcore CFO, she had made dramatic changes, and she had made sure that she and she alone got the credit for them. Undoing the perception of her that she had found Rupert had fostered – namely, that she was an airhead heiress with no business skills – had taken a lot of time. Moving the company to Yorkshire had been a dramatic move; slashing the over-staffed personnel roster had been another one. The long, boozy lunches in smoky City of London wine bars had been trimmed from the expense accounts of the men that had stayed, and when perks like company cars were suddenly tied to performance, there was a fresh round of resignations. Becky was glad. It saved Ken and her from having to fire more executives, which, despite them being bad at their jobs, overpaid and underworked, was still the part of her business she liked the least. The regime was draconian, and the banking community responded. They had been able to obtain desperately needed financing. Productivity crept up, and costs dropped sharply. For the first time in more than eight years, according to Stone, Lancaster was able to show a modest profit.

The only trouble was that 'modest' wasn't going to cut it.

In her heart, Becky knew that she could turn the shipyards around, given enough time. She could shift production away from the large, oil-guzzling industrial ships that the world was starting not to want and towards luxury goods, like speedboats and cruisers. She could sell off the tin mines, and use the profit from that for the shift. But to get there, she had to have time to find buyers and set up an entirely new distribution arm.

And to do that, she needed money. Her modest operating profit wasn't anything like enough. The interest from back debts was crippling. Unless they had more money to pay it off, they would have to sell or fold. And this was her father's company. Becky would never sell it.

There was only one acceptable result for her. Getting another refinancing loan, getting the money she needed, and finding a buyer for the tin mines. She thought that with another five years, the new, streamlined, luxury-goods Lancaster could start to once again build its way to dominance. Maybe add some more hotels. Her time in that tiny Oxford room had not been altogether wasted. Becky's hotel was now a gem, admittedly a small gem, but a gem nevertheless. It was making a nice profit, and bookings were up substantially. But getting a hotel business was for the future.

Today was about impressing these suits. Today was about survival.

The phone by her bedside jangled with that double ring the Brits used. She would never get used to it. Becky picked it up.

'If you're ready, Miss Lancaster, we're in the lobby.'

'Yes, thanks, Ken. I'll be right down.'

Becky hung up. She had dark circles under her eyes, but that couldn't be helped. She had worried about this meeting until late into the night and, anyway, the traffic noise had kept her up all night. Ken wouldn't let them check into an expensive hotel. This one was in Lancaster Gate, and it had depressing faded wallpaper and no air conditioning. But they had to lead by example. Becky didn't want to sack thousands of working men and then stay at the Ritz. It would have been better if the bankers had come to Yorkshire, but Becky was the one with the cap in her hand. She travelled to meet them.

She picked up her briefcase and headed downstairs.

The head offices of the Limburgh Bank were located in the City. They had their own brand-new concrete monstrosity, complete with hideous pebble-dash 'textured' walls next to the dark glass revolving doors. Their lobby was full of pot-plants and trees in earthenware tubs with pebbles around the base. It reeked of money and impersonality. Becky composed herself and mentally retuned her pitch. These men wouldn't care in the slightest about Lancaster's history, about the ships it had turned out at breakneck speed for two world wars. None of that would matter.

Harold Boise, her director of mining, walked forward and announced their party to the receptionist. Becky had learned to let the men she employed do all the small errands. If she did it, she looked like a secretary or an intern. And that was still how most men liked to think of her.

Boise walked back. 'They're ready for us. Twelfth floor.'

The Industrial Loans Division was just as bad as the lobby. Aspidistras everywhere and ficus trees with waxy leaves. The men wore grey pinstripes, and Becky saw one lonely woman in a boxy green suit with a little shoelace tie at the neck of her shirt. Probably the office manager, she thought to herself rather bitterly. All the other skirts in here were parked behind cubicles, typing. She made a note to call her own personnel manager when they got back up to Yorkshire. Next time Lancaster did any hiring, she would send someone to the universities and pitch the jobs to women. If they ever got to actually hire anyone again.

'Miss Lancaster?' A lanky man in his fifties, with Coke-bottle glasses and neatly combed white hair stepped forward. 'I'm Matthew Ripon, Vice-President of Finance.'

'You know Kenneth Stone, I believe, and these are Harold Boise, who runs our mining division, and Miles Clark, head of shipping.'

He shook hands limply with all of them. 'Follow me, please.'

The soulless meeting room had been furnished with every modern convenience. There was an urn of coffee, a yellow legal pad and pen next to each place setting, a projector and a plate of biscuits. Becky refused everything. She was introduced to a parade of bankers, and promptly forgot their names as soon as they were announced. But the important ones she wasn't likely to forget. They sat at the head of the table, ranged opposite the Lancaster executives like politicians negotiating a peace accord, and stared intently at the figures Miles Clark was projecting on to the screen at the end of the room.

Sir Quentin Hope, the chairman of the bank. His presence in this meeting indicated how important it was. Matthew Ripon, whose City nickname was 'Scrooge'. He thought Britain was heading into industrial disaster, and he had a terrible reputation for pulling the bank's money out of any loan that looked even remotely shaky. And here was Becky asking him for more. Great. And finally there was Desmond Ferris, their best hope. He had been at Eton with her father and now headed the industrial investing team. She had smiled at him, hoping for a sympathetic glance, but so far nothing. There wouldn't be any free rides here. She had to hope she could pull it out with just her numbers.

'Yes, thank you.' Ripon spoke up as Clark sat down. 'Those projected sales are very interesting, but they are only projections. How can the bank be sure that you could complete your transformation on time?'

'We will have excellent motivation. Your loan will enable us to find the time to sell the mining division,' Harold Boise said.

'That is all very well, but—'

'But you prefer more concrete figures.' Becky spoke up, and her throat felt dry. Every man in the room swivelled to stare at her. 'Let me see if I can help you there. Limburgh Bank will have our recent past record to go on. Mr Clark has prepared for the bank a summary of our cost savings over the past year, our return to profitability and our productivity increases. This dramatic programme will continue at the same rate.'

'Indeed.' Sir Quentin's voice, silent during their whole long presentation, finally rolled out in a deep bass. 'But, Miss Lancaster, your operating profit is small.'

'Yes, Sir Quentin, but compared to our large operating loss before Mr Stone and I took control, it is not a small achievement. If we improve at the same rate, we will make dramatic profits for ourselves and this bank in less than five years.'

'You are proposing to dismantle one of Britain's oldest companies, Miss Lancaster,' Desmond Ferris said disapprovingly. 'I wonder whether your father would have approved.'

Becky shivered. It was working against her. She looked the old buffer right in the eyes.

'I think he would. I think he would have wanted me to save the company. In its hey-day, Lancaster was progressive. I want it to stay that way. And besides . . .' she turned to Sir Quentin and smiled warmly at him . . . 'my father was a gentleman, and gentlemen always pay their debts. Selling the tin mines to a company that can better use them will enable us to do that. Turning the shipping company into a more modern operation will then enable us to become truly profitable.'

'How long do you think you will need the loan for?'

'A year, no longer, Sir Quentin.'

The older man seemed deep in thought. Finally he nodded and stood up. 'Very well, then. One year, to the day.'

'But, Sir Quentin, the bank's exposure—' Ripon hissed.

'One year. And the interest rate will be a full point above prime.'

Becky felt Ken Stone stiffen beside her. She gently kicked him in the shins. This was no time to argue. They were in no position to. She jumped to her feet.

'Thank you, Sir Quentin,' she said.

'Don't thank me, Miss Lancaster. Make the bank some money.'

Becky sent her executives back to Yorkshire without her. Ken Stone knew what to do, and Harold had put together an attractive analyst's report which would let them sell the mines. She hoped. She had made it easy for him to be motivated by tying a quarter-million-pound bonus for him into a successful sale at the right price. But whatever – she had to sit back now and let them do their thing.

The relief was so overwhelming that Becky felt wiped out by it. It was probably something like a marathon runner or a Boat Race oarsman, she thought as she jumped into a taxi for Paddington station. Your body put off all the exhaustion and aches until you were done with the crisis, and afterwards you wanted to sleep for a week.

Well, she didn't have a week, but she might have a weekend. She wanted, desperately, to get back to Fairfield, to be away from her phone and her secretary's buzzer and company reports and tours of the dockyards. She wanted not to see any union shop stewards, not to have to spend more hours with Ken rejigging their figures after the latest electricity shortage. It was May, and it was sunny for once. She thought she might go out into Fairfield and check the gardens out. Maybe take a long bubble bath with some Floris bath essence. And after that, sleep.

She couldn't even be bothered to go back to the shitty hotel and pick up her case. Miles Clark could do that for her. It was one of the small perks of being the boss. One day, she might even stop feeling apologetic about giving orders.

'You can't be serious.'

Lita looked at her lover through that thick fringe of her dark hair he loved so much. Maybe because he could control her with it. He liked to wrap its silky strands round the rough, thick skin of his fists so that he could move her head like a horse is moved by its reins. Lita would wriggle underneath him on his silk sheets, and her glorious, dark-nippled tits would bounce as she squirmed, making him harder and hotter. Edward Kahn couldn't believe how this woman made him feel.

Sensations and lusts he had buried in business since the death of his wife more than twelve years ago. She was achingly young, but her determination matched that of any fifty-year-old senator he had ever met. He was addicted to her.

'Why do you always say that to me?' Lita fired back.

Edward drove her mad. He was ruthless and demanding and smart and infuriating. When she came over to the Olympia offices, most of the time he wouldn't even see her. And he didn't apologize for it. He expected her to make appointments, to run around him. Another man she would have dumped. But that wasn't an option with Edward.

He had helped her start New Wave advertising agency. Provided her with her first four clients and funding.

'But I want to do it on my own,' Lita had said mulishly.

Edward had looked at her as if she were mad. 'Oh, OK. I thought you wanted to succeed. Advertising is about contacts. But if you don't want help, feel free to fail as independently as you like.'

She had bitten her cheeks with fury, but she knew he was right. Doheny never turned down a client that came on the recommendation of somebody's friend. Or boyfriend.

Her first campaigns were for high-powered clients. Lita worked her magic, and increased sales and market share. She got more commissions after that. Her first act with her new money was to pay Edward's loan back. Her second was to hire Harry Weiss to run her office.

'I believed you, you know, Lita,' Harry told her flatly.

'I know. You couldn't have done anything else.' And as she talked to him, she realized she did know it. Edward had pointed this out to her, and he had been right.

'I'm glad you saw the light. What changed your mind?'

She didn't want to admit it had been Edward. 'I just knew, Harry.'

Hiring Weiss made all the difference. He creamed off the best, most undervalued executives at Doheny. It gave her particular pleasure to hire Janice. But from the second she had founded the firm, Lita had only been marking time. She had known she was going to do this. And she was prepared to battle Edward over it.

He wanted to marry her. She knew it. He had already talked about it, and two months ago she had found the ring, in a coat pocket, one morning when he left at six to go to his office and she'd had a headache. Lita had tugged on the tiny silk robe he liked her to wear around the house, she thought because it barely skimmed the cheeks of her ass, and started to check out his pad. She had an insatiable curiosity to know everything about him. The thick chest and muscled arms and big, hard thighs were just the start. His dark eyes that swept over her, that felt like they could strip her nude when she was fully dressed, didn't tell her anything like enough. She wanted to understand what drove him to such perfectionism, why he was trying to teach himself Latin, why, whenever he wasn't at Olympia, he was out socializing and networking. He only seemed to stop for her.

It was intense to be pursued so relentlessly. Edward would walk through the door and grab her without breaking his stride, shoving her down on to the rush matting and pulling her clothes from her breasts, shoving up her skirt, plunging into her as though he'd had a raging hard-on all day and couldn't wait even one second. He took her against the fridge, thrust her over her desk in the office when he came to pick her up late. He talked to her while he fucked her, low, breathy words that made her see herself the way he saw her, that turned her on so that she was slippery wet and impatient for him. Edward cupped her ass lightly while he talked about it, firm and flaring out, round, and jutting at him. He said he thought about her ass all day. He put his mouth above her nipples but didn't kiss them, didn't even flick his tongue over them, just stared at them, his breath hot over them, until Lita was moaning and writhing underneath him, begging for his touch, for him to take her.

But after all that, he hadn't proposed. She was still waiting. And now she was about to challenge him.

Lita had the English papers delivered to her office in midtown every day. She had looked for stories on Rupert Lancaster, but he had disappeared. These days it was the snotty girl, Becky, who was getting all the press.

And Becky was in trouble. Lita knew everything about Lancaster Holdings. She had even obtained a copy of the annual report, flown over to her from Companies House in England. For a few sweet months, as New Wave got off the ground, Lita had thought Becky might be bankrupted. But no. She had gotten herself a meeting with her???U pg278 bankers. She might be able to pull the whole thing out.

Lita was not going to allow that to happen.

'But, darling, I am serious,' she said. She looked Edward right in the eyes. 'I'm going to have to go to England.'

Chapter 26

Fairfield was quiet. So quiet that Becky had to unlock her front door with the old, huge, iron key they kept under the statue of the hind on two legs that guarded the entrance to the kitchen garden. Of course – the first Friday of every month, Mrs Morecambe took off. She'd be on her own today. She sighed with pleasure. It was exactly what she wanted.

Inside the fridge there were a few essentials that Mrs Morecambe kept there in case Becky ever came home. Slices of smoked salmon, whole lemons, brown bread and a half-bottle of Moët. There was also an entire, sinfully moist and rich-looking chocolate cake. Becky's mouth started to water. It was three p.m. already and she hadn't touched any of the nasty British Rail food on the grimy train. She buttered a couple of slices of brown bread and heaped the salmon on them; it was wild, of course, none of that farmed rubbish at Fairfield. Despite the early hour, she also cracked the champagne. Sod it, Becky thought. She was going to enjoy herself today. She finished the salmon and deliberately cut herself a slice of cake. That was good, too. She ought to indulge herself more often.

Once she'd eaten she kicked off her shoes and slipped into the pair of green wellies they kept by the back door. She couldn't be bothered to change. She tugged on the quilted Husky that Mrs Morecambe insisted she wear outdoors, and poured the rest of the champagne into a chipped china mug. The sun was blazing over the garden, and she drank in the glorious scent of new-mown grass and flowers, lots of flowers. Lavender and roses and God knew what else. She opened the door and walked out on to the back terrace and breathed in deeply, loving the country air, getting the gritty taste of London out of her mouth. The garden was in full bloom. It looked different, though. Gorgeous, but a little different. What was it?

Becky's eyes focused on the walk at the base of the terrace, where her garden bordered the apple orchard. There was a yew hedge there.

She blinked. Was she going mad? There hadn't been a hedge there before. It was clipped and dark and thick and very beautiful, but it was also new. Wasn't it?

She held herself still and heard, as though it were a confirmation, the sound of clippers. Snip, snip, snip. Hand-held clippers. Becky took a great swig of chill champagne from her mug and wondered briefly whether or not she should call the police. But tell them what – that she had a mad hedge-installer in her garden? Maybe not. She walked down the steps.

'Hello?' she called, loudly. Keeping her distance just in case.

'Hello,' a voice replied. It was male and English and had what Becky now knew was a Yorkshire accent. But no head appeared. The snipping noise continued. She started to get a little aggravated. She walked down on to the lawn, right up to the hedge. Behind it there was a man, a tall, rugged-looking man, she thought in his mid-thirties, holding a huge pair of clippers and slicing at the leaves of the hedge with great concentration. He didn't so much as look at her. Becky angrily cleared her throat.

'I'm Rebecca Lancaster. I own the place.'

'That's nice,' he said mildly, continuing to snip.

'Who are you? And what are you doing? And what is this hedge doing on my lawn?'

He sighed with an aggravation almost equal to her own and lowered the clippers. 'I'm Will Logan. Your gardener. You hired me.'

Becky racked her brains. Oh, hell, this guy was the gardener she'd hired back when she was dating Rupert. She'd wanted to impress him with how well she was looking after Fairfield, and Sharon said this man was making a good name for himself locally.

'Yes. But . . . that was a year ago.'

'I was busy,' he said unapologetically. 'My last job took longer than I thought. If you don't want me now, that's fine. Just say the word.' He suspended the heavy clippers lightly from his hand, looking at her steadily.

'Why did you put this hedge in?' Becky asked curiously.

He shrugged. 'The first fifteen rows of your apple trees have to come down. They got blight. They'll be affecting the rest of the orchard.'

Becky looked down towards her orchard in dismay. 'But . . . that'll look so bare.'

'The alternative is an orchard full of dead trees.'

'Oh, no,' she said, genuinely upset.

The man regarded her for a few seconds, and seemed to soften a little. 'You like this garden?'

'Like it? It's glorious. I wanted to protect it.'

He gestured to the yew hedge. 'I have several more to come. I'm going to plant a small maze here. Seems right for the old house. Then there'll be a paved path leading into the rest of the orchard behind it. And you'll get all the old trees chopped up for firewood in your log-shed. All right? And it's going to be expensive. Your boyfriend told us money was no problem.'

'It isn't. And he's not my boyfriend,' Becky said defensively.

'I see.' He grinned at her. Becky got the uncomfortable feeling he found her amusing. A small trickle of sweat ran off his neck down into the thick muscles of his collarbone. It didn't seem to bother him. He was well built, but his hard muscles looked natural, not the narcissistic hairless look of the jocks she'd left behind in the States. He obviously got them from lifting trees and stones all day long. She couldn't help glancing at his hands. They were powerful, with the skin thick and roughened from the elements. His eyes were light green, incongruous with his dark hair, and he had thick, dark eyelashes. 'So, you're in charge, Miss Lancaster.'

'That's right,' Becky said defensively. 'I own Fairfield and I run Lancaster Holdings.'

'I plant gardens,' he said solemnly. She coloured – he was teasing her. He hadn't asked for her CV.

He set the hedge clippers to one side on the grass and wiped his hands down on his pants. She thought he was going to shake hands with her. Instead, he put his hands on his hips and looked her over in a way that made her drop her eyes. Shouldn't this guy be at least a bit deferential? she thought, aggravated. She was the boss. He worked for her.

'Just so there are no misunderstandings, let me explain what I do. As I told your ex-boyfriend before.'

'I think that would be a good idea,' she said as stiffly as she could manage.

'I make gardens. I don't mow lawns and pull up weeds. I already hired a teenager to come here once a week and do that for you. It will go on your bill. I plan the way the space looks, and I don't take advice. If the client doesn't like my plan, that's the end of the job. Gardens are too important for clients to mess up.'

God, he's arrogant. I should tell him to get lost, she thought. But she said, 'So what is your plan for my garden?'

He looked around. 'It doesn't need much. The maze will cover the dead trees. And then I'm putting a formal rose garden with planned walks over there.' He pointed to the croquet lawn on the west side of the kitchen garden.

'But we play croquet there.'

'No, you don't.' His green eyes stared hers down. 'I checked the hoops. They're at an angle and they're almost rusted through. Your croquet equipment is in the garden shed. One of the sticks has cobwebs all over it.'

'What if I don't want roses there?'

'Then you pay my expenses and we part company. I've only been on this job two days, so I won't have wasted much time.'

She felt like stamping her foot. 'You're very arrogant.'

'So I'm told,' he said calmly.

There was a pause.

'Why a rose garden?' she asked, despite herself.

'This house is Elizabethan. It should have a garden that suits it. You need more colour in that spot. And besides, there was once a formal garden there. I can see the traces of walks and beds under that boring manicured lawn you have there now. It was probably a rose garden. I see this as a restoration.'

She was impressed.

'I know gardens,' he said simply. 'Now, Miss Lancaster, are we working for you, or not? Because I have a waiting list months long.'

Becky wanted that garden. She loved the idea of putting Fairfield back the way it was. She swallowed her pride.

'You're working for me, Mr Logan.' She smiled and waited for him to ask her to call him Will.

'Good. And the fee for the lawnmower boy is extra,' he said, and picked up the hedge clippers again.

Becky had been dismissed. She turned on her heel and walked back to the house so he wouldn't see her colour again.

So much for her relaxing weekend.

She went upstairs and ran herself a warm bath, turning on the taps viciously. She emptied half a bottle of Floris gardenia into the hot water, but not even soaping her long limbs, shaving and rubbing half a bottle of lotion all over her skin stopped her feeling annoyed. Maybe she had buckled. Maybe she should get dressed, go back downstairs and tell him to get off her property.

She took her white silk robe off the hanger and walked to her lead-paned windows that looked out over her grounds. He was still there, working. Now he was next to the hedge, digging a trench along a stretch of ground. Presumably for the next hedge. He had his shirt off, and he was working in the blazing sun. The thick muscles of his back rippled; he was tanned, a golden brown, strong, well proportioned. He turned, and she saw that his chest had a wiry mat of brown hair. He was gorgeous. And she had a feeling he knew it, too. There was an easy confidence in that thick Yorkshire burr that said that girls had been flinging themselves at him for quite some time.

What are you thinking? she chided herself. He's ten years older than you, easy. And he's just a gardener. You're running a company. You couldn't have anything in common. He was what Sharon would call a 'bit of rough'. Not that she had time for them in her life.

He could cut her off, Becky reminded herself, but she was the one with hundreds of people reporting to her. She was the one saving her father's company. She was the one that had just pulled a refinancing deal out of the fire in London. So what if he knew about rose gardens? He worked for her. Bottom line.

She dried her long blonde hair and let it hang loose. Then she went to her wardrobe and chose her tight-fitting blue jeans and her crisp white shirt with the three-quarter-length sleeves. She buttoned it up tightly and took off her earrings. No make-up for this guy. Of course, concealer and blusher didn't count. That was just to make her look normal. Mrs Morecambe wasn't in; he had to have something to eat and drink.

The quicker I take it down to him, the quicker I can get away, Becky reasoned to herself. She searched through the fridge and rustled up the rest of the smoked salmon, some bread and butter and a slice of cake. She got out the ice tray and made him a tall glass of Ribena, arranged it all on a tray and pulled on her boots again.

He looked up as she came over, and straightened up. Becky tried not to let her eyes slide over his chest. He was sweating, and small beads of it trickled over the brown hair on his chest which thickened distractingly down to his navel.

'Thanks.' He took the glass of Ribena and drained it in one go, wiping his mouth with the back of his hand. 'I needed that. And you might have to bring me some more. Lunch, huh? How thoughtful.'

'You're welcome,' Becky said.

'Oh, and in the future, Miss Lancaster, you'll need to leave some place in the house open for us. I'll be bringing in workmen, and they need access to a loo.'

'Right,' Becky said.

He sat down heavily on the grass and patted it, as though inviting her. 'Join me?'

'I ate already,' Becky said.

Logan considered her. Yeah, the rumours were true. Gareth, his mason, had teased him in the pub last night that he'd only taken this job to get a look at the Yank chick who owned the mansion. Not that that was true – he'd been itching to get at the grounds of Fairfield for years, and when this commission had come up he'd jumped at it, even though his books were full and he was getting a lot more money than this would pay. Fairfield was an almost pure Elizabethan garden. It was a nice change for him from the eighteenth-century landscaping that was fast becoming his speciality. But sure, he'd been curious. Ever since he'd come to this part of England last summer, he'd heard talk about her. American, and an heiress. It was almost enough to put him off taking the work, but not quite. He dealt with rich, spoiled owners every day. And he was getting successful enough that if he didn't like one, he could tell them to stuff it. That had been his insurance.

And now here she was. Young, definitely. Mid-twenties, with soft, buttery skin and long gold hair that invited a man to play with it. She was young enough that her insecurity was obvious. Her combative attitude was actually kind of sweet. Idly, he imagined her in a bikini, with those long, lean legs resting against white sand on some beach somewhere. Maybe a yellow bikini, or a string one, contrasting against her tan and her long flaxen hair. She was the kind of girl that painted her toenails. He imagined that waterfall of blonde hair playing over her little apple breasts, teasing the pale pink nipples, getting them erect before he even touched them.

She was a bit young for him, but that never stopped Will Logan from mentally stripping a woman. He did that for any female that was even remotely attractive, and Rebecca Lancaster qualified in spades. He hadn't seen many girls like her in Rosedale, that was for sure. Or anywhere else, for that matter. Logan's mind flickered to the old boyfriend. He'd been a lord. He'd also been a pussy. Logan could tell that right away. Urbane, charming, nicely dressed, and a coward. Logan was a fighter, and he could smell another fighter like he could smell an aroused female. Rupert Lancaster hadn't been one. There was something small and mean in his eyes and, besides, he must have been about one-eighty, soaking wet. Tall and lanky, looked like he'd never lifted a weight in his life. He wouldn't have been able to handle this girl.

He liked the way he could unsettle her. He saw her blushing and trying not to stare at his chest. He got that reaction a lot when he took his shirt off.

'Maybe you should wear a T-shirt,' she said.

He took a bite of the salmon and chewed. It was good. For this princess, nothing but the best, he supposed.

'No point. It'd get soaked in sweat.' He winked at her, which made her blush harder. 'Nothing wrong with having your shirt off in hot weather, Miss Lancaster. Maybe you should try it.' Logan glanced at the high-buttoned white thing she was wearing. The buttons would pop off easily enough if he ran his hand down through it. He imagined what her bra would be like. Virginal white cotton, with the little bud nipples straining against it . . .

Ah, that had been a daydream too far. He felt himself stirring inexorably beneath his jeans, which fitted him snugly. Annoyed with himself, he turned aside abruptly. It had been over a fortnight since he'd had a woman, since he had sent Elsie packing. He shouldn't take risks with silly little twenty-somethings.

'Don't be silly. And you can call me Becky.'

'OK, Becky,' he said abruptly, 'thanks for lunch.' He put the plate back on the tray and handed it to her. 'I have to get back to work.' And he picked up his spade so there could be no further argument on the matter.

I wish I had a dog, Becky thought furiously as she stomped back up to the house. If I had a dog, I could go for a walk with it. Get away from him.

If she went for a walk on her own, Will Logan might imagine she was running away from him. And she couldn't bear to have that happen.

She retreated back into the house and got out a book from the library. Something totally distracting, one of her shelf of modern paperbacks. Jackie Collins, *The Bitch*. Perfect. And exactly how Logan made her feel. She tried to concentrate on work, go over in her mind what she might do with that extension, but it was no good. Whereas before she'd had trouble getting her mind off Lancaster, today thinking about it was just impossible.

She sat on the sofa and tried to read. Mostly, it didn't work. Her gaze kept slipping to where he worked in the sunlight, shovelling mountains of earth, tearing up the ground. She thought about offering him another drink, but she was too proud to go out there. When the phone eventually rang, just as the long shadows were beginning to fall over the orchard, she was pathetically grateful for the distraction.

It was Ken Stone.

'Yes,' he said, once they had gotten past the pleasantries. 'I'm afraid it seems as though we may have a bit of a problem.'

Chapter 27

Their name was Wilson Shipping, and she knew all about them.

Jocelyn Wilson had started the business from scratch twelve years ago, and he was one of the seventies' hottest stories. He specialized in what the City boys called 'bottom fishing'. He liked to buy failing shipping companies for pennies on the pound, liquidate their assets, sell their real estate and integrate the better parts – whatever they had – into his company.

Wilson loved the recession. He even loved the soaring inflation, the strikes, the power outages, because they made his targets go bankrupt. He sold enough of an acquired company to keep his loans low, and so he could afford what they could not – the cost of money. Meanwhile, he had started Wilson Ferries. He ran both passenger and industrial ferries, no-frills operations which his firm advertised as money-savers. And in Britain, in the seventies, you needed every penny you could get.

Wilson Shipping was a huge success.

And now it was after Lancaster.

Becky shuddered at the thought of it. She would have loved to have bought back enough of the stock to make her a majority shareholder, but she simply didn't have the money. Lancaster would struggle to sell the mines in time to cover the bridge loan they had just negotiated. Well, so much for her relaxing weekend. She had pulled on her coat and purse and called for a cab. Once she was in the train, heading north, Becky had thought of Will Logan, sweating in the hot sun, without anything else to drink. Oh, well. Let him sweat, she thought crossly. If he walked out on her, she wouldn't care. She could hire someone else to install a maze and a rose garden. Right now, she had to figure out a way to deal with Jocelyn Wilson.

'It shouldn't be that hard,' Ken Stone had told her, trying to stop her from coming up to Whitby on her weekend. 'Just something we have to take care of. Persuade the stockholders not to sell.'

'Why would they? Our plan gives them full value for the stock. And it's going to appreciate.'

'They wouldn't. Lancaster isn't a failing company. I think you can handle this on Monday, Rebecca.'

Ken steadfastly refused to call her Becky. It had taken some work to pry him off 'Miss Lancaster'.

'I'm still coming up. Put together a take-over defence package, Ken. Initial thoughts. We'll meet at my flat.'

'On Sunday?'

'Wilson won't be taking the weekends off, Ken.'

'Well?' Lita asked.

Edward took a long look around. Lita felt herself tense, waiting for his judgement. She felt an intense need for him to approve, to back her. To forgive her for having done this.

The fight they'd had about her coming to England had been epic. The sex they'd had afterwards even more so. Edward hadn't even let her get two steps from him, crushing her to him, tilting her face upwards, trapping her lips in a kiss, his hands cupping her through the thin fabric of her silk pantsuit, stroking her lightly with his fingers, brushing over her sex until she was absolutely frantic. He'd made her wait, too, unbuttoning each fastening of her satin shirt agonizingly slowly, bending his salt-and-pepper head to the lace La Perla bra that struggled to confine her olive-skinned breasts, breathing on her nipples until they were so swollen with blood that the lace chafed against them mercilessly. Lita had been almost whimpering when he finally let her clothes slither to the floor in a soft rustle, and pushed himself inside her. She was hot and slick for him, the blood pooling in her belly, and he knew it, his hands tracing a line on her skin.

But then, as he started to thrust, and sweat, and his breathing became as ragged as hers, Lita took her revenge. Her hands crept down to tease his feathery skin, her nails brushing so lightly against him as they slid down to the floor, making love on the mess of clothes littering his priceless Persian rug. He groaned, and she knew she had him. With her pleasure there came a sweet sense of power. Lita swung her lithe, curvy body around so that she was mounted on top of him, her full breasts swinging over him as she rode him, her dark nipples jet black and hard with blood, pointed out at him, making him fight to keep his control, and she tightened herself around him, flexing the hot, wet heart of her around him.

The pleasure that had started to build in her was tightening, her body feeling each shuddering wash of ecstasy build up into a block of tight, hard bliss, and Lita had to bite down on her lip to stop herself from surrendering. She looked down at Edward, her future husband.

Goddamn him! She leaned forward so her large tits were brushing against the grey hairs of his chest, her glossy hair was teasing his skin and he could smell the heat of her. One hand snaked downwards to toy with him further, the other raked his burning skin with her nails, and Lita rocked him with a merciless, driving rhythm, until Edward could no longer bear it and exploded inside her with a deep groan, and she was able to let go, her whole body juddering with the force of the orgasm that rocked her, before she slumped against him, kissing him hotly.

That had been the last time they had made love. The hunger for Lita that had seemed so urgent in him had been replaced by a simmering anger that she was really leaving.

'It'll only be for six months,' she promised him. 'Just enough to set up the European offices. Find some talent, and set it up to run itself.'

'We'll see,' he said flatly.

That was why she was so glad that Edward had agreed to come and see her in London. She'd arrived here two weeks ago and found a place in less than a day, a tiny jewel of a mews house, in Kensington, a two-bedroom house with a minute paved garden in the back. Lita had rented it for six months. She wanted to show Edward the short lease to prove her bona fides, but he hadn't been interested. Now he was here. In the UK on another acquisitions trip, this time to buy some paintings by the hippest artists – Jackson Pollock and David Hockney. He had called her from his room at the Ritz.

'I might as well see what you've done with the place.'

Lita, newly unpacked, had tried to hide the excitement in her voice. 'Come on over.' She gave him directions, and ran out to her favourite Indian restaurant for take-out, which she was now keeping warm in the oven. The champagne was chilling. And he was here.

'Interesting,' Edward said eventually.

Lita smiled. From Edward, this was high praise.

He looked down at her. That glorious smile lit up her whole face. God, she was young, though. So goddamn young and stubborn. It was why he had fought back that crazy impulse to propose. Bull-headed Lita, single-minded and defiant.

His life was in America. It was inconceivable that hers might not be. He was sure this new pet project of hers would burn itself out in a couple of months. New Wave wasn't even well established enough in America for her to be over here.

'It is pretty cool, huh? I didn't want anyone to think I'd come to England and turned stuffy.'

He chuckled. 'Nobody could ever think that about you.'

Lita had furnished her pad in the latest style. It was a complete break from the delicate carpets and mahogany sideboards of his place in New York – you opened the old-fashioned English oak door and you stepped into a James Bond fantasy. It looked like Blofeld's lair. Lita had thick shaggy rugs in cream that your feet sank into when you stepped on them, low-slung coffee-tables stained a deep shade of chocolate brown, a TV that rose up from its black wooden stand when you pressed a button on the remote control, and large mirrors everywhere, the one in the bathroom lined with light bulbs. Her face, he thought idly, might be just young and beautiful enough to take it. She had piles of magazines stacked on her dark glass occasional table. *Vogue* and *Elle* and *Tatler* and *Harper's*, and in the bedroom, with its large, industrial steel-framed king-size bed, she had glass cupboards topped with her make-up in a sleek metallic case. In fact, he loved it. It was young and fresh and, considering she was here in grey, wet London, refreshingly shocking. Like his girlfriend.

Kahn reflected on the relief some of his partners had felt when he told them that Lita was moving to Europe. They liked having him free for the social circuit, free to flirt with all the society matrons. Not that he needed it. The company was too prestigious now to need the help of flirtation.

'Are we going out to dinner?' he asked.

'No. We're staying here.' Lita took his hand, tugging him through to her kitchen, which had an eat-in island in the centre of it. Yes, a perfect place for a single girl. 'You like Indian food?'

'I like it in India.'

'This is almost the same thing. Trust me, you'll love it.' She opened her oven door and spooned dishes from little foil containers on to her china, which was, incongruously, Royal Doulton. 'Chicken Tikka Marsala, vegetable dahl, lamb Basan Paranda . . .'

The scent was delicious. 'I'll try it.'

Lita opened her fridge and cracked the bottle of champagne. Perrier-Jouet, he noted approvingly. Well, she certainly didn't seem as if she was suffering unduly out here. She filled his champagne flute, offering him the first glass, then clinking her crystal to his in a toast.

'What are we drinking to?' Edward asked.

'Oh, I don't know.' She shrugged. 'England. Life. Everything.'

It had taken half a bottle of wine but, Lita thought, she had finally got him to relax, or at least to unwind a fraction. They were now on their second bottle of ice-cold champagne, sitting coiled against each other on the deep, soft, buttery leather sofa she had installed opposite her large TV. She had a small, fully stocked bar in one corner of the room, complete with barstools, but she didn't think she'd need to use it tonight.

'You're sure about this,' he murmured.

Lita brushed her lips against the skin of his neck. 'Yeah, babe. You have to understand. I want New Wave to have a global presence.'

They had only just gotten a New York presence, he thought, but successfully managed not to say. She looked good tonight. It was a sunny evening in May, just at the time when spring started to shift into summer, and it was warm in London, with lots of clear light streaming through the windows, tinged with the reds and pinks of sunset. Lita was taking advantage of the good weather. She wore a white dress, a tight, halter-necked thing made of very fine jersey. It was distractingly snug around her large breasts, tapered down across her waist and then flared out a little, but not enough to hide the firmness and roundness of her glorious ass. It stopped halfway down her thighs, which, he couldn't help but inventory in his mind, had stayed just as firm and silky smooth to the touch as when he had last caressed them. The dusky tones of her golden skin were dramatically accentuated by the dress, to the point where you longed to peel it off her just to check everything was equally delicious underneath. He didn't want to blow it by saying something stupid. Or thinking too much about their relationship and what she was doing.

When Lita Morales looked like this she had his brain in a fog.

'So who's going to be your first client?'

She stood up and walked over to a sleek white filing cabinet. Kahn watched the high, round ass muscles rolling under the white fabric and felt his groin tighten up again. Hell. She was like a sweet addiction.

Lita pulled out a clipping and handed it to him. She had cut it neatly, he noticed, and it was as carefully preserved as though it had been a banker's draft. Her steely determination shone through in everything she did.

'This guy. Jocelyn Wilson.'

'Does he know that?' Edward asked mildly, with one of those flashes of perception that she found so unsettling.

'He will.' Lita drained her champagne glass and leaned into him, brushing her nipples, tight under the fabric of her dress, against his shirt. She took his glass from him and kissed him, those thick, plump lips capturing his, her tongue darting across his mouth like it was on a search-and-destroy mission. 'Come on, let's go to bed.'

Jocelyn Wilson's offices were located in a nondescript, attractive building in St James's Street in Piccadilly, near Hatchard's and all the exclusive shirt-makers and cobblers that Edward liked to buy his clothes and shoes at. It reeked of quiet money. Old-fashioned money. Not the kind of money that liked to hire twenty-something Latina girls from New York.

Lita had walked past it twice. Research. Knowing what the client was all about was an essential part of advertising. She had gone down to Companies House and pulled the annual reports of both Lancaster Holdings and Wilson Shipping. Then, from her house, she had put calls back to the New Wave offices in New York. Janice managed to dig out UK press clippings through their contacts in the media, and Lita spent a weekend reading up on Rebecca, Rupert and their little family empire.

It must be great to be born with a goddamn silver spoon, she thought bitterly as she flicked through the inky pages. Lord Lancaster beaming out at her from the decks of yachts, lounging next to his Rolls-Royce . . . Rebecca throwing a ball at her vast country estate, full of snobs with titles and fur coats. She saw the reporting of the split. Like other people gave a damn about their pathetic love lives. Lita was only sorry Rupert Lancaster had disappeared. The *Daily Mail* said he was in St Moritz, skiing. She expected he was out there trying to weasel cash out of some other Eurotrash sugar mommies. But in the meantime, she had Rebecca Lancaster, who obviously had never had to work a day in her life.

Painstakingly, Lita pierced Rebecca's life together. Aristocratic parents, inherits a mansion and a fortune in infancy, swans off to the States. Lita knew girls like her. Boston Brahmins in the Hamptons, never working, playing tennis all summer with little white sweaters knotted around their necks and diamond bracelets dangling from their wrists. Her colour rose as she read up on the Honourable Rebecca Lancaster and thought of her own start, cleaning Pappy's tiny apartment obsessively because it was the only way to keep the roaches out. And dragging herself up by her bootstraps in advertising, to the point where she ran her own small firm. Of course, there had been nothing like that for Miss Lancaster. She had swanned straight into a CEO job in Daddy's baby conglomerate, and then let her dissolute titled boyfriend run it into the ground.

Lita wasn't fooled by the small amount of good press Lancaster had gotten recently. This Mr Stone, not Becky, seemed to be responsible for some cost-cutting measures, but judging by all the earlier post-mortems the British press had published, it was going to be too little, too late. Jocelyn Wilson had never lost a target yet. And she would see to it that he didn't lose this one.

The thought of Rebecca, standing at the top of the stairs,

dispassionately watching as she sobbed her heart out in front of Rupert, burned in her belly like pure acid.

Well, she had waited for years. And now it was time to get even.

It took Lita almost a full week to get an appointment with Wilson. This wasn't surprising. The man was a workaholic, filling every moment of his day with business. He liked to delegate everything, too. But Lita wasn't going to take a chance on being turned down by some faceless suit. She would make her pitch to Wilson alone.

He finally agreed to give her ten minutes at 4.40 p.m. on a Friday afternoon. Lita chose a sober, tailored suit in dark green, with a skirt that came to just over the knee, and a pair of neat low-heeled shoes, together with Wolford hose and light, fresh make-up. She twisted her hair up in a French pleat in an attempt to make herself look older and added a pair of neat pearl studs. Lita wanted Jocelyn Wilson to see her as a kindred spirit. True, he was upper class, like the Lancasters, but unlike them he'd been born poor. A father who'd been a degenerate gambler meant that his mom had had to work at low-paid, back-breaking jobs to support the family, including being a shop girl. Now, instead of serving at Harrods, she shopped there. Wilson had skipped university to start earning money right away. And he'd been very good at it.

Lita admired him. He hadn't let the recession and strike-bound Britain's industrial woes slow him down. She knew he didn't deal with a lot of businesswomen, but she preferred to suppose he was open-minded.

It all depended on whether he'd think she could make him some money.

She had prepared as well as she could. She had a briefcase full of clippings, previous campaigns from New York and costings. She had planned every aspect of this meeting right down to the scent she was going to wear. Now she sat in his outer office on a mahogany chair, her heart thudding at a million miles an hour.

Wilson's fifty-something Scottish secretary, terribly prim and proper in tweeds, came to fetch her. Her voice had the quiet solemnity of a librarian.

'Miss Morales? Mr Wilson will see you now.'

Showtime.

Chapter 28

'You'll appreciate, Miss Morales, that it's very unusual for me to be discussing my business with . . .'

Wilson, a fifty-something guy in an immaculate suit, gestured at Lita. His office was everything she had expected – sober, with dark red wallpaper and oil paintings on the wall, the desk a dark, glossy wood, the chair she was sitting on black leather.

'A young woman?' Lita supplied.

His eyes narrowed. 'Are you one of the women's libbers, Miss Morales?'

Lita shrugged. 'My only cause is my company. New Age is a small agency, Mr Wilson, but we have a prestigious client list owing to my previous work for Doheny Inc. in Manhattan . . .'

He coughed gently. 'I know your bona fides, Miss Morales, or I wouldn't have agreed to meet you. In fact, our ferry route to Scandinavia has lost a little market share recently, which is an unacceptable state of affairs, and providing your fees are substantially lower than your competitors' I am prepared to consider a pitch for that account.'

'Substantially lower?'

'You'll need to take a fee dip in exchange for establishing yourself on this side of the Atlantic, which I presume you are in a hurry to do.'

Lita grinned before she could stop herself. Cheeky bastard. She liked the way he thought.

'If you will allow me, Mr Wilson, I would prefer to make a counter-proposal. It relates to the bid you recently announced for Lancaster Holdings.'

'I hardly need advertising for that,' he said dismissively.

'Sir,' Lita said, slightly nervously, 'if you will allow me to present my proposal, I can wind up this meeting in less than eight minutes.'

He leaned back in his chair and steepled his fingers, indicating that she could go on.

'Lancaster Holdings is a slightly unusual case for your company. They are making a small profit, they have financing in place, they are looking to sell and slash costs. Presented well, it might appear to the shareholders as though hanging on to the stock would be worthwhile, even though they haven't paid dividends for years. You are looking to buy at an extreme discount. You have also not lost a take over yet. Your reputation causes smaller outfits to simply fold in their cards and sell to you.'

Wilson raised an eyebrow minutely. She could see he was impressed. She ploughed on.

'Thus, going after Lancaster is a risky proposition for you. You could gain a company very cheaply, a bigger target than your previous ones. Or you could lose your invincible reputation. Something to be avoided at all costs.'

'Not at all costs, Miss Morales. I take costs very seriously. I don't like them.'

'Understandable, sir. Your key to this deal, then, is persuading the stockholders that the Lancaster reorganization is like arranging the deck chairs on the *Titanic*. They can get rid of the pain and misery of endless loss-making company reports by simply selling to you at your reasonable offer. They must be convinced that the Lancaster restructuring effort is doomed. I can help you with that.'

'How?'

'Mr Wilson, corporate public relations is limited. It usually involves pictures of a chairman next to a giant cheque his company has donated to some charity or other, preparing a report, or possibly organizing sponsorship of some sporting event. I propose to do something different for you. Attack PR. I will find out, and I will make sure the press finds out, every problem in existence with Lancaster, their holdings, their unions and their executives.'

'And how do you know there are problems?'

'There are always problems,' Lita said. 'If I go to the union foreman in their shipyards, he could help me look for them. If I ask pointed questions about spending at the company's public meeting, I can create some. There are always plenty of problems. The interest rate is a problem.'

'You are an advertising agency.'

'That's true. But we're branching into public relations. It will help us to start with a high-profile success.'

'And how do you know you'll be successful?'

Lita thought Wilson had a slight twinkle in his eye. The corners of his mouth twitched slightly.

'I just know it,' she said firmly. 'And here's the best part. It won't cost you anything.'

He blinked, looking surprised for the first time since she had walked into his office.

'We'll charge you expenses, of course. But that's all. And what we get out of it, if you get the company, is an exclusive contract to represent you for one year. At whatever you are currently paying your ad agency.'

'Less five per cent,' Wilson said.

It took Lita a second to realize he was actually agreeing to it.

'Yes,' she said, trying hard not to smile. 'Less five per cent.'

'I was taken,' Jocelyn Wilson told her when he took her out to dinner at Claridge's that night, 'by the fact that you knew so much about my company. Usually, advertising agencies only brush up on the project.'

'I believe in preparation.'

'Try the smoked salmon to start with, why don't you? I think it's some of the best in the world. And a bottle of Krug.' He handed his menu to the waiter. 'The usual, please.'

'Very good, Mr Wilson. Madam?'

'Oh, I'll have the grouse,' Lita said, enjoying the soft candlelight and the pianist softly rippling out ragtime jazz. Not to mention the air of quiet luxury everywhere. When they weren't being patronizing assholes, she liked the English.

I could get used to this, she thought.

'I know you believe in preparation. That's why I'm letting you try this.'

'And because we're free.'

'That, too.' He nodded. Wilson kept a couple of very expensive and discreet mistresses in flats in Chelsea. Mentally he compared them to the American girl. They dressed a little better, but no amount of expensive Chanel suits could compensate for her sensational tits, handspan waist and perfect curvy arse. The sober thing she was wearing couldn't hide any of it. Of course, she was achingly young. He indulged in a brief fantasy of Lita straddling him, her breasts bouncing, heavy, still firm, dark-nippled. Mmm. Of course, he would never say anything. Business was business. You could get high-end call girls anywhere, but the money that paid for them was more valuable. And Morales made some excellent points.

After she left, Jocelyn Wilson had called a few people in the States. She was quite well known in New York, though Doheny was trying to blacken her name. On Madison Avenue, he was told, Ogilvy & Mather had already tried to buy out her fledgling agency. It was true that he was taking a risk, going after Lancaster. But maybe she could help. She was aggressive and pushy, but that was the seventies woman, wasn't it, at least in America.

'What do you know about Lancaster?' he asked, squeezing the lemon wedge over his fish.

'Quite a bit. I think your best asset there is Rebecca Lancaster.'

'The heiress. She seems to have done reasonably well in turning the company around.'

His companion leaned over the table, her heavy-lidded eyes narrowing dangerously. 'She dated a playboy, she's in her twenties, she's practically a foreigner, she has no business experience, and she's just the latest scion of the family that spent this company into the ground. She's a liability.'

'You're in your twenties, Miss Morales.'

Lita smiled wickedly. 'Ah, Mr Wilson, but I'm not front and centre here. She is. At least, for as long as she opposes this take-over.'

He nodded. 'Well, the bridging loan they received recently is designed to let them sell off some tin mines in Cornwall.'

'That won't happen.'

'Why not?'

'I don't know,' Lita told him, 'but I'm going to find out.'

'What will you need, do you think?'

Lita grinned. She had already thought about this. 'Space in your offices, about five of your analysts, and a large enough budget to entertain any journalist I want to, lavishly.'

'You have it,' Jocelyn Wilson said, without hesitation. He took a sip of his champagne, delighted. He suddenly had a very good feeling about his investment.

'There has to be something we can do,' Becky said.

She felt physically sick. Nothing so far had prepared her for this kind of onslaught. Not the bitter negotiations with the unions, not relocating the company and selling the London offices, not even firing all those extraneous workers and executives. All the late nights with Ken Stone and his team of financial Rottweilers had toughened her up. Or so she'd thought. But the attack from Wilson Shipping had been vicious, swift and thorough.

The press. She was just a businesswoman, she was used to a short paragraph in the financial section, the odd inky photograph on the back pages. Not the hailstorm of nasty publicity that had descended upon her. The tabloids had been sold a 'human angle', as her recently fired head of publicity had put it so helplessly. She was suddenly being written about in gossip columns, in Sunday supplements, in features sections, and none of it was good. They portrayed her as a brash American playgirl, a foreigner who had swanned in, put her boyfriend in charge of the company, let him spend millions, then tried to make it up by firing people. Husbands and fathers. They wrote up sob stories about dock workers she'd sacked because they were on the take, except in print they looked like the Tolpuddle Martyrs, and ran them next to lurid accounts of the dance she'd thrown at Fairfield. Somehow they'd found a few pictures of her in her white pantsuit, looking like Jerry Hall, and another couple of her with her arm through Rupert's, holding a glass of bubbly. Great. She wasn't sure if his face, or the story underneath it, made her sicker. And whatever Lancaster sent out, the press wasn't interested. They had a nice angle, and they weren't going to let it go.

Reading it, Becky hated the person they were describing, too. The fact that it wasn't her didn't seem to matter.

'I don't think there is,' Ken Stone said quietly, 'Miss Lancaster.'

There hadn't been any selling, of course. The stock price had risen. But only because of the ever-present shadow of a take-over looming over them.

Stockholders were wavering. More than that. Rebecca's secretary had had to take on two assistants to deal with all the hate mail, and some of it came from shareholders. One of them wrote that he had 'forgotten what a dividend looked like'.

In other circumstances she might have found that quite funny.

Stone and his team had rallied to her side. They had told her to forget about the press and concentrate on selling the stockholders their plan. His sober, matter-of-fact financial figures and projections told a story of solid recovery and possible future growth. They had mailed them out *en masse* and for a short while it looked as though the Lancaster stockholders might just hold steady.

And now this.

'But they can't prove that there's any safety violations.'

Becky thumped the files of letters down on her desk furiously. They came from the Health and Safety Council of Truro, Cornwall. Residents of the villages near her tin mines had suddenly claimed they were getting sick. They alleged the mines were poisoning the water supply. The Council was going to hold a full investigation.

'They don't have to. That's what's so beautiful about it, from Wilson's point of view. The investigation will take at least a year, and nobody's going to buy the mines for the price we need with liability hanging over their heads.'

'Fuck.' Becky swore, uncharacteristically. 'Shit. I'm sorry, Ken.'

'I feel exactly the same way, Miss Lancaster,' he said solemnly.

She flopped into her chair. It was hard to breathe. 'Goddamn bastard. I guess the bank has been calling?'

'Incessantly. They want us to come in for a meeting.'

'They can wait.' She pressed her hands to her head. 'Ken, is there any chance we can find a white knight? Someone else, a partner instead of a take-over merchant?'

'There's always a chance,' he said doubtfully, 'but our investment bankers have already looked everywhere. With the mines and the interest on the loan . . .'

'I know. We'll default. We could beggar our stockholders.' Becky stood up, tears in her eyes. She blinked them back. 'There are some people out there who have their whole net worth in Lancaster stock. I can't be responsible for ruining them.'

'What are you going to do?' Stone asked.

'I'm going to meet with Jocelyn Wilson,' Becky said softly. 'Set it up, Ken, would you?'

Wilson set the terms, and Becky knew she had to put up with them. He asked her to lunch at the Dorchester, and selected the most visible table. She had expected that. Wilson had taken on his biggest target, and his victory was almost assured. Becky had slept in London the night before, backing off her austerity policy to take a suite at the Ritz. There was no point in austerity any more. But there was a point to looking her best. She picked a light-hearted outfit, a sunny dress in layers of lemon chiffon that showed off her tan and her long blonde hair, together with kitten heels and light, natural make-up. She didn't have to try and pass for forty any more. She went early to the Dorchester, and was sipping a champagne cocktail when he arrived at her table, middle-aged, respectable-looking, exactly what she had expected.

She stood and shook hands with him, giving him a beaming smile. She was pleased to see that this seemed to surprise him a little.

Wilson was shocked. The girl looked positively radiant. He breathed in a delicious waft of L'Arpège. What could she have to be so happy about? He had destroyed her. He sat, exchanged pleasantries with her and ordered their starters. Once the waiter had brought over a bottle of Pouilly Fuisse, he decided to broach the obvious.

'You asked for this meeting, Miss Lancaster?'

'I did, Mr Wilson.' He saw she wasn't going to ask him to call her Rebecca. 'I have a proposition for you.'

'Nothing you propose will alter my purpose to take your company over, Miss Lancaster.'

'Indeed. But I can still affect the price at which you obtain it. I can save you almost two pounds a share.'

Now he was very interested, the goddamn vulture. Becky looked him right in the eye.

'The backing of the board for your bid will make it a slam-dunk. The longer we delay and fight, the more debt you'll be saddled with when you eventually take us over. Money is important to you; Lancaster is important to me. I don't want the name being traded out of my control. If you will assign the name to me, and the hotel division, I will assign the assets to you.'

'The hotel division? I thought you only had one.'

'We do.' She grinned at him disarmingly. 'But maybe I can turn it into something real. At any rate, I will have the opportunity, and nothing with my father's name on it will do something I disapprove of.'

He thought about it for a couple of moments.

'Done,' Wilson said, and shook her hand.

She wanted to cry, but she kept the smile fixed tightly to her face. 'You know, Mr Wilson, Kenneth Stone is my CFO. He did a wonderful job, almost rescuing us from the hole we had dug ourselves into. You might want to consider hiring him.'

Wilson dabbed at his mouth. 'Was, Miss Lancaster, was your CFO. I will certainly think about it but, please be aware, I neither want nor expect any advice from you on how to run my company. You can take the name and the hotel, but that is all. Your ties to the rest of it will be completely severed. Once a target is mine, I never allow the slightest interference from anyone else.'

Becky swallowed hard. It was as bitter as hell to have to sit here and take this. But she had no choice.

'Very well, sir,' she said.

I'm coming back from this, she thought, as she turned her attention to the delicious food that tasted like ashes in her mouth. This is not going to be the end of the story. I swear it.

She lifted her glass of wine and offered Wilson a toast.

'To the future,' she said.

Chapter 29

She decided to retire and lick her wounds.

Wilson wasn't sentimental. Nor had she really expected him to be. Becky had spent the next two weeks being humiliated – trotted out to mouth platitudes about how good for Lancaster's shareholders Wilson's bid would be, forced to endure photo opportunities shaking his hand, like she was the young kid handing over management to the adults. In exchange for this, she was deeded, in 'compensation', the name of Lancaster Holdings and the single hotel in the Scilly Isles. She was also granted six months' salary. As Becky had never drawn much of a salary, ploughing everything back into Lancaster, this amounted to less than twenty thousand pounds. She also, of course, received Wilson's price for her personal stock. That was when she got her real financial shock.

Her holdings were worth less than a hundred thousand pounds.

Ken Stone confirmed her worst fears. 'I thought you knew. Lord Lancaster sold off some . . . well, most . . . of your personal holdings, his and yours, in order to reduce the debts of his marketing programme. That held off speculation for several months, as I recall. He had papers with your signature on them. The authority was perfectly legal, or I would never have authorized [illegible]'

'No, that's quite OK.' Becky calmed him. It wasn't his fault. It was Rupert's. And hers, for letting him do it. That was the last time she would surrender any control. It was still coming back to haunt her, all these years later. She thought of the bills at Fairfield, and what would happen to the house if it weren't heated through the winter. There was no question of selling paintings. Her lack of money terrified her.

Heiress. What a joke. She had lost almost everything in one generation.

She put her Yorkshire flat on the market at once. Someone from Wilson Shipping bought it, and Becky couldn't even refuse to sell it to them. She was told that it was 'very convenient for the head office'.

Well, Becky thought, that's why she had bought it.

But they were prepared to pay full price, and she couldn't afford pride. That sale netted her another ten thousand in profits, once the fees were paid off. She went to a branch of her bank in Yorkshire, and deposited every last Penny.

The sum total of her estate – one hundred and twenty-seven thousand pounds, a small hotel and a country mansion. Not a bad haul for most people, as she tried to remind herself. But for Lord Lancaster's only child, it was a hell of a comedown.

She shook hands with her team, and saved the goodbyes to Ken for last.

'You don't seem too cut up, Ken,' Becky observed, shaking his hand.

'I'm not. I've had plenty of offers.'

She was a little hurt. 'Oh. Well. That's excellent.'

'Don't worry,' he said, smiling warmly at her. 'I'll be working for you again in the future. I know it.'

Becky bit down hard on her lip. She had avoided crying throughout the whole process, but having one person left that actually believed in her might put her over the edge.

'Goodbye, Ken,' she blurted, and rushed from the room.

Now she was in a train heading south. First class, of course. Not because she wanted to waste money, but because she had to. She didn't know how long she could keep this act up, and she didn't want any of the press watching her dissolve.

'Welcome home, miss,' Mrs Morecambe said when the taxi deposited her at the front door of Fairfield. 'I just put the kettle on. The van with your stuff came yesterday, and it's all unpacked.'

'Hey, thanks, Mrs M.' Becky kissed her on the cheek. 'I'd love a cup of tea.'

Mrs Morecambe brightened. 'That's what I like to hear. You need fattening up.'

Becky looked at her flushed face and knew she wanted to say something. 'About the papers—'

'It's murder, that is.' The words burst out of her. 'Them – them . . .'

'I know. But sticks and stones, right? We won't worry about them.'

'Then everything's OK, miss? My salary?'

'Your salary will always be paid here, Mrs M.' God knows how, Becky thought. She could hardly afford six grand a year for a bloody housekeeper. But this woman had worked for her family since she was a little girl. She'd have to find a way to keep her on.

Mrs Morecambe looked as though she might say something emotional, but she settled for, 'I'll just get you that cup of tea, miss.'

'Thanks.' Becky followed her into the kitchen. 'Then I think I'll take a bath.'

She suddenly wanted one, urgently. Longed to wash the dirt of her disappointment and fear right off her skin, to cleanse herself. The older woman filled a bone china mug with fragrant Lapsang Souchong, her favourite, and she retreated back upstairs. Becky went into her room, shut the door and peeled off her clothes. It was already twilight out there, the pale blue sky of a late summer evening, and there was a slight chill in the air. She ran herself a piping hot bath with masses of Badedas. No more Floris for her. Waitrose sold cheap bubble baths, and that was what she would be using. Becky took her time, soaping her long, lean legs, rinsing the grit of the journey from them, looking out of her bathroom window, which she had opened to let out the steam, over her garden.

Her garden. It had been what, almost a month since she was here last, and her place was totally transformed. The orchard had been halved, and there was a glorious, dark green, thick-branched little yew maze, maybe an acre, with curving, tricky paths, mossy statues hidden inside it and a small stone bench with wild roses climbing in the gazebo on top of it. Half thrilled, half panicked, Becky looked to the west. No, the croquet lawn was still intact. She could see tape measures and flags laid out over it in some kind of pattern. Well, at least she could save some money there. Logan would probably be back in the morning. She could get his bill then, and that would be that. She repressed a pang of regret. She wasn't a millionaire any more.

'I did promise you a rose garden,' she muttered to herself, 'but you can't have one.'

Becky finished her bath, slipped into her Janet Reger pyjamas in pale coffee-coloured satin and tied her matching silk robe around her. She washed off her make up and tied her hair back in a ponytail, then selected a pair of embroidered black silk slippers with gold detail. Maybe there was something good for supper. She could have a nice meal and a mug of hot chocolate and then go to bed with a trashy novel. There would be time enough for figuring out her next move in the morning. She padded downstairs and went into the kitchen.

'Mrs Morecambe, I—'

She stopped dead. Will Logan was sitting in her kitchen, drinking a mug of tea. He was wearing dirty boots and had bits of yew hedge in his hair, and his once white T-shirt was sticking to his chest with sweat. She could see all his muscles defined under it. His dark eyes, with their ring of thick lashes, regarded her, his gaze sweeping up and down over her clinging satin outfit approvingly. Becky instantly blushed scarlet. She felt as good as nude.

'I – I thought you'd left for the evening.'

'No. 'Appen I hadn't.' It took her a second to decipher the thick Yorkshire burr. 'It's only half-seven,' he pointed out.

She guessed it was quite early to be dressed for bed.

'I'll just go and change,' she murmured.

His eyes danced. 'Don't bother on my account, love.'

Becky fled.

She raced into her bedroom and tugged on the most shapeless outfit she could find – a pair of skinny blue jeans and a sweatshirt. Yeah, much better.

Man, she's delicious, Logan thought when she reappeared, racing down the wooden stairs in her bare feet. With that scrubbed face, the long, swinging blonde ponytail, those huge blue eyes, she looked like a tanned, golden advertisement for a holiday in L.A. The predator in him enjoyed her discomfort. They both knew Logan had seen her in her lingerie, distractingly feminine, clinging to her little bud curves, her slim body, saying as much as it did about her sensuality. He constructed the slight curve to her tiny waist, the coltish delicacy of her body, and imagined his hands, rough and calloused, running over the smooth, nut-brown skin of her.

'OK.' He grinned at her attempt to be brisk, which seemed to aggravate her even further. 'Mr Logan, I need to talk to you about your work.'

'There's a problem with my work?' he asked. Becky steeled herself. Logan's tone was a silky, dangerous challenge.

'Not that I can see.'

'The crew and I are glad to hear it.'

'Your crew aren't here, are they?'

'No. They left a few hours ago. I had some things to finish up.'

'OK.' She twisted her fingers. 'Mr Logan, I'm not going to be able to have you finish the rose garden.'

He frowned, annoyed. 'You agreed to the rose garden and you agreed not to interfere with my work. I'm not putting anything else in that space. I thought we had discussed that.'

'No, you don't understand. I can't afford to have you complete the rose garden. There's been—' she blushed again—'a change in my circumstances.'

He shifted in his seat, not taking those dark eyes from her. 'Aye, I read something about that.' The guys in the pub had taken an avid interest, and so had the boys on his crew. Their pay was at stake. He'd had to gesture to the huge house behind them, to the oil paintings and antiques that surrounded them when they tramped through the hallway on their way to the downstairs loo. 'You'll be covering the bill so far, though.'

Becky prickled. He flung that out like a challenge, like he thought she was going to try and weasel out of it, and that he'd sue her if she did. God, what an arrogant bastard. She drew herself up rigidly.

'Yes, Mr Logan. You will be paid in full for your efforts so far, as soon as I have inspected your work and found it to be satisfactory,' she snapped. 'Kindly draw up an itemized bill and present it to me tomorrow. I'll have a cheque for you by the end of the day. *Assuming* your work is of a sufficient standard of quality.'

Logan leapt to his feet, furious. Who did this little twenty-year-old Yank chit think she was? He had sweated, toiled, slaved over this job, some of his finest work in years. He had taken on a job that was too small for his company and put off other, more lucrative clients, just to have the opportunity to work creatively on this ancient garden. It was almost a mercy job. And now she was spouting bollocks about the quality of *his* work?

'I don't think I can take a personal cheque, *Miss* Lancaster.' Two can play at that game, Logan thought. 'Given what happened with your company. We'd prefer you go to t' bank and get a certified cheque. Or cash. We'll write you out a receipt.'

His words stung Becky like a whip. 'Very well. Mr Logan. Tomorrow at ten o'clock will be convenient.'

'Fine. When you "inspect" my work, I'll walk around it with you. That way, any *legitimate* complaints you can address with me actually there.'

'Very well,' Becky said.

Logan set the cup of tea down on her kitchen counter. 'I'll see you tomorrow, then. Ten sharp.'

He strode past her into the hall and left the house without looking back.

Becky was waiting for him at ten o'clock the following morning. She had prepared a receipt, waiting for the amount to be filled in. She had called the bank and told them she would be needing a bank draft. Then she'd washed and blow-dried her hair, made herself up and selected one of her most expensive outfits, a fitted dress in pale pink by Christian Dior, with a matching cardigan in fine jersey wool and a rope of thick, lustrous pearls at her neck. She also slipped on one of her pieces of heirloom jewellery, a fine Kamcha sapphire ring the size of half a quail's egg. She kept her make-up soft and neutral, but she also spritzed herself liberally with the rose and sweet-pea scent that had been custom-blended for her in Paris. Will Logan was accusing her of being a deadbeat. Well, screw him. She'd show him.

It was no surprise that he turned up at ten a.m. on the dot. Her bell rang just as the grandfather clock in the hall was chiming the hour. Cocky jerk, she thought. He probably walked up the drive then waited there until his watch said the exact second.

'Hello, Mr Logan,' she said coolly as she opened the door.

He was wearing an immaculate black suit and a pair of thick-soled, rich-looking walking shoes. His shirt had a thin stripe of palest blue to it and he had plain gold cufflinks at his wrists. Becky struggled to control her surprise. She was so used to seeing him in jeans and T-shirts, with mud spattered on his clothes and skin, that this was a total shock.

'Is there a problem?'

'Why?'

'Because you're staring at me.'

Shit. She was.

'I'm sorry. I suppose I didn't expect to see a gardener . . .'

She gestured at him.

'Oh?' His tone was hostile. 'I told you, Miss Lancaster, I don't mow lawns. Logan Gardens does landscape gardening, and I own the firm. When I'm not working on site, I like to dress properly.'

'Of course.' Please, not another blush, Becky thought. She had been completely wrongfooted. 'Come in. We'll go into the library.'

She looks hot, Logan thought. A bit Jackie O., but hot as hell. The sound of that accent was cute, so out of place in this house. He followed her into the library, watching the slight, suggestive curve of her ass under that well-fitting pink thing. A waft of flowers hung in the air where she moved, mixing with the smell of her skin. Stuck-up little madam. He glanced around the library – ranks upon ranks of leather-bound books, a glorious old fireplace with gargoyles and oriental rugs on the floor. Hell, yeah. He'd like to have a place like this. He promised himself that one day he would. Money bought everything, and the rich kids that inherited it didn't value it, and spent it on drugs and yachts and couldn't hang on to these kinds of houses.

Logan had big dreams. He looked around the room to remind himself just how big.

'This is incredible,' he said, then stopped. He could have kicked himself. He wasn't meant to be acting impressed in front of this little princess.

'Yes, it's beautiful. This room dates from the fifteenth century. It's the earliest in the house.' Becky walked over to her writing desk, and Logan reached inside his jacket and drew out his bill in a crisp white envelope. Smythson's stationery, she noticed at once.

'Here.'

She examined it. The bill was for a whopping five thousand pounds, but it was perfectly, mercilessly presented, with raw materials, transportation, mark-up, labour costs, design fees . . . It looked like one of her shipyard reports, it was so dense.

'This seems to be in order,' she said faintly. She wanted to argue with him about the cost, but she couldn't bring herself to. Her own voice floated back to her, saying boldly that she was in charge and that money was no object.

'Let's go and inspect the work, shall we?' Logan suggested.

'Fine with me.' Becky tossed her head, in a slight, almost unconsciously arrogant movement that set her platinum mane moving around her shoulders. Logan forced his eyes to slide off her. He walked out of the front door, leading her through the kitchen garden down on to the lawn and towards the maze.

'You'll see that, as discussed, your infected apple trees were cut down and chopped up for firewood. They should last a couple of winters.' He gestured one thick hand at the wood-shed. 'Then the ground was dug into ditches and mature yew hedges were planted and clipped, following my design. Statuary, a bench and roses were also introduced.' He kept the explanation clinical as he led her into the maze. It was a warm, summery morning, and a drowsy fat bumble bee was already buzzing through the fragrant green scent of the leaves. The grass underfoot was flat and smooth, the hedges clipped so close and even it looked as though they had been cut with razors. At the end of the first fork, there was a mossy statue of Persephone, clutching her gown around her as she fled.

It was enchanting, and it looked as though the whole thing had been planted back in the days of Elizabeth I.

'Keep to the left, otherwise you might get lost. It's small, but tricky. A plan of the maze is attached to your bill.'

Becky followed him silently though the maze. It did seem to meld into one glassy corridor of smooth emerald lines. It was perfect. The statues were exquisite, and unexpected, and when he finally took her to the bench, she couldn't suppress a gasp of admiration. In the full, warm light of day, under the sun, the twisted arch of roses, a spray of dripping scarlet against the dark green yew, it was so romantic that it took her breath away.

Her reaction wasn't lost on Will Logan.

'You like it,' he said.

It was a statement more than a question.

'Yes. I love it. It's perfect. Thank you,' Becky breathed.

His dark eyes looked at her impassively. 'Not at all. Happy you're pleased with the work. The address to send the bank draft to is on the invoice. I would say I hope we'll be working together again, but I think it's highly unlikely.'

He stood up and turned away from her.

'If you follow me, I'll lead you back out.'

Becky did as she was told, feeling ridiculously small and rebuffed. Not that she had made any advances, but still.

She looked at Logan's broad back and decided that she hated his guts.

Chapter 30

She had more important things to do, she knew that. The costs of running the house had to be calculated, the profits from the hotel had to be sent over so that she could see where else she could cut costs and what kind of a salary she could draw. Was she going to go and take a place in the Scilly Isles, for example? It seemed like a long way away. Sailing back to the mainland and then getting a train every time she wanted to come back to Fairfield would be costly, and it would take for ever.

Thinking about her new situation made Becky's head throb.

It was the first time in her life that money had ever been a problem.

She had to fight to keep herself detached. Unemotional. And on top of all this, she couldn't stop thinking about Will Logan.

The supreme cockiness of him. He was only a goddamn gardener, she told herself. A fancy gardener, sure, but ultimately that was all he was. Becky told herself that he was the male equivalent of a snotty assistant in a designer store.

The trouble was, she didn't believe that.

She made casual enquiries. Asked Sharon to ask her friends in the village. Rupert had hired Logan, so she knew nothing about him.

The answers surprised her. He was from Yorkshire – well, she knew that – and his service was in demand. Hot demand. He had been in her area working on something else, the grounds of a local castle being renovated by the National Trust. There was a long waiting list to get Logan Gardens to do your property, and they didn't work on ordinary gardens.

'He's a landscaper, really,' Sharon told her over tea and Marmite toast in the kitchen. 'Like they used to have in England. I forgot the name of that guy, the famous one.'

'Capability Brown?'

'Yeah. Him. Well, Logan does that sort of stuff. And they charge through the nose for it. I don't think he makes much dosh himself, though.'

'Why not?'

'Because he spends so much on the gardens. Hires large crews of men, sometimes even architects. Buys the best plants and prefers organic plants, which cost a bomb. So he doesn't clear that much.'

'He clears enough for a nice suit,' Becky snapped.

Sharon blinked. 'Don't bite my head off, I'm just the messenger. What, did he rip you off or something?'

'He charged me five grand to put the maze in.'

She looked surprised. 'That's all? He must have made a mistake.'

'What are you talking about?'

'Well, think about it.' The toaster pinged, and she jumped up to slather more toast with butter. 'A mature yew hedge, how much does that cost? *Especially* organic. You've got about twenty in that maze. Then his crew, that stuff's heavy, and he must have hired equipment to cut down the trees and an architect to plan the design of the maze. I'd say he's out about three or four grand, easy.' Sharon shrugged. 'My uncle runs a nursery.'

Becky was horrified.

'You don't think he cut me a break?'

'Either that, or he's really, really bad at sums,' Sharon told her.

Becky buried her head in her hands. 'Oh, God.'

'What's the problem? You got a nice little discount. Can't you use the money right now?'

'That's the point. He was such a bastard. I don't want his pity, I don't want him doing me any favours. Why the hell would he, anyway? I live . . . here.' Becky waved her hand at the Elizabethan splendour all around her. 'And he was aggressive about me paying his bill.'

'He's got other people to pay. He probably insisted you cover their salary.'

'I have to find out now.' Becky shook her head. 'I have to call him. Oh, maybe you could do it for me, Sharon. Just ask him if there's been a billing mistake.'

'Keep me out of it, cheers.'

Becky demolished her last piece of toast half-savagely.

Sharon left around one. Her estimates on the cost of keeping Fairfield maintained, even at a minimal level – maintenance and repairs, lawn-cutting and hedge-clipping, Mrs Morecambe's salary and heating at least a part of the house in the winter – were depressing. 'And don't forget, that's not everything.'

'What else is there?'

'You. You have to live. Food, drink, transportation. It's actually pretty expensive being alive. Something you probably haven't noticed up till now.'

It was. Becky didn't think the remnant of her cash would last her any more than three years, maybe four if she really skimped. She'd never had to skimp, and she didn't relish the prospect.

'The hotel is pretty profitable.' Ignoring the sinking feeling in her belly, she tried to put a bright face on it. 'I worked on that at first. Before I wised up to what Rupert was doing. It's only one hotel, but it makes money.'

'You want my advice?'

Becky looked warily at her friend. 'What makes me think I'm going to get it anyway?'

Sharon grinned. 'Your wisdom and experience, my dear. I think you should sell it.'

Becky was horrified for the second time that day. 'It's all that's left of my father's company.'

'Lancaster Holdings isn't a hotel, Becky. It's you. If you sell the hotel now, while it's doing well, you'll have enough money to tide you over until you can figure out what business you want to be in. You can live off the interest if you're careful. You own that hotel free and clear?'

'No.'

'Pity. But you'll still have a profit.'

'Not as much as you think.' But Becky was wavering. The thought of starting over, starting completely fresh, was intoxicating. Maybe nothing less than that could get her out of this blue funk she was in.

Starting over involved clearing her debts, though. And that meant calling Mr Logan.

'He's not available.'

Becky stood by the phone in her hall, resisting the urge to stamp her feet. 'You said that last time I called.'

The girl had an irritating, whiny voice.

'Yes, miss, well, he's on another job, ain't he?'

'Don't you give him his messages?'

'You saying I don't do my job?'

'Did you tell him it was important?'

'I told him what you told me. He's not available. Sorry.'

There was a click on the phone and the line went dead. Seething, Becky marched through to her library and snatched Logan's invoice out of its file. Yes, there was an office address at the top.

'Mrs Morecambe.'

'Yes, miss?'

'I'm going to be out for the rest of the day.'

'Very good, miss.'

Becky grabbed her bag and went out to her car, the little Renault Five that Sharon had insisted she buy. Enough of his weaving and dodging. She was going to track him down, settle up and get on with her life.

The journey took a frustrating three hours. Even though she hadn't driven in the States for years now, using the wrong side of the road was confusing, and she had to swerve away from oncoming cars, their horns blaring, twice. She had to pull into a lay-by to consult her map three times, then took a wrong exit, got lost in the back roads and finally reached her destination over an hour late.

Buxted was a sleepy little village in Shropshire, not far from the Welsh border. It had white signposts, with black lettering, which tilted against overgrown hedges that were green and thick, with honeysuckle and bindweed competing for space. It had a small post office with a red-tiled roof and a couple of thatched cottages, and the rest were stone houses with the odd weathered building in cosy red brick. Becky couldn't see anything remarkable about it. There was a pub, the Queen Charlotte, but she didn't stop for lunch, despite the fact she was starving. See Logan first, then eat. And get the hell home.

The village was too small to have its streets marked out on the map, but that was no problem – there were only four of them. Becky found Swan Lane and turned down it. The address on the neatly produced letterhead was Third Floor, 26 Swan Lane. Very well. That had to be it – the slightly taller, boxy, brick building on the corner. It was the only one that looked as though it might have three floors. She parked the car, got out and walked up. The front door was unlocked, and there was a dentist's office on the ground floor.

'Help you, miss?' the receptionist asked.

'Logan Gardens?'

The girl jabbed upwards with her thumb.

'Thanks,' Becky said. She walked up the wooden stairs, noticing that the carpet was frayed and the walls could do with a new coat of paint, possibly two. The whole place looked cheap. Not tacky, maybe – it was too rural to be tacky – but cheap, worn and wholly inappropriate for a 'hot' firm of any description.

There was a sturdy oak door on the third floor with a small brass nameplate next to it, announcing that it was Logan's offices. Becky took a deep breath and pushed her way in.

The space was small, and clearly inadequate. The walls were ringed with steel filing cabinets but, despite this admirable level of storage, there were little nests of paper everywhere – letters, bills, catalogues of roses and vegetables and garden implements. There were also open boxes of sample trowels and other tools, and even a couple of sacks of fertilizer.

There was a teenage girl chewing gum at the front desk. With a little thrill of dislike Becky realized it was the same one that had been blowing her off this morning.

'Can I help you?'

'I hope so. I'm looking for William Logan.'

The girl's eyes narrowed. 'You that lady that was talking to me before?'

There was no point in denying it. How many Americans did they deal with?

'Yes. I thought I might have better luck if I came down here myself.'

'Look, miss.' The girl sighed. 'I don't want to be rude or nothing, but I don't think he wants to talk to you. I gave him your message and he crumpled it up and threw it in the bin.'

Becky felt the blood rush to her cheeks, but she persevered. 'I'm sure he doesn't want to talk to me. However, I want to talk to him. There's a problem with his bill.'

'A problem?' The small amount of sympathy she had just displayed vanished instantly. Now she was openly hostile again. 'Do you even know how cheap he did that job for you? We're almost two months behind on the rent and the nurseries are calling, and you think there's a problem? I'll tell you the bloody problem—'

'And what would that be?'

Becky jumped out of her skin. The receptionist had been half shouting and she hadn't even heard him come in. Logan was standing behind her, wearing black corduroy pants and a black T-shirt, with thick Doc Marten boots. His clothes picked out his dark eyelashes and hair. In the tiny room, he was right up against her, his handsome face clouded with anger.

'I'd prefer to discuss it with you alone.'

'Anything you've got to say you can say in front of Tracy.'

She glanced at the hostile chick. She really didn't want to discuss her affairs in front of this girl. But Will Logan was gazing down unrelentingly into her eyes.

'Please.' She said it softly. 'Mr Logan. I drove here for three hours to speak to you about this. Can't we go to the pub?'

He was hungry. 'Very well.'

'Thank you,' Becky said. She felt an amazing sense of relief. She put it down to wanting him out of her head.

Logan carried their drinks to the table. The pub had a pretty back garden, with a large buddleia bush covered in butterflies and dog roses everywhere.

'What's this?'

He nodded in disgust at her white wine spritzer.

'I'm driving.'

'So you are.'

'I thought real men didn't eat quiche,' she said, from a childish desire to get him back.

'I happen to love quiche.' He pronounced it ''appen'. 'Now, you said you drove three hours to see me. And you won't discuss it in front of my secretary. This must be good.'

'It's about your bill. It's too low.'

He paused with a forkful of Quiche Lorraine on the way to his mouth. 'What do you mean?'

She looked him right in the eyes. He wasn't going to stare her down this time. 'I mean I did some research, Mr Logan. I found out what yew hedges cost and your labour costs and the thing about the architects. I found out you took my job on as some kind of – of horticultural charity case.'

Logan was astonished. He burst out laughing.

'Don't laugh at me,' Becky snapped. 'You know what I mean. You normally only do industrial-style things, and you don't make any money because you spend too much on quality. And yet you undercharged me by thousands of pounds despite—'

'Despite what?' he asked softly, his dark eyes twinkling.

'You know. The fight. Anyway, I don't need your charity. I've got more goddamn money than you and I want to pay my debt. I don't want to be owing you for any favours I didn't damn well ask for.'

Logan paused for a moment, then took a deep, refreshing pull at his gin and tonic. Over the glass, his gaze travelled lightly over her body, the way it had done before. Becky suddenly wished she had worn something other than a white cotton dress. What if the sunlight was making it translucent and he could see her bra and panties? They were pale blue lace. What if he could see them?

'Don't you have anything to say?' she demanded.

Will Logan looked her over. She was incredible, this chick. He thought of feminists as those ugly women that stormed university campuses, wearing no bras and refusing to shave their under arm hair. This girl was exactly the opposite; tanned and long-limbed and golden-haired, a blonde bombshell right off the Pirelli calendar. So what the hell made her so pissed off and proud?

What was it the Yanks said? Feisty. Yeah, feisty.

She was ten years his junior, he reminded himself. Hadn't he decided she was definitely too young? And yet she was a challenge. She was rich, aristocratic, lived in a mansion, had run a company – run it into the ground by the sound of it. But still, she'd had a taste of 'yes, madam, no, madam' – she wasn't the kind of girl who dated the likes of him. She was reserved for *Lord* Lancaster, and other chinless wonders of that sort. But he liked her spirit. Even though she needed taking in hand, like an unbroken mare.

He had read about her fall from grace, and he had cut her a break on the bill. Maybe that was stupid. She was right, she had a lot more money than he did. But he'd folt a bit sorry for her. Proper little princess though she was.

'I'm surprised.'

'Just let me know what I owe you, and I'll be on my way.'

'It'd take a while to figure out. Besides, I don't want the money.'

'Goddamn it.' She was like a wildcat, fairly hissing at him. 'Your wishes don't count. I want to pay.'

'You can't force me to take a penny.' Logan grinned. 'Tell you what. I'll toss you for it. If you win, I'll send you a bill, clean and simple. I'll bank the money and you'll never see me again.'

'And if I lose?'

'I'll still take the money. I need to pay some bills.' Becky grinned. 'But,' Logan added ruthlessly, 'for the price I come back to Fairfield and plant your rose garden *and* you have to go on a date with me to the venue of my choice.'

'Excuse me?'

'Yeah, that rose garden's been nagging at me. I can't stand to leave a job unfinished.'

'I meant about the date.'

He looked her over in that relaxed, confident manner she found so disturbing. 'It would amuse me to see you forced to be civil to me for an evening. Besides, you're very attractive, as I'm sure you're aware.'

Becky shot to her feet. 'I don't sell my body for the privilege of paying your bill, mister.'

His eyebrow lifted. 'Who asked you to, sugar? I said a *date*. Maybe date means something different on your side of the Atlantic. Or maybe you're too posh to go out with a working man?'

'No. Of course not.' She pulled out a coin from her pocket and tossed it high in the air, slapping it down on her slender wrist.

'Well?' Logan challenged.

Becky looked right at him. 'Tails. It's tails.'

She lifted her hand slowly from the coin. 'Shit,' she said.

Logan chuckled, a low, throaty sound. 'That'll be three thousand pounds and one date, please, Miss Lancaster.'

'You can call me Rebecca,' she said miserably.

'And it's Will.'

'You'll let me know when this date starts.' She wrote out a cheque and stood up. His hand shot out and grabbed her wrist, lightly but firmly.

'Where are you going?' Logan asked. 'The date starts now.'

Chapter 31

Lita had the clippings framed, all of them. She hung them in her nice new office in Dean Street, Soho, behind her kidney-shaped chrome desk with the glass top. Her sheepskin rug lay on polished hardwood floors, and the sleek metal vase was permanently filled with hothouse sunflowers. Every day, when she came into work, Lita saw the pictures of Rebecca Lancaster's stricken face. She had the whole story told in pictures and headlines, from the 'safety problems' in the tin mines down to 'Lancaster Broken Up: Surrenders to Wilson'.

She didn't know why that wasn't enough. But she still felt restless.

Edward wanted her back in the States, and she went. They made love in his apartment, and that was the moment she knew it was over. There was a distance between them, and she took no pleasure in it.

'But I thought you were going to come home,' Edward said, his handsome face angry.

'And I thought you were going to marry me,' Lita said sadly. 'I found the ring. Edward. Months ago.'

He shook his head. 'I was going to. I still want to. As soon as you make the arrangements to come home.'

'Don't you see, Edward? I can't be tied down like that. I want New Wave to be more than a boutique agency. I'll need to fly back and forth.'

'This isn't about business.'

'But it is. It's about you not telling me how to live my life.' Lita stood up. 'I'm young, and I have to do stuff my way. I've worked too hard to wind up someone's rich wife.'

She got her stuff out, and bought her own small townhouse in the Village. There were tears, but she was too busy to cry much or to pay this fresh heartbreak much attention. Breaking up with Edward was bitter-sweet. It hurt, but Lita knew it was the right thing.

Maybe she was a ball-buster. But Lita wasn't about to make the same mistake twice. She had let Rupert tell her what to do, and he'd ruined her. If Edward couldn't take her as she was, he had to go.

Harry Weiss was thrilled to have her back. He showed her their campaigns for Rich-Milk chocolates and Panda lemonade. The clients were delighted, the products had made impressive gains. Lita thought she could have done better, but she knew she couldn't design every campaign herself.

Harry had always found good talent. If she wanted to become a major player, she had to let him continue to do that.

'Alternatively, you can design every ad yourself, and we can take on twenty-five jobs a year,' Harry said dryly when he saw the shadow of doubt on her face.

'You're right.'

'I know I'm right.'

'I'll be taking another three months in London, to hire staff, start with the Wilson account, feed blind items to the trade journals.' Lita flipped through the stack of congratulatory notes from clients. 'This is great, Harry. You need a larger bonus. How about another five per cent?'

'I'd rather have stock options.'

'Why?'

'Because I'm not stupid, Lita.' Harry grinned at the younger girl. 'I see where this is going.'

Lita had arranged to get her stuff out of Edward's place when he was at work. She unpacked carefully and put everything personal in storage in her basement. Then she went to a rentals agency and put her place on the market for a corporate let for two months, furnished.

'I can't believe you bothered with that,' Harry said as he drove her out to the airport.

'Take care of the pennies, man.'

'Whatever that means.' Harry wrinkled his nose. 'Are you gonna be OK in London, Lita? You don't know anyone there.'

'I know Jocelyn Wilson.'

'I meant like friends.'

'I can make some. Besides, who has time for friends? I'm gonna be stuck to my desk.'

'My wife has some London friends. She can call them for you.'

'That's sweet, but—'

Harry waved aside her protests. 'You've got to have some social life, or you'll have a nervous breakdown.'

Lita tossed her glossy chestnut mane. 'Nervous breakdown? You make me laugh.'

'Don't tell me. You don't have time for one.'

Jocelyn Wilson was as good as his word. He kept Lita busy. There was the ferry company account. Lita managed to sell holidays on that like they were exotic Nordic cruises. There was corporate PR, and fall-out from the planned sales of Lancaster's bones, with the vultures from various industries hovering around. She spent the mornings interviewing and hiring staff; young, hungry, talented kids that liked T-Rex and Bowie and the Who and weren't getting on at the big PR and advertising agencies.

Lita expected them to know her name. If you were an ad guy, you had to know the pulse of the business. She was hot in New York, and New Age, with its core of Doheny refugees, was a comer. If they knew that, and they dressed hip, she'd hire them. She made the London branch of New Age in her own image, and it wasn't long before they got their first non-Wilson client. It was a contractor that built identical tract houses, red-brick little boxy things, each the exact specifications of the next.

'Hideous,' Trisha Wood, her newly hired number two, a former unpromoted but brilliant copywriter from Y&R, pronounced, when flipping through the brochure.

'Secure. Convenient. Modern,' Lita corrected her.

'But of course.' Trisha winked.

Their campaign for that one was a great success. Now, as it had always done for Lita, the phone started ringing off the hook. Not only was she the hot new girl in town, she made it a policy to charge at least twenty per cent less than the big agencies.

The only problem was her personal life.

Lita couldn't sleep. Often she didn't get back to her flat until ten at night, and then, even if she had a quick bath and bolted her supper so that she was in bed by eleven, rest eluded her. Counting sheep didn't work, neither did the non-prescription sleep aids with cutesy names like Nighty-Night that just made her feel ill. She ignored it, of course, but after a month she found herself spacing out in a planning meeting.

'Wake up, boss.' Charlie Wall, one of their account executives, was shaking her. Lita blinked and came to. Two young creative executives were standing by their presentation and looking despondent. 'I thought this stuff was great, and it's making you fall asleep?'

'Damn it.' She passed one slender hand through her dark hair. 'No, I'm sorry. The material was great. I've been sick. I have insomnia. Can we do it tomorrow? I'll go home and take a nap.'

'Here.' Charlie scribbled a name and number on his yellow legal pad and shot it across the table to her. 'This guy's supposed to be fantastic. My sister went to him last month and he cured her.'

'Thanks,' Lita said. She excused herself and had her secretary make an appointment. His name was Dr Mark Conran, and he'd had a cancellation that morning. Could she come round right away?

Lita could. Despite her tiredness and her aching eyes, she really didn't want to take a nap. Trying to sleep filled her with dread.

Dr Conran had offices in one of the old, elegant Victorian buildings in Queen Anne Street. Lita took an old, impossibly elegant elevator made of wrought iron twisted into interlocking fleur-de-lis that was hauled smoothly up an open stairwell by its thick cables, to a third-floor suite with a discreet-looking brass nameplate outside. His reception room was decorated with Colefax and Fowler wall fabrics in deep, luxurious red. The magazines were ranged neatly in a mahogany rack, and the couches looked antique.

Yeah, Lita thought. This is going to be expensive.

'Miss Morales?' A middle-aged receptionist in a stout tweed suit opened the door for her. 'The doctor will see you now. Please, come in.'

'Thank you,' Lita said. She walked into his offices, and the woman closed the door quietly behind her.

The inner office was decorated with similar masculine taste, all dark burgundy leather chairs, an examining bench and medical equipment hidden in dark mahogany cabinets. The doctor was sitting behind a walnut desk. He rose as she entered.

'Miss Morales, isn't it? I'm Dr Conran.'

Lita placed him at about thirty-six. He had light brown hair, green eyes and under his starched white coat she detected an immaculate dark suit. He had a small gold signet ring and plain gold cufflinks. He was an imposing man, tall but not lanky, perhaps six feet two, and he had an aquiline nose and square jaw, aristocratic and highly attractive.

Suddenly she wished she didn't look quite so much of a wreck. It was a mild September day, and she had pulled on a light and simple pink wool dress and matched it with a sleek pair of heels, but that wasn't going to change anything. Not with her skin sallow and her eyes reddened from lack of sleep. The circles underneath them were so dark she looked as though somebody had given her a couple of black eyes.

'Hi, Doctor.'

'So you've been having trouble sleeping. Take a seat, please.' He indicated the cavernous leather armchair in front of him. 'Is this normal for you?'

'No. It's only been for the last month.'

'Open the buttons on your dress, please.' His cool eyes swept over her as she obediently peeled the ivory buttons apart, and he placed a cold stethoscope on her skin. Lita winced.

'I'm sorry. Just a second.' He listened for a few moments, then took it away. 'When was the last time you had a full medical check-up, Miss Morales?'

'Uh.' She blushed. 'Actually, I've never had one. I've been too busy.'

'For what?' He looked her over. 'Twenty-six years?'

'Well, I was a model and then an advertising executive. It's very busy work,' she said sheepishly.

'I see.' He frowned. 'And so, as a child, when were you last checked out?'

'I wasn't. We didn't have health insurance,' Lita explained, and her blush deepened on her smooth olive cheek. She hated telling this man with his obvious wealth that she had been poor.

He shook his head and wrapped a tube around her arm. 'Make a fist, please.'

'You're taking my blood pressure.'

'Correct,' he agreed.

'What does this have to do with my sleep problem?'

'You need a full medical check-up, Miss Morales. Blood work, everything. Now,' he added in a voice that did not brook argument, 'please tell me about your work habits. Have you recently changed your routine?'

'Well, I'm setting up an office in England.' Lita shrugged. 'It takes work. I guess I'm working late. But I get into bed by eleven whenever I can.'

'And when do you get home?' he asked perceptively.

'Ten,' Lita admitted.

Dr Conran looked at her sternly. 'Do you try to catch up with your sleep on the weekends?'

He unhooked his blood-pressure gauge. 'One-twenty over eighty. Excellent. I'm going to draw some blood now. Make a fist, please.' He swabbed her vein with alcohol, and the green eyes bored into hers.

'Not really. I guess I try and cat-nap. But I work weekends.'

'Saturday and Sunday?'

Lita nodded. 'Nobody's in charge but me, Doctor.'

Dr Conran pulled the needle out of her arm, filled with rich, dark blood. Lita glanced down and saw he had done it so precisely there was barely a visible puncture mark.

'Miss Morales.' He sounded severe. 'You can't sleep because you're working yourself into the ground. You can't return home at ten and hope to have unwound by eleven. You need to digest your food and have a little relaxation. Moreover, you can't work seven days a week and hope to maintain mental and physical health. I want you to take a holiday at once, and in the future, structure your working day so that you're back home no later than seven p.m.'

Lita blinked, then laughed aloud.

Dr Conran looked at her levelly. 'Something amusing?'

'Sure, very amusing.' She waved one hand dismissively. 'It might be news to you, Doc, but I can't work that way. My company isn't going to establish itself, and you have no idea of the time pressures I'm under. Please, just prescribe me some drugs and let's be done with it, OK?'

In response, Dr Conran pressed a button on his intercom. 'Mrs Rogers, Miss Morales is just leaving. Please, get her address so we can send the results of her blood tests to her.'

'You're kicking me out?' Lita demanded furiously.

His expression was tight and unrelenting. 'Yes, Miss Morales. I don't prescribe drugs where none are needed. If you haven't got time for your health, I haven't got time to waste treating you.'

The door opened a crack and the secretary came in, holding a form.

'Please, give us a minute,' Lita said.

'Certainly, madam,' she said, and withdrew.

Lita wasn't used to being spoken to in that manner. The doctor's gruffness was a wake-up call. He was sincere enough to lose a rich patient over this.

'I'm sorry, Doctor. I'll try and do what you suggest. If you'll treat me.'

He nodded slowly. 'Very well. Now . . .' He consulted his watch. 'I's already past two. I want you to take the rest of the day off.'

Lita wanted to say, But. She stopped herself.

'Go to the Dorchester that's my suggestion. They have a spa there. You should get a massage. It's ideal for stress relief. And consider taking up exercise.'

Lita shivered. 'Aerobics? Jumping around with Jane Fonda? It's really not me.'

'I swim. You might want to consider that.' He shook her hand in a firm, dry grip. 'Come back and see me next week.'

Lita took Dr Conran's advice. It was hard not to. He was so sure of himself, she felt she'd be taking her life in her hands by doing otherwise. She had a massage, and while the masseuse gently kneaded her flesh she found herself thinking about him. She half drifted off, and in her unwary state, thoughts that would usually never surface bobbed up unchallenged. Like how tall and aristocratic-looking he was, how piercing those green eyes were. She loved the unusual striking good looks, the noble Roman nose and the air of command . . .

Stop that, she finally admonished herself. A crush on your doctor. That's ridiculous.

But she found herself looking forward immensely to the next week's appointment.

'Welcome back.' Dr Conran looked her over critically. 'Let me see. Yes, the circles have gone. You've been following my instructions?'

'Yes, Doctor,' Lita said meekly.

She'd gone the full hog this time. She was wearing a skin-tight black leather catsuit, perfect now the weather had acquired a sudden chill. She'd added a little blush to her cheeks, had had her eyebrows freshly waxed, a manicure and a blow-dry at Vidal Sassoon. Her long, luxuriantly thick brown hair rippled over her shoulders.

'Can you tug down your lower eyelid for me, please?' he said, apparently unfazed by her wild lavender-and-emerald eye-shadow.

'But I'll smudge my mascara,' Lita protested, then kicked herself. What kind of a bimbo would he think her?

'Nevertheless, I need to see your lower eyelid. Yes, very good. You aren't anaemic. I like to confirm first-hand what my blood work says.' He went to sit back behind his desk, cool and impersonal. 'Here's your report.' He handed her the test results.

Goddamn him, Lita thought. He could at least notice my outfit. I spent two hours on this.

'Oh, and about your outfit, Miss Morales.'

'Please, call me Lita, Doctor.'

'Very well, Lita.' He smiled at her, and it was like his whole face lit up. 'That outfit isn't good for the circulation. It's too tight, and it might disrupt your blood flow. That's all.'

Lita tried not to let her crestfallen face show. She beat a hasty retreat to the door, then smiled at Mrs Rogers in the outer office.

'So, when do I see the doctor again?' she asked. 'Next week?'

'Oh, no, madam. You won't need to see him again for another year. Good morning, Mr Harris,' she added to the old man behind Lita. 'The doctor will see you now.'

Shit, Lita thought as she left the office.

Oh, well. It was sophomoric to be infatuated with a physician. Maybe there just weren't enough cute guys at work for her to think about, Lita told herself the next Saturday. She had been obeying Dr Conran's orders, and she felt so much better for it that it wasn't even funny. If she knew she had to be home by seven, she just worked harder. Or, at least, smarter. She managed to let some of her talented new employees pry just a little control from her iron grip, and as a result they got more done, better, because Lita was free to concentrate on the big picture.

Now she would come home, cook something for herself, eat it with a large glass of wine and listen to Mozart or watch *Top of the Pops*. She was relaxed and rested, and she worked better. She actually had a life. If you overlooked the lack of a man.

So here she was, on her way to the Century Health club in Chelsea Harbour, her neat little Louis Vuitton carrying-case packed with a towel, a cashmere robe and other necessary items. They had a warm, Olympic-sized pool in the brand-new, modern gym. Lita had started swimming and found it pretty relaxing. At least her health was improving. She waved to the receptionist who nodded at her to go through. Other members had to sign in, but not Lita. Everyone recognized her. She slipped into the women's changing room, with its bamboo matting and oversized lockers, and changed into her swimsuit, a lemon-yellow Lycra number, cut high on the thigh. She tied back her long hair and tugged on the tight little cap, then walked through the sterile footbath out to the long, echoing cavern of the pool, built under glass, with hothouse plants dotted back against the walls.

'Hello,' said a voice.

Lita jumped out of her skin and almost lost her balance on the slippery tiles. A strong male hand reached out to steady her.

'You don't want to crack your head open.'

Her mouth opened slightly.

'Dr Conran! What are you doing here?'

He was wearing a pair of tight, and therefore very flattering, black shorts. Lita dragged her eyes away from the tell-tale bulge in his crotch, but didn't know where to put them. It was hard not to stare at the thick, ball-player thighs, the tight muscles of his quads, the defined crunch of the stomach muscles with their thick silky knot of hair trailing down to his waistband, or the worked-out pecs covered with dripping, beautiful black hair.

'I'm off duty. Call me Mark.'

'And it's Lita,' she said, fidgeting. A stab of intense desire was blasting through her stomach.

'That's a beautiful name.' And that's a beautiful body, Conran thought. Damn it all. He was going to have to get the woman another doctor. As professional and smooth as he'd fought to appear with her, it was not every day such a fox strutted through the doors of his office. To his horror, his groin had started to stir the first time he put a stethoscope between those awesome soft breasts. That was not supposed to happen to doctors.

Now he was toast. You could stick a fork in him. Oh, shit. Look at her, with that olive skin and perfect-ten body, her ass in that yellow suit jutting out behind her, perfectly rounded and lifted, and that tiny waist and then the swollen tits, with the nipples winking at him from under that tantalizing suit. She was short and curvy, in ideal proportion, everything from the sexy hollow in her throat to the turn of her ankle, on which she was wearing a tiny gold bracelet. He could never safely examine this woman without being struck off the register. He'd have to hurry to get out of there. Once there was water trickling between those breasts . . .

Oh, God. There it was again, that tell-tale tickle in his crotch. Hurriedly, Conran half ran to the edge of the pool and dived straight in.

Lita watched his body curve tautly and part the water with incredible precision. If he hadn't been a doctor, he might have been an athlete.

It was no good. Her nipples hardened mercilessly. She walked to the edge of the pool and slipped into the water herself, for safety. She couldn't continue to see this guy. Lita racked her brains. He was swimming back towards her. But what the hell did you say? Not, Oh, Doctor I can't see you any more, you're too gorgeous . . .

Maybe she had been referred to a specialist. Yeah, that was it. Lita took a deep breath. He was swimming towards her like a very muscular otter. His head surfaced, and he stood up, towering over her.

'Lita. I'm afraid I won't be able to treat you any more, but I can give you a referral to another very good doctor.'

'B-but . . . why not?' Lita stammered. It was one thing for her to make an excuse, quite another for him to blow her off.

He smiled, and his lips had a slightly crooked quirk to them that she found enchanting.

'Because I feel the urgent need to ask you out instead. Not that I expect you to say yes, but . . . might there be any chance you'd consider having dinner with me at Blake's tonight?'

Chapter 32

'Where are we going?'

Logan looked over at her and chuckled. 'Now, now. Patience. It's my date, and I set the agenda. You don't want to be a sore loser, do you?'

Becky scowled at him. 'I guess not.'

He handled the car like it was a horse, Becky noticed, his hands easy on the wheel, coaxing the old banger almost smoothly round the narrow twists and turns of the back country roads. His car was a piece of shit, but she couldn't pretend she wasn't enjoying this. The trees overhung the roads with a carpet of emerald, pierced through with shafts of sunlight. Soon they fell away, and the car took a steep climb up a hill, with fields and copses stretching below them.

'God, this is beautiful,' Becky breathed.

Logan winked at her. 'Just wait.'

He finally pulled the car into a stop on a bare patch of gravel. They were at the top of a ridge, which banked down steeply below them. The view was fantastic – lush fields in a patchwork of grass green and arable yellow, and then behind them, dark, massed woods, with a glittering river snaking into them from the left. The horizon shimmered slightly and shivered a little dance in the heat.

'This is . . . incredibly romantic.'

He grinned. 'Yeah, it is, rather.'

'Don't tell me. They call this Devil's Leap.'

Logan laughed out loud, a rich, deep laugh that lit up his entire face, and Becky couldn't keep up the barriers that she had shoved between them. She smiled back, and he thought her face was like a morning glory flower opening up to the sun.

He moved closer to her, until Becky could smell the faint masculine tang of him and feel the heat of his breath on her face. She halfclosed her eyes, waiting for him to kiss her. In fact, she wanted him to kiss her. And maybe she secretly had for quite a while.

There had been nobody since Rupert. She'd had no time, and she hadn't even wanted anyone else. But now . . .

he lifted weights, he even boxed. When he took her out to dinner parties, he was gregarious, rather cynical, dry and witty. The other women there looked at her with envy and muttered obviously catty things behind her back, which Lita, tossing her glossy mane and giving them a long, arrogant smile, rather enjoyed. As her client list widened, she had to start socializing. She found, to her surprise, that she quite enjoyed it. Giving a dinner for important clients and their wives was as good for business as a late-night session in the office – in fact, better – and now Mark was sternly supervising her health, Lita was forced to do it more often. Only she was good at it. These weren't the days back in New York with Rupert, when she was trailing around after him, hoping desperately to be found good enough. Lita was confident in her own skills and her new company. And she had that American-abroad style that the London wives seemed to long to imitate. It was the seventies, and Britain was bound in strikes, stoppages and power failures, while America revelled in Charlie's Angels and oil money. It endowed Lita with instant glamour, and she made the most of it.

Mark helped her to do that. Unlike Rupert, he needed nothing from her success, and unlike Edward, he didn't resent it. He supported her, but he also demanded that she support him. They were falling in love, independent of each other, but protective of each other. He made her laugh, he made her feel safe, he made her sweat with longing to have him inside her.

And that was the problem.

Mark had never been to bed with her. Not once.

She didn't think he was gay, though the thought had crossed her mind, and it made her feel physically sick, almost panicked. This was only the third relationship of her life. Rupert – well, the fire of hatred in her for him still burned. Her first love, and her first hate. One day she would deal with him the way she had dealt with his snotty girlfriend. Edward – physically intense, but emotionally dead. She still felt slightly dirtied from that love, because he had been dominant to the extent that he wanted to crush her spirit, and she had fought too long and too hard for that. And now Mark, younger, more vital than Edward, funnier too, more loving, more of a friend. One she ached for. And it was almost as if he didn't want her.

Lita didn't want to confront him about it. But she knew she had to. They had been dating now for almost two months. And she didn't want to believe that she had chosen wrong again with Mark, too. Because then she might never be able to trust her own judgement again.

She planned and plotted but could never bring herself to say anything, and then finally she blurted it out in the street, when they were walking down Piccadilly on their way to Hamley's to look for a doll for Mark's niece.

'Yes, I need to talk to you about that.' He sighed. 'I've been putting it off.'

'Oh, God,' Lita said, looking horrified. 'You're gay.'

'What?' Mark's eyes rounded with shock, then he started to laugh. 'Dear God, no. What the hell would I be doing dating you if I were *gay*?' His eyes flickered over her body appreciatively. 'Let me tell you something, honey, you're no Twiggy. No gay man wants anything to do with those curves.'

'Then what the hell is it?' Lita demanded.

'Let's go and have lunch,' Mark said.

He took her to a pub, the Duke of Sussex, and settled them into one of those dark, musty-smelling banquettes with the polished wood sides and faded velvet seats that Lita was coming to appreciate, in a back room far away from the jukebox and the TV set showing Arsenal vs. Coventry. Mark ordered scampi and a couple of pints, then sat opposite her and started to fidget.

'You don't need to be nervous,' Lita said, though her heart was thudding. 'We can work through it, whatever it is. Are you . . . you know . . .?'

'Impotent? Nope. I'm in perfect working order.' His eyes trickled over her breasts again. 'And dating you, that can sometimes be a trial.'

'Then I don't get it. I thought you found me attractive.'

'I do. God, you don't know how bloody much. I think of you all the time. I'm glad I'm not a surgeon – I could get distracted any minute. I'd be a menace to the poor sod on the operating table.'

The waiter came and laid down their food. Lita's fingers drummed on the table with impatience. She couldn't wait for him to leave.

'The thing is.' He sighed. 'I'm a Catholic.'

Lita stared at him. 'I know. What difference does that make?'

'I'm practising. I actually believe in it. I want to wait until I get married.'

'You're a virgin!' she almost shouted.

Mark grimaced. 'A bit louder, babe, I don't think they heard you in Scotland. And actually, no, I'm not. When I was a teenager . . . But now . . . This is what I want.'

'But . . . we could be waiting for ever,' Lita said.

He looked at her wolfishly. 'That depends on you, doesn't it?'

She paused, then let the blush spread richly over her face. 'You're kidding. You *want* to marry me?'

'Why wouldn't I want to marry you?'

She thought of Rupert and Edward. 'I don't know. The other guys I were with . . .'

'The other guys you were with were arseholes,' Mark said. 'And I'm not.'

Logan drove her back late, as the sky's red and gold streaks were already fading to blue and the twilight darkened across the Shropshire hills. Becky couldn't stop looking at him, could hardly bear to take her eyes off him. She felt his touch across every inch of her skin, where he had caressed her like he wanted to feel every part of her, from the firm, smooth skin on the inside of her thighs to the delicate bone of her ankle and the high dancer's arch of her instep.

'I want to come back with you, but I can't.'

Becky suppressed a stab of disappointment. 'I understand.'

'I already blew the whole day off, and I have to get back to the office and make calls. But I'll be down to Fairfield tomorrow, day after at the latest.'

'OK.' She picked a few grass strands from her clothes. 'I guess I'll see you there, then.'

She wasn't going to get too stressed about it. Logan was the one for her. There was no doubt in her mind.

When she got back, he called to apologize and say there had been a delay. It would take six weeks to finish up the job he was on currently, because the owner had messed up a garden wall and it had collapsed, wrecking his hothouse. Becky was wretched, more so when Tracy took the phone from her boss and asked Becky to send the new cheque.

'Of course,' she said coldly, and put it in the mail that day.

'Will you come down on weekends?' she asked Logan when they next spoke. His low chuckle was maddening, sexy and too far away.

'No, baby. I want to get t' job done, so I can spend the right time with you. And we'll figure it out from there. Besides, you'll be flying off to t' Scilly Isles soon.'

'That's right.' She had spilled her guts out to him on her plans for selling the hotel and starting a new business.

'Better I do this than twiddle my thumbs. I'm not good on the phone, sugar. I'll see you soon, all right?'

'Calm down,' Sharon said when she saw her face. 'My God, I've never seen a man get you like this.'

'He's a jerk,' Becky said, furious at being blown off.

'I thought he was the best lover in history.'

'I must have been dreaming. Come on, get in the car.'

'Where are we going?'

'We're going to the Scilly Isles,' Becky said angrily. 'I've got a hotel to sell.'

They wrapped up the deal quickly enough. Becky stayed in the hotel while she took investors round it, talking to her lawyers and watching how her improvements had worked in practice.

'This was what the place was like before Lancaster started the remodelling,' Martin Drasner, the general manager, told her, showing her a large album of photographs and wall plans.

Becky winced. 'Yes, I remember.' Hideous chintzes and faded patterned carpets. Her new style, neutral beige carpeting and walls, each room hung with different and inexpensive paintings for distinctiveness, had given the place a much more modern feel with less cost. Some of the old, early adrenaline she'd felt had started coming back to her.

'I'm surprised it took you this long to sell,' Drasner said. 'The hotel has a ninety/sixty-five per cent split in occupancy, season to off-season, because of the promotions you run in winter.' He dropped his voice. 'Scilly Isles tourism is off in general, though. The big chains have been circling this hotel for a couple of years now, but it's really the time to sell.'

'I agree.' Becky snapped the book shut. 'You said you wanted to resign?'

'I want to work on the mainland. Besides,' he shrugged, 'the Hiltons of this world like to use their own people.'

Drasner was an early hire of hers, Becky recalled. He had helped her lay people off and keep the costs low by making contractors bid for their business.

'You might want to consider coming to work for me, Mr Drasner,' she said.

'You have another hotel, Miss Lancaster?'

'Not yet. But I'm going to,' Becky said.

His smile was polite, but regretful. 'Call me when you make your acquisition. I don't really have time to wait.'

Becky travelled back to Fairfield one week later and two hundred grand richer. That was the profit once all the debts had been settled. She had money to live on, and almost enough to start a new company. But not quite.

The hotels she targeted for improvement were ready to sell, in good positions, and trammelled by uncooperative union labour and winter vacancy rates. So far, so good. However, the banks refused to give her the mortgage necessary to buy any of them outright.

'You have no experience of running a hotel, Miss Lancaster.'

'I ran one very successfully at Lancaster,' Becky said for what seemed like the hundredth time. 'Look at my goddamn record.'

The commercial loans manager at Lloyds frowned at her language. 'Your record, Miss Lancaster, frankly, does not inspire confidence. A company broken up . . . well . . .'

'Those aren't the facts,' Becky said, colouring.

'Mr Wilson's press people sent us detailed factual statements, Miss Lancaster. I did my research on this request,' he said smugly. 'Would you like to see the dossier?'

Not trusting herself to speak, trembling with rage, Becky held out her hand.

The firm that had put it together was called New Age. There was a glossy mock prospectus, and everything in it was true. It concentrated on Uncle Henry, Rupert and the high rates of refinancing she'd had to agree to for the bridge loan. It was damning, and vicious, and her blood pressure rose as she read it.

Careful not to let her emotions show, Becky flipped to the back page. There was a picture of Wilson looking sober and trustworthy, and a picture of a young, beautiful woman with dark hair and olive skin . . .

I know her, Becky thought, and the recognition flashed into her mind so strongly she almost dropped the report.

'Thank you for your time,' she said automatically, hardly looking at the banker. She almost ran from his office, and couldn't compose herself until she was out on the street.

She had forgotten the name of that woman. But she would find out. And she would break her.

Chapter 33

Lita knew he was the right guy when she took him home and he managed to do something with Chico.

'Jeez. Another limey,' her brother muttered sullenly, sitting at the table in his ill-fitting suit. He made sure the words were loud enough for Mark to hear. 'What the hell is wrong with American guys?'

Mark leaned across the table and winked at him. 'The thing is, I bench two-fifty and I'm hung like a horse.'

Chico blinked in astonishment then burst out laughing.

'You're OK, man,' he said.

Pappy inspected the ring that Mark had put on Lita's finger. It was a three-stone, round cut, sleek, modern design from Cartier in platinum, with a two-carat stone in the centre flanked by half-carat stones. When Lita's hand moved, the whole room glittered from the light it threw off.

'Hmm.' He grunted his satisfaction. 'You're a doctor? Doctors got money.'

'Pappy,' Lita protested, blushing richly. 'I make my own money.'

'A man should be able to take care of his woman,' Pappy said unrepentantly. 'Not like that lord guy.'

'Mr Morales, I brought you a copy of my bank statement,' Mark said easily, 'as well as pictures of my house in town and my place in the country.'

Lita blinked at him. 'You did what?'

Chico was laughing at her, which made a nice change from his usual sulky, resentful stares.

'Your father is concerned that I can keep you in the style to which you have become accustomed. So I brought proof,' Mark said, grinning.

'Yeah. That's good.' Her father glanced over the papers; to Lita's mortification he was actually checking the figures. 'I like this guy, Rosa.'

Mrs Morales came back with her roast lamb and put it on the table.

'God, that smells good,' Mark said, sniffing hungrily.

Her mother beamed, and Lita squeezed his hand under the table. In exchange, Mark deftly slipped his hand up her thigh, keeping his eyes fixed on her father.

The wedding took place in America. 'Bride's home,' Lita had insisted, and Mark had shrugged.

'As long as we get married soon, I couldn't care whether it's Oxford, New York or sodding Timbuktu.'

He didn't even blink at flying in hordes of his family and friends. New Wave negotiated a good rate at the Victrix, and Lita invited Janice, Harry, Mrs Harry and her other friends from the company. The girls oohed and aahed over her diamond.

'He must be loaded,' Janice said.

Lita thought of all those first-class tickets for Uncle Jacob and Aunt Camilla. 'You know, I kinda think he is.'

The girls giggled.

'Business is pretty good. You're not doing so badly yourself,' Janice reminded her.

'I know.' Lita resisted an impulse to hug herself. 'It's finally all coming together.'

They held the ceremony in St Patrick's Cathedral.

'That's going to be impossible,' Lita said when Mark told her his plans.

'I've got connections,' Mark said.

And he had. They found them an impossible-to-get slot, and Lita had to practically stop her mother from fainting with glee. She got to invite a few of her friends from Queens, sitting in the pews in big dresses and too-tight shoes and green with envy. Lita was thrilled for her mother. Mama almost got more joy out of this than Lita did.

Almost, but not quite.

Lita's style on her wedding day was the same as her normal style – fresh, light, modern. She wore a slim sheath dress with sheer organza sleeves and a draped, cowl neck in heavy cream satin with no beading or fuss. Her bouquet was fresh grasses, arum lilies and white tulips, and instead of a veil she had a circlet of orange blossom woven into her loose, glossy dark hair. She kept her face almost bare of make-up – just a little concealer under the eyes to hide the excitement of the night before and gloss on her large, soft lips, which Mark found so erotic. Her lashes were so thick and dark they needed nothing, and beyond that, Lita decided to let her young, clear skin speak for itself.

Mark wore English morning dress, something that involved a waistcoat and tails, and he managed to look as comfortable in it as though it were a pair of jeans. After the ceremony, which passed in a

Lita, limos picked them up and drove them a few short blocks to rix, where Mark had hired the ballroom. The place was covered in tumbling fountains of pale pink roses and huge, cloudy bunches of babies' breath in square crystal vases. The chairs were covered in crisp white cotton, the waiters served roast Long Island duckling with a bitter orange sauce, and the cake, taking centre stage, was an eight-layer pale blue and gold affair. Lita's family and her guests moved from stately shuffling around to the string quartet to drunken congas once the third bottles of Tattinger Rosé had been drunk.

After Pappy's mercifully short speech, Mark tugged at Lita's hand, and they slipped out through the throng to the ballroom's large terrace, carved of solid white marble. Mark shut the doors and circled his arm possessively around Lita's waist as they stared out over the magnificent view of Central Park and uptown. It was a glorious New York summer day, with the sky as clear blue as a robin's egg and the sun glittering off the lake in the park, while tiny stick figures of humans ran around below them and the constant river of traffic crawled up the tarmac streams of Manhattan.

'Don't you miss it?' Mark murmured in her ear.

'Sometimes.' Lita shrugged. 'I have to build up in Europe before I can come home. With wages and stuff, it's going to take me a few years to see any actual profits. I'd like to make more than just a good salary. Besides . . .' She kissed him on the cheek. 'I can't come back, because now there's you.'

Mark smiled dryly.

'I'm portable. Sick people are everywhere.'

'This wedding has been perfect,' Lita said.

Mark tugged at her sleeve. 'Mmm. Yes. Now, can we get the hell out of here?'

To escape the crowds of their families, Mark had booked them into the Plaza. They had a suite on one of the higher floors, looking towards the Park – that was if you ever managed to escape from the bedroom. Roses were crammed into silver vases, and there was a magnum of Krug chilling in an ice-bucket by the bed. The bathroom was a fantasy of gold and ivory, and the bed was king-size and made up with silk sheets.

'We never have to leave this room if we don't feel like it,' Mark said. He tipped the valet twenty dollars and shut the door firmly behind him. 'Mrs Conran.'

Lita blushed. For some reason, she suddenly felt nervous, almost self-conscious. This would be her first time with Mark, and even though she was sure she loved him, she didn't really know how to handle it. What would he be expecting, and what . . .?

He was looking her over, slowly, deliberately.

'You're tense. I thought I was the one who was supposed to have jitters.'

'I am not,' Lita lied, reaching for the champagne.

Mark's firm hand came down across hers. 'No, no medication. I want you fully conscious for this.' He walked across the room and drew the inner chiffon curtains so that they were protected from the eyes of any stray pervert with so binoculars but so the warm sunset light still spilled into the room, washing Lita's ivory gown with the faintest suggestion of rose. Mark walked up to her and stood behind her, tugging at her zip so that her wedding dress slithered off her in a rustle of silk and satin, sliding down the taut, olive length of her calves and pooling around her ankles.

Lita stood there in La Perla snow-white lace, a little demitasse bra, strapless, that fought to contain her breasts. They spilled out deliciously over the top, and Mark found his breath catching in his throat. Her small waist tapered down to flat stomach, lean from exercise, then flared out again as the swell of her ass was caught in another wisp of white lace, cut high on the thigh, that seemed to make her more naked than bare flesh alone would have, because it teased him unmercifully. Bisecting the firm, creamy flesh at the tops of her thighs were the lines of her garter belt, matching cream against her tawny skin, with see-through white stockings running down to her kitten heels, sheer enough so he could see the colour of her smooth thighs through them.

'Mmh,' Mark said. It was more of a grunt. He swooped up her dress and flung it unceremoniously over the back of a Louis XVIII chair. 'I could eat you. In fact, I think I will.'

Lita felt a prickling of desire crackle over her skin, raising all the downy hairs on the back of her arms and legs. She reached out and tugged at his tie, but Mark's hand brushed hers back.

'Not yet.'

He stretched out one finger and traced a light, teasing line down the line of her jaw to her bra, circling just above her nipple, which was red and peaked through the lace. Lita gasped faintly, little tendrils of desire shooting from her breasts down to her belly and between her legs, burning there. Mark expertly unhooked her bra, letting her full breasts bounce slightly free. Lita heard his own breath shorten. His hands moved forward, but didn't touch her, maddening her. His eyes dwelt on her swollen, dark nipples, and his hands slid down her waist, snapping her garter belt free. He gently tugged the stockings from her slim legs, his thumb and forefinger rubbing against the arch of her foot.

Lita suppressed a moan in the back of her throat. Mark was making her wait, touching her everywhere that wasn't obvious, lighting up her whole body, her whole skin. Tiny hairs rose everywhere. She became desperately conscious of the sensation of the soft carpet under her toes, of the whisper of inadequate lace between her legs, where she was completely moist and slick. Mark was fully dressed, even to having his shoes on. His eyes trailed possessively over her body, where she stood in front of him, trembling.

He was on his knees now and he raised his hands, tormentingly slowly, up her calves, touching her, massaging her, keeping his eyes level with them, until he drew up between her legs and his stare bored right through the tiny snatch of white fabric. He inserted his two thumbs under her panties and rubbed the sides of her hips, tugging the tiny triangle free so that she was completely naked, and she could feel his hot breath against her skin . . .

'Mark. God,' Lita panted.

He pressed his mouth closer and trailed the tip of his tongue over her. Lita sobbed and bit against the sides of her cheeks to keep herself quiet. When she was squirming hard against him, he stood up, grinning, and kicked off his shoes. Lita wanted to tear the buttons from his shirt, but her fingers were shaking so much she knew she wouldn't be able to control them. Mark stripped off his clothes fast, working efficiently, like he had total control of himself. His body was the way she had known it would be – wiry and hard, with his erection thick against the dark silky hair of his groin. He moved back closer to her, pressing himself against her, not taking her quite yet, his hands ranging over her skin, lightly brushing over the nipples, then darting down her back, cupping the firm swell of her ass. His breath was hot against her skin. Lita writhed in his arms.

'Mark, Mark . . .'

'What?' His voice was a whisper in her ear. 'You didn't expect this? You have to be prepared. You see, I'm a doctor. I know how your body works. Every inch of it.'

He lifted her up and carried her lightly to the bed. Her weight was as nothing in his arms. He laid her down, and she felt the satin coverlet against her body.

'You're mine, Lita. I waited to claim you, and now you're mine.'

He kissed her hard and pulled her hands over her head, pinning her wrists together with one hand while the other one strayed over her thighs, gently pushing them apart. Then he thrust, hard, into her, still controlled, his mouth working its way along her jawline and down her neck, the little butterfly kisses contrasting with the hard movement of his hips pressing into her. Lita's back arched with sheer pleasure. She was so primed, so ready for him. Her nails dug into his back, but Mark didn't stop, didn't even seem to notice. Small waves of pressure broke from the centre of her, her pleasure building up relentlessly, until she was moving with him, gasping out his name. Mark twisted his hips, angling his thickness even deeper into her so that he pushed against the small, melting, white-hot spot in the slick walls of her which Lita hadn't even known was there, and she shuddered into a huge, relentless orgasm, and somewhere felt Mark gasp and surrender himself inside her, until they were sweating and panting in each other's arms.

Becky placed a call to Ken Stone, who had refused a position at Wilson in favour of a directorship at KPMG. He told her the name of the woman. Rosalita Morales, the president and founder of New Wave, apparently over in England to expand a New York business. Becky called Aunt Mindy, who knew a friend that worked on Madison Avenue, and she relayed that New Wave was a well-regarded boutique.

Not for long, Becky thought bitterly.

Her sunny nature had retreated behind clouds of anger and disappointment. Logan didn't call. He had sent her one card, a beautiful Victorian valentine with a pressed four-leafed clover inside it. Becky had never seen a real one. She looked at it, then tossed the card out.

Then there was Rosalita. You goddamn bitch, Becky thought. She knew, deep in her heart, that the woman had come here to destroy her. A little digging confirmed this fact, at least in Becky's mind. Her hatchet job on Lancaster had been the first thing her stupid little firm had done in England. Probably with the blessing of Rupert.

That was OK, Becky told herself. Lita would get hers. But until she had some power, she couldn't do a damn thing to her. Becky longed for Logan, the bastard, but the drive to reinvent her father's company was ever-present, and the only thing that could distract her.

'You can't get a hotel?'

Sharon was supportive and dismayed for Becky.

'No.' She shook her head, and her long golden hair gleamed in the sunlight. 'But I have an idea.'

'Why does that not surprise me?' Sharon blew out her cheeks.

'I already have a building.' Becky gestured to the house behind her.

Sharon looked horrified. 'You can't be serious. The government will never let you touch this place. This is Grade I listed.'

'I'm not going to touch the place. At least, not much. I'm going to get permission to install plumbing in a couple of the rooms, so that they can be bathrooms. This isn't going to become a Holiday Inn. I'm thinking super-luxurious, high-end clientele, and not many of them either. Perhaps room for ten couples. We have six spare bathrooms right now. I won't touch the walls, I'll just run in some new pipes. I bet if I call English Heritage and ask them to design a plan in keeping with the house, I'll get permission.'

'That's a bloody good idea,' Sharon said slowly. 'You would make them feel you gave a damn about their opinions, so they wouldn't block you.'

Becky was enthusiastic. 'I have enough money not to need financing from anybody. Sure, it'll wipe me out, but what the hell. There's a market for that kind of luxury.'

Sharon looked doubtful. 'I don't know . . . Inflation . . . strikes, taxes . . . Nobody's spending much on luxury here.'

'Not in the UK. But that doesn't apply to the States.' Becky smiled. 'I know both places. And I know enough about conventional hotels to be able to run this well.'

'Go for it,' Sharon said. 'Bags I be Vice-President.'

'I don't know,' Becky said, looking her friend over critically. 'Just how cheap will you work?'

'Cow,' Sharon retorted, grinning.

After all the humiliations with the banks, this plan worked perfectly. Becky had her own money, and she knew how to kowtow to mandarins. Her plan for four more bathrooms was approved, and she spared no expense. The fixtures were designed to look like antiques but to work like new, with freestanding iron baths on little lion legs in the corners of the rooms, hot, powerful showers encased in glass but inlaid with marble and stone carvings of the Lancaster coat of arms. Becky kept records of every last penny she spent for tax, and Sharon helped her find labour – reliable friends who were maids, cooks and musicians. She knew a girl who had opened a professional massage salon, and drafted her in too.

'They'll expect a certain level of luxury.' Becky showed Sharon an old, musty storeroom in the back of the house. It had large, dirty bay windows that looked down towards the maze. 'I'm going to clear out this rubbish, spruce this up and set up a massage table, speakers for soothing music, a manicure desk, foot massage . . . Ellen will stay in the house every day while the guests are here, so they can have beauty treatments twenty-four seven.'

'I know a make-up artist that's on the dole,' Sharon suggested. 'She'd be glad to come, too. If I were a rich lady on vacation I'd love to have my hair washed and my make-up done professionally every day. Seduce the husband, like.'

'History and hairstyling. I love it. Can she do hair, too?'

'She can't cut it, but I think she can set it.'

'That'll have to do.'

Becky asked Mrs Morecambe to arrange for the old chauffeur, Jenkins, to be ready to make airport runs, and she used Irish linen for the sheets and Royal Doulton for the dinner service. Mrs Morecambe had a cousin who was a butler. Unemployment was ridiculously high in Heath's Britain, and people jumped at the chance of a new job. When she thought she was ready, she booked herself on a flight to New York, first class there and back.

She couldn't afford it, but that didn't matter. She was selling luxury, and that meant she had to think luxury.

Thank God she wouldn't be charged to stay at Aunt Mindy's

Chapter 34

Becky spent the first week catching up with her family. That was fun, almost too much fun. She didn't want anybody to know she found she had nothing in common with her old classmates, though. The girls were mostly full of plans to marry; rich bankers and lawyers were favoured. She found the old crowd, with their endless tennis matches and talk about nothing, to be completely uninteresting. But Becky put herself through it. She went horseback riding, put on her little white tennis skirt and sneakers, and chatted idly about the weather, movies and who was having whom to dinner.

She waited for her opportunity. She would spot it when it came.

'God, I'm *so tired* of Mauritius,' Katherine Simpson drawled one night over the pheasant and claret.

They were staying at Philip Simpson's 'farm' in Dutchess County. Simpson ran one of the more exclusive hunts in New York State, and owned exclusive health and racquet clubs in Manhattan. Becky was dining with her cousin Susie and her husband Bob, who shot game birds at the Simpsons' country club. They had twenty couples ranged around a long, seventeenth-century farmhouse table, all of them social register types, with a couple of nouveau Wall-Streeters thrown in for good measure. Becky liked the Wall Street types best, but she wasn't going to be fussy. She'd had to endure a bunch of needling from the others as to why she wasn't married yet, not to mention forcing polite conversation when seated next to the bespectacled, weedy nerds they seemed to think were good 'prospects' for her.

'It's so *crowded*. You simply can't find a decent exclusive place to stay any more. Princess Margaret's crowd are OK, but what about those awful rock stars? Mick Jagger, and so forth. I want something *quiet*.'

I'll bet you love hanging out with Mick Jagger, Becky thought silently, but her heart was hammering. If Katherine wanted to play that game, Becky could oblige her. It would just take a little bit of balls.

'I know exactly what you mean,' Becky said lightly. 'I have a vacation place, but it's not . . . shall we say . . . *suitable* for the common herd. Strictly invitation only. We're keeping the list *extremely* tight.'

Katherine's eyebrow lifted. 'Where is it?'

'It's my manor house in England. It's about five hundred years old, and the public have never been inside it. The English authorities have it listed, so I can't afford to advertise. Unacceptable applicants, you know.' Becky carefully lifted her glass of wine and turned to the spotty youth on her left, as though she was done with that topic.

'Hold on a moment, Rebecca,' Katherine Simpson said. Becky recalled Katherine – she had famously been an air hostess when she met Philip on a first-class flight somewhere. She was a huge social climber – the very thought of her being in on something others couldn't have was enough to make her drool. 'Tell me a little about this place.'

Becky turned to her hostess, and lowered her voice confidentially. 'It's the family seat. My mother, Lady Lancaster, was the first American ever to set foot inside it, if you can believe that.' That was good; she could see Katherine's eyes glitter at the title. 'I offer complete relaxation. Masseuses, manicurists, a private hairdresser and make-up artist all complimentary and twenty-four hours a day. A chauffeur on standby. Tours to stately homes other people can't get into.' How the hell was she going to pull that off? Becky wondered. What the hell, she'd find a way. 'It's a spa treatment for the very discerning, for people who appreciate European elegance. There will be private concerts, chamber music before dinner, horse-riding . . . all the gentlemanly and ladylike pursuits. Of course, you understand, I can't offer this to anybody but a very *select* group of people.'

Katherine Simpson was hooked. Her heavily mascara'd eyes were narrowing acquisitively.

'How big is your place?'

'Well, it's huge,' Becky admitted, 'but we'll only be accepting ten couples at a time. I don't believe in crowds. Of course, it will be . . . *premium* vacationing, and only for those that can afford that sort of thing. The price helps with the exclusivity.'

'And are you open for business?'

The uniforms weren't quite ready, she had no trips lined up, and no horses, and . . .

'Absolutely. I have someone in mind for the opening celebrations, but I haven't talked to them yet.'

'Oh, but you must give it to me.'

'To *you*?' Becky did a creditable job of looking surprised. 'I don't know, Katherine, the price . . .' She looked pained. 'It's ten thousand a week. Pounds, not dollars, per suite.'

Katherine laughed brightly. 'Goodness, very reasonable. I'll take all the rooms for two weeks. I've been meaning to put together a party of girlfriends for simply *ages*.'

Becky had a brainwave. 'You can have all the rooms but one. I've agreed to allow a photographer and journalist from *Town and Country* to take a few snaps of guests at the opening week.'

Katherine Simpson lived to get her picture in *Town and Country*. She couldn't stop the smirk from spreading across her face.

'Well, I *suppose* that would be all right,' she said, reluctantly.

Becky made her excuses after dinner, kissed her aunt on the cheek, and rushed back to JFK. Her ticket was transferable, so she caught the red-eye back to Heathrow. There was no chance of snatching any sleep. She jotted down her ideas on the back of the air-sick bag. First, call the press. Well, that wouldn't be too much of a problem. She could sell the American society magazines on this, no problem, super-exclusive, invitation only, ultra-expensive. She remembered a couple of titled bods who had been to her first ball. She would stick one of them on the welcoming committee and call some owners who hadn't surrendered to the National Trust and offer them a thousand pounds for the use of their halls for one night. Throw a dinner, with musicians . . .

She was still writing furiously when the plane touched down on the tarnac.

Katherine Simpson was the perfect guest. She gleefully reported to Becky that she'd had girlfriends in tears because she had no space for then to buy tickets. She also took two weeks and had all her guests send over their money in advance Becky instantly gave small bonuses to all her staff, with the promise of more to come if the guests were satisfied. She took the same trouble with the non-paying journalists that attended as she did with the wives of the bankers and senators, greeting then with vintage champagne and Charbonnel and Walker chocolates in their rooms, providing caviar and vodka, and filling each room with a huge bouquet of roses, each room having a different colour bloom. Finding the private houses was easy – everybody wanted money towards their heating bills. Becky organized a dinner with musicians in Elizabethan costume in the hall of Caerhaven Castle, she hired an impoverished academic from Oxford to offer a tour of the prettiest colleges, and went one better, paying drama students to put on a private performance of *A Midsummer Night's Dream* on her lawn.

The weather co-operated only fitfully, but Becky made a virtue of the autumn chill. She had warm fires laid and blazing in every room, she served liqueurs and she brought in soft lambswool robes from the Shetlands. One day, when there was an unseasonal hailstorm, Becky declared it 'Beauty Day', and the women were rubbed and primped and made up all day long.

It was an incredible success. The next set of guests were ringing Becky and begging to be admitted before the first set even left. Becky paid her staff handsome bonuses and set about putting together a winter holiday – an English Christmas package, with trips to Paris and private shopping in London, West End shows, boxes at Covent Garden and three more massage therapists.

She was busily negotiating with a local florist for a year-round rate when there was a rap at her door.

'Come in, Sharon,' Becky said, covering the phone with one hand.

It wasn't Sharon. It was Logan.

He was wearing a faded pair of jeans and tough work boots for the garden, along with a crumpled T-shirt that looked as though he had slept in it. He was unshaven and his hair had bits of grass in it.

He looked sensational.

Becky couldn't stop herself jumping out of her skin. She hated herself, but her nipples started to contract at the mere sight of him. Thank God she was wearing her thick leather jacket today. Her body, the traitress, remembered, as if in a flash, every last second of his caresses, the way he had stroked her from the inside, the way she had lifted up her body to meet his tongue.

The heat of sex with him, because God knew it wasn't 'making love', at least not for him, felt sick and wrong now.

'Six weeks,' he said simply. 'It had to be finished. And now here I am.'

'That's fine,' Becky said icily.

Logan's dark eyes bored into hers. 'You didn't get the card I sent?'

'Oh, yes. The *card*,' Becky snapped. 'It was so long ago, I forgot all about it.'

Will Logan looked her over, then shrugged. 'You want to fight? I told you, I don't do well on the phone. I rather thought we were too serious for a telephone relationship. I prefer to wait until I can talk to my women in the flesh. If you have something, you only find that out face to face.'

'Or body to body, in your case.'

He regarded her calmly. 'Did anybody ever tell you're a petulant little brat? I can't be the first. But never mind. I'll get on with the garden.'

'That's fine,' Becky said. 'And, please, let's keep our relationship strictly professional. I think we've both moved on from that mistake. Don't you?'

'Aye, lass,' Logan said. His voice moved into a thicker Yorkshire accent the angrier he got, Becky noticed. He moved to leave.

'Wait.' She gestured imperiously for him to stop. 'Your money. I want to pay you in advance this time.'

He nodded. 'I see you're taking in boarders.'

'Not *boarders*,' Becky said, furious. '*Guests*. This is a hotel now.'

'I'll take the money,' Logan said, holding out his hand for the cheque she ripped off and practically threw at him. 'If only because it means I won't have to see you after I'm done.'

He folded the cheque up neatly, put it in his jeans pocket and walked out.

Becky waited till he had gone to slam her fist against the wall.

Goddamn him. He took his sweet time, Becky thought as she watched the team of workers on their knees in the chilly autumn air, digging and sweating and planting what looked like an unimpressive mass of greenery. She knew enough about his talent to understand that it would be sensational when it was finished, though. And now Fairfield and its grounds were her business, she felt she needed him.

She tried to concentrate on work, but it was hard. Sharon was very competent at carrying out her vision. Becky had meetings with banks, showed them her new figures and raised some money. But she couldn't get the thought of Logan out of her mind.

She made a point of coming home after he would have left, to check that all was running smoothly with her guests and to work in her study. Today she had been finalizing a loan for a small, dilapidated theatre in the West End. Becky couldn't afford hotels, so she had been forced to think laterally. Theatres were priced differently. She had enough to convert the structure now.

Becky pulled into the small garage at the end of the drive, locked her car and got out. The sun was setting, and she tugged her cashmere scarf round her neck for warmth. She had washed her hair this morning and was wearing it loose; her make-up was light and simple. There was no need to have to dress older than she was now. Her heels pinched, though, and she was longing to slip them off and get into her own, unrenovated bath . . .

Suddenly she went crashing to the ground, a thick male body on top of her.

'Hey.' Two hands shot out, Logan holding himself above her. He wore black work pants, there was a faint masculine tang of aftershave and sweat about him and his chest was bare, the way he usually worked in the sun. 'Are you OK? Are you hurt?'

'No more than usual when somebody uses me as a rugby ball,' Becky said. She found Logan's body on top of her incredibly disturbing. 'Where's your shirt?'

'Why? Does this body offend you?' Logan teased. 'It never used to.'

He rolled off her, propping himself up on the grass. 'I was running into the house. You walked out in front of me.'

'You should look where you're going,' Becky snapped.

'You look good like that,' he said idly, trailing rough fingers through her hair.

'Leave me alone,' Becky said, but her voice cracked annoyingly in her throat.

'No,' Logan said slowly, 'I don't think I will.'

He reached up one calloused paw, slipped it behind the silk of her platinum hair and pulled her mouth towards him in a kiss. His lips half crushed hers, his tongue slipping between them, barely touching her upper lip, lightly brushing the skin. A silver fire of wanting him slid from her throat down to her breasts, instantly swelling the nipples, dampening her between the legs. There was just too much of his bare skin next to her to resist. She made a half-hearted movement to push from him, but Logan, merciless, raised his left hand and touched her little hardened mud through the fabric of her dress. His slightest touch rocked pleasure through her breasts, down between her legs.

'You want me.' His low murmur in her car was supremely confident. 'You've been thinking about me all the time. The way I've been thinking about you.'

Becky couldn't even manage a lie.

'Let's go somewhere,' he suggested. 'You don't want to be an extra entertainment for your guests.'

'There's a back entrance to the east wing,' Becky muttered. She had grass stalks on her clothes and skin, and there was a suspicious bulge in Logan's tight jeans she'd never be able to explain.

He led her round the back, his hand locked on hers, roughly begging her along. The small wooden door opened easily and Logan had to duck as he had her through the winding wooden passage, up to the back of Becky's bedroom.

'Wow.' He emerged into the master bedroom suite and took the beam across the ceiling, the priceless Persian carpet in pale blues and gold the lead-panelled windows and the antique furniture. 'It's good to be you.'

Becky was fumbling at the buttons of her dress. 'I guess.' She was hot and impatient.

'What was that little doorway doing leading into here?'

Becky smiled. 'To smuggle in the servants maybe?'

Logan stopped dead. It was as though a shutter had been lowered over his eyes. 'What?'

Becky was oblivious. 'Maybe the master of the house used it to bring up his kitchen maid.'

'Fuck,' Logan swore softly. Her head lifted. 'I should have known. Your kind is all the same, *milady*. That's what I am to you, right? A servant?'

'Of course you're not,' Becky said angrily. 'Don't blow this up into something.'

'Something like being the hired stud? The gardener? Yeah, very *Lady Chatterley*.' Logan shook his head. 'I don't think so, Becky. You'll have to get your diversions somewhere else.'

'Just get out,' Becky said, frustrated and furious. 'You bastard.'

'My pleasure, *ma'am*,' Logan said. He touched his forehead in ironic deference, then walked out.

Becky flung herself on to her bed and burst into tears. Unreasonable, unlikeable, proud son of a bitch. She hated him. And she hated that she wanted him so badly.

When she woke up in the morning, Will Logan had cleared out. His head planter told her that he had gone to supervise another job.

'Don't worry, Miss Lancaster. Mr Logan designed the whole project already. All we have to do now is the final bedding in of the rose plants.'

'That's fine.' But she couldn't stop herself asking, 'Where is the other job?'

'In France, miss.'

Chapter 35

'Welcome back, *Mrs Conran*,' Janice said, teasing her with a big grin.

'Thank you, thank you.' Lita took a little bow and smiled at her staff. 'Though my honeymoon was too good. I almost wish I hadn't come back.'

'You'll wish that in a minute,' Harry Weiss muttered.

'Excuse me?' Lita asked.

The smiles had faded from the New Wave staff's faces, and there was a mutual shuffling of feet and staring at the table.

'Somebody spill,' Lita said firmly. 'I know I took two months off, but this place can't survive without me for two months? Harry?'

'It's not that. In fact, it seems that it's you that's the problem,' Weiss said bravely.

'Harry,' Janice protested.

Harry cut her off. 'Somebody has to tell her. Look, Lita, New Wave has lost six new accounts, including United Newspapers.'

Lita looked dismayed. That had been her biggest coup, the large regional publishing group that put out papers in Manchester, Liverpool and Birmingham.

'Why the hell . . .?'

'Bad press.' Harry opened his briefcase and poured a spill of clippings on to the table. Lita picked one up at random. It was a *PR Weekly* article implying that she was sleeping with Jocelyn Wilson, and that New Wave had got its start by ripping off Doheny. It brought up the charge of Lita's 'plagiarism', and insinuated that she had only been promoted there by doing 'sexual favours' for Harry.

Lita felt a huge rush of adrenaline as she read it. She flushed darkly, her heart started to thump and sweat broke out on the palms of her hands.

'We'll sue,' she whispered.

'You can't.' Weiss was matter-of-fact. 'I've already consulted libel lawyers. This is a "blind item". It just suggests without stating it outright.'

Lita rummaged through the rest of the clippings. It was all equally damaging. It made them look like sleazy nouveau *arrivistes* who were out to take British jobs and who ripped off other firms for campaigns.

She saw that her hand was trembling slightly with the force of her rage.

'Who's behind this?' Lita demanded.

Weiss shook his head. 'Lancaster Holdings. As far as I can work out, they hired three individual tabloid hacks from Fleet Street to dig dirt, then send it on to their pals in the press. It worked out a lot better for them than hiring a PR firm. In fact, you have to give it to them—'

'Goddamn it, no, you don't, Harry.' Lita blinked. 'How the hell can it be Lancaster Holdings? I destroyed them. They sold everything to Wilson Shipping.'

'Everything except the name.'

'What the hell use is that?'

'She rebuilt. She's working at lightning speed. A luxury hotel in her own house, then a theatre conversion in London and a lodge house in Edinburgh right next to the Palace of Holyrood House. Where Mary Queen of Scots—'

'Enough already with the history lesson!' Lita snatched up the profile of Becky's company.

'She has guests lining up to pay astronomical prices to stay in these places. The banks love her. And she wants your blood,' Harry said succinctly.

'Well.' The white-hot rage was replaced with an icy calm. 'That's fine. If she wants blood, she's got it.'

'There's a call for you, Miss Lancaster.'

Becky tightened her plastic headscarf against the icy wind and drift of snow that was whipping down Edinburgh's Royal Mile towards her site, an historic lodge house, fallen into disrepair, which she was given permission to restore with the aid of the local authority's historical buildings commission.

Other developers were frightened off by the need to retain original features. Becky wasn't. She knew that was what would sell it to her guests.

The beauty of the Royal Mile, with its twists and turns and small shops set into the ancient stonework, was worth fighting for. And she wasn't scared of paperwork.

This hotel would go down great with all the Scottish-Americans. 'Come and be neighbours of the Queen at the Royal Thistle Hotel.' Perfect. In fact, she had money in the bank already from guests who wouldn't get there until the conversion was complete in May.

Becky ducked into the small field office to take her call. A wave of nausea rocked through her, and she pressed one small hand to her mouth. Oh, God. This was happening more and more frequently as her successes spread. The joy of winning contract after contract, and the satisfaction of ripping those assholes at New Wave into pieces, was offset by all the travel and the stress. And her inability to get Logan out of her head.

'Who is it, Freddie?'

Her foreman passed her the receiver. 'I think she said her name was Rosalie or something, miss.'

The nausea doubled. Becky steadied herself. She knew exactly who this was.

'Can you give me a minute, Freddie? I need to take this call.'

'Is this Rebecca Lancaster? This is Rosalita Conran. I'm President of—'

'I know who you are, Ms Conran.'

'You're making a big mistake,' said the voice at the other end of the line. Becky recognized, dredging it up from her memory, the slight Bronx tang.

'A big mistake, huh? Like when we tried to sell the tin mines in Cornwall, and there was an "environmental hazard"?'

There was a pause.

'No,' the other girl said slowly. 'More like when you stood at the top of the stairs and watched me cry like I was your private freak show. You'd better back off, lady. I ruined you once and I'll be happy to do it again.'

'Oh, I get it.' Becky grinned to herself. 'This is all about Rupert. You must have gotten him back, you must be in this with him. Well, I'm more than a match for both of you scumbags.'

The girl laughed. 'I'm married. Unlike you. And you can't fool me, Rebecca. We both know you were the little society playgirl with that bastard. Now you have money, maybe he's back with you. But money isn't going to be able to hide you from me if you don't draw that head back into your shell.'

'You don't scare me, sister. Not one tiny bit. If I were you, I'd head down to my travel agent and book the next flight back to New York. You can get a discount if you book in advance, you know. And pretty soon you'll be needing the money.'

'I see, *chiquita*. It's like that, huh?'

'See you around, Rosalita,' Becky told her. She hung up, but not before she heard the little click that announced the other woman was doing the same thing.

Becky smiled to herself, despite the churning in her stomach. Bring it on! She was ready for it.

Lita picked up the phone in Mark's townhouse in Park Street, and started to dial Harry.

Mark reached over, took the receiver out of her hand and gently replaced it. 'You can do that tomorrow.'

'Honey—'

'Tomorrow, I said.' His fingers started to undo the buttons at the top of her silky blouse. 'Doctor's orders.'

She didn't dare protest and, anyway, she didn't really want to. Mark's hand was already tracing little teasing patterns on her bra. He made her feel her sexuality every second of the day. He rang her at work and told her exactly what he was planning on doing to her when he got home, in a detached, almost clinical voice that made her belly warm and her nipples hard. Lita had thrown away every piece of functional underwear she possessed, and dropped five hundred quid buying little thongs and high-cut French knickers at Janet Reager's, in every colour, so that she felt, under her tight little business suits, that she was preparing for him constantly. Mark hired a maid to keep their place clean, and they ate out almost every night because, he said, 'I don't want you being tired with small things when you should be hot and ready for me.'

'But a maid is so extravagant,' Lita had protested, as his hand slid up her skirt, feeling her smooth, lean thighs.

'No, she's a necessity. I don't want housework on your mind.'

Now he was lightly, tormentingly, touching her nipples the way he knew drove her crazy, forestalling any further conversation. Lita gasped. The bra today was pale gold satin, but even its silky caress was almost painful to her when her breasts swelled like this.

Mark brushed her blouse half-off her soft shoulders and freed her heavy, soft breasts from their bra, dropping it on to the ground. He bent his head close to the warm, sweet scent of her, and his tongue darted out, flickering across the dark, taut peaks, taking her nipples into his mouth so she groaned lightly, aloud.

'Let's have a look at you,' he said, and lifted up her skirt, where her tiny golden G-string was pressed against the trimmed, silky V of her crotch. 'Yeah, those panties are very nice.' He slipped a finger inside them and stroked the wetness of her. 'I really don't know why you bother to wear them . . .'

His thumbs hooked into them and slipped them free of her thighs. She wasn't wearing any tights, nothing but a stacked pair of slides that threw out the rounded curves of her butt.

Even his control was lost.

'God, you're beautiful,' he said breathlessly.

'Mark,' Lita moaned. She tugged off his T-shirt, looking at his muscular, lean chest, her nails lightly raking the wiry hairs there.

'Hold on,' he said. He loosened his zipper and kicked off his socks and shoes, and Lita's hand came out, for revenge, cupping him, taunting him. He grabbed the small of her back and pulled her closer, their lips and tongues tangling, until Lita lost her footing and they tumbled back on to the soft sheepskin rug at the bottom of her desk. Mark thrust himself unceremoniously inside her, and the waves of pleasure began before she even began to thrust back at him, as he angled himself inside her deeper and harder, his rhythm coming faster and more furious, sending the silver lines of ecstasy running up to her nipples and down through her flat belly to her thighs, as he reached behind her to grab her butt, stroking it, toying with it, using it to pull her deeper against him, until she was gasping his name and clutching at him, and the bright wall of pressure inside her exploded, and her body crunched into orgasm, and everything except Mark fell away from her.

'Oh, Rupert, *darling*, roll the dice again.' Madame la Baronne Marie d'Escalier clapped her slightly wrinkling hands, which made the gaudy rings she wore on each blood-red finger sparkle in the light of the chandeliers.

They were playing craps in the Casino Lowenstein in Monaco, on the Rue de la Croix. Rupert knew to stay away from all the big houses. His credit rating was for shit there, and he had to keep appearances up. The mortgage on his tiny one-bedroom apartment, which he called his '*pied-à-terre*', was killing him. Lita's money had been spent or gambled away long ago, and now he was surviving on presents from rich 'girlfriends', like the Baronne, if indeed she really was one. That didn't matter to Rupert, though – just soft enough lights, and enough coke and booze, so that it became bearable to get into bed with her occasionally.

He obeyed and rolled the dice. His luck had been in today. Baronne Marie liked to laugh and peel him off some notes from her winnings, as though he were some floozy hanger-on that needed a tip. Rupert didn't have enough pride to turn her down. That burned his insides worse than the ulcer he had developed.

'*Sept, Monsieur le Baron*,' said the impassive voice of the croupier.

'Oh, Ru-u-pert darling, you are *fantastique*,' Marie purred. 'Here, for you.' She tossed him a couple of shiny red chips.

'I'll get the champagne,' Rupert said, pocketing them and winking at her. He sidled off to the bar, anything to get away from that awful old hag. 'Bottle of Moët,' he said, snapping his fingers. They understood English here providing you spent enough money.

There was a tap on his shoulder. Another older woman, this one about fifty and with a bad dye job on reddish hair, and a skirt at least two inches too short for her dumpy legs.

'Lord Rupert Lancaster?'

Rupert was high, but he still clocked the sharp London accent, middle-class with a trace of Cockney.

'Yes,' he said, not bothering to correct her on the title. Who cared in this hell-hole, anyway?

'Doreen Evans, the *Star.* Would you have time for an interview, my lord?'

'No, I bloody wouldn't,' Rupert snapped. 'Sod off.'

'We pay,' said the harridan softly. 'A thousand pounds for half an hour.'

Rupert beckoned a waiter over and told him to send the champagne to the Baronne. 'Put it on her tab,' he muttered.

'Now.' He turned to the woman and smiled at her, his most seductive smile. 'What exactly did you want to know?'

He got drunk that night, not enough to render him incapable but just enough to help him through banging the Baronne. She was starting to whine about 'doing it with the lights on'. Thank God he had taken a couple of thousand from her tonight, because he couldn't hack this for much longer. Rupert splashed water on his face, back at his own flat, trying to sober up. The cheque from the journalist was lying on his dressing-table. As soon as the bank opened, he'd be there, paying it in. They shouldn't have a chance to cancel it.

He ran some numbers in his head. With the cheque, and the small amounts he'd managed to skim off Mrs Ashford, last month's 'companion', he probably had enough for a trip to the States. What that journalist said burned him.

'It's a human-interest story.' She had waved her tall glass of gin and tonic around, sloshing the ice cubes dangerously near the rim. 'You know, the two women, both young and sexy, you should see the pics, and we heard they have a history and the history is *you.*'

'Possibly,' he'd agreed. Guarded, but she'd want something for that grand.

'Both of them feeding dirty stuff round Fleet Street. Real juicy. Rebecca Lancaster was a back-page story, but she's society, and the other girl is from the Bronx . . . it's good copy.' A tongue darted out and slicked her too-red lips that were starting to feather at the edges. 'Now, we asked around New York, and some of the page-six types that feed Liz Smith and the other gossip columnists said you were once engaged to Rosalita?'

'Lita.' Rupert sighed theatrically. 'Yes, I was, but briefly. It ended by mutual agreement. We just didn't fit.'

'Was that the real reason?'

'Well.' He winked at the old soak. 'Let's just say a gentleman doesn't like to tell tales.'

'She's very successful now. Made a ton of money, married a society doctor, big house, nice car – Aston Martin, I think. Like James Bond.'

Rupert stewed over this. Bloody Lita. How was it that she'd made money when his life had fallen apart, just due to bad luck? Bitch.

'Of course, Rebecca Lancaster is trying to stymie her. Out of revenge for the Lancaster thing. You must know about that.'

'The way she ran . . . No, let me say instead, the way my family company was run into the ground? Destroyed? Yes, I heard something about it.' His tone was bitter.

'Well, Lita helped Wilson Shipping do that. And with this PR war, the only connection my editor could think of was you.'

'Very likely.' He preened a little. 'They were both madly in love with me. I'm sorry it didn't work out. And that it seems to have degenerated into a cat-fight.' Rupert shook his head. 'The title seems to attract some women. I don't know why, it's so unimportant. Anyway, you say they are both successful businesswomen?'

'Rebecca has a nice little hotel business going, which she started in Fairfield Court.'

The journalist drew back. The fire in Rupert's eyes was icy. He looked as though he might be going to hit her.

'That house is a listed building,' Rupert hissed.

'She got all the permissions. We checked.'

'My God. She's ruining the family seat.' His fingers gripped the bar rail. 'Who does she think she is?'

'It's been very successful,' the journalist pointed out.

'Yes? Well, if she's such a successful wheeler-dealer, what's the point of this petty feud? It's rather bad for business for both of them, wouldn't you say?'

'Yes, I would,' said the woman, clearly delighted. She pulled out a pre-printed cheque and handed him a grubby card. 'Here you go, Lord Rupert, and don't hesitate to contact me if you want to say anything else. We pay good cash for *real* leads.'

'Tell me something. Do you have these things they've been sending to the press about each other?' Rupert asked, quickly pocketing the cheque.

'I can get them to you,' she said.

'Why don't you do that?' Rupert said. 'It might jog my memory.'

'Delighted, milord,' she said, smirking.

Chapter 36

'I have to put a stop to it.' Becky bit down on her lower lip, furious.

It was only one story, but it was devastating. Smarmy, patronizing, with large photos of her and Rosalita, Fairfield and Rupert. She cringed as her blue eyes flickered over the lines describing Rupert's embarrassment, his 'gentlemanly' unwillingness to tell tales out of school, and his 'polite dismay'.

> Lord Rupert Lancaster bowed his head as he sat in the ultra-exclusive Monte Carlo hotel, obviously upset that love of him caused two women to behave like hissing cats, or perhaps like spoilt children. Lord Lancaster tried and failed to hide his disgust at the American heir to an old English country manor turning it into a common guest-house for money, and then running to the press . . .'

This was disastrous. Becky's exclusive competitors on the luxury-holiday circuit would make sure people saw this. It would make a terrific blind item on page six, back in New York. She had to staunch the bleeding right now. Sharon and her other workers didn't know what to say to her.

Rosalita – apparently it was Lita – would have to see it her way. Becky didn't think it would be hard, because the woman ran an advertising and PR agency, and corporate clients hated this sort of thing. But, still, she couldn't risk a phone call. She had to go and see her.

'I know you do, but reading it a million times isn't going to make it go away,' Sharon said.

Becky felt the familiar, revolting rush of sickness. 'Oh, God, I can't take this.' She bolted into the small loo next to the library, which was out of bounds to the guests and acting as her office. She barely made it to the bowl before she was retching, dully and violently ill. It felt like she was puking out her entire guts. She stood up and wiped her mouth; her face looked pale, shot to hell.

She didn't think she'd had a good night's sleep since Logan had left.

'Becky? Are you OK?'

She wiped her mouth and went back into the library. 'I don't know, to be honest. Maybe I just can't hack the stress.' Miserably she admitted, 'Maybe I'm lovesick. Oh, God, Sharon, I can't stop thinking about him. And I never even went out with him, not really. Isn't that pathetic?'

'Have you considered,' Sharon said slowly, 'that it's not that at all?'

Becky look dismayed. 'I don't have time to get sick. You think I'm sick?'

'I think you might be pregnant.'

'Don't be silly, that's impossible.' Becky stared at her. 'I use a diaphragm . . . Oh, God . . .'

'It wasn't exactly planned that time, though, was it?'

'Give me the phone. I'm calling the doctor.'

'No need to rush it, Becky—'

'Forget it.' Becky held up a hand. 'I have to know, and I have to know now.'

The Caterham clinic was set in a small bungalow with a red slate roof that had been converted into doctors' offices. There were comfortable, faded chairs, a table with a stack of ancient magazines and a rounded nurse at the front desk in a neat uniform.

'I have to see Dr Ellison right away,' Becky panted, with Sharon hovering anxiously behind her.

'Is it an emergency?' The nurse peered doubtfully at Becky's tall, healthy frame, with her glossy platinum hair and sparkling colour.

'Not exactly, but—'

'Then I'm afraid you'll have to wait. Name, please?'

'Rebecca Lancaster,' Becky muttered.

'We'll call you when we have a slot, madam,' the nurse said brightly.

Becky tried to be patient. She read faded copies of *Punch* and issues of *Country Life*, the *Lady*, and *Horse and Hound*. Sharon gave up on the magazines and went outside to smoke.

Eventually, after the shuffling old man with the hacking cough had been despatched, Dr Ellison poked his grey head through the doorway.

'Rebecca Lancaster? Come through, please.'

She followed him into a small room with posters of children with measles on it, a desk and an examination table covered in a smooth white sheet.

'What seems to be the trouble?' he asked, hardly looking at her.

'I throw up in the mornings. I think I might be pregnant.'

'Well, we'll soon find out. Do you and your husband practise birth control?'

A feeling of shame crept over her. 'I'm not married,' Becky half whispered.

'I see,' Dr Ellison said amiably, his brown eyes twinkling. 'Might have to move the wedding up, eh? Who is the lucky chap?'

'Do I need to pee in a cup or something?' Becky asked desperately.

'What? Oh, yes.' He handed her a plastic tumbler. 'Urine sample, please. There's a loo at the back there.'

Sharon drove her home in merciful silence. Becky was worrying her lower lip, staring out of the window.

'What time is he going to call?' Sharon asked eventually.

'God knows. I can't wait by the phone,' Becky burst out. 'I feel like I'm suffocating. I'm going to London to see the Morales woman.'

'Well,' Sharon said sensibly, 'at least take the train. You shouldn't drive. You're too stressed out.'

Becky sat in first class and ordered a glass of Coke to steady her nerves. Thank God for Coke, so reliably American. She pressed her hands to her head and wished that she could just transport herself back to Aunt Mindy's. Back to the States.

Well, nagged a little voice in her head sarcastically, you'll be getting a little slice of the Bronx right now.

As the green fields of England slipped past her, she tried not to think about Logan and the baby. There was no way, if she was pregnant, that she wanted an abortion. If it was alive inside her, her baby, she just couldn't do it . . . But, God, she didn't want to be a single mom either, didn't want to have the press at her door, baying about her 'fast' lifestyle, hurting her child with their foul stories . . .

Oh, God. She'd have to call Logan. There was absolutely no way of getting around it.

By the time the train pulled up at Paddington she was almost glad to be on her way to see Lita.

At the New Wave offices, Becky didn't give her name. She simply said she had a message for Rosalita Morales.

'It's Conran now.'

'Oh, right. Yeah.'

'She's on the fourth floor.'

Becky rode the elevator up. The offices were decorated well, a funky, cutting-edge style, like something out of a movie, a little slice of Manhattan here in Chelsea. She didn't have far to look for Lita. The girl was pacing around in her offices, yelling and waving a copy of the same paper that Becky had been agonizing over earlier.

She saw Becky through the glass walls of her office, and stopped cold. Her staff, following her eyes, rushed out of the office.

'No, it's OK.' The girl's voice carried loud and clear into the outer office. 'Let Miss Lancaster in. And hold all my calls.'

'Thanks,' Becky said, sweeping past a hostile Janice.

Lita was wearing a pair of scarlet leather pants that cupped an impressive booty and a little, sexy, black shell top. She had on high-heeled boots, and her hair was down, and she looked like she was prepared to take on the Devil single-handed right now.

Becky took a seat without waiting to be asked.

'Well.' Lita admired the elegant beige pantsuit with the fitted jacket and butter-coloured silk shirt. 'This is a surprise.'

'It shouldn't be.' She gestured to the paper tossed on to the table. 'You've read it. Now, I intend to be brief.'

Lita arched an eyebrow.

'I've got personal business I need to take care of. So let me just say, first, that I can't stand Rupert, and he almost beggared my business before I kicked him out. Second, that I can't stand you either, but this is killing my business. I'll back off if you will.'

'Fine. Settled,' Lita snapped back. 'But I still owe you. It just won't be this way. And I want *you* to know that I hate Rupert Lancaster. He dumped me by telegram, and then he stole all the money I had in the world.'

'Perfect.' Becky got up to leave but, despite her preoccupation, curiosity had started to gnaw at her. 'I have to say, it didn't look like that when you turned up at Fairfield. Which, by the way, was when he had just started to ask me out.'

'Of course. You had the house. Look, I just refused to believe it.' She laughed. 'I loved him, can you believe that?'

'I'm afraid I can,' Becky said. 'What do you mean, "You had the housed"?'

Lita made an airy gesture. Her long, painted nails gleamed in the weak autumn sunlight.

'You know he had that court case . . . He was winning it when he was with me. So I guess he thought he'd inherit a lot of money and the house. Then, when he lost, he bailed, just bailed, and flew to England to pick you up. Not that you minded.'

'I didn't know.' Becky sighed. 'You know, that's exactly what my girlfriend told me. That he had to get the house back through me.'

'She was right.'

There was the start of a thaw in the air, but both girls suddenly flashed on the sobbing Lita in Fairfield's entrance hall. Becky stood awkwardly.

'I think this temporary truce will benefit us both. I can see myself out.'

'Goodbye,' Lita said coldly.

The relief Becky felt as she got straight back on the train was minimal. Yes, that danger was gone from her business but, despite her love of it, her mission to rebuild her father's empire faded out of Becky's mind compared to what might be about to happen to her.

She tried to read on the train, and she tried to nap. Nothing worked. She stumbled out at Caterham station and got into a local cab, fending off the driver's good-natured observations about how filthy London was, and how glad she must be to be back in the country. She felt as though somebody were suspending her over a vat of boiling oil, and the rope was fraying.

Unless you counted her dreams, Will Logan hadn't been back, not once. His men had completed the glorious, formal rose garden, planting organic, original flowers, mulching the bushes in for winter and, after that, leaving. The company had sent her a nice formal bill, which she'd paid, and then there had been nothing but silence.

Becky had spent weeks telling herself that it was totally pathetic to fixate on Logan. He was just a gardener, for heaven's sake, and a proud, arrogant bastard who'd never been to college even, who'd just screwed her and then disappeared for six goddamn weeks with nothing but a shitty card . . .

And a baby. Oh, Jesus.

She burst into Fairfield, walking straight to her office, and dived on the phone to the clinic. It was just before five. Hopefully the doctor would still be there . . .

'I'll see if I can catch him, madam.' There was a pause, then the soothing, impersonal voice of Dr Ellison on the phone.

'Congratulations.' She steadied herself on the soft green baize of the desk so that she could stand up while the dizziness rocked her. 'You're going to have a baby, Miss Lancaster.'

'Yes, he will be calling into the office at some stage.'

Becky had forgotten how much she loathed that arrogant voice. Of course, the girl probably had a hopeless, spotty teenage crush on Logan. Becky knew she did, why not this girl? No wonder she sounded so much like she hated her.

'But I really don't know that I can transfer you. Or tell him. He said he didn't want to be bothered with you.' There was a note of triumph in her voice. 'He was most particular, like.'

'Listen to me. This is very serious.' Becky hated having to beg and plead. 'This isn't about bills or anything trivial. It's – it's – a matter of life and death, OK? A matter of life and death.'

'Are you OK?' Tracy said, reluctantly concerned, then, more panicked, she went on, 'There's nothing wrong with Will, is there?'

'Not with him. Just get him to call me. It's important.'

'OK, miss,' the girl said, hanging up.

Becky went and made herself a cup of tea. The British had built an empire on cups of tea. Maybe one would help her now.

It didn't.

She was sipping disconsolately when the phone rang. It was probably Sharon, but she still jumped on it.

'Hello?'

'Becky?' It was Logan, and she half jumped out of her skin. 'What do you want? Are you sick?'

He was half shouting at her, like he was really mad. 'This had better be good.'

'That depends on your definition,' Becky said, and her voice sounded like it belonged to another person, coming from far away, calm and measured. 'I'm pregnant.'

'What?' he shouted.

'I'm pregnant. The doctor confirmed it to me today.'

'And you think I'm the father?' he said, after a pause.

The question pierced her right in the heart, with an almost physical stab.

'Who else could be?'

'How the hell should I know?' His voice was gruff.

Becky fought back the sob that rose in the back of her throat. 'There's been nobody but you ever since I split up with Rupert. Actually. And now we're going to have a baby.'

He was silent at the end of the phone. 'I make you three months gone, then.'

'I suppose so.'

'You're at Fairfield. I can't get there till tomorrow. I'll be there then.'

'Why are you coming here?'

'Why not? We've got things to discuss, don't we?'

'I'm not having an abortion,' she said, and now the tears did start to fall, and she bit her cheek, so glad he couldn't actually see her.

'I didn't bloody ask you to,' he said, and slammed down the phone.

Becky was left holding the receiver and a dial tone. She gently replaced the receiver, then went outside to find the small back stairway that led up to her private bedroom. She bolted the door, flung herself on to her bed and burst into tears.

Rupert gave Kathy Donalds a full-wattage smile. Despite his fatigue and jet-lag, he knew he looked fantastic – one of his old, sober, Gieves & Hawkes suits, his John Lobb shoes and cologne from Floris. He didn't have a woman's advantage of concealer for the shadows under his eyes, but he carried a pair of thin glasses set with non-prescription glass for just such an emergency.

He had wasted all his money, and now all he had left was the title and the looks.

But that could be changed.

The article he had seen pleased him immensely. It made both of those stupid bitches look like the spoilt wastrels they were and, of course, it had emphasized what Becky was doing to Fairfield. *And* pointed out that Lita's first dabbling in PR had come at *his* expense. Why, with giving her her shot at TV, *he* had made her. And he deserved something for that . . .

As for Becky, she was a common thief. Whatever the courts said. A thief, and now a vandal.

Rupert burned with righteous indignation. He didn't want to have to move down to the last resort. That was to marry money. To marry some older woman with pots of cash and no class, the kind that would pay for a title and agree to settle money on him in his own name. Because he'd rather be a whore than be poor, he thought bitterly.

God, imagine a lifetime of screwing the Baronne, or equivalent, and maybe having her open the curtains. He couldn't take it, there wasn't a strong enough drug in the world.

But while he was here, he was fishing madly. His old society pals, unaware, perhaps, of his fiscal status, were welcoming him back with open arms. Perhaps he could find some rich, desperate debutante with a forgiving disposition, one desperate for love who would refuse to look too closely at his nights away from home. His chances would certainly be helped if he could show he had legitimate business interests.

Lita and Becky had plenty. They owed him, and he intended to collect.

And a couple of calls had persuaded him that this man would be willing to help him.

Kathy Donalds smiled dreamily up at him.

'Mr Bessel will see you now, your lordship,' she said.

Chapter 37

When he came down the drive, Becky was waiting for him. For the first time in her life, business became completely uninteresting to her. She let Sharon deal with the fall-out from the Rupert article. Sharon persuaded her to dig up a distant relative, a dowager countess, to come and stay free, to fill the gap created by one of the morally upright guests who had pulled out and demanded a refund.

'She had three rooms. That's going to put a big hole in our budget. And she didn't cancel in time.'

'It doesn't matter.' Becky had looked like she couldn't care less. 'Give Mrs Feuerstein her money back right away, and the same to her guests. I mean today. And send them one of those silk cushions filled with lavender from the garden, with a note saying we hope to see them at Fairfield or another Lancaster hotel in the future.'

'OK.' Sharon nodded. 'Actually, you're right. We can't get a reputation for anything other than—'

'Effortless luxury. How we deal with this situation will make the rounds in Palm Springs, Malibu and the Hamptons.'

'I follow you, boss-girl.'

'And fill that room.'

Sharon was starting to understand Becky's philosophy. The Countess was ideal. The old lady was as pleased as Punch to be wined and dined free for a week, and the Americans and Canadians that were left were thrilled to be mingling with a real aristocrat every day. Bookings that had trailed off were suddenly, magically reconfirmed. Lita was as good as her word – there were no more damaging stories in the press.

The Edinburgh hotel was close to completion, and the outfitting of the London property was coming along on schedule. Banks that wouldn't give Becky the time of day before were suddenly tripping over themselves to lend her money.

But she didn't give a damn.

There was a new life inside her. Her child and Will Logan's child. Becky's emotions ran so deep, she could hardly figure out where to start obsessing. Over the baby? Had the wine she habitually drank at dinner harmed it yet? Over Will? Would he refuse to acknowledge paternity? He hadn't actually done that yet. And what if he did, what then? Would her baby be subject to sullen, angry visits once a month from its Yorkshireman father, and trips to some poky town to visit with Logan, his wife and all his *legitimate* children? Maybe with that snotty teenage secretary of his. Would Logan tell the child it was the product of a one-night stand? Surely somebody would.

Becky had to fight herself not to hang her blonde head in shame. Bastard. A word they would always throw at her baby. And the tabloids would just love it, wouldn't they? It would follow the kid around all the time. 'Tom Lancaster, the bastard child of the last Lancaster heiress . . .'

She knew she shouldn't care, but she did. She cared desperately. Since she had made the first decision not to sell Fairfield, Becky had been trying to restore her father's name, her father's rights. And now she was about to embroil his name in a public scandal. Knocked up from a one-night stand.

She brushed away the tears that threatened to trickle down her cheeks. Logan was here, finally. And Becky would die before she'd display any weakness to him.

She ran into her bathroom and quickly dropped some of those blue drops from Boots into her eyes to get rid of the redness. She took deep breaths to get the blood out of her nose, and rubbed a little oil of Llouy into her face. A slick of bronze powder made her pallid face look a little healthier.

Yeah, that was better.

She heard the front door's heavy swing, and Mrs Morecambe's voice talking to Logan. She couldn't make out the words, but even the low, masculine timbre of his accent sent shivers racing through her. She picked up her L'Arpège and spritzed herself lightly; scent as armour. Then she walked downstairs.

Logan was wearing black corduroy pants and a black T-shirt. He had stubble, and he looked even more muscular than she remembered. Perhaps he'd been working in some garden somewhere, hoisting stone to build a terrace, or carting statues about. The T-shirt was tight over his pecs and sliced off at his biceps.

She didn't dare look at him in case she started to want him even now.

'Hello, Will. Good of you to come.' God, she sounded like she was offering the vicar another round of cucumber sandwiches. 'I thought we could have some privacy in the office.'

'Fine.'

His eyes looked dull and defeated. It was torture to Becky. Was having a child with her *that* bad? He looked like he'd been sentenced to life.

'Mrs Morecambe, will you see that we're not disturbed on any account?'

'Certainly, miss,' Mrs Morecambe said stoutly.

Becky showed Logan into the library and shut the door. Then she picked up the phone and took it off the hook.

'Have a seat.'

Logan sat. He sat on the edge of her Louis XVIII chair, like he wanted to get the hell out as soon as possible. His dark, gorgeous eyes stared into hers, challenging her.

'I assumed you were on the Pill.'

'Well, I wasn't. It's your baby, Will.'

'I know that.' He sighed.

'I don't want your money.'

'Oh, no,' he said sarcastically. 'Lady Rebecca doesn't need anything from the hired help.'

'I hope you can be reasonable about this. I just want what's best for the baby.'

'And what's that? To have a couple of married parents that actually give a damn about each other?'

That was almost too much for Becky. She felt the tears surge implacably in the back of her throat. She had to take thirty seconds before she could force them back down through sheer will-power, and even then her voice was quavering.

'We have to deal with the situation the way it is.'

'Agreed,' he grunted.

'So . . . I guess I need to know what part you want to play in the baby's life. I don't want it to form an attachment if you're not going to be there.'

'I'll be there the entire time.' Logan frowned thunderously. 'You think I want a child, *my* child, teased and bullied because we didn't use protection?'

'They're going to call her a bastard,' Becky said, and a tear trickled treacherously down her cheek.

'It might be a boy.' He sat there and stared at her. 'I want to get married.'

Becky stared at him. Her heart started to race furiously, surging with hope that she couldn't suppress. 'What? What did you say?'

'Just temporary, like. For the child. I'm not expecting us to be tied to each other for even a year. We get married now, get a divorce six months after the birth. That way the baby has a name, and we don't have to see each other. After that, I'll visit him once a week. We'll tell him it just didn't work out.'

The fire of her hope flickered and died. Becky pressed her hands to her forehead. It was like having a bad acid trip. She was going to marry the man she had fallen so hopelessly in love with, but he still hated her.

But it was an offer she couldn't refuse. Her happiness wasn't important. For a year of suffering, she could eliminate the tabloids, the nicknames, the gossip, from this baby's life.

Becky hated this idea, but she had to jump at it before he changed his mind.

'That's fine,' she muttered.

'And we shouldn't do it shotgun either. You want to stop them talking, you can't run and hide. Not that you need to have a big expensive wedding, but you've got to announce it, you've got to invite relatives.'

Becky shivered at the thought of her family seeing her misery. Logan noted it, and his face darkened.

'I hate the idea as much as you do. But it will be one day, and it won't last long. We should rent a place together so that people don't talk when they see the separate rooms.'

'There's a small cottage at the end of the orchard I already thought about buying.'

'Fine. You can sell it once we're through.' Logan stood. 'I'll get a ring today and send it to you in the post. You can make the announcements and put the wedding list together. I'll send you a list of my guests.'

'It doesn't have to be huge, does it?' Becky almost whimpered. She didn't think she could hack that.

Logan shot her a look of pure disgust.

'Just big enough to stop talk. Family and a couple of friends. You'll have my numbers. Let me know the arrangements, and pull something together as fast as you can.'

He left her without a backward glance.

After ten minutes, Mrs Morecambe crept into the library carrying a tray with a pot of tea and a slice of jam sponge.

'You need to eat something, miss . . .'

She had expected to find her sitting weeping in a chair, but Becky was dry-eyed and cold, writing at her desk.

'Thank you, Mrs Morecambe. Could you get me the telephone directory? I need to call *The Times*.'

Becky had no idea how she got through the next two weeks. She pulled a wedding together in record time, paying Smythson's extra to rush through the invitations, placing engagement announcements everywhere, even posing for photographers with a glassily smiling Logan. She held out the hand with the simple, one-carat diamond he had sent her in the mail as though he had slipped it on to her hand in some flower-strewn meadow. She wasn't showing at all yet, but there was no time to get a custom wedding gown so Becky had a local seamstress attach an antique lace train to a stately, long white shift dress.

'You can't be serious, Rebecca. Why, the man is a *nobody*. He's *working class*. He's a *gardener* . . .'

Aunt Victoria's harrumph of dismay echoed down the line.

'He's going to be my husband,' Becky finished calmly. 'If you can't come, Aunt Victoria, I understand. Aunt Mindy will be there.'

'And so will I.' She sighed bitterly. 'I have to. But, Rebecca, you're disgracing your family.'

'Nice to talk to you, too, Aunt Victoria,' Becky said, hanging up. She no longer cared about Victoria and Henry. She was miles past the stage where their rejection could hurt her.

Now it was only Logan's rejection she cared about.

She booked the local village church, a glorious fourteenth-century affair built of grey stone, with mediaeval frescos still visible on the ceiling, and had it decorated with the fruits of the season – gourds and nuts spray-painted gold, chrysanthemums in wonderful shades of ochre, yellow and white, hollyhocks, asters and trailing, fragrant masses of clematis. She paid the local caterer double to whip up a six-tiered cake with pale blue icing with a white trim, like a piece of Wedgwood china.

The actual wedding ceremony was mercifully brief for Becky because there was so much to do. Aunt Mindy, in a pretty green silk suit, was her matron of honour, and Sharon came behind in a matching dress carrying a bouquet of dried lavender and rose-hips with lilies. Becky smiled at stone-faced Aunt Vicky, at Ken Stone and at Logan's parents, his mother, a small, friendly woman with a harried air, in tears in her purple tweed suit and straw hat with a large bow at the front. The vicar read from a Gospel text about Jesus changing water into wine at Cana, gave a short sermon, which Becky had particularly requested, the words were pronounced, and it was all over.

They processed out of the church, the small congregation smiling approvingly, to the strains of a choirboy she had tipped thirty pounds to sing 'Panis Angelicus'. Anything to avoid having to belt out some hymn. When she had said, 'I do,' Becky had, for a second, let her control slip, but she thought that was OK.

Brides usually cried at their own weddings.

Just not for this reason.

Becky thought how ironic it was. This was her wedding day, the day she had dreamed of ever since she'd draped a handkerchief over the head of her first Barbie.

And it was the worst day of her life.

She managed to smile and keep busy through the champagne reception in the walled kitchen garden, which they had closed to hotel guests, and to circulate throughout the delicious buffet lunch which she didn't touch. But when Logan tugged at her sleeve, she couldn't stop herself jumping out of her skin.

He smiled, but it didn't reach his eyes.

'We have to go.' His voice was a whisper. 'It's three p.m.'

'OK.' Becky kissed Sharon, clapped her hands and made the announcement. Barkin drove the little horse and buggy decked out in white asters, which they had hired, around to the terrace, and Logan helped his wife up to it while the small crowd cheered and clapped.

She tossed her bouquet, and Logan's cousin Francine caught it. Becky felt Logan's thick body next to her wince almost imperceptibly, and at the fresh snub, the tears sprang to her lashes.

'Oh, look, she's crying,' Mrs Logan said.

'I'm just so happy,' Becky said miserably, through a rictus grin.

'Drive on, for God's sake,' Logan hissed at the driver.

Barkin snapped the reins, and they drove away in a cloud of fragrant blossom, cheering and heartbreak.

The dirt road that ran down the side of Fairfield led directly to the little cottage. Becky supposed it might once have belonged to a worker on the estate. It was small and comfortable, with an idyllic thatched roof and a minute garden of its own at the back. She hadn't been able to buy it, but the London owner had agreed to a year's rental. It was furnished simply, with coarse linens and plastic-handled cutlery, but it would have to do.

Barkin pulled up.

'Here you are, Mr and *Mrs* Logan, and I wish you much—'

'Mmm. Thanks,' Logan said. 'Here you are.' He gave the man a twenty-pound note.

'Much obliged.' Barkin grinned. 'I'll leave you to it, then.' He clicked, and turned the horse away.

Becky said, 'There's a key under the pot-plant.'

Logan bent down. 'I'll get it. Don't want you to dirty your dress.'

'I couldn't give a damn about this dress,' she snarled. It was as though the lid was off, and all the tensions of the last fortnight were about to pour out. 'It means nothing to me.'

'You're such an unbelievable brat,' Logan replied, in a chilling tone of quiet contempt. 'Can't you wait till we're inside? You want to spoil everything we just did?'

Becky paused. 'I'm sorry, you're right.' She handed him the key, and Logan unlocked the door.

The place had been scrubbed since she saw it last. There was a hamper on the table; she could see fresh bread, brown eggs, a whole cheese, bottles of champagne, truffles, fruit . . . In the small sitting room, a fire had been prepared in the hearth, artfully stacked with kindling, coal and crumpled newspaper. The sun had gone down, and it was already starting to get cold.

'They've only made the double bed,' Becky mumbled, 'but I can make the single room up for you, if you want.'

He arched a brow. 'You know how to make a bed?'

'Oh, sod off,' she snapped.

He sighed. 'You're right. Look, we both hate this, but it's for the kid. Right? So if we have to live together, we might as well be civil.'

Becky nodded, not trusting herself to speak.

'You make the bed, and I'll see to the fire and the hot water and supper.'

She hadn't eaten all day. She was suddenly starving. 'Sounds good to me.'

Chapter 38

'Tell me about Fairfield,' Pete Bessel said soothingly, 'my lord.'

'You can call me Rupert,' he said, swinging his brandy glass around with dangerous abandon so that some liquor spattered into the fire and caused it to flare briefly. Rupert was slowly getting drunker, and he really didn't give a shit. He liked Bessel. Man was a Yank and a grubby little advertising wonk, but he knew his place. He also treated Rupert properly, arranging for him to stay at Bessel's *pied-à-terre* on Madison, a luxurious studio flat decorated with erotic prints on the walls, wood floors stained black and an abundance of animal-skin rugs. It was a love-nest for a mistress, maybe a succession of them, but it was sumptuous, in a trashy way. Bessel sent Rupert gifts of champagne and small vials of cocaine with glass stoppers and tiny silver spoons. He'd made a lot of money, and he wasn't averse to sharing it, Rupert thought with satisfaction.

Not like those two bitches back home.

'Historic. Family seat. *My* seat. Now she's . . .' Rupert grimaced '. . . *whoring* it out as a hotel. And she's making a fortune with *my* property. 'S not fair. She's a *woman*. She can't pass on the family name.'

'Did you see this, Rupert?'

Bessel unctuously passed over a folded sheet of newspaper, a report from *The Times*. Rupert blinked in horror.

'Wait . . . She married William Logan? A *gardener*?'

He went so pale Bessel hastily gestured behind him to the exit for the bathrooms. He didn't want this drunk asshole throwing up in the Oaks, the gentleman's club in midtown to which Bessel had only just been admitted.

''S OK. Not gonna be *sick*. *Feel* sick.'

'Understandably,' Bessel soothed. He was really interested in Lita; whatever he could use to destroy Lita. Maybe the Becky woman could help. But Rupert Lancaster was essential to his plans, and Rupert needed to be listened to.

Like most failed drunks, Bessel thought with contempt.

But Lancaster had one thing to recommend him besides his name, and that was a certain amount of low cunning. He had managed to get money and power from both these women. The only reason it hadn't destroyed them was because Lancaster had had no idea what to do with that money once he'd got it.

That wouldn't be the case with Pete Bessel.

He'd invested wisely with the bonus he'd received for winning that ad campaign, and once Lita had left he'd become the star of Doheny. And that was about the last good thing that had happened.

Pete had been ticking along, sure. He was good, and he knew it. He retained his own clients. But the accounts that hadn't jumped ship with Lita weren't satisfied with his work. Slowly, they had defected to New Wave or other agencies. Slowly, the innuendos about Lita stealing his work were replaced by sneaky suggestions that she had always been the big talent after all.

He hated that. He hated it more when Harry Weiss left. It looked like a vote of confidence in Lita. It looked like an accusation of him.

Doheny was still a big player, but it was leaking. Prestige. Accounts. Clients.

Destroying New Wave had become Pete's wet dream. But he had no idea how to do that – until Rupert Lancaster showed up.

With Rupert's ideas and Bessel's management, he thought it would be a piece of cake. And if he could harm Cousin Rebecca as a sop to the limey, so much the better.

'I think the press would be interested in that, don't you? The blue-collar help and the rich heiress? And it's on the record that you won big orders for her company. And that Lita started out as a partner in your firm.'

'That's right.' Rupert took another deep swig of brandy. The warmth of it mixed with the crackling fire and the comfortable leather armchair. There was an icy arctic wind whipping through the canyons of Manhattan outside, and he was enjoying the toasty sensation. He smiled blurrily at Bessel, suddenly gripped by an idea.

'You know, Becky started out in the hotel division at Lancaster.' He laughed. 'One shitty little hotel. And . . . I helped her with that.'

'Of course you did,' Bessel prompted him. 'She stole all your ideas, right? And Lita also walked off with your business plans?'

'Absolutely,' Rupert agreed firmly. He dropped his voice. 'But it might be hard to prove.'

'For a hotel business catering to an exclusive clientele, and for a commercials house, you don't have to.' Bessel grinned. 'That's the beauty of it. All you need to do is make enough of a stink.' He smiled. 'And maybe Becky will pay you to go away, once she's seen what we do to Lita. Her clients will flee that little shop like cats with firecrackers tied to their tails.' He stared at his guest. 'I just need you to be with the programme.'

'No problem there.' Rupert smirked. 'You can rely on me.'

'Good man,' Pete said. 'Another brandy?'

Becky avoided Logan as best she could, but it wasn't easy. He transferred to doing work for local clients, but he arrived back at the cottage in time for supper. Winter was right around the corner, and there were Christmas and New Year's events to organize, a full Hogmanay programme for the Edinburgh hotel and a Dickens *Christmas Carol* – themed week for the London property, but nothing could change the fact that Becky came home to Logan every night.

Distant. Cold. Arrogant Logan.

He left her notes instead of talking to her. 'We need more logs. We're out of bread.' He left the room when she was sitting by the fire and read in the ancient rocking-chair in the guest room, usually with a bottle of wine that he didn't ask her to share.

It hurt Becky like all hell, but she was proud of herself for not showing it. When the post slipped through the letterbox, and she had to pick up congratulatory cards addressed to 'Mrs William Logan', she didn't let him see her wince.

Tonight she was in late. She had just come in from London, where they were putting the final touches to the London property, seamlessly sleek and elegant. The designers wanted a name for the front, and Becky had decided to simply call it The Lancaster. She would build a chain. The Scottish property would be The Lancaster, Edinburgh. Only Fairfield would never be called a Lancaster hotel.

Becky got out of her Mercedes and shivered. It was an icy night, because the sky was cloudless. In the country the stars were so bright they glittered like diamond chips over the arc of the inky heavens above her. Somewhere she could hear the faint hoot of a barn owl floating over the neighbouring fields. Behind her, Fairfield's stately silhouette was lit up with the windows of the current crop of guests, her first Europeans – an Italian racing family with pots of money who were presumably bored by endless sunshine. Becky didn't care where the guests came from. As long as they paid in full, and went home happy, telling stories to all their rich friends. There were lights on in her little cottage, too; she could see the cheerful fire through the lead panelled window, and the light in the kitchen . . .

Logan was in. Of course.

Becky let herself in and shut the door behind her. 'Will, I—'

'God!'

Logan was standing there, naked. He had just walked out of the tiny bathroom. His body was hard, chiselled, his stomach muscular and lean. Steam from the warm water lifted off him. The black, wiry chest hair was plastered to his skin, with water dripping off it in tiny rivulets. His thighs looked as hard as a rugby player's, and he was as large as she remembered.

'Seen enough?' he said dryly.

Becky snapped out of it. 'You can't use a towel?'

'I put a wash on. They aren't dry yet.'

Logan disappeared, ducking back into the bathroom, while she composed herself. Becky knew she was blushing. She hoped the firelight would camouflage it. He emerged a few seconds later, wearing his jeans, barefoot, his chest still wet.

'I thought you were going to be in London tonight,' he said.

'Sorry to disappoint you,' Becky retorted.

'All this travelling must be hard on you.' He didn't rise to her bait. 'You should try and take it easy for the baby. Pregnancy is no time to get stressed.'

Becky tried not to let her eyes wander back on to those sharp muscles. She gestured to the tiny cottage. 'It's kinda late for that, don't you think?' There *was* nowhere else to look. His body was like a magnet. 'Please, put some clothes on,' she insisted.

Logan's response was to move to the fire and stretch out in front of it, rather like a puma or a lion, all sinewy grace. His eyelids narrowed, regarding her.

'If I didn't know better I'd say you found my chest disturbing.'

'Of course I find it disturbing.' Becky had been going to cover herself, but what was the point? 'You're the one that stormed out on me, remember? You rejected me.'

His eyes widened. 'You're joking, right? I rejected you? You said you didn't want to know. When I came back.'

'You left me to twist for six weeks,' Becky said, and her voice was cracking. 'You slept with me and then you just let me hang. You fucked me and then you forgot me. Like I was some piece of trash to you.'

Logan stood up, pressing on the balls of his feet. He took a step closer to her. 'Is that what you thought? That I just wanted to have sex with you?'

'Why not? You left Fairfield. When you came back and jumped me, you wanted to jump my bones, too. Or maybe just to tease me. To take offence at – at—' she was so angry she was spluttering '—at *nothing* and then just *leave* me?'

'Because you started talking about some servant, some shit like that.'

'That was in the past. That wasn't about you, you stubborn asshole.'

'And I suppose throwing out that Valentine I sent you wasn't about me either? That was my great-grandmother's, Becky. My great-grandfather gave it to her during the Boer War. My family has kept it for ever.'

Becky gasped. 'I'm sorry. You didn't say . . .'

'I didn't think I'd have to, to stop you throwing it away.'

'But you just sent me a card, Logan. You didn't even call. Nothing.'

He looked perplexed. 'You thought I was blanking you? But didn't I tell you that I hate the phone? Didn't I say that something as important as us shouldn't be done in a long-distance way? Because that's just bullshit. I don't love someone down telephone wires.'

'You said love someone.'

'Of course. I was madly in love with you.' Logan shook his head, as though amazed. 'Ironic, wasn't it, to think that the gardening boy could ever be a suitable match for the squire's daughter? I found out that much when you gave me the cold shoulder for asking to be paid.'

'You loved me,' Becky whispered. 'You really loved me.'

'Pity you never felt the same way about me. You always let me feel I was only in it for your money, like I was the stud getting used.'

'I do love you.'

'Pull the other one, sweetheart,' Logan said wearily, 'it's got bells on it.'

Becky walked over to the windows and pulled the curtains shut. Not that anybody was likely to walk past their little country lane, but just in case. She didn't want anybody rubber-necking right now.

'A man I was with once dated me for my money . . .'

His eyes were ice.

'So that's it, was it? The poor lad from oop North after your money. It may surprise you to learn, princess, that I make my own.'

'Yeah, but hardly – I mean, look at your offices, look at how badly you needed to pay . . .'

Logan shook his head. 'Incredible. You call yourself a business-woman, but I guess it never occurred to you that other people can have cash-flow problems. I took that space while I was waiting to get paid on . . . God. Why the hell am I justifying myself to you? Do you realize the scale of my normal jobs, the work we're taking on now? The calls are coming from Italy, from France, from Spain, from the Arabs. The Saudi Royal family called me the week before you dropped your little bombshell. The King wants a garden created in an oasis.'

He shrugged. 'Not that it's any of your business, but Logan Gardens ken off. Just like I knew it would when I first came to work for I never had any doubt. My commissions this year will hit a quarter of a million in fees, not including expenses. Next year it'll be more.'

'Then how come you did the rose garden for . . .?'

Logan didn't smile. 'Because it was *your* rose garden, and I wanted something to keep me close to you. How dumb can you get, right? I thought we had something.'

Becky sat down in one of the soft armchairs. That brought her right next to his thick thighs in those jeans. She stared determinedly into the fire.

'Are you OK?' Logan asked, dropping to his knees.

'Why wouldn't I be? Oh, you're worried about the baby. I'm just a baby-carrying device.'

'And I'm just the sperm donor.'

Logan's face was right next to hers now. His dark eyes were softened slightly. His thick jaw was up against her lips. He was gorgeous, and Becky bit down on her cheeks to stop the whimper of pain and wanting. Did he really *have* to put that muscled chest right next to her like that?

'Logan,' she said firmly, mustering every ounce of self-control, 'can you, *please*, go and put some—'

He kissed her.

One hand came behind her head, grabbing it through the silken strands of her blonde hair, the other reached up to her cheek and lightly traced a path down the bone, slipping from her face to her neck, trailing lightly, touching the hollow at the base of her Adam's apple. His lips were rough, though; hungry, crushing her, his tongue probing her mouth insistently, his body pushing her back against the chair. Becky sobbed in the back of her throat, her starved body responding instantly, her nipples taut on her small breasts, her slim waist moving in the chair, pushing closer to him.

'What about the baby?' she whispered.

Logan muttered, 'It won't hurt the baby. It's natural. It's how the baby got here.' His breath was hot on her throat, his lips moving over the hollow there. 'Besides, you're my wife. I'm going to consummate this marriage.'

His hands unbuttoned the top of her dress, freeing her smooth shoulders. Becky's breath came hot and ragged as she reached to undo her silk bra. Logan batted her hands away.

'Don't touch. You're mine.'

He slipped his thumbs inside the silk of her bra and started to stroke, lightly, to tease the soft flesh around the nipples without actually touching them. Becky moaned, softly. Logan unsnapped the metal strap and tugged the tiny cream silk strap. It slipped from her skin, dragging at the tiny golden hairs which were prickling on her arms, her back, everywhere, her body warm and flushed, sensitized to his slightest touch.

'My breasts are too small,' Becky whispered.

Logan grinned. 'They're perfect. They're like plums. You're so beautiful.' He extended one fingertip and touched one tiny pale pink bud, tight against her ivory apple-breasts, and watched as it swelled slightly and darkened. The grin faded. She saw that his breath was starting to become heavy. Logan tugged impatiently at her dress and tights and the matching, tiny, cream panties. His erection was straining, chafing against the rough denim of his jeans.

'Let's get upstairs.' He was insistent. 'I'm not waiting.' He placed his hands flat against the firm, satiny expanse of her inner thighs and slid them relentlessly upwards till he was cupping her, feeling the downy golden fur and her damp slickness against his calloused palms.

Becky tried to stand up, but her knees were shaking.

Logan smiled, that sexy, slightly cruel smile that made the lust squirm in her belly, sending little darts of need through her aching nipples and down to the sweet nub between her legs.

'I guess I'll just have to do it the traditional way,' he said.

He bent down and scooped her up. Becky gasped. He hefted her weight in his arms as though she were made of thistledown. She was pressed against his hard chest, locked in his arms. Logan carried her up the wooden, polished staircase of the little cottage into her bedroom, now their bedroom. He lowered her gently down on the old-fashioned bed carved from cherry wood and made up with cool white sheets. Becky reached up and snapped the metal buttons down the front of Logan's jeans. He kicked them off furiously, freeing himself, large and thick against her slender legs. Becky's hands reached out to touch him. He was so gorgeous. Thick, almost stubby, rock-hard, velvet-soft skin that leaped against her. But Logan wasn't going to permit her to take control. He slipped his finger inside her, feeling the warmth, the wetness, the damp of her.

'Please,' Becky gasped. She squirmed on her back, rocking herself against him.

'Not till you're ready,' Logan said. He could hardly get the words out, but he forced himself to take his time. On her slim left hand, clawing at his back, he saw his ring flash and glitter. He put his hands on her arms, pinning her down on the soft coverlet, then moved lower, lower, his lips and tongue relentless. When he reached her hot core and lightly dragged the edge of his tongue over the pulsing centre of her Becky reared up against him, half screaming, and he had to put a hand over her mouth. Unable to control himself a second longer, Logan thrust inside her, slipping instantly into the tight, wet heart of his wife. He moved with total abandon, the need to explode urgent in him, his lust for her body, for her wild eyes and damp tendrils of hair completely overwhelming. He pressed his mouth to hers, kissing her savagely, feeling her belly and groin spasm against him, holding her slight body down with his, her responsiveness milking his cock until he couldn't stop it, didn't want to stop it, and his hands gripped Becky shuddering beneath him, and he exploded in a burst of white-hot pleasure so intense that he could think of nothing but him and her, and everything else fell away.

Chapter 39

'It must be her.'

Dr Conran adjusted his tie and tried not to salivate at the sight of his wife, furious, gorgeous and highly fuckable, sitting up in bed with her black silk Pratesi sheets pooling around her olive skin, her brown hair loose and tumbling around her shoulders, and her glorious tits swaying as she moved, cat-like, on the bed.

'I thought you had resolved this,' he said. He had an eight o'clock meeting with Dr Jackson this morning to discuss the new lease of their building. Jackson was a short-tempered old curmudgeon who hated to be kept waiting.

Unfortunately, Lita's tits, with their dark nipples still hard from this morning's tussle in the sheets, were hypnotizing him. Mark felt sixteen with her. Fifteen minutes after they were done, he was ready to go again. He felt his cock stiffen relentlessly.

'I thought so, too. But obviously not,' Lita half hissed, her heavy-lidded eyes narrowing. 'Harry Weiss called from New York. New Wave lost six accounts last week, including Costa Coffee.'

She stood up and turned around to where her silk negligee was hanging in the walk-in closet. Unfortunately, that didn't help Mark much. He was now exposed to Lita's firm, jutting ass. He loved to rub his hand over those dangerous curves. It got him hard instantly, and it made her body leap in response. Men stared whenever she wore so much as a pair of jeans. Mark didn't mind – who could blame them? He groaned aloud.

'Now, now.' Momentarily distracted, Lita turned around, the silk robe clinging to her skin, a flash of dark, wobbling breast visible through the lacy opening. Her nipples were clearly delinated through the liquid material. 'Husbands have to get to work, too. What about Dr Jackson?'

'Screw Dr Jackson,' Mark said, frantically tugging at the tie it had taken him five minutes to align perfectly. 'He can wait.'

Lita had to call the office to say she was going to be late. Making love with her husband was incredible, but once he had left, and she had showered the sweat from her body, the limp, relaxed sensation of her crashing orgasm was slowly replaced again by simmering rage.

Fuck Becky Lancaster. She'd thought they'd come to an agreement, a truce, if not an entente cordiale. Obviously not.

Lita was confident. Her business had been booming – hiring more staff, getting new accounts, more column inches in *Ad Weekly* and the other trade publications. She had even toyed with opening up more branches, maybe a boutique in Australia, something in New Zealand and Canada. She was making something of herself. Something big.

And now it was being threatened.

She fixed herself a pot of the cinnamon coffee she imported from the States. Lita liked it in England, but they knew nothing about coffee. Or bagels. She missed bagels. She let the dark liquid brew, savouring the heady scent that filled her gleaming kitchen. While the coffee perked was one of her favourite times to think.

There was no way those accounts had defected because of some legitimate reason. Lita had personally flown back to the States, had deprived herself of Mark's body for almost a week, to secure that Costa Coffee account. She had charmed the head of the company, reminding him that she got her start as the Costa girl.

'I knew how to sell your coffee then and I know how to sell it now,' she'd concluded her presentation, to grins and handshakes all round. Taking that account from Doheny had been a real coup. Costa was a family brand, and family brands were where the real dollars were in advertising.

Just ask Procter & Gamble. The groceries giant spent more on advertising than any other firm in the world. Lita wanted New Wave to get those kinds of accounts, because there was only so far you could go selling scents and boutique lipsticks.

Costa had been her first. And now they were blowing her off, after less than a month, without a single commercial making it on the air. Lita had had the Costa acquisition trumpeted to the skies when it had happened. It had been in every trade publication. And so would this.

You could go that quickly from being the hot new agency to being tainted with the stench of failure.

They would all be asking *why* Costa had fired New Wave. Shou'd *they* reconsider, too?

But Lita knew why. There was a reason, and it was a tall, skinny, Boston Brahmin with long blonde hair and a country mansion. And Lita wasn't having it.

If Becky wanted war, she was going to get it.

It took almost two weeks for Becky to find out. Sharon had a good explanation, but it didn't help her much.

'You were on honeymoon,' she'd said, shrugging. 'Nobody wants to be arsed on honeymoon, do they? And besides, you were so happy. I couldn't bring myself to bring you any bad news.'

Becky was mad, but she understood. She was so in love with Logan she could hardly see straight. After that first hot, sweet session with him, they hadn't left the cottage for the entire next day. They had made do with whatever food was in the house. Logan had gone downstairs to fetch thick slices of crusty bread and cheese and glossy red apples.

'I don't want you moving from my bed,' Logan had half growled, and the food had tasted perfect, almost as though she had never tasted apples before, never tasted sharp, crumbly Cheshire. They needed the food for more grappling. Though she loved Logan, was madly, exquisitely, almost painfully in love with him, when he grabbed her slim frame and pinned her down, stroking her thighs, her butt, licking between her legs and thrusting himself into her, it was raw and animal, and Becky sweated, and panted, and needed food.

They took showers together that wound up with more sex, Logan getting so aroused from soaping her belly and breasts with his hands that he couldn't even make it back to the bedroom. The curtains stayed drawn, and they made love in front of a roaring fire downstairs in the tiny drawing room. The following day they decamped back to Fairfield, but Becky didn't do any work. How could she, when there was a huge double bed in her room? Logan and she had eventually emerged, holding hands, to get food and new clothes, but he had been all over her, stroking her butt through her jeans, nuzzling at her neck, breathing in the scent of her, like an animal claiming possession. And Sharon had tried to keep out of the way, run the hotels and not bother her boss.

Only now she had to.

'More cancellations.' That had been putting it mildly. Over fifty per cent of the guests at the Lancaster London had asked for their money back on the Dickens holiday that Becky had bust her ass organizing, and in the Lancaster Edinburgh the Valentine's Day bookings they'd had just pulled out – nine guests, a party from Palm Beach, Florida – with no explanation. 'I'm hearing bad things from New York, apparently. That kind of thing. I sent the money back. I thought you'd want that. And the cushions,' Sharon added hastily.

'Yeah, yeah. You did the right thing.' Becky had a sudden impulse to bite her nails. They had been doing great, but they had also been spending a lot of money. Without the guests and their huge payments,

Lancaster would experience what was politely referred to as a 'cash-flow' crisis.

With guests or without them, staff had to be paid. Mortgages had to be paid. She had a cushion, of course, but this took a big bite out of it. Any more, and she might start needing a bridging loan.

They hadn't been operating long enough to avoid a crisis. Becky's whole business was word of mouth. If it went bad . . .

She paced up and down the library.

'This is Lita Conran. That goddamn bitch. I thought we had an agreement.'

'Maybe truce time is over.'

'Maybe.' Becky's face was grim. 'I'm not going to let her destroy me. Sharon, call the banks. Set up a meeting on a line of credit. I can play this game as hard as she can.'

Sharon nodded and went to pick up the phone, but it rang as she was reaching for it.

'Good morning, Lancaster Hotels,' she said. Her eyebrows shot up. 'Hold on a second. I'll see if she's available to speak to you.'

She cupped her hand over the receiver.

'She says it's Rosalita Conran.'

Becky snatched the phone from her.

'The reservation is under Lancaster. Baron Lancaster,' Pete Bessel said. He was standing at the entrance of Wilton's, in Piccadilly, the famous fish restaurant that was a preferred haunt of the London upper classes and politicians. He already hated it. For one thing, he wasn't big on fish. And for another, the dim light and low-pitched, polite hum made him feel shabby, as though his shoes didn't fit right. He shifted a little in his expensive Saks suit and wished he was wearing something, well, more British. More Savile Row.

But whatever. Rupert wanted to be met here, and right now Rupert's giant, whiny ego had to be placated. He was close to bringing his whispering campaign out in the open. The recapture of Costa Coffee had already gotten Pete a huge bonus from the Doheny board. Everything was proceeding according to plan. With the lawsuits and the press interest, gun-shy clients would avoid New Wave like the plague. He didn't give a shit about the Becky situation, but the press here might, and that would help Bessel destroy Lita.

'His lordship is already here, sir. Let me take you to him.' The *maître d'* led Bessel through the tables to one at the back of the room. Normally Bessel would be insulted, but he had figured out that the Brits didn't care about tables being visible. In fact, they seemed to prefer discretion. Whatever, there would be no more discretion for Rupert Lancaster.

He saw Rupert had already gotten himself a large Martini. That guy was shaping up to be a regular soak, Bessel thought disapprovingly. And he loved the fine-milled white powder just a little *too* much. Give the guy a spoon and he wants to snort the whole vial. They had been at Tramps last night, the hot night-club, and Rupert had been loud, talking ten miles a minute on the drugs, his arms each around a couple of common little tarts with big tits . . . girls that looked barely out of school.

'Hi, Pete,' Rupert said, not getting up.

'Hi, there.' Pete sat down. 'I'm starving.'

'Really? I don't think I can even manage a salad,' Rupert gabbled.

Of course not, you coke-head. You're on that Colombian diet powder, Bessel thought. 'I think I'll try the bouillabaisse. Now, dreary thought it might be, we have to talk a little business.'

'Her guests are cancelling,' Rupert said. 'There are expenses.' He actually rubbed his hands.

'I've arranged for another interview with Doreen Evans, as well as Felicity Manners and Richard Farringdon. The last two write for the *Daily Mail* and the *Express*. They're interested in the romance angle, your side of the story. The gallant English peer forced from his ancient home by the American upstart,' Bessel said, unable to contain a sneer. Luckily, Rupert wasn't paying any attention. 'And then his company stolen from him by another American girl, his fiancée. Who betrayed him.'

Rupert nodded. 'And Becky also stole my hotel plans.'

Bessel grinned. The peer was on the same page at least. He dropped his voice. 'Yes. I've sent some documentation to your hotel room. It looks very realistic. We found a guy in Brooklyn that can fake postmarks. He stole some postal equipment. It looks like you registered both business plans years ago. After the interviews, we file the lawsuit. Then we hold a press conference to announce it.' Bessel grinned. 'Whatever happens with the suit, their businesses will die. Neither one of their client bases likes controversy. But remember, today you have to look, like, heartbroken. Not vengeful. Saddened.'

Rupert looked contemptuously at the little man. He had Brylcreem on his hair, like some witchdoctor hawking snake oil.

'I think I can handle it,' Rupert said.

Lita arrived at Fairfield at eight p.m. that night. She had spent a day in the office trying to project total unconcern, not even calling the Costa executives. She told everyone but Harry Weiss that this was expected, that it was nothing to worry about. But she still seethed.

Becky Lancaster's wild accusations, her denials – should she believe them? Or were they just a ploy to stop Lita taking revenge?

She drove down to Fairfield herself to find out. She took her own car. The long drive, the rearing lions on pillars, were everything she remembered from years ago. It was a bitterly cold country night, with bright stars, and Lita even screeched to a halt on a wooded road as a startled doe ran past her, its big eyes lit up, terrified, in the glare of her headlights.

Chapter 40

Logan heard the crunch of tyres on the drive.

'She's here,' he said. He put one hand on Becky's shoulder, his thick fingers rubbing her smooth skin. She could feel him standing behind her protectively, his body braced firm against the threat. 'Want me to stay?'

'Not unless she came down here with muscle.' Becky smiled faintly, although her stomach was churning furiously. 'I'll be OK. I need to find out where I stand with this bitch.'

'Let me at least let her in.' Logan grinned. 'I'm curious.'

The bell buzzed. They both leapt out of their seats, but Logan was faster.

'*Will*,' Becky hissed. Too late – he had lifted the latch and opened the ancient, heavy wooden door.

A girl stood there, about Becky's age, almost a foot shorter. She was curvy, with an hourglass figure poured into tan leather pants with fringes and a matching cashmere jumper that clung to impressive tits. She had matched them with high-heeled boots that made her almost as tall as Becky, and her dark hair tumbled loose and sleek around her shoulders, with a slight, tousled kink to it. She had dark, flashing eyes, *café-au-lait* skin and full make-up. Logan's eyes flickered over the thick mascara, the glossy, lined lips and the sheer blush on her cheeks.

'I'm—'

'Yes, I know.' Logan looked down into her eyes coldly. She returned his stare with just as much steel. 'My wife is waiting for you in the office.'

'Thank you,' Lita said, striding past him. 'I know the way.'

Logan admired her butt on the way past. He almost wanted to watch. She was everything his wife wasn't – flashy, modern, sassy, over the top. Tons of make-up, skin-tight clothes. She looked good; she just wasn't his type. Logan flashed on Becky's tiny, delicate breasts with their rosebud nipples, high and tight and pink . . . He felt a stiffening between his legs, and beat a hasty retreat up the stairs. You couldn't go around comparing Becky with other chicks, certainly not while they had company. He wanted her again now. Cold-shower time.

Logan wasn't worried about Lita. She was a wildcat, but so was his wife if you scratched the surface. Becky could handle herself. Maybe Lita should have brought reinforcements.

Becky sat in her favourite burgundy leather armchair with a file on her lap, pretending to be reading. She looked up idly as Lita Conran stomped in and shut the door firmly.

'Have a seat,' Becky said.

Lita stood there and glanced around the room. 'I see the place hasn't changed much.'

'Not in this part of the house.' I'll be damned if I get up for her, Becky thought. 'Our guest rooms have bathrooms, but they're discreet.'

'Discreet.' Lita rolled the word around her tongue sarcastically. 'We haven't had much of that, lately, have we?'

'Apparently not.' Becky had to fight to stay seated. 'I've had three sets of bookings cancel. Each guest pays up to ten thousand pounds a week. I've had entire parties blow me off at the last minute. And my costs stay constant. I assume you know what constant costs plus less revenue equals?'

'Hmm, let me see.' Lita frowned, as if she were trying to figure it out. 'Could it be . . . the same thing that's happening to New Wave when my accounts cancel? I know you're connected on the East Coast, Lancaster, through your mom's family. Don't tell me you had nothing to do with Costa.'

'Who's he?' Becky asked blankly. 'And technically the name's Logan now. But most people still use Becky.'

'Who's he? It's not a he.' Lita's dark eyes narrowed. 'Are you seriously trying to tell me you don't know what's been happening to New Wave? That you had nothing to do with it?'

'Oh, and this "attack is the best form of defence" is all you could come up with?' Becky shot back. 'Like you didn't send one of your PR snakes out to the States and Europe to spread God knows what rumours around Lancaster Hotels?'

'You haven't read anything in the press, have you?'

'No, but I'm sure you're spreading private rumours. Yourself.'

Lita stared at her in astonishment. 'Me, sugar? I'm a girl from the Bronx. I don't mix with your tennis-playing, weak-chinned set. I can't stand that social register crap.'

'And I don't know who the hell Costa is.'

'It's a company.' Lita tried to assess the blonde girl's posture. She didn't look like she was lying but, then again, she might just be a hell of an actress. 'Costa Coffee.'

'Whatever. It had nothing to do with me.' Becky was impatient. 'I care about Lancaster. I've worked too hard on this goddamn company to watch it thrown away because you—'

'I've done nothing.' Lita stated it so flatly that Becky was forced to believe her. 'Nothing. Except try to build my client list. So let's just assume, for the moment, that you've done nothing either.'

'OK,' Becky said guardedly. 'In that case I see two possibilities. One, coincidence. Two—'

'Rupert.'

'Exactly.'

'There is no other connection between us.'

Becky stared at her guest for a long second, then said, 'Would you like a drink?'

Over bourbon – 'Jack and Coke. I can't stand that aged malt liquor stuff. It tastes like a pile of mouldy wood,' Lita said – she gave Becky the whole story. Everything from walking into Rupert's office, to the shoot, the kiss, the dinner with her family, and then the fiasco with Modern Commercials.

'You gave him an open line of credit?' Becky asked, horrified. Lita actually blushed.

'I was in love with him. And he's a smooth talker.'

'I hear that.'

'He presented it to me like it was the best thing for *me*. Like he didn't need a big lump sum, he could use a line from my account to take "only what he needed".' Lita shook her head. 'My father saw right through him, you know.'

'I like to think mine would have, too.' Becky hesitated. 'Do you think he ever . . . loved you?'

Lita smiled at the look on the other girl's face. 'That's cool, you don't have to tread on eggshells. Excuse my language, but I don't give a shit.'

'Excuse your language? I'm not Princess Grace,' Becky said.

'No, you just look like her.'

The two girls managed a small smile. The ice cubes clinked in Lita's glass.

'I think he liked the look of me. I don't think he loved me, I don't think he's ever loved anyone. I had looks, and I was making a lot of money. The way I figure it, at that time he was pretty certain he was going to win his case and inherit this place. He still wanted my money. But when your lawyers pulled it out, he knew there was only one possible bride, I guess. I was out, but not before he'd cleaned out my bank account.'

'Yeah, you told me last time. The telegram was pretty cold.'

'And that meant *you* were to be the lucky lady,' Lita said, pointing one blood-red talon dramatically at Becky.

'Yeah, real lucky. Lucky enough to bring him into Lancaster and make a terrible situation absolutely disastrous.' Becky grimaced. 'I let love blind me, or what I thought was love.'

'He's a good-looking guy.'

'After Logan I find him a bit wimpy,' Becky said, 'and terrible in bed, of course.'

Lita burst out laughing. 'I thought it might just be me.'

'All mouth and no trousers, as they say over here.' Becky grinned.

'Well, no mouth either, unfortunately,' Lita said.

Becky chuckled. 'You think he might really have had something to do with this?'

'If it's not you and not me, then you bet your ass, *querida*. I don't buy coincidences. Rupert is sly and conniving and money-grubbing. He's quite capable of being vengeful.'

'Yeah, but he's not capable of sound business thinking. As I found out to my cost,' Becky said, thinking aloud. 'He has to be working with someone.'

'That shitty article proved how much he enjoyed sticking it to both of us.'

Becky turned around and slid open one of the drawers of her walnut desk. 'I kept a copy, for the record.' She skimmed it. 'He was supposedly in Monaco, at some club.'

'Gambling? Debts?'

'He left England, sold the London house. Quite possible.'

'So he'd be looking for money, right? And looking for a way to get you out of this house. He's always looking for that.'

'Yes. And if he is working with someone, I guess we'll find out later who.'

'But how can you counter whatever he's doing if you don't know what it is?'

'Between the two of us, we must have enough on Rupert to make him wish he'd never been born,' Becky reminded her.

Lita shivered, despite the warmth of the room. 'But that's publicity. My business is dead with a lot of sleazy publicity, Becky.'

'And that's what he's counting on. That we'll be too camera-shy to talk. He won't expect anything else.' Becky winked at her.

'We'll be playing a game of chicken.'

'I like it,' Lita murmured. 'And he won't expect us to work together either.'

'Would you like to stay the night? I have an extra guest room.'

'Due to cancellation?' Lita stretched. 'You know . . . it *is* a long drive back down to London.'

'Why don't you call your husband? I'll get you some night things. We already ate, but you can order room service.'

'Room service, huh?' Lita said. 'I bet it's excellent.'

'It is,' Becky replied, with a hint of pride.

Mark wasn't pleased that she wasn't coming home. 'I understand,' he said.

'That's a lie, isn't it?'

'Yes. Get back here. I miss you.'

'I've only been away five minutes.'

'Thirteen hours and twelve minutes, to be exact. What are you doing now?'

'I'm lying in a canopy bed,' Lita said.

'That's American for a four-poster. What are you wearing?'

'Nothing,' Lita said maliciously.

He groaned. 'You love to tease me.'

She smiled. She could almost hear him smiling back at her down the phone.

'That's OK. You just spend the whole day tomorrow thinking how I'm going to pay you back.'

He hung up, blowing her kisses, and Lita relaxed on her bed. She was impressed. Old world charm had never been her style, but even the most modern miss couldn't fail to be taken aback by this. The bed was antique mahogany, with heavy drapes in a chinoiserie silk, and the furniture matched it – there was a chair carved out of solid ivory, a delicate ottoman, a chaise longue, and a Bokara rug in golds and palest blues. The lead-panelled window looked down towards a manicured lawn and a large pond, with the ancient maze to the right. She felt like Anne Boleyn at Hampton Court.

There was a knock on the door and a uniformed maid entered with a tray on wheels.

'Dinner, madam,' she said.

'Thanks.' Lita scrabbled around for a tip and fished a pound note from her coat.

'*Thank* you, madam,' the girl said, delighted, and retired. Lita sniffed hungrily and lifted the lid on the food. It was roast pheasant with stuffing, wilted spinach with lemon, and roast potatoes. There was a salad with fresh peas, half a bottle of champagne, and a small chocolate parfait that made her mouth water just to look at it. Then there was a silver pot of coffee with a tiny heavy card that said 'Decaffeinated' propped against it, and a small flowered box of Charbonnel and Walker chocolates. She noticed that the cutlery was solid silver. Lita carved off a slice of pheasant. It was moist and incredibly good, probably wild.

She was blown away. No wonder all these rich folks paid king's ransoms to stay here. If you were rich and bored, there were worse ways to blow your cash.

Becky's problem was that she was relying on word of mouth. That made her vulnerable to someone like Rupert, in fact to anyone that wanted to start a whispering campaign . . .

Lita uncorked the champagne and poured it into her crystal flute. She felt a familiar frisson of excitement.

She was starting to get an idea.

Becky slept badly, despite Logan putting his hand over her mouth to stop her worrying aloud about Rupert and slipping inside her, forcing her to forget everything while he made love to her. When they were done, she felt relaxed, like she normally did, and Logan fell asleep, his muscled arm draped over her. But despite the warmth of him and the aftershocks of her orgasm, the echoes of her physical pleasure, Becky couldn't fall asleep.

Having Logan beside her made her feel she was so close to everything. And now Rupert was resurfacing. It *must* be him. And she had no idea what he was going to do.

She slipped out of bed at six and made herself coffee, wrapped herself up in a cashmere robe and went for a walk in the rose garden, now full of bright red hips that offered a splash of colour in the cold morning air. Maybe she would make some rose-hip syrup, she thought idly. The guests loved all the old English touches, like the jars of crab-apple jelly she liked to serve. God, but Fairfield was beautiful. And now she was in debt on the other two properties, might she, in the end, lose the house, lose everything?

She could have retired and licked her wounds, lived small, lived on a husband's income and protected her birthright. But instead she had gambled. And now it might all go wrong.

Becky sipped at her coffee and watched the steam from the hot liquid mingle with the white smoke of breath rising from her mouth as her shoes crunched on frosty grass. She felt fear, yes, but more than that, deeper, she felt anger.

Rupert would always be back. She had to find a way to destroy him. To ruin him. And to protect herself against this kind of *bullshit*. I've got English courage and American chutzpah, Becky thought. And that's more than a match for him.

She walked back up to the house feeling a little better and waved, seeing Lita in the kitchen, poured into one of her looser dresses. They could have breakfast and make some more plans. She opened the kitchen door and walked in.

And then the phone rang.

Rupert sat with Pete Bessel in the small conference room in the Dorchester, wearing his best pinstriped suit with that sober Hermès tie and his John Lobb shoes, his plain gold cufflinks and his signet ring sparkling under the lights. He was sober but, despite that, he was enjoying himself thoroughly.

There were an impressive number of tabloid hacks here and a couple of financial writers. Bessel had made calls, had instructed lawyers, had done a decent job. Rupert was happy to give him Lita.

'But why have you taken so long to come forward, Lord Lancaster?' asked one pretty hackette from the *Daily Mirror*.

Rupert turned a half-wattage, sexy, regretful smile directly on her. She blushed.

'Because I was hoping that it wouldn't come to this. That Miss Morales – Mrs Conran – and Mrs Logan would do the decent thing by themselves. They knew they had taken proprietary information. I suppose I should have known when Mrs Logan started to blame me for the collapse of Lancaster, which happened under her management. However, after a period of intense reflection, I feel I owe it to my family and myself to pursue what is, after all, mine.'

'You went out with both those women?'

'Yes,' Rupert responded gravely, 'which makes this so sad. To have to sue for damages.'

'Are you seeing anyone right now?'

'I'm a little soured on love, as you can imagine,' Rupert responded. There was laughter, and he grinned.

'So you've really filed suit?'

'That's a matter of public record. Regretfully.' Rupert stood, sensing the moment had come to call a halt. 'That's all, ladies and gentlemen.'

'I have copies of the motions for you,' Bessel cried, waving them at the pack of hungry reporters who were yelling more questions at Rupert as he walked out the door.

He grinned. That was perfect.

'Yeah, I got it. I understand.' Becky grimaced at Lita, who was making motions for her to hang up. 'I'll call you back.'

She replaced the receiver and yelled for Sharon not to put any more calls through.

'That son of a bitch. Pete Bessel. That asshole,' Lita spat. 'He's from my old firm. He must have found Rupert.'

'I knew he had to have help. You've got a history with this Bessel?'

'Let me tell you about it in the car,' Lita said. 'I think we should go to London together. And I've got something to run by you.'

The New Wave offices were gloomy when Lita arrived with Becky in tow. The receptionist wouldn't even meet her boss's eyes, almost as if she was afraid she'd get fired. There was a sense of fear and dejection in the air that made Lita mad enough to spit. The two women got into the elevator together and rode up to the main office, where Lita stepped out to find Harry Weiss deep in conversation with Richard Feinstein of Costa Coffee, his solemn tone injected with a pleading note.

Lita's eyes flashed. She motioned for Harry to wind it up, and he managed to say something nice and be off the phone in less than thirty seconds.

'Everyone.' She clapped her hands. 'Get off the phone and get over here and listen up. We have a situation with Doheny and Rupert Lancaster, and here's what we're going to do.'

Rupert's fantastic mood had started to dissipate. He'd gone back to the hotel, enjoyed a champagne brunch with Bessel that was more champagne than brunch, and then, when the oily little Yank had departed, he'd chopped out a couple of lines just to keep the party going. Only now they had run out, and he couldn't hook up with a candy-man until he started to hit the clubs later tonight. And now reception was saying that there was somebody there to see him. Bloody tiresome.

'Well, who is it?' Rupert barked.

'It's a Mrs Conran and a Mrs Logan, my lord.'

'What is this, some kind of joke?'

'There's also a man here that wants to speak to you, my lord.'

There was a pause, and then Bessel's voice on the line, subdued. 'You better let us up, man. They have some stuff to say.'

'Whatever. Come up. Room 256.'

Rupert hung up and felt the stirrings of a new buzz begin with the news. Bessel wouldn't make a scene in the Dorchester, of course, but he had made quick enough work of it, hadn't he? They were actually here, those two bitches? In person? Ready to beg and plead for their stupid little companies, ready to offer him a cut? And what else would they be offering? The cocaine was still singing in his blood. He started to fantasize about Becky and Lita blubbing and making a scene and begging him not to destroy them. He might want to test just how far that naked ambition would go. Maybe, in exchange for letting them keep a part of it, they would drop to their knees and give him a blow job. Both of them. One for him and one for Pete, he didn't particularly care which. Rupert started to get hard as he imagined this, himself and Bessel sitting on the couch chatting about the case as Becky's and Lita's blonde and dark heads bobbed up and down on them. Yeah. Now, that would feel like *total* victory.

He was only sorry he hadn't found Bessel before.

There was a knock on the door. Rupert stood up and went to answer it. Well, well, and there they were – Becky wearing a clinging, silky dress of jersey that stopped above the knee, displaying those gorgeous slim pins, with her blonde hair flowing down her back, and Lita in black cropped pants that hugged her tight, round ass, paired with a black leather jacket and a black satin T-shirt that outlined her glorious tits. If anything, she looked better now than when he'd last seen her. A little polish added to the beauty.

'Come in, ladies,' he said, smirking. They were a couple of peaches, weren't they? And he'd got to fuck them and then fuck them over. 'Bessel, take a seat.'

Pete Bessel sat in the corner, staring at his shoes, but Rupert wasn't focused on him.

'I take it you've heard about the lawsuit. I suppose it's a bit of a shock—'

'Rupert.' Becky cut him off. 'Let me tell you our counter-proposal. You withdraw your lawsuit and apologize, saying you've been under a lot of emotional stress recently. Then you get out of England and you never come back. You never bother Lita or me ever again. You never use the Lancaster name for any business purpose, ever. How does that sound?'

He gave a short bark of laughter. 'You crazy bitch. A little publicity and your luxury-hotel bookings will go all to hell. We *know* it's already started to happen. Right, Bessel?'

'Oh, shut the fuck up, Rupert,' Bessel hissed.

'You might be right. About the negative publicity, at least in the short term. Only the thing is, we've decided we're prepared to start over rather than let you do this. So, if you proceed, here's what we do,' Lita said. 'I've talked to my old bank manager who has the financial records for what you did to me. At the time, you were right, I couldn't have afforded a lawyer. Guess what? It's not the same now.'

'And I go to the press and say you hit me.'

'I'll sue,' Rupert said nastily.

'Maybe you've forgotten Sharon,' Becky said calmly. 'I have a witness. You wouldn't get anywhere.'

'I already told Pete that I'll give *Ad Week* a long, exclusive interview talking about his plagiarism of my work, not to mention his sexual harassment and discrimination. My deputy Janice knows a bunch of girls still at Doheny. She made some calls – they're prepared to testify. He knows he can't risk that. The bleeding would be huge. And I can start over, take small accounts. My work speaks for itself. Besides . . .' Lita coughed. 'Once we get you on the stand and it's clear you don't know the first fucking thing about advertising, not only will the judge throw out your case but we'll sue for perjury.'

'That's a criminal offence,' Becky said.

'And what have you been doing over in Monaco? We looked up that Baronne you were with. She's old enough to be your mother, Rupert. An English lord turned gigolo,' Lita said, grinning. 'The press would love the human-interest story there, wouldn't they?'

'She wouldn't say anything,' Rupert managed.

'Oh, yeah?' Becky was triumphant. 'And would any of them, do you think? How confident are you? They can't be all that pleased, anyway.'

'What the hell do you mean?' Rupert spat, colouring darkly.

'I mean, my lord, that you are the worst goddamn lay I've ever had,' Lita said. 'You can't keep it up and you last all of two minutes.'

'That long?' Becky asked, looking at her.

Lita smiled maddeningly at Rupert. 'And don't think I won't tell them. Because I'm not a shrinking violet. Though I seem to recall that *you* were. Now, do you really want that in the papers?'

'Bessel?' Rupert barked.

Pete Bessel looked at him with open loathing. He had never believed that any of the bitches at Doheny would talk. Never thought Lita knew about that, or that she would contact them. Goddamn women sticking together. He couldn't operate there any more. He'd have to resign.

'I told you to shut the fuck up,' he snapped.

'You can't do this to me. You wouldn't dare,' Rupert whispered.

'You think not?' Becky shrugged. 'Here's a copy of the press release we'll be distributing if your suit isn't withdrawn in the next half-hour.'

She handed over a copy of the paper, and Rupert's face darkened further as he read it. He steadied himself against a great rush of nausea.

'I'll withdraw,' he muttered.

'I know you will.' Lita smiled again. 'And you'll get the hell out of

England. And don't bother trying New York either. I have an office there, and I never want to see your face again.'

'We have things to do. You see, you did us both a favour. You made me realize my operations were *too* exclusive and boutique. What if some two-bit piece of shit like you comes along and tries to make more trouble? What I need is advertising. A little more of a base. That way, there won't be the cancellations.' Becky patted Lita's shoulder. 'New Wave is going to take care of that for me.'

'We'll be working on a commission basis. I think it's going to be very profitable.' Lita looked at her former fiancé, his face ashen, slumped back against the chair. 'We'll be going now. Goodbye, Rupert. I'd say, See you around, but I know I'm not going to.'

'So long,' Becky said. 'If you want my advice, you'll find a pliant girl with money and keep quiet for the rest of your life.'

'How do I know you won't publish that stuff anyway?' Rupert said, and even to himself his voice had a terrible whiny catch to it.

Becky looked him right in the eye. 'Because we're second cousins, Rupert. As long as you disappear, I won't have to.'

'I can't stand you,' Rupert snarled. 'You know that, right?'

Lita giggled.

'You know what, Rupert?' Becky said. 'I think I'll get over it.'

Then she walked out and shut the door.

Lita slipped her arm through Becky's as they walked to the elevators. 'That was fun,' she said.

Becky shook her blonde head, and even her Boston Brahmin accent didn't bother Lita any more. 'It was. I think we're going to make a lot of money.'

'I *know* we are,' Lita said. 'They just expected us to act how they think women act. They never expected us to fight fire with fire.'

'Well, that's not my problem.' Becky reached out and tugged one of Lita's curly dark tendrils. 'There was a little girl, and she had a little curl, right in the middle of her forehead. And when she was good, she was very, very good—'

'And when she was bad, she was horrid.'

Lita finished the rhyme, and they both started to laugh.